W9-DCM-642

Praise for L.E. Modesitt's *Timegods* Novels

"A most skillful interweaving of old Nordic legends with a new conception. I am most intrigued with Modesitt's timediving immortals."

—Andre Norton

"Time and the universe have been taken apart and put together into a dazzling combination of word power, adventure, and sharp thinking—exceptionally brilliant and original. L.E. Modesitt takes his place way up there with the sf and maybe some other immortals."

—A. E. Van Vogt

"The cosmic concepts are often fascinating, the action fast, and the prose sometimes chilling . . . a lot of fun."

—*Science Fiction Chronicle*

Tor Books by L.E. Modesitt, Jr.

THE RECLUCE SAGA

The Magic of Recluce
The Towers of Sunset
The Magic Engineer
The Order War
The Death of Chaos
*Fall of Angels**

THE ECOLITAN MATTER

The Ecologic Envoy
The Ecolitan Operation
The Ecologic Secession

THE FOREVER HERO

Dawn for a Distant Earth
The Silent Warrior
In Endless Twilight

The Green Progression (with Bruce Scott Levinson)
The Hammer of Darkness
Of Tangible Ghosts
The Parafaith War
The Timegod

*forthcoming

The
Hammer
of
Darkness

L.E. MODESITT, JR.

A TOM DOHERTY ASSOCIATES BOOK
NEW YORK

To my parents, for the gift of words
and the love of reading

NOTE: If you purchased this book without a cover you should be aware that
this book is stolen property. It was reported as "unsold and destroyed" to the
publisher, and neither the author nor the publisher has received any payment
for this "stripped book."

This is a work of fiction. All the characters and events portrayed in this book
are fictitious, and any resemblance to real people or incidents is purely coin-
cidental.

THE HAMMER OF DARKNESS

Copyright © 1985 by L.E. Modesitt, Jr.

All rights reserved, including the right to reproduce this book, or portions
thereof, in any form.

Cover art by Greg Call

A Tor Book
Published by Tom Doherty Associates, Inc.
175 Fifth Avenue
New York, NY 10010

Tor® is a registered trademark of Tom Doherty Associates, Inc.

ISBN: 0-812-56322-0

First Tor edition: March 1996

Printed in the United States of America

0 9 8 7 6 5 4 3 2 1

Part I

The Planet of Eternal Light

I

In toward Galactic Center, the myth implies, there is a star so hot it is a mere dot in the sky of that planet where the God of Darkness and the Lady of Light live. Just as this sun has only one planet, so is there only one God, the God of Darkness.

In fact, stars that hot, FO or hotter, don't have planets. And if they did, the star wouldn't last long enough to allow planetary development of a terrestrial environment.

Even if such a god existed and if he could build a planet from scratch, why would he be humanoid or interested in humanity?

—*Lectures on Pan-Humanoid Myths*
Prester Smythe Kinsel
University of New Augusta
1211 A.O.E.

II

The young woman sits on the edge of the ornate bed where she is being watched.

"Everyone watches the Duke's daughter," she says in a low voice. Even the Duke's security force. More since the accident, she suspects. She cannot remember much of what she knows she should know.

The Duchess was solicitous, and her father the Duke growled. Yet he cares.

She frowns and leans forward, letting her long black hair flood over the shoulders of her pale blue travel suit.

Why should her memories be so cloudy? She can remember everything since she returned so clearly, but the people around her, the rooms, they all have a clarity that the past does not have.

Yet she belongs. The well-thumbed holobook in her father's study shows images of her growing up, standing at her father's knee, holding his hand.

Perhaps her studies at the Institute will help. Perhaps time will remove the awkwardness of relearning her past. Perhaps . . .

"Back into the fishbulb," she says out loud, crossing the room that would have held five of the single sleeping room she had occupied at Lady Persis'.

Somehow, the long row of garments hanging in the wardrobing room does not surprise her, although she has not remembered them. She walks through the wardrobe to the tiles and direct light of the bath.

Neither does she remember its luxury.

Half shrugging, she catches sight of herself in one of the full-length mirrors.

"Disheveled," she observes, looking at her hair. Something is right about it, for the first time in a long while, and something is not, nagging feelings she cannot place.

She squints until her eyes close. She opens them again. Her reflection awaits her.

III

"I don't understand, Martin. You're not registered . . ."

Not registered . . . a Query on your name . . . blocked even from the Duke's code . . .

Kryn's words are clipped, and even without the underlying concern he can sense, Martin knows of her unrest from the shortened speech.

The courtyard, the one where they always meet, is chill, as chill as the weather controls ever allow on the Planet of the Prince Regent of the Empire of Man. The little winds shuffle the small needles from the miniature cone-pines back and forth along the interior walls. No shadows, for the overcast is heavy enough to block the winter sun, and the climatizers have not succeeded in dispersing the clouds.

Kryn shivers, and the blue-clad guard involuntarily steps forward out of the corner, then back into the columns.

Always the guards, Martin reflects, *always the trappings of power.*

His eyes flicker over the communit bracelet that links her into the Regency data system, the blue leather overtunic that costs more than his total tuition, the sunpearls on her ring fingers.

He clears his throat.

"It's not that simple, Kryn." Not simple at all. He cannot register for further grad study, not with the Query stamped against his name.

No reason is given, and the junior registrar with whom he'd managed to get a face-to-face appointment had not known anything . . . . nothing except a few vague thought fragments unvoiced to Martin.

. . . has to be dangerous . . . deadly . . . not even Darin will meet him . . . why me? . . . Darin's ex-Marine . . . afraid of a student . . . why me?

"The real reason?" Martin had pressed.

"Imperial Security, Citizen Martel. That is all the University is told." Her smooth dark brow and open thoughts had revealed nothing else, even when he had probed deeply. And no one wanted to talk to him.

That had been it. Someone, somehow, had fed the results of the damned paracomm tests to Imperial Security, and he was out of grad school and on his way to the mines or the Marines ... the only employment open to someone who was Queried.

"Why not?" snaps Kryn, her cold words bringing him back from his thoughts into the chill of the Commannex courtyard.

"Because I can't get a job, any job, on Karnak. With no credits, I can't free-lance. If I could, no one could hire my services. So it's either off Karnak, or the Marines and off Karnak shortly. That's the choice."

"There has to be another one." Her voice is matter-of-fact. So are her feelings, Martin can tell, and she is as calm as her mother, the Iron Duchess, in telling a subject he is mistaken. Kryn will be Duchess, or more, Martin knows.

"If you could be so kind, Lady Kryn Kirsten, as to suggest another alternative for your obedient subject, Martin Martel, I would be most deeply obliged. Particularly since my student status will be terminated rather shortly."

"How soon?"

"Tomorrow ... today ... perhaps three days. The term is over, and the minimum guarantees of the Regency toward a Free Scholar have been met."

He looks down at the flat white of the marble pavement, then lifts his eyes to watch the dust devil in the far corner scatter a small heap of cone needles.

The sunlight floods abruptly into the courtyard.

"The climatizers succeed again," the ex-Scholar remarks, "bringing light into darkness, except for a few of us."

"Martin!"

He realizes that she wants to stamp her foot but refrains because the action would be unladylike.

He chuckles, and the low sound eddies through the columns. The guard in the shadows, now that there are shadows with the full winter sunlight beaming down, edges forward.

"What will you do?" Her question comes almost as a dismissal, an acceptance.

"I don't look forward to spending five years in the ore mines . . . and I don't have the heroic build of the successful Imperial Marine. So I'm somewhat limited."

"You aren't answering the question."

"I know. You don't want to hear the answer."

"You could leave the Empire . . ."

"I could. If I had the creds for passage. But no one can hire me to pay my way, except an outsider, and outsiders aren't allowed to downport here. And I don't have passage to the orbitport."

"I could help."

"I've already made arrangements."

"You didn't!"

"The Brotherhood is looking for comm specialists, so . . ."

"But"—her voice sharpens—"that's treason."

"Not unless the Regent changes the law."

He ought to. Brotherhood is nothing but trouble.

"Perhaps he will," Martin supplies the follow-on to her thought. "But they do pay, and will clear me from Imperial space, if necessary."

"Why?"

"Because, Lady Kryn Kirsten," Martin answers the question she meant, "I came off the dole, and I will not spend five years at slave labor in the *hope* that a black mark will be lifted from my name."

"May be Da—, the Duke, I mean, could take care of that." Martin refrains from trying to read her thoughts.

"I doubt that even the Duke could remove the Prince Regent's Query. And why would he? For a penniless scholar who's attracted to the very daughter he's planning to marry into the Royal Family?"

"Martin Martel! That's totally uncalled for." *How did he know? Never said . . . paracomm?*

"Realistic," he says in a clipped tone, trying to allay her suspicions. "Duke of Kirsten holds the most powerful House on Karnak next to the Regent. What else?"

So obvious, so obvious even to poor sweet Martin.

He cannot keep the wince from his face.

"Martin . . . what, how do you know?" *He reads thoughts, I know he does. How long? What does he really know?*

"Nothing that the gossip tabs haven't already spread. Nothing every student in the Commannex hasn't speculated."

Sweat, dampness, runs down Martin's back, with the perception that the guard is drawing his stunner, edging the setting beyond the stun range toward lethal.

Martin concentrates on the energy flows in the stunner, puzzling how to divert them, to distract Kryn from her iron-cold purpose, to just leave without raising any more fear and suspicion.

Aware of his sleeve wiping perspiration off his forehead, strange itself in the courtyard chill, he stammers.

"Nothing . . . nothing more to be said, Lady Kryn, time to depart . . . fulfill my contract to the Brotherhood . . . and then if you hear of a newsie named Martel on a far planet . . . think about corel."

No . . . no! Treason? Corel. Romance and flowers to the last. But a Duchess is as a Duchess does.

Her hands touch the stud on her wide belt, the stud that screams "emergency" to the guard. The tight-faced man in blue aims the stunner.

Zinnnng! The strum of the weapon fills the courtyard.

"I wish you hadn't, Kryn. Wish you hadn't," mumbles Martin, knowing that he has bent the focus of the beam around him, knowing that such is impossible.

The guard knows it also, looks stupidly down at the stunner, then raises it again, only to find that the blackclad student has disappeared, and that tears stream down the cheeks of the Lady Kryn Kirsten.

Along the courtyard wall, behind the black marble bench, lit by the slanting ray of the afternoon sun, the dust devil restacks the pile of cone needles.

IV

Aurore

No shadows has the noon; no darkness has the night,
And no man wears a shade in that eternal light.

The night has not a star; the sky has not a sun,
Nor is there dusk nor dawn to which a man can run.

No breakers crash at night, nor fall on sand unlit.
No lightning flares the dark where coming years might fit.

No dawn will break like thunder; no eve will crash like
    surf.
No shadows seep from tombs to mark its golden turf.

And if that's so, then why does darkness stalk the sky,
And only one god cast a shade to those who die,
And only one god cast a shade for those who die?

V

The overhead is pale yellow. The color is the first thing he
notices. That, and that he is on his back, stretched out on a
railed bed of some sort.

The second observation is that he wears a loose yellow
robe, nothing more, that is hitched up close to his knees.

There is no pillow, no sheeting, just a yielding surface on
which he lies. He lifts his head, which aches with the pain he
associates with stunners. Kryn's guard had missed, but not
Boreas.

"You'd think you'd learn, Martin," he mutters.

You'd think you'd learn, Martel.

He scans the room. No one else is present. The portal is

shut. A single red light on the panel next to the portal is lit.
The unlit light, he presumes, is green.

The railing lowers with the touch of a lever, and Martin
swings his legs over the edge and eases himself into a sitting
position. Rubbing his forehead with his left hand, he continues the survey of his quarters.

"Wonder if I'm being monitored."

Wonder if I'm being monitored.

Besides the bed, there are two chairs, a low table rising out
of the flooring between them, a higher bedside table, an
opaqued window screen, and a closet. The sliding doors of
the wardrobe/closet are half open, and Martin can see that his
few belongings have been laid out on the shelves or hung up.
The travelbag is folded flat on the top shelf.

He shakes his head, winces at the additional pain the
movement generates, and studies the room silently.

No speakers, no inconsistencies in the walls that could conceal something.

As he lowers himself to the floor the room wavers in front
of his eyes.

"Not again!" He recalls the paratest that led to his confine-
ment, that test which seems so distant, even though just days
past.

Not again! The echo pounds into his skull.

Slow step by slow step, he covers the meter or so from his
bed to the wardrobe, putting each foot down carefully, unsure
of his perceptions and his footing. By the time he puts out a
hand to lean on the wall edge of the wardrobe, he is dripping
sweat.

He shivers.

The robe, which had felt almost silky when he awoke, grits
against his skin like sandpaper. Martin fingers the cuff, but
the material still feels smooth to his fingertips.

He shivers again, but ignores the chill to concentrate on the
personal belongings laid out on the chest-level recessed wardrobe shelf.

Two items leap to his eye. The first is the solidio cube of
Kryn, which glows with a new inner light.

The second is the Regent's Scholar belt clasp. Before, it

had been a dull maroon. Now it glowers at him with a crimson malevolence.

One hand against the wall, still propping himself up, the former scholar and present fugitive/prisoner checks the garments. The robes provided by the Brotherhood have all been replaced with simple pale yellow tunics and trousers, three sets, and two new pairs of soft brown formboots lie on the floor.

After wiping his forehead with the back of his cuff, still looking silky and feeling gritty, he checks through the underclothes and folded personal items.

Most are missing . . . anything that might have linked him to the Brotherhood or to his time as a Regent's Scholar.

"But why leave the clasp?"

But why leave the clasp?

. . . leave the clasp . . .

. . . leave the clasp . . .

The room twists upside down, then right-side up, then upside down.

Martin closes his eyes. The brochure he'd been studying before Boreas had stunned him had mentioned disorientation. But this wasn't disorientation. It verges on torture.

He opens his right eye. The room is right-side up. He opens his left eye, and the room jumps to the left and stays in the same place, all at once, so that Martin sees doubled images.

He concentrates on fixing the images into one, just that, keeping his visions of things firmly in place. The images merge.

The sweat streams from his forehead again.

Suddenly the floor looms in front of his face, and pain like fire screams from his nose. And darkness . . .

The overhead is still pale yellow, and his head still aches. So do his nose and a spot on his forearm.

Again he is flat on his back on that same pallet, in the same hospital, if that is what it is.

"Flame!" he mutters without moving his head.

Flame!

He closes his eyes and tries to think.

He must be on Aurore. So why is it so painful? Aurore is

a vacation spot, a wonderful place to visit, where sensuality has its special delights and where some people gain extra powers. So why is one Martin Martel having such difficulty?

Too aware! The idea flashes into his thoughts. For whatever reason, his body is more sensitive to the environment.

Eyes still closed, he begins to let his thoughts, his perceptions, check out his body, starting with his toes, trying somehow to dampen the ultrasensitivity, to dull that edge, to convince himself that such perceptions should be voluntary, not involuntary.

He can feel the sweat again pour down his forehead, scented with fear, fear that he will not be able to regain control of his own body.

Others do it, he thinks, suppressing the urge to talk aloud.

The headache and the soreness in his nose and neck retreat. Martin opens his eyes. The room is a shade darker now, and yet the light levels from the walls have not changed, he realizes.

He lifts his head slowly, turns on his side, and fingers the rail release. After a time, he again sits up, legs dangling over the edge of the bed, heels touching the cold metal of the lowered rail.

He wills his vision to lighten the room. Nothing happens.

He relaxes the iron control on his perceptions.

The room wavers; his back itches; the soreness across the bridge of his nose throbs; the light intensifies.

Martin clamps down on his control.

Not a matter of will, but of control. Of perception.

He experiments, trying to isolate one sense after another, until the room begins to waver. He lies down, lets himself drift into a sweating sleep.

He dreams. Knows he dreams.

He is on a narrow path, except there are no edges, no walls, and the path arcs through golden skies. In front of him is Kryn. Her golden eyes are cold, and her mouth is tight-lipped.

Martin does not care, and yet he does. He takes a step toward Kryn, and another one. With each step he takes, she is farther away, though she has not moved.

Soon he is running toward her, and she dwindles into the distance. . . .

He sleeps and, presently, dreams. Again.

Martin watches a mountain spire, covered with ice, which thrusts up from a floor of fleece-white clouds. A part of his mind insists that he watches a meteorological impossibility, but he watches.

In the thin air above the peak, from nowhere appears a black cloud, modeled after the Minotaur. Across from the bull-cloud stands a god, male, heroic, clad in sandals and a short tunic. His crown is made of sunbeams, and it hurts Martin's eyes to look at his perfect face.

Between the two arrives another, a full-bearded barbarian who carries a gray stone hammer, red-haired, bulky, fur cape flowing back over his shoulders. He sports leg greaves and a breastplate, both of bronze.

Above the peak hovers another figure, which is present, but not. Martin strains to see, and after a time penetrates the ghostly details. She is slender, golden-haired, golden-eyed, and glitters. Beyond these details he cannot see, and his attention is distracted by the appearance of another god, also ghostly.

Where the goddess is golden, the latecomer is black-shadowed.

Unwanted, as well, because the three older golds strike. The barbarian throws his hammer; the sun-god Apollo casts a light spear; and the bull-god sends forth a black mist of menace.

Precog? questions someone, somewhere.

Perhaps.

Martin loses his dream, drops into darkness . . .

. . . and wakes screaming!

The scream dies as he moves his head, discovers he is on his side, holding the railing of the bed. Discovers his fingers are sore. He releases his grasp, and knows he should be surprised. He is not.

The metal is crushed, with eight finger impressions and two thumb holes clearly visible.

Martin scrambles to his knees, ignoring the wavering effect, to study his handiwork. He grabs the railing in a new place, farther toward the foot of the bed, squeezes with all the force he can muster.

His palms and fingers protest, but the metal does not yield. He lets go. Tears well up, sorrow and frustration.

"Mad, I'm mad. Crazier than Faroh."

Mad, I'm mad, mad, mad. Crazier, crazier, than, than, Faroh, Faroh.

He closes his eyes, presses balled fists against them to shut out the double echo, and the incredible flare of light that accompanies it.

"You'll get used to it," a calm voice comments.

Martin hops around on his knees, feels awkward, embarrassed, and almost pitches over the side of the bed as the nausea strikes him in the pit of his stomach.

The glare dies with the closing of the portal.

The speaker looks like the sun-god of his dreams, with short and curly blond hair, even features, cleft chin, piercing green eyes, heroic body structure, wide shoulders and narrow waist, under a gold tunic and trousers.

Martin nods for the man to continue.

"You're going to have more trouble than the others. There are two reasons for that. The first is that you're an untrained, full-range esper, and fully masked. The second is that you have, shall we say, a certain potential."

The golden man clears his throat, and even that sounds oddly musical, matching the light baritone of his clear voice.

"During the times ahead, for a while you'll know you're going mad, Martel. At times you will be. You have a great deal to learn. A great deal."

The speech bothers Martin, but he cannot pin down why.

"Who are you?"

Who are you?

Martin winces.

"You can either sync your thoughts to your speech or put a damper on them to eliminate the echo. The resonance makes any long conversations impossible, not to mention the headaches, until you get your thoughts under control. That's a function of the field. It tends to amplify stray thoughts and reflect them. Really only a nuisance, but without controls you could upset the norms and the tourists pretty strongly."

Norms? Dampers? Field? And what about the glare from outside?

He settles on the simplest question, trying to block his own thoughts at the same time.

"Is it that bright outside all the time?"

"No. It isn't bright at all. Normally the intensity is about that of early morning on Karnak. Bright, but nothing to worry about."

"But . . . when you came in?"

The golden man smiles. "It only seems bright to you. You don't see me at all. You're perceiving paranormally, and any light hurts your eyes. Except for the solidio cube, the belt clasp, and the port light, your room is totally dark. We've even screened out the glittermotes."

Martin gulps.

"I'll put it another way. Off Aurore, you have to make a conscious effort to use esp. Here, you have to make a conscious effort not to. As I mentioned a moment ago, when you really weren't paying attention, you are a full-range esper, one of a double handful in the entire Empire. That's fortunate in ways I'll not explain, and unfortunate in others. Unfortunate because the Empire would want you dead off Aurore, and because your adjustment to Aurore will be difficult at best, assuming you do make it."

The golden man is lying. Martin cannot explain which statement is wrong, decides to let it go, and tries to keep his doubts about the man buried.

"You're doubtful, Martel?"

"Why do you keep calling me Martel?"

"Because that's your real identification. Subconsciously you think of yourself as Martel, and not as Martin. I would advise you to cut some of the confusion short and go with Martel. That's an easy problem to solve."

When the other makes no move to leave, with the silence drawing out, Martin/Martel clears his throat.

"Call me Apollo. I'm here because I can't resist danger, however removed, and because someday you might decide to help me."

Not exactly the most helpful answer, reflects Martin/Martel, but it rings true.

"What sort of help?"

"I'd rather not say. You'll find out."

Another true statement, according to Martel's internal lie detector.

There are too many fragments. Norms, glittermotes, strength he doesn't have, but has. Seeing in total darkness . . .

He closes his eyes but wills himself to see. The room does not change, is still visible through closed eyelids.

As he realizes he can see behind the half-closed doors of the wardrobe, he begins to itemize the small personal trinkets.

He stops, half bemused, half frightened, when he realizes that Apollo has gone and that the portal had not opened.

The ceiling begins to glow, shedding a real light.

"Flame. Just beginning to tell the difference."

Just make it habit. The thought comes from far away. Apollo?

A low note chimes, and the green light above the portal illuminates. Martel braces himself for the glare, but with his eyes slit, the increase is bearable.

A thin older woman carries a small tray into the room. The mental static that surrounds her announces that she has some sort of shield or screen.

She does not look at him.

"Good morning. Is it morning?"

Her face narrows. The frown, her black hair, and her thin eyebrows all combine to form a disapproving look. Martel studies her, decides she is younger than he thought.

"It's morning. How do you feel?"

Despite the mental screen, Martel can sense her puzzlement.

"Confused," he admits. "How long have I been here? Asleep?"

"Two standard months. Not always asleep."

She puts down the tray and steps back, eyes taking in the bent metal railing.

"What do you mean, not always asleep?"

She backs farther away.

"That's something the doctors need to discuss with you. I will see what can be done. You're not scheduled yet."

Martel frowns to himself. Not scheduled? Scheduled for

what? Two months? From a stunner? Has he been here ever since Boreas stunned him?

She drops a folder on the low table and scuttles for the portal.

"If you read that, it will give the right perspective." She darts out. The door irises shut, and the amber light replaces the green, but the ceiling glow remains.

Apollo had said that using paranorm powers was easy.

Martel reaches for the folder with his thoughts and is still surprised when it floats up from the table into his hands.

The folder is not what he expected. Rather than a general brief, it is an excerpt from a technical article: "Dealing with Fullphase, Full Awakening of Paranormals in an Ultrastimulatory Environment," selections from the full and uncompleted works of one Sevir Corwin, S.B., P.D., M.D., S.P.N.P., etc.

There is one introductory paragraph that catches Martel.

Inasmuch as Dr. Corwin did not live to complete his work, and could not be consulted on the selections, the editor has attempted to include those portions most likely to help clinical personnel working in high-risk situations.

Martel studies the folder. Cheap reproduction, right from an ordinary copy unit. More questions.

He reads the entire folder. Twice, despite the odd turn of technical phrases, while he eats the fruit and the protein bar and the flat pastry that the aide has brought.

Phrases ring in his thoughts.

Ultrastimulatory environments can be dangerous for newly aroused paranorms . . . transition under sedation . . . subconscious realization . . . LR_{50} for intervenors during I.P., . . . de facto ban on paranorm transfer to ultrastim (read Aurore) . . .

He leans back on the pallet, closes his eyes, tries to list what he knows, tries to get it in some sequence, something that makes sense.

Item: He is considered paranorm.
Item: Paranorms arriving on Aurore are dangerous as flame, to themselves and to those around them.

Item: Boreas has stunned him en route, under Brotherhood
      orders.
Item: The Brotherhood definitely wants him on Aurore.
Item: For two months he has been out of his mind.
Item: While dreaming, he had literally crushed a heavy
      steel railing.
Item: Apollo isn't afraid of Martel.
Item: The woman is.
Item: He is getting sleepy.
Item:

His last thought on the listing is *Don't you ever learn, Martel?*

Again, the dreams . . . but more confused, this time, these times.

He is floating above the same ice peak, but no one is around him, and there are no clouds, but the upper levels of the mountain are still in shadow.

He turns to move closer to the peak, but from his left a golden thunderbolt blasts in front of him. On his right, a dark thundercloud materializes.

He contemplates the needlepeak, waiting . . .

. . . and finds himself sitting at a table, across from a golden-eyed and golden-haired woman. She is speaking, but he cannot understand the words; though each is a word he knows, her sentences form a pattern and a puzzle he cannot assemble, and as he wrestles with each word the next catches him by surprise.

Finally he nods, and looks past her over the railing toward the golden sands that slope down to the sea. He touches the beaker by his left hand. Jasolite. A jasolite beaker. Jasolite, jasolite . . .

. . . LIGHT! . . .

. . . and he is strapped down on a cold metal table, under the pinpoint of a telescope. The telescope is gathering starlight, and that light is coming out of the pinpoint needle just above his forehead.

He twists, but the heavy straps and metal bands do not bend.

The light coming from the instrument burns his skin, and he wrenches his left hand free, then his right, and cups them under the enormous telescope to catch the torrent of light. But his hands overflow, and the burning light cascades over his palms and blisters his forehead.

Finally he throws the light back into the telescope, which melts, collapsing away from him.

Then he curls up on the metal table, and sleeps . . .

. . . and wakes in a lounge chair. For a long time, he is not certain if he is awake. A woman is stretched in the chair next to him, but he cannot turn his head. Perhaps he does not want to.

He is near the sea. The salt tells him so, and the slow crashes of the breakers do not confuse him, not the way the words the unseen woman speaks do.

She speaks slowly, and the words are in order, he knows. But some he hears twice, and some he loses because of those he hears twice.

". . . you, you, understand, stand, sedated, sedated . . . if, if . . . remember, remember . . . dream . . . dream . . ."

The strain of pursuing the words presses him back into the lounge, and he lets himself float on the vibrations of the incoming breakers.

". . . god, god, you, you . . . forget, get . . ."

The urgency of her tone chains him, whips across his cheeks like a blizzard wind, and he drowns in the sounds, drifting into a darkness.

Thoughts boom like drums in the darkness, out of the black.

This one troubles me.

As well he should.

That upstart?

Boom! Boom-boom! Each letter of each verbal thought brands his brain, and he screams, and screams . . .

He wakes.

The clarity of his surroundings announces that he does not dream, and may not be drugged.

Although his eyes focus on the pale yellow overhead, someone waits. Another woman. He knows without looking.

Instead of sitting up and reacting, he remains motion-

less, thinking. Deciding if he can sort out what he has
dreamed from what he experienced under the sedation. Deciding that sorting can wait, and filing the memories in a corner of his mind for more scrutiny.

His thoughts scan the room.

The woman wears a mental screen. Both a laser and a full-
range stunner are focused on him from the ceiling, and the
thickness of the walls argues for a prison rather than a hospital. Idly Martel lets his perceptions change a few circuits in
the laser and stunner to remove their immediate threat.

Then he stretches, slowly, and begins to sit up.

The woman is red-haired, and radiates friendliness.

Martel notes that she has appeared in his dreams, and files
the note. He senses that her friendliness is genuine, and lets
himself smile.

"I'm Rathe Firien, and I'd like to welcome you formally to
Aurore. I suspect you know you've already been here for
some time."

"Delighted," responds Martel, with a twitch of his mouth
preventing a full smile. "How long?"

"Five standard months."

"Wonderful."

He puts his feet over the edge of the bed, lets them dangle,
lets his mind range through the room again. The room is not
the same one, but built like a Marine bunker, meter-thick
plate behind the walls, and ferroplast behind that.

He shakes his head.

"Something the matter?" She is concerned.

"No. Just a little amazed. Do you go to this extent for all
paranorms?"

She hesitates.

"Special instructions, huh? From the Brotherhood?"

"Brotherhood?" Confusion there.

"Apollo?" he pursues.

Fear, but validation.

He decides to change the subject.

"What's next on the agenda?"

"For you?"

Martel nods.

"I suppose you could get dressed . . ." She grins.

"I meant . . . in general terms."

"Once you're dressed"—and she grins again, and Martel cannot resist smiling back—"we'll get you out of here. Then we'll go over the things you need to do to get settled in."

Martel wraps the one-piece robe around him as he realizes that it has started to fall open, then relaxes. Obviously, the woman knows all about him. He shakes his head.

"Does it always take this long?"

"What?"

"Getting adjusted, or whatever this process is called."

"For a paranorm it varies."

So many questions . . . He gives up, and decides to work on one thing at a time. He stands up, feeling fit, stretches, and sees Rathe's mouth in an O, suppressing a laugh. He suspects he has grown somehow, until he discovers he is floating a good ten centimeters off the floor, and lets himself down.

"Sorry. Not used to this."

"I'll meet you outside. The fresher's next to the wardrobe. Touch the plates next to the portals to open them."

She leaves.

Martel discovers that he does want a shower. After cleaning up, he pulls on one of the yellow tunic/trouser outfits and a pair of the formboots.

He doesn't like the yellow. When he can, he will have to replace the clothes selected for him.

Wonder of wonders, the outer portal opens at his touch, and Rathe Firien is waiting.

VI

Outside the portal is a balcony, and from it Martel can see a town spreading down a gentle incline toward the silver/green/gold expanse that has to be the ocean.

He still must squint against the unaccustomed strength of the light, indirect and unfocused as it is.

A light breeze ruffles his hair, and he notes that it is neither warm nor cool, but bears a faint scent of pine.

He is conscious of Rathe Firien, who has stepped back as he moves to take hold of the black iron railing.

The roofs of Sybernal are white. Some sparkle; some merely are white.

A wide dark swath of trees halfway between him and the sea breaks the intermittent pattern of roofs and foliage.

Must be some sort of park.

. . . some sort of park . . .

He shakes his head, trying to remember to hang on to his control.

"Is something wrong?" asks the woman.

"No." He pauses. "The dark stretch there?" He points.

"That's the Greenbelt. It surrounds the coastal highway where it cuts through Sybernal."

" 'Coastal,' and not on the coast?"

"It is, except in Sybernal. You can walk the Petrified Boardwalk there. You'll see."

Martel supposes he will.

He studies the grounds beneath the balcony. The grass is nearly emerald-colored and short. Roughly half the trees are deciduous, which seems wrong.

Why?

He knows it is "wrong," but also knows he is not thinking clearly enough yet to pose the question correctly, much less answer it.

The streets are little more than paved lanes, suitable for walking and for the electrobikes he sees under a covered porch at the far end of the building.

The square paved space in the middle of the lawn, he assumes, is a flitter pad, which would make sense for a hospital, or whatever institution he is confined in.

"What's next?" he asks.

"I've called a flitter."

"For what?"

"So you can leave."

"Just like that?"

"Do you want to stay?" She favors him with a half-smile, one that reminds him of the friendliness she radiates.

"I can't say that I do, but that's not the question. Don't I have to check out? Or see someone? Or sign something?"

"That's been taken care of. You're ready to leave."

Taken care of. Right. You've been taken care of. And how! What's next? A quiet little trip to another secluded hideaway?

"Just a flaming instant! Just what other little tricks do you all have planned? If I'd been hospitalized, or institutionalized, anywhere for this long, I couldn't possibly be let go the minute I woke up and the first pretty nurse to come along said, 'You. All right. You can leave now.'" He takes a deep breath.

Rathe Firien just waits for him to continue. Her smile is even more amused.

"Here I am, drugged, doped, and dreaming for months on end, and now—snap, bang, yes, sir, Mr. Martel, time to check out and get on with your business. Of course, we haven't told you where you are, why you've been here, how long you've been here, and where we want to take you. But let's get going!

"Now! Just what the flame is going on in this place? And what's the sudden hurry?"

He completes the last word with a slam on the iron balcony railing. The twinge that rips up his left arm reminds him that he is awake and that iron bars do not bend at his touch.

He looks down at his wrist, uncovered and pale, and at the yellow cuff of the tunic. Both are too light.

The woman stands just beyond his reach, waiting for him to insist on an answer.

"I won't," he whispers, understanding that his refusal only hurts himself.

. . . won't, won't, won't . . .

The day is still, and the breeze has died. The pine scent is gone, replaced with a heavier smell of flowers and freshly turned earth. A single bird chirp breaks the silence.

Swallowing, he finally looks up. "Would you care to explain?"

"If you'll listen."

Martel nods.

"First, you're on Aurore. You know that. Nowhere else is like Aurore, and you don't seem to understand that. You're leaving because your mind is ready to cope with Aurore. With your background, the sooner you leave here the better.

Besides, when He says you can go, you can go. I don't question Him, and neither should you.

"It may be months before you understand why, but please take my word for it now. If you don't agree, you can always ask your questions later." She purses her lips, licks the upper one with the pink tip of her tongue, and goes on.

"For the time, being, please remember that you are *totally* responsible for the results of your actions. If you keep that in mind, you won't do too badly."

"*Totally* responsible for the results of my own actions?"

"There are a few exceptions, but, yes, that's a fair statement. This isn't the time or the place to get into that discussion. Wait until you've had some time."

He senses bitterness behind her statement and refrains from pushing that line of questioning.

"So what comes next? Where are we going, and why?"

"On a quick aerial tour of Sybernal, to help you get your bearings, and then for something to eat. After that, I'll help you look into lodgings, though that's scarcely a problem."

Scarcely a problem? Then what is? He keeps the questions to himself and looks toward the flitter pad in reaction to the *flup/swish, flup/swish* of a descending flitter.

Rathe Firien is already at the end of the balcony and headed down the wide stairs toward the lawn and the waiting aircraft.

Martel misses seeing the incoming pilot, if there is one, because when he arrives, breathing heavily, Rathe is at the controls.

"Whew! Out of shape."

"You'll recover, I'm sure," she observes with a twist of her lips.

By now the flitter is airborne, and she begins her travelogue.

"Sybernal is laid out like a half-circle around the bay, although it's really more of a gentle arc in the straight coastline than a true bay. Most of the beaches are straight, and those that do curve are generally perfect arcs. You can see the Greenbelt from here. That's the coast highway running through the middle."

Martel follows the direction of her free hand. As far as he

can see, the so-called coastal highway, which rejoined the coastline south of Sybernal, has very little traffic on it.

"Not much travel."

"Natives and norms don't travel that far or that much. The touries use flitters. This one belongs to Him. For special use. Now, on the beach side of the Greenbelt, that's where the plush houses and the better restaurants are. This side is the trade district, and closer to us is where most norms and natives live."

The flitter's nose swings northward.

"There are a few large estates in the higher hills north of Sybernal. You can see the white there ... and there? The owners keep to themselves. For all I know, some may be gods or demigods."

"Doesn't anyone know?" asks Martel, aware that his voice carries a waspish note. "Doesn't the government keep track?"

"Private property is private property, and trespassing is strictly forbidden."

Martel frowns. Rathe Firien's response doesn't exactly qualify as a direct answer.

"I'm not sure I understand," he finally says, pulling at his chin.

"Let's just say that the right to privacy from one's fellows is fully respected here. Generally, even the gods leave you alone. So long as you don't hurt anyone else."

"But—"

"I'll explain later. Right now you're getting a quick tour, remember?"

Martel can sense her amusement, as well as an underlying sense of fear. He reflects, and decides that the feeling is not just fear. As the flitter cabin swirls around him he breaks off the mental stretching and concentrates on regaining his equilibrium.

Aurore is going to take some getting used to, Martel.

"Wouldn't gods have palaces on mountaintops?" The question sounds stupid even as he asks it, and he shakes his head.

The pilot lets the question pass, and swings the flitter back toward the town.

Martel studies the terrain beneath.

In the distance to the southwest of Sybernal, a flash of

light, brilliant red, catches his eye. He strains to make out the regular and angular shapes nearly on the horizon, shapes that seem familiar. His memory dredges up the map he had studied and supplies him with the answer—the shuttleport, one of only two on all Aurore. The flash has to have been an in-beacon call.

. A single highway, no bigger than the thin strip called the coastal highway, arrows away from the city-town of Sybernal toward the port. Martel cannot spot any traffic at all on the roadway to the shuttleport, and only a few dwellings lining it.

The homes beneath the flitter cluster closer together the nearer to the center of Sybernal they are, Martel notes, although even those most closely packed have individual lawns and foliage surrounding them.

For all the whiteness of the roofs, for all the emerald green of the grass, the gold-green sparkle of the sea, and the darker green of the trees, something is missing. Martel cannot decide what it is, but there is a subdued drabness about Sybernal as seen from the air, a certain lack of color.

"There's the CastCenter, where you'll be working once you get fully adjusted."

"What?" Martel has not been following her gesture.

"Over to the right. The circular building on the low hill with the roof grids? That's the CastCenter."

Martel picks out the structure, notes its position, slightly to the northwest of what would be the center of Sybernal if one were that clearly defined. If his estimate of distances is correct, he could probably walk the distance from the farthest point in Sybernal to work in less than a stan.

Sybernal is not exactly the largest of cities, not a booming metropolis, particularly after Karnak. But his briefings had indicated that Sybernal is by far the largest city on Aurore.

He shakes his head again. He has questions, too many questions.

"Not looking forward to work?" asks Rathe, apparently misinterpreting his headshake.

"It's not that. It's just that I've got more than a little adjusting to do."

He turns away from her and stares out through the bubbled canopy toward the south. Is it his imagination, or is there a snowcapped peak just over the horizon? He can feel that there ought to be just such a mountain, but is there?

The land that stretches away from Sybernal toward the south lies in gently rolling hills, composed of roughly equal sections of cultivated fields, forest, and golden grass meadows.

The emerald lawns of Sybernal are at odds with the golden field grass.

Another contradiction, unless the city grass is an import.

The air is clear, cloudless, yet the high golden haze, uniform from horizon to zenith, conveys an impression of mistiness. Martel knows that impression is false by the clarity of landmarks, such as the hills to the north, and the sharpness of the thin highways angling into the distances.

They are nearly over the coastline now, and only faint traces of whitecaps streak the ocean. The breakers streaming into the beaches are sternly narrow.

"We're going to land near the South Pier and have something to eat. I'll answer some of those questions you had, and then we'll look into housing for you."

"Oh . . . fine."

Fine, right, Martel? Not much in the way of formality here, is there?

She eases the stick forward, and the flitter responds, dipping toward the pier.

VII

"Before we really get started . . . the first and most important point is to defer to the gods."

Martel sets the jasolite beaker down on the transparent tabletop.

"Let's have that again. About the gods."

About the gods.

He rubs his forehead at the mental echo. Any lapse of control has immediate results.

"You're tired."

He hears the concern in her voice and senses the compassion. He hates it, hates being pitied. He hated being understood when Kryn had felt sorry for him, and he hates it now.

"Not tired. Careless. Go on. Why must one be so careful with the gods?" He picks up the beaker and takes another sip of the liqueur that warms his throat on the way down and seems to dull the ache in his head. Springfire, Rathe had called it.

A stray glittermote, a shining black rather than the usual gold, settles on his shoulder, flickers twice, and vanishes.

"You know about the gods, Martel. The ones like Apollo who can kill with a gesture, manipulate your feelings with a song, throw thunderbolts if they feel like it . . ."

Martel looks away from her freckled face and east toward the incoming surf. According to his scattered knowledge, Aurore shouldn't have tides as substantial as it does.

"Apollo can't do all that," he mutters, not caring totally, but knowing that what he says is true.

"No, probably not all that, but each god can do at least one thing out of the ordinary, and by that I mean beyond the normal range of esping. Now, technically speaking"—she stops to purse her thin lips before continuing—"there are distinctions between potentials, demigods, gods, and Elder Gods. For a newcomer, even as esper, all god types are dangerous."

Martel doesn't believe it, half doesn't care. But Rathe is so earnest, and he is expected to ask. He does.

"Why?"

"They all can tap the field, and that's an energy source not open to nongods, not even to you."

According to his chrono, it is approaching local midnight, but the light level has not varied. While the tables on the balcony are only half occupied, those who are there keep their own schedules. Martel has observed three breakfasts, several midday meals, and after-dinner liqueurs delivered by servitors since he and Rathe had been seated so much earlier.

"Does everyone keep their own schedule?"

"You weren't listening?"

Another black glittermote settles on the pale gold collar stripe of Martel's tunic.

"I am, and I was. So many things to ask."

"All right." She sighs. "Yes. Everyone keeps his or her own schedule. How could it be otherwise? It's always day. Some stick to an arbitrary day/night schedule. Some follow standard Imperial. Others take naps around the clock. Gods never sleep."

"Gods, gods, gods. All I seem to hear is about gods."

She sets her expression. "And it's all you will hear until you show some signs of understanding who they are and what they can do."

She is serious. Martel can tell.

He spreads his hands in surrender. "So tell me about the gods."

"If I only could . . ." she starts.

Martel opens his mouth.

"No. Don't interrupt. Please. I'm not used to espers. Why you were assigned to me—Don't look into my thoughts . . . just listen."

He nods, seething at the idea that he would indiscriminately rummage through anyone's mind, wondering if he can, really can, at the same time.

Rathe sips her own liqueur, looks out at the breakers, and begins to talk, the words falling in a rush.

"Everyone says that Aurore is the home of the gods, and lets it go at that. Everyone thinks it's nice we don't have big government or much crime. Or that assassins can't even get off a shuttle here. Or Imperial spies or agents. I guess it is. But no one mentions the other side of the cred. We don't have a choice. The gods do. We don't."

"What do you mean?"

She goes on as if he has not spoken.

"We don't have any police, you may have noticed. No courts. No written laws."

Martel has not noticed. The brochures and infopaks he had read hadn't mentioned this aspect of Aurore.

"We have gods," Rathe Firien pushes on, "and they punish criminals. Rather, the demigods do. If the demigods exceed their rights, they get punished. By the gods. Simple, Right?"

"If you say so. But who judges the gods?"

"Other gods, all of them, or so I've been told. But that really doesn't concern you."

"What does?"

Rathe does not answer. Just shakes her head. Her short, fine hair fluffs out momentarily. With the light behind her, she seems to wear a crown, an image incongruous with the warmth and approachability she radiates.

The warmth is why she has the job she does.

Martel cannot think of anything to say, and the silence stretches out. As Rathe purses her lips prior to speaking an answer strikes Martel.

"Severe punishment?" he asks.

"Not necessarily severe, but certain. Unavoidable. Just."

"You didn't mention merciful."

"Mercy isn't the question. Justice is."

"But how?"

"The punishment fits the crime. Common thieves lose their right hand."

"That's punishment?" asks Martel, thinking about bionics and full-clone grafts.

"It is when the nerves refuse to take a graft. Ever."

"Oh . . . oh." Martel understands. Anyone who can alter the nerve structure to such a degree, the chromosome patterns, has powers beyond the normal.

"What about the more severe crimes?"

"Most don't get committed. They screen all incomers. People who have committed minor crimes get blessed. Very few criminal types escape. That leaves crimes of passion, and even a lot of those are headed off. Gods can sense trouble, when they choose to."

"Total conditioning."

"Not exactly. Just if you're antisocial or antigod. And it's not really conditioning. An absolute prohibition locked into your soul. Or a compulsion. A pyromaniac can't touch matches. He couldn't even light a signal fire to save a life. A man with a violent temper can't raise his voice or lift a hand in anger . . . even to stop a beating or a theft."

Martel shudders. Imperial justice is bad enough. But an absolute justice? He shudders again.

"It isn't bad. Really, it isn't. It works. You won't get cheated. You won't get mugged. Very civilized."

If it's so civilized, dear Rathe, why do you sound so bitter?
He holds the thought to himself.

"And everyone has a job, and is happy to have one." She paused, then added, "Except mothers of small children."

"You will work, and you will be happy. Is that it?"

"Not exactly. If you want to work without a blessing, you'll never draw attention. If you don't want to work, and don't cause problems and can pay your service taxes, that's fine, too. You can't expect to live off society."

Martel squeezes his lips together. Somehow, Aurore doesn't sound quite so ideal, quite the paradise he'd imagined. All this was just the first lesson.

He drains the last of the Springfire.

"What about the second lesson?"

"You've already heard it. Two rules. Defer to the gods. Don't hurt anyone. That will cover most things. That and paying for what you use. That's it."

"That's it?"

"Does there have to be anything else?"

He thinks, looks out at the too-regular breakers, then back at the red-haired woman.

"I suppose not. What if you hurt someone accidentally?"

"If it's unforeseen and unintended, nothing. If you are careless, you'll be judged and punished."

Why do you know so much, Rathe? Why so much sadness beneath the friendly surface?

She pushes a small infopak across the table to him. Against the transparency of the surface it hangs in midair, along with the two beakers.

Martel ignores a faint bead of sweat on the woman's upper lip. The sea breeze has stopped momentarily.

"Possible lodgings. Available singles. You can choose house, conapt, or room."

"What would you suggest?"

"For you, I'd think a small house, as far away from others as possible. Until you have your mental defenses built."

"How could I pay for it?"

"No problem. The owner or seller knows you'll pay, and you're already on salary at the CastCenter."

Martel hadn't understood that section of his contract when

it had been presented . . . why the pay had started when he arrived on Aurore, rather than when he started work. It made more sense now. But he felt guilty about the back pay, if there was any.

"Back pay?" he ventured.

"That's a crossover. Paid for your treatment."

It figured. He pushed the infopak back at Rathe. "Pick out some very small houses for us to look at."

"I'll suggest several."

Rathe pointed out two in the hills behind Sybernal, and one south of the town/city.

Martel didn't even leave the flitter for an inside view of the first two.

In the end, he settled on the hillside guesthouse with the view of the sea. He liked the idea that by walking fifty meters up the hillside he could look down the other side at a sheltered bay.

The landlady, a gray-haired woman of indeterminate age, Mrs. Alderson, offered no objection to Martel's immediate occupancy, and even supplied linens . . . for a deferred payment.

Rathe Firien pointed out the slight differences in the appliances, then sat on the bed as he unpacked his single bag.

"Don't know why I bother," Martel mutters as he hangs up the gold-and-white tunics and trousers that have been furnished for him.

"The colors, you mean?"

"Um-hmmm. Not mine."

"Yours is black."

"How did you know?"

"You said so."

"When?"

"When you were under treatment."

"What else did I say?"

"Who's Kryn?"

"The girl I loved. The one I thought I loved."

"She love you?"

"No." Martel folds the collapsible savagely, jams it to the back of the high shelf at the back of the built-in wardrobe. "Don't ask me!" he growls, afraid Rathe will ask more.

Don't ask me! Don't ask me! He cannot block the thoughts.
"I'd like to help." Her voice is low.

... have to help ... The thought fragment is clear.

Martel turns toward Rathe, watches as she unbuttons her
blouse, watches as she shrugs out of the tight trousers and
stands, breasts firm, nipples erect, arms half outstretched, almost pleading.

... please ... have to ... gods are just ... be merciful ...

Her eyes do not meet his, and he wants to turn away, to
bury himself in the memory of Kryn, in cool blue, even she
who held a hot stunner. Instead, he lets his thoughts enfold
the red-haired woman, who knows him while he scarcely
knows her, lets his mind fall around hers, trying to understand.

As he takes a step toward her the pictures flood him, first
one at a time, then in a tidal wave.

A red-haired young woman, a girl, swimming with a
friend, sunning themselves on a deserted beach with even
waves, the friend of a young man. Blond, handsome. An insistent young man, with insistent hands, hands knowing of
her desires and her resistance, trying to trigger the former and
brush by the latter. Kissing, leading to touching, and her
breaking away, out into the water, half laughing, half crying,
half wanting, and half turning away. The man's reluctant acceptance.

More pictures, blurring.

Another scene, high above the sea, on a ledge over white
cliffs, secluded. More kissing, more touching, and again the
girl breaks away. This time the man grabs for her, tries to
force her back into his arms. She half turns, falls. He falls
onto her, breathing hard, and she kicks at him. His feet go out
from under him, skitter on the white gravel, and he loses his
balance, bounces, and falls. Falls out over the hard rocks and
down, down onto the jagged edges and foam hundreds of meters below ... his scream ... her tears ... barely started before the thunderbolt, the god appearing, sunhair so brilliant
his features obscured ... his judgment ... seared into her
thoughts ...

Martel tries to break out of Rathe's thoughts, tries not to, all at the same time, understanding at first/second hand what she alluded to in mere words.

Let the punishment fit the crime. Because she led on one who wanted her, who loved her in his own way, killed him, even accidentally, she had to pay, and pay, and pay, by easing the hurts of those who are lost, the Martels and who knew how many others, forever and ever and ever . . . world without end.

He stands there, his body nearly next to hers, but not touching her naked skin, with his own tears and hers streaming down his cheeks, shaking, wanting to touch her, wanting her to hold him, and unable to bring about either. He touches her hands, finally takes them in his, holds her, and she presses against him, gently, undemandingly, and their cheeks touch, their tears meet.

After a time he cannot measure, he lays her upon the low bed and holds her more tightly. Lips brush, and more, and they fold and enfold each other.

After the instants, after the quiet, in the silence that is no longer empty, sleep finds them, finds her.

In the day-lit time that seems like night, she tries to pull away, but asleep and awake all at once he will not let her go, strokes her short red-silk hair, touches her thoughts, touches the line of judgment within her soul and finds he cannot remove it, finds he can add something, a small something, restore a small sense of pride, and does. Holds her through the day that is morning.

And sleeps.

When he wakes, she is there, dressed, sitting at the foot of the bed.

"Leaving?"

She nods. Touches her fingertips to her lips, then to his forehead. She stands and leaves without a sound, having given, having received.

Martel wants to cry, cannot, will not, and feels the shadow within him grow.

After instants that feel like hours, he rolls over, stares at the open doorway.

More time passes before he sits on the edge of the bed, head down and resting in his palms.

Should he have let her walk out?

Martel stands and surveys the room, the empty shelves, the wardrobe where three outfits hang, the window that opens on the grassy hillside with its scattered pines and a single quince.

Tell me now, and if you can,
What is human, what is man?

The lines of the old song seem singularly appropriate, though he knows not why.

He pulls on trousers, tunic, boots.

The portal, which is really an old-fashioned doorway, beckons, and Martel follows it.

On his right, as he goes out of his bedroom, is an even more expansive window that frames the hillside running down toward the coast road and the sea beyond. To the left is a set of louvered panels that screen off the small kitchen. Straight ahead are a settee, a low table, and two stretched-fabric chairs. Behind the arrangement of furniture is a dining area with another, higher table and four chairs.

Walking around one of the fabric chairs, Martel stops in front of the window.

"A long day . . ."

A long day . . .

He rubs his forehead. The control is not automatic yet, not on this, his first day of return to the land of the living. From five months of drugged existence to a friendly face, a warm person, who greets you in the most intimate way possible, and then feels she must walk out?

Rathe Firien, Kryn or no Kryn, memories or not, will be part of his life. For now, for who knows how long. And who knows how long for anything?

Martel holds two images up in his mind, compares.

Kryn: long dark hair, light complexion, high-breasted, slender, blue girl. Mind and thoughts like a knife ready to cut. Fragile and strong as plasteel, uncertain, yet ambitious and ready and willing to stab for hers. Cold, and passionate.

Set the record straight, Martel. You think she's passionate.

He makes the mental correction with a half-smile.

Rathe: short red hair, narrow-waisted and full-breasted, friendly, open, and vulnerable. Strong . . . he didn't know, but her mind said she was. Ambitious—no. How could anyone be ambitious with a compulsion like that laid across her soul? Passionate . . . yes, with reservations.

He shakes his head.

Are the gods really gods? Or men and women with larger-than-life powers playing god over a planet that wasn't really a planet? Playing with Martels and Rathes of Aurore, like toys in an endless game?

Does he, Martel, really want to find out? And risk the outcome for himself, for Rathe, for Kryn?

Does he have any choice?

And what about Kryn? Is she real or an inflated memory? Will she be part of the future? And Rathe? How long? How?

He turns from the window.

VIII

Reason would indicate that death either represents no state or a changed state, nothingness or somethingness, if you will.

Humanoid cultures, almost universally, represent death as a dark and grasping figure, which does not follow logically. Is there something about the source of this representation of which we are unaware?

The Dark Side
Sidney Derline

IX

A glittermote lands on his left arm, the one sprawled out on the sand next to his head.

Without looking up, he knows it is black. The black ones

feel different, more attuned to him than the normal white or gold motes that seem to be everywhere.

He leaves his head on the sand, eyes closed, lets the diffused warmth soak into his bare back. For whatever reason, he can get a light tan at any time of day or night. Logically, whether or not the field diffused light, the tanning effect should have been limited to the technical "day." As with many things on Aurore, though, logic is wrong.

Martel corrects himself: Apparently sound logic is wrong.

Crunching sounds, footsteps, intrude.

He lifts his head, rolls over and into a sitting position.

A tall man, blocky, black-haired and dark-skinned, dripping ocean, walks from the foam at the water's edge straight up the beach toward him.

The black glittermote stays perched on Martel's arm. A second mote appears next to the first.

Martel half smiles ... the first time he had seen two together. Black ones, that is.

So you're the one.

Martel blocks the thoughts and answers, "The one what?"

"If you want to handle it this way, it's your choice." The stranger stares at Martel, the sharpness of his study disconcerting.

Martel stands and wishes he hadn't, as the other towers a full two heads taller.

"Black glittermotes? Never seen any before. Must be something new, not that there hasn't been time for that."

Martel gathers his defenses, mental and physical. Will some sort of assault follow the verbal onslaught?

"Who are you?"

"Just a curious bit player. You can call me Gil Nash, if you want. It's close enough."

To what? thinks Martel, simultaneously blocking it from the other while drawing energy from somewhere, somehow.

A small cloud of black glittermotes appears from nowhere, circles Martel, and a handful array themselves across his shoulders, their feather touch electric.

"Don't draw any conclusions!" counters the tall man, backing up several steps. "I'm just watching."

Martel shakes his head to clear his sight from the momentary disorientation, focuses on the other's face as a stabilizer, finds himself reaching, evading the other man's sievelike screens, and picking up fragments, mostly images.

A tall ice-pointed peak ... Apollo the sun-god ... oceans and brass chains with links to dwarf a man ... a sword that flames when drawn ... a dark cloud that is a bull and a man and a god ...

Martel retreats from Nash's thoughts, finds he can see the energy of the man, his ties to the field. Those are what the lines of energy have to be.

Nash retreats another step, far enough down the sloping beach that he and Martel are almost at equal eye level.

"Take your time, Martel. You have forever, and they don't."

"What about you?"

"Another century of causing tidal waves won't hurt, and that's what I'll get."

"What? And who are 'they'?"

"It's a long story. But since the thunderbolts haven't hit yet, how about a drink?"

Martel shrugs.

None of what the crazy giant says makes sense, but maybe it would. What seems logical isn't. So what isn't might be.

"My place is up the hill. All I've got is some local beer and Springfire." He turns and digs his toes into the sand as he starts upward, mentally reaching out and letting the towel sweep itself off the sand and over his arm.

"I'll take the beer. Springfire's the last thing I need at the moment." Nash does not comment on the acrobatics of the towel, as if they were only expected.

Either an esper or familiar with them, reflects Martel, letting his extended perceptions track the bigger man as he follows Martel out of the sand and onto the grassy hillside.

The two chairs and table on the covered deck wait for them, as well as a beaker of Springfire and a frosted mug of beer.

Martel gestures to one chair and seats himself in the other, the one closer to the door into the cottage. The nearly dry Nash, wearing only what seems a metallic loincloth, sinks into the chair, which bends, but does not give. Martel revises his estimate of the man's weight and strength up another notch.

The other downs nearly a full liter in one gulp.

"Not the best, but damned fine after all that salt water."

"Could you explain?" asks Martel. "None of this makes any sense. Black glittermotes, bit players, thunderbolts, chains, and drinking salt water."

"Young one, when you've been around as long as me, you take things for granted. It all seems so simple. Some things I won't tell you, because you won't believe them, and my telling will make it even harder. That'd hurt me. So I won't tell. Some things you're about to learn and half believe, and those I will tell you. And some things you won't understand."

Martel waits, but the tall man, who physically does not appear more than a handful of years older than Martel, drains the rest of the mug. Martel refills it without leaving his chair. He does not like using so much esping, but has the feeling that the stranger might disappear if he takes his eyes off him.

"I might, too—" the man grins—"but not quite yet. It's like this. First, the glittermotes. They're simple. They congregate around those who can or do tap the field. But in . . . say a long while . . . I've never seen black. Only gold and white. Not even . . . anyhow, that's the glittermotes.

"Bit players, demigods, bystanders, all the same. Strong enough to endure, but not to influence the game. Once in a while, we can point things out to the new ones. That's you. My chains rattled free before they were supposed to, and I won't say how, on the condition I have a beer and a chat with you. No illusions about that. I'll be back throwing waves shortly."

Martel listens, trying to accept the information, to take what is offered and sort it out later. In the back of his mind, he senses a change in the weather, a storm brewing over the hills to the west.

"You're educated. Talk about the chains of the sea. I've something to do with that. If you're in the chains of the sea, you drink salt water, and that doesn't do much for your thirst. Now ask why I don't try harder to get free of my chains. I do, every once in a while, for an adventure or two. But I don't stand up well against the storm-gods or their thunderbolts, and they don't stand up well to the Elder Gods, which says where I stand in the grander scheme of things. You're different, or will be, once you get the hang of it. You've got some of them stirred up. Can't see why exactly . . . seem too peaceful to me."

Martel stands, the blackness boiling out of him like night, the glittermotes clinging to him like a shadow cloak.

Explain! His command strikes the other like a whip.

Young god . . . and the older gods fear you. You are not ready to face them . . . by their own laws they cannot strike you down . . . but will tempt you to your own destruction . . . or to attack them all . . .

The perpetual day turns sudden dark, brooding smoke-yellow dusk, with the swiftness of a razor knife slicing day into night, and the thunder rolls in from the west and down the hillside like a war wagon to shake the cottage. The windows chatter with each quick drumroll.

Gil Nash freezes whiter than the white roads to Aurore, whiter than the white roofs of Sybernal, whiter than the snows of winter and the sands of Sahara.

Nash's eyes dart toward the clouds.

Martel throws a mental shell around himself, trying to gather all the energy he can, but as he draws he feels the golden bolt descending from the clouds in a blaze.

"Mr. Martel . . . Mr. Martel . . ."

Coldness, wetness . . . water across his face.

"What . . ."

He opens his eyes. He is sprawled on the deck on his back, looking up at the circular charred hole in the roof, and at the gray face of Mrs. Alderson.

He checks himself over, lets his unsteady perceptions review his body. The report is sound. No overt injuries. He sits up, concentrating on keeping everything in focus.

The chair where Nash has been sitting is a heap of ashes. The one where Martel sat is untouched. There is no sign of the demigod who called himself Nash, nor any remains.

"Thought there weren't any thunderstorms on Aurore, Mrs. Alderson." He sits up.

"There aren't, 'less the gods are involved. You be messing with what you oughtn't, young man?"

Probably, thinks Martel.

"Don't think so, but the fellow I met at the beach may have been."

Martel stands up, uses the back of his hand to wipe the water off his forehead.

The table lies on its side, the beaker next to it. The beer mug, a glassy lump now, is coated with the ashes from the fired chair, and has rolled almost to Martel's feet.

The landlady follows his glances, sees the melted mug, connects it with the ashes of the chair and the hole in the roof, and gasps.

"Called himself Gil Nash. Swam out of the water and asked if he could have a beer. Didn't see any harm in it. He seemed nice enough."

"And that goes to show you, Mr. Martel, what happens on Aurore when strange people arrive from the sea. Like as not he was a ruined demigod trying to escape his just punishment. Lucky as not you're an innocent. Knowing mortals who help the wicked uns, the gods have no mercy on them."

Martel shakes his head slowly. No innocent, just fast enough with an energy screen . . . and yet . . . how long was he unconscious? Certainly long enough for anyone disposed to do him in to do so.

What had Nash said? Tempting him to strike out?

He shakes his head again, more violently. No striking out, period!

"Luck, I guess," he answers the waiting woman. "I'll pay, as soon as I can, for the damage. Not on purpose, but, as you said, I should have known better."

"No, Mr. Martel. How would you know, being new and all? It's not that I'm short on funds. You are, and I should have warned you. Just be a mite bit more careful what strangers you strike up with. Time comes and you'll sense the queer ones."

"I will. Certainly will."

He sweeps the ashes into a bag, where he deposits the lump of glass that had been a mug, and carries the bag out to the recycling pickup next to the coast road below Mrs. Alderson's house. By the time he climbs back up the long steps, she has rearranged the porch furniture and placed another chair next to the table. Except for the hole in the roof and a darker shade of decking where Nash's chair had been, the setting is again as it had been.

Most people, reflects Martel, wouldn't see the difference unless they looked up. And who makes a habit of looking up?

"Thank you again, Mrs. Alderson." The words feel awkward, but he doesn't know what else to say.

"No problem, Mr. Martel. We all have to get used to new places, now, don't we?"

He nods, trying to repress a smile. Some individuals, like Mrs. Alderson, like Rathe Firien, have a down-to-earth friendliness that puts everything in perspective.

Rathe . . . He purses his lips.

"Do you have a directory? For Sybernal?"

"Aye, and so do you. Second drawer, under the vid." She picks up her broom and with quick steps is halfway down the porch steps before he can speak.

"Thank you again. I appreciate, I really do, your understanding."

She smiles.

"Without that, wouldn't be much, would I? But you do be careful, Mr. Martel." She turns, like a sprightly terrier, and marches back down to the main house.

He shakes his head. *Of course, she's right, Martel.*

He does not know if it is his thought or another's. It doesn't matter.

The directory is in the second drawer under the vidfax, and he does find the listing: Firien, R., NW of Sybernal.

His fingers tap out the codes.

There is no answer as the beeps pulse and pulse and pulse.

"Not even an answer slot?" he mumbles.

A check of the instructions reminds him that autoscreens are not available on Aurore.

He tries again, but she is still not there.

Next, he surveys the drawers in the small kitchen, mentally inventorying each utensil.

He taps out the number again, and there is no answer.

He reads the autochef manual, cover to cover, beginning with the installation date stamped inside the front fold and ending with the recipe for time-roasted scampig.

Rather than try her number again, he looks for some cobwebs to dust, but his memory reminds him that Aurore has no spiders, and therefore no cobwebs. He keys Rathe's codes into the limited memory of his faxer, then jerks his hands off the access plate.

Should he have let her go?

No.

Was he going to let her go?

No.

Thinking about it, he smiles. Listening to the soft chittering of birds through the open windows, the muted swash of the sea beyond the hill, and, feeling the sharp edge of the salt air, he smiles.

X

The receive channel on the relay ship opens for nanounits.

The monitor blinks green, signifying that the relay has been completed.

The Brother at the controls touches one plate, a stud, begins the quick sequence to take the ship into underspace to wait for the next transmission.

Once the small ship is underspace, he stabilizes the controls, touches the replay stud, and waits for the equipment to return the message to real time.

The image on the screen is that of Brother Geidren, current domni of the Council.

"By order of the Council, all Brothers and Sisters of the Order are hereby requested to give their full prayers to the Congregation of the Fallen One, in accordance with the Writ of Perception.

"Though all will not be accomplished that might, though the hours of the very stars are numbered, still we persevere until each is weighed and numbered."

The screen blanks.

The Brother frowns.

Like all Brotherhood quicksends, it has a double message,

and for the first time in many years, he does not understand the logic behind the second message.

In effect, the Brotherhood is being disbanded, being told to join and fully support the Church of the Fallen God while continuing the basic goals of the Brotherhood.

The relay pilot pinches his fat lips together.

The command releases the ship to him, for whatever purpose, and the same effect apparently will take place throughout the Brotherhood.

He rechecks the authentications, and taps a query into the sender. The whole idea of the message is absurd. There will always be a Brotherhood, Empire or no Empire.

To go underground even more thoroughly has been expected since the ejection from the Empire, but to join such an offbeat group of lunatics as the Church of the Fallen One?

He readies his ship for the real-space transfer to send his query.

XI

CASTCENTER—a simple bronzed plaque over the portal.

Martel steps through.

The foyer on the inside is small. Indirect yellowed lighting combines with the brown plasteel to convey a clean dinginess. The entry console is vacant, as are the two armless chairs across from it.

Martel sits down, lets his perceptions range through the small building.

There are, from what he can tell with a quick scan, three studios, several smaller rooms, four or five offices, a larger screening room, plus fresher facilities, editing rooms, and the reception area.

He picks up three people in the entire circular building. One engineer, one caster, and one administrator. A man and two women.

The administrator, female, is walking down the corridor toward Martel.

Martel stands up.

"You must be Martel. Certainly took your time in getting here."

He frowns. He is reporting eight weeks earlier than he has to.

"Does everyone report early?"

"I forgot." The woman smirks. "You had adjustment problems." She has sandy hair, cropped straight at chin level, and bangs that are trimmed squarely above her eyebrows. The washed-out gray of her eyes matches the gray tunic and trousers she wears.

Martel wonders about her obnoxiousness, but answers evenly. "That's right. I had adjustment problems. But I'm here and ready to work."

She slouches into the lounger behind the console.

"Aren't you the chiever-beaver. Just like that."

Martel waits.

"Sit down. Sit down. Farell's on the board, will be for the next two stans. Few comments from KarNews on the in-feed. That's about it. That's all it ever is, except for the specs and the logos, the gossip pieces, the once-in-a-god-year storm warning. Feed the touries their home-planet news. We handle Karnak."

Karnak? The one fax outlet on Aurore handling Karnak, and that's where the Brotherhood has placed him? He files the point for reference, and turns his attention to the woman.

Her eyes are bright. Too bright. Cernadine. Do the demigods allow addiction?

Why not? So long as it doesn't impair performance or hurt anyone else. Cernadine is safe and available. And explains the washed-out look in her eyes.

"Fine. Farell's on the board. You are . . . ?"

"Hollie Devero, at your service, Masterfaxer Martel." Her mouth quirks upward even farther, then twitches into a thin line before she continues. "And how did a Regent's Scholar with a masterfax rating end up on Aurore, the punkhead of faxing?"

"You seem to know all the answers. Since I'm not sure, you tell me."

"You're right. I do know full feed on you, Marty Martel.

How you actually put a little love into a greeter's life, and how you really like to take long walks alone on the sands, and how you avoid people. And how the first things you bought were black tunics and trousers. And you had to special-order them!" She laughs and the sound is brittle.

Martel bites his lip. No one should be greeted like this! No one!

"Then you know why I'm here."

Her voice loses its edge. "No. I don't. First new faxer in ten standard years, first one not even a Guild prentice, and the Guild approves you . . . and no record marks."

Martel probes at the fringes of her thoughts, gently, uncertain how cernadine affects her sensitivity, unsure how sensitive she is.

. . . say that? . . . Did I . . . what . . . Martel . . . the one . . .

Her curiosity is building against the damping waves of the cernadine, but Martel senses she does not know what she has just said. How? Why?

Someone else is walking down the corridor from control area—the engineer.

Danger. Danger! *Danger!* DANGER!

Martel strikes, lets his mind go in a blast of energy, lashing at the man in a way he only half believes.

"Gods! *No!* . . ." The scream from inside and outside Hollie Devero catches at the edge of his attack, and he holds back the darkness . . . finds himself staring from a slumped position against Hollie's console at a man lying facedown, antique slug-thrower gripped in his hand.

Martel knows the man is dying or dead. Maybe.

"You . . . you killed him . . ." Tears, real tears, tears not from the cernadine, well from the corners of her eyes.

Even from under the blanket of the drug, he feels the grief, her ties to the dying man.

Can he do anything? Has he done too much?

Martel sends his perceptions out, touches the heart, adds strength to the beat, oxygen, repairs a torn artery, a stripped vein, and, standing back in his mind and watching himself do the miraculous, finishes by rebuilding a damaged nerve chain.

His knees wobble as he staggers up and over toward the now-unconscious man. His vision blurs momentarily as he bends to pick the slugger from a flaccid hand. He removes the shells and drops the empty weapon on the console.

"You . . . owe . . . me . . . one . . . Hollie."

He sits down heavily, concentrating on breathing for himself. Half watches the woman as she kneels beside her lover.

"I thought you'd killed him."

"No." *I did, but I undid it, and flamed if I know how.*

"Why?"

"Why, yourself? Why did"—and he picks the name out of her thoughts—"Gates want to kill me? Given the demigods, maybe you owe me two."

Her eyes widen. Her face crumples, gray to match her washed-out eyes. "Why? Why? Why?"

Martel echoes her thoughts silently, blocking them as well.

Gates Devero had been primed to explode as soon as one Martel, faxcaster, student, Brother, showed up at the CastCenter. But the attempt had been direct. Too direct.

Gates was supposed to fail. That meant Martel had been set up to kill the engineer, which meant . . . Martel shivered.

He remembers something Rathe said.

"The gods are jealous, Martel. Jealous."

"Jealous" seems an understatement.

Martel finally answers the question Hollie asked. "Because he was supposed to fail, Hollie, because he was supposed to fail."

"Oh, gods, no! Why us?"

"Not you. Me. Don't worry. You're safe. So's Gates. A second time would be too obvious." *For now.*

"Second time?"

"Forget it. Just tell Gates he tripped."

Martel lurches to his feet, knees solid at last, picks the weapon off the console, and drops it into a pocket.

"Tripped?"

"Got any better ideas, smart lady?" His voice burns, and the anger in it turns the gray-faced administrator grayer.

"But the gods . . ."

Martel swallows, hard. *Only the thoughts count.*

"Gates tripped, Hollie. That's all that happened."

And with that his thoughts follow, changing the pictures in

her mind, then in Gates'. Both would remember that Gates tripped.

Martel is sure that the gods will know that the memories are false, should they check, but what really happened is erased, gone, except in his own mind.

"In answer to your other question," he goes on as if nothing has occurred, "I'm here—"

"I don't need to know. I don't want to know."

"—because I was Queried by the Emperor and the Grand Duke of Kirsten."

Hollie turns her head from side to side, slowly, still on her knees by Gates.

"And the only ambition I have is to get paid for being a faxer while I sort things out."

He looks at the time readout. Almost a full stan has passed since he walked into the CastCenter.

One stan? One whole stan?

He tightens his lips. Apparently his mental excursion into the physiology of one Gates Devero has taken longer than he has realized.

"You'd better help Gates up," he suggests mildly as he lets the engineer wake and groan. "By the way, am I expected to follow Farell?"

"No. She'll brief you, give you a handful of procedures, and walk you through. Double duty for her. Double pay. Doesn't happen enough. So she won't mind."

Martel can tell her thoughts are on Gates, her genuine worry about the fall he has taken. Martel heads down the corridor toward the control center.

He scans Farell from outside the control room.

She is dark-haired, from her own mental image relaxed, and, so far as he can tell, untrapped.

He waits until she finishes the locals and is into the KarNews feed before opening the portal.

"Martin Martel," he announces quietly.

"Swear I'd locked that."

He looks vacant.

"Guess not." She gives him a half-smile, accented by naturally red lips. "You're Giles' replacement. Our new wunderkind from Karnak."

"Green from Karnak," he admits, "and so far as faxing goes, green as gold. Lots of ratings, a few degrees, and no more than the minimum uncontrolled airtime."

"No illusions, at least." She gives a fuller smile.

Her arm sweeps the circular room. "This is it. All older than you or me. Just a reader-feeder op, with enough of us in it to assure the touries that they're seeing real, live people before they get the latest from home."

The control center is clean, and from his mental runover Martel knows that the equipment all works, everything except a disassembled line feed on the end of the counter where the portable faxers are lined up.

"By the time, I'm Marta Farell. You ready to start, or is this just social?"

"Ready to start. But let me get a few things straight before we start on technicals."

Martel gestures at the old but clean equipment around them.

"From what you just said, there's no local base to the operation. No, if you will, native support. Who foots the bill?"

Marta pushes a loose strand of hair off her forehead, carefully pats it back into place.

"Not much of a bill, really. We don't have any of the extras here. No image enhancers, no multijection feeds, no strictly outside faxers. We all do the outside work. Not really news usually, but the froth." She shrugs. "Learn a lot about the basics here. That's all we've got."

"So it's a small bill. But who pays it?" Martel resists the urge to snap. Like everyone else Marta Farell seems to avoid straight answers.

"You do. Partly. The rest is from fees and donations."

"Me? Fees?"

"Wait . . ."

Farell eases into the focal seat, uses the finger-touch controls, and settles herself into a position as the holo scanners focus on her.

"That's the stan update from Karnak. I'm Marta Farell with CastCenter . . . official fax outlet for KarNews on Aurore. At the chime, stan time will be fourteen-thirty, Aurore Standard, Imperial Central, Karnak Regent.

"Next we'll be taking you with Gates Devero on a tour of the eastern beaches, and a look at a few out-of-the-way spots you may have missed."

Martel admires the way she slips into the local feed. He wonders if the Devero slot is a repeat.

"Repeat?"

"Right. Geared on the Karnak tourie. Run it twice a bloc month. Once you get the feel of things you'll be out there as well. Interests?"

"Not using my full name," slips out before he thinks. *Flame! Why did you say that?*

Marta Farell only nods. "You a drinker, adventurer, a shopper, anything like that? Rockgrubber or sailor?"

"Loner, I guess. Would a slot on places to really escape fly, really fly?"

"Martel, we got more stans to fill than you dream, and you're only the fifth faxer for a round-the-clock operation. Even an extra half-stan slot a week would help."

"And who pays the bills . . ."

"If you're that persistent about faxing, half my problems will be solved. All right. There's a standard ten percent deduction from all pay on Aurore. To pay for services. And we're a service. About one-tenth of one tiny percent goes to the four faxcenters. Mostly for power costs. The fees are from docuslots. The one that's running now was picked up by both KarNews and the MatNet on Halston.

"One of mine ran prime on Tinhorn. You never know. We back-feed regularly, and sometimes they catch. You get two percent commission on the back-feed sales."

"What's the rate?" Martel doesn't have the faintest idea of what the majors would pay for a backwater documentary.

"Average is maybe a hundred thousand credits a quarter-stan."

Martel figures. The faxer would get two thousand Imperial credits for each quarter-stan, or four thousand for a standard half-stan bloc. Two full blocs equaled his annual contract. There had to be a catch.

"How many have you had picked up?"

"In the past ten years, I've averaged three full blocs a year.

That's the problem." Farell turns in the seat, waiting as if to see whether he can solve the puzzle.

He spreads his hands, admitting his bewilderment.

"Really good faxcaster can buy out his contract in five years, with enough left for first-class passage anywhere. But you've got to be good, because we can't doctor the tape. Edit, yes, but no image enhancement, viewpoint realterations, threshold emotionals, none of the fancy techniques they taught you at the Institute."

"Why not?" *Stupid question, Martel!*

Farell looks around the studio.

"With what? We've got two portaunits that are up, and one that sometimes works." She catches her breath and plunges into the next sentence, again unconsciously patting a stray hair back into place. "The reason why we don't have the latest equipment is that the Empire doesn't send it. We buy second-, third-hand. Besides, I doubt that propafax is wanted on Aurore. You'll notice that our relay doesn't carry the emotional bands."

Martel wants to ask why, but Marta Farell doesn't pause.

"Don't ask. Just say it's not wanted."

"Stet." It isn't all right, but what can he say? "Why don't the majors send their own teams?"

"Expensive. Fuel costs once you break sub are twice any other planet in the Empire. Second, let's just say that outside fax teams aren't exactly welcome."

"Sort of like Imperial agents aren't welcome?" Martel asks with a grin.

"Yes. Not something I'd advise smiling about."

Martel frowns, turns toward the monitor, rubs his forehead with the middle three fingers on his right hand. He senses the hostility his last remark has triggered.

Why? Awfully sensitive. Just take over the shift and let her go. Right? Wrong. You don't even know the feed parameters.

"Is there a center manual and a set of engineering specs I could study?" he offers.

The woman does not answer, walks over to the console, and pulls out two discs.

"Here. Why don't you use the vidfax in the lounge, second port on the right as you leave. Ought to be able to go through those in a stan or two. Then I'll check you out on the system."

Martel feels her relief, but does not go into her thoughts to double-check.

The control lock snicks into place as he steps out.

There! Her thought is as clear as if she had spoken.

Martel smiles. The lock had been engaged when he entered.

Gates Devero, recumbent in a recliner, nods at Martel as he enters the blue-paneled lounge.

"Martel . . . sorry I was so clumsy when you came in. Don't know what came over me. Really upset Hollie."

The younger man scans the room.

Gates picks up the inquiring glance and answers. "She's left. Be back later. Getting me a coldpak for this flamed bruise."

The cheek below Devero's right eye shows the beginning of a dark blotch.

"I hope it wasn't my fault, being later than you expected."

"No. Need another faxer. Understand your problem. You also carry a second-tech cert?"

"Right."

"Good. We're only a Beta Class. Means you can handle swings by yourself, long as I'm on call. Better for everyone."

"Fine with me, once I know what's where." Martel lifts the discs thrust on him by Marta Farell. "Where's the console?"

"Corner."

Martel spots it before the engineer finishes his directions.

"Not much," Gates adds. "Dates from the First Republic."

Martel's mouth drops open. That would make the unit more than an antique. More like a museum piece.

"Not really." Gates smiles. "Just what it feels like. Older than anything else in the station. About a century old, if you don't count all the replacements. And don't believe everything I say . . ."

Martel shakes his head, not fully listening to the engineer's patter, trying to remind himself to doubt things, not to be so flamed accepting.

". . . more than one way to do a story, make it good without all the fancy gear those Imperial automatons deck themselves with. Hades! Done better stories myself. So's Hollie. We can't hold a pinlight to Farell or Boster. Probably not to you, if what the record says is true. Even half true."

"Don't believe all the records, either." Martel forces a laugh. "I've had all the courses, but no experience."

"You'll get that quick here. Another thing those big flames on Karnak don't understand. Go there and hold faxers' disccases five years before you get a three-clip slot on your own. Farell'll have you out doing half-stan slots in days. 'Course, she won't use it all. Rip you pretty good. But you'll learn."

Another voice, Hollie Devero's, breaks in.

"She already has you out of the control center?" Her tone is pleasant.

Martel automatically lets his perceptions check her over, but her pleasantness is genuine, as if her "forgetfullness" has taken fully. He hopes so.

"Not exactly. She suggested that I learn the rules, procedures, and schematics."

"Funny, she is," Gates comments. "Good editor, good teacher. Has to be, to get a dumb engineer like me to run sub. But sure doesn't want anyone in with her when it's hot. In the other studio, the one she uses to train, another story." He shrugs. "All got problems. What's yours, Martel?"

Martel returns the shrug. "I suppose my biggest problem is that the Regent and the Grand Duke Kirsten don't like me."

Gates claps his hands. "Bravo! A step ahead. Don't like most of us till *after* we get here. Why? Offend the Imperial pride? Student prank?"

Martel fingers his chin before answering. "It has something to do with the Grand Duke's daughter."

"The goddesses will love you!" roars Gates Devero, breaking the laugh off sharply to touch his bruised cheek.

"I didn't know he had a daughter. I'm sure he doesn't. Not one old enough, or young enough, for Martel." Hollie's voice conveys absolute certainty.

"But I went to the Institute with her," protests Martel. "And why would the Duke . . . and why all the body-guards . . ."

Hollie shakes her head once. "I know what I know. There was no sign of a daughter ten years ago."

"But the Duke wouldn't chase me, Query me, and the Brotherhood wouldn't—" Martel breaks off, realizing his gaffe in referring to the Brotherhood, but neither seems to care, and the reference only succeeds in increasing Hollie's confusion.

"Maybe he had her hidden away. Maybe . . . well, the Duchess wasn't much for children."

"She went to school in New Augusta. Didn't come back until my second year at the Institute. That's when I met her."

"How long ago?" asks the woman.

"About five years, I'd guess. You see, I only saw her in the corridors at first. I wondered who had the bodyguard with the matching colors. But it wasn't until the middle of my third year that we had a class together or I ever talked to her. Dr. Dorlan warned me about her father, but I never really did much except talk to her."

I'll bet! The thought from Gates takes Martel off guard.

"But she seemed to like you?" asks Hollie.

"I thought so."

Gates shakes his head. "That's more than enough, Martel. The Dukes don't like Regent's Scholars until *after* they're rich or powerful. In this Empire, you don't marry into money."

"Especially with a mother like the Duchess," adds Hollie. *Especially her!* The thought has a trace of bitterness, and a touch of nostalgia, but the deepest feeling is repugnance.

Martel closes his eyes, trying to sort things out. Hollie was convinced that there is no Kryn, no daughter of the Grand Duke, and the strength of her feelings and even her surface thoughts show she knows something she is not telling and does not want to tell about the Duke. The depth of those feelings, which his perceptions can only sense generally, also tells Martel that she has buried those memories from herself, and especially from Gates.

"Kryn didn't seem to care much for her mother," Martel temporizes.

"That must be it. Still . . . well, the Duke would act like that if he cared enough." *Which he didn't always*. She waits a moment, then lifts her head. "Before you start studying all those discs from Marta, I have some forms for you to author-ize. We need to report that you've started work."

Martel nods. The less he says the better.

Hollie Devero marches out through the portal, expecting Martel to follow.

Gates gives a half-wave, and Martel returns the gesture be-fore hurrying after Hollie. As far as he can tell, their false memories have stuck.

Now all he has to do is learn how to be a decent faxer, if he can avoid being distracted by all the contradictions that keep popping up.

XII

Despite the multiplicity of the theories regarding the "seed-ing" of the known Galaxy with so-called *Homo sapiens*, no satisfactory explanation exists which can adequately describe why so many human and humanoid cultures apparently began at the same absolute point in time, or why a number of hu-manoid remnants have been discovered on habitable planets with no evolutionary train which would have led to such be-ings.

With centuries of concentrated archeology behind us, we have yet to discover any real traces, besides the so-called fleet anomalies, of a star-spanning civilization which predates our own. Yet the odds of two separately evolved humanoid races possessing genetic compatibility, let alone the hundreds with absolute interlockability, and the other handful which are close enough for sterile crossbreeding, are prohibitive. . . . One might as well leave it to the "will of God" as attempt any rational scientific explanation at this time. . . .

> —*Essays*
> Fr. Adis SterHillion
> New Augusta, 2976

XIII

Martel watches the monitor of the direct feed from Karnak. The feed is a wasteout, and is displayed on the aux screen, because it features a ballad singer. A redisc of Gates Devero is the actual on-air program.

Martel has seen Gates' tape twice, and three times would be too much. So he watches the unused feed from Karnak.

Unusual as it is for him, he is tired, with another five stans left on his shift.

The singer, a young man with kinky black hair, pointed mustache, and a fluorescent green bodysuit, warbles the words in a false tenor, thin but true. The song was old, Martel knew, a variant on words that predated the First Republic, which had predated the Empire by a good millennium.

". . . and where have all the poor men gone,
Gone to slavers, every one.
Ah, where will they ever turn, where will they ever turn?"

Good Question. Where have all the poor men gone?
On Karnak, the answer was simple enough. Gone to the sewers, the Brotherhood, before it was driven underground and off-Empire, or gone to the wellhouses.

The Fuards make their poor cannon fodder. Who knows about the Matriarchy?

Martel leans forward in the swivel to check the remaining run time against I.D. schedule. He wants to have everything ready, because he will have to give the I.D., with a cube scene of the ocean, voiced over, before switching to the upcoming news feed from Karnak.

"The poor ye shall always have."

Wasn't that the antique quote? What about the poor on Aurore? Couldn't be as many, not with the nearly mandatory work ethic Rathe had pointed out.

He smiles.

Strong-willed lady.

She knows more than he does. Even so, he has to discount all the hints that he is much more than a bright faxer with a bit of esp. More than that . . . absurd.

Is it? Really? He pushes away the nagging question, decides to think about the poor.

But he doesn't have the time, yet. With the units flicking off the downcount, he touches the feedmesh and begins to fade over the scene-cube.

"CastCenter of Aurore. Path station from Sybernal. Gate Seven."

He drops his vocal an octave, easy enough for those with the right relaxation techniques, and begins the scene logo fade to prep the newsline.

"Straight from Karnak, Imperial Regency News Central, comes the latest update. From Gate Seven, here's Fax Central."

As he completes his last word the switches to the outstation signal, an eight-frame of the Fax Central logo, and from that to the mainline cut, featuring the slim figure of Werl K'rio, silver-voiced and silver-clad.

"Brief power failure at the Regent's Palace . . . described as not serious. Concerns that the Grand Duchess is failing . . . and a dedication."

Martel takes himself fully off-line, but continues to watch the story on the power outage at the Regent's Palace. No one could explain the failure of both the main and backup systems, and the outage lasted nearly a full stan. No details were forthcoming. A Regency spokesman dismissed the occurrence as "a freak happening." Rumors of a strange appearance co-incident with the blackout were dismissed by the Major Doorkeeper as "absurd."

Have to wonder what was behind a power outage in the palace. What ambitious officer suffered an unfortunate accident? Or "perished" in protecting the Prince Regent?

Someday, the mere tradition of the Prince Regent wouldn't be enough. Someday, someone like the Grand Duke would succeed.

Wonder what that will do to the Empire? And Karnak? And Kryn?

He shies away from the thought of her, grasps at the earlier questions, the one of the poor on Aurore.

Had he ever seen any?

He concentrates, trying to drag up memories of shabby clothes, a beggar on a corner, unshaven faces outside a crowd of touries or happy norms.

Martel squints, looking through his console, but cannot drag up that kind of image.

But there have to be poor on Aurore. Have to be!

Where else would they be? Where would they be hidden away? Or is Aurore so prosperous or so conditioned that none are in need?

Ding! The warning chime interrupts his mental search, reminding him that he has to go local.

First, the I.D. and the logo. He'd dragged an old one from the cube library, featuring a woman who could have passed for a goddess—golden hair and golden eyes, and a voice that could have sold freezers on the poles of Tinhorn. The phrasing wasn't current, but complied with the stat requirements. The date on the cube made it over forty stans since it had been used last, but Martel's tests showed it was technically acceptable. Besides, it would be a nice change from the scenery that Marta Farell used.

She'd said he could use whatever he wanted from the library, provided it wasn't sealed. Not that anyone would notice, not on his shift.

Despite the eternal daylight of Aurore, most of the norms and all of the tourists stayed with standard Karnak time, which meant that Martel's shift ran through their "night." Most faxviewers were touries, with a few norms.

Martel wonders if he is a norm or a native. No one had ever described the difference, except Hollie Devero.

"Natives understand Aurore, live with it. Norms don't. That makes Gates a native, and me a norm." That was what she'd said, and it was all anyone had said to Martel, including Rathe.

He refocused on the board in front of him, matching the frame counts, then precisely plugging in the I.D. cube.

"The CastCenter of Aurore. Gate Seven. From Sybernal and for your information and your pleasure."

Even after forty standard years of storage, the cube fires a bolt, and then some.

Martel wonders who she was, whether she will see the cube and not recognize the woman she once was. But his fingers are busy. As he feels the gut-level impact of the face and voice, he is already triggering the next program.

Again he matches the frame count to perfection as he brings the title logo of the holodrama on line.

A "romantic and escapist" plot, the summary had indicated, called *Yesterday, the Stars*, the drama featured a junior cruiser commander in the Imperial Fleet forced to choose between his career, which he loves, and a young Duchess, the woman he loves.

The cube was on the list Marta had suggested as suitable for his time slot. For now, he was relying heavily on her guidance. Sooner or later, he'd have to strike out on his own, he supposed.

Martel sets the warning chime and eases himself out of the control chair to head for the index for the station cube files. He hopes to find some more interesting I.D. spots, or some standard dramas that hadn't been faxed to gray oblivion.

Buzz!

The incoming fax line was lit, for the first time since he'd been doing night shifts.

He leans over the console and taps the accept stud.

"CastCenter."

The screen remains black, only the green light beneath blinking to indicate the caller remains on the circuit.

"May I help you?" he tries again.

"Do not show HER again. This time it is ignorance. Next time will indeed be blasphemy." The low voice sounds feminine.

"What?"

The red light blinks that the connection has been broken.

Martel touches the stud, frowning.

Strange. Most strange.

Buzz!

Two in the same night? Incredible, when for months no one has faxed at all.

He accepts the second call more tentatively.

The caller is Marta Farell, disheveled hair pushed back off her forehead, a robe thrown around her shoulders, and close up to the screen, as if to block off the view into the rest of the room.

Is there a faint golden glow visible over her shoulder? Martel wonders why anyone would need artificial light.

He keeps his smile to himself. At least in private Marta is human, and in the hurriedly thrown-on robe, she even looks desirable.

"That I.D., Martel? Has anyone faxed?"

How did she know?

"Uh . . . yes. Blind. Said if I ran it again, it would be—"

"Blasphemy," she finishes.

"Right."

"That one's not sealed. Gates ran the other one like it once a couple of years ago, and the same thing happened. I didn't know we had another. Don't run it again. Or any other one that has Her on it.

"Her?"

"I think it was the Goddess in one of Her lighter moods. She probably wouldn't mind, but Her followers certainly do. I'll talk to you about it tomorrow."

As she reaches down to sign off, her eyes flicker to the side, and the robe parts slightly, enough to show that she had indeed thrown it on hurriedly.

Strange. Why would Marta interrupt what she was obviously enjoying to warn you? The Goddess? What goddess? Ridiculous.

"You're saying words like that too much." His words echo in the empty control room.

Obviously, some people take the god and goddess business seriously. Very seriously.

He looks down at the small vidfax unit, but the amber light stays amber. No more calls.

The poor? What about the poor? Do we always have them? And what does that have to do with "Her"?

Just as he thinks he is learning something, another series of questions pops up.

He pushes the poor out of his mind, and turns back to the index to see what else features the golden woman and to find another I.D., hopefully one that won't be classified as blasphemy by one cult or another.

XIV

The sand is warm, even without the directness of sunlight, and Martel turns over onto his stomach.

Rathe lies facedown, her head on a small towel, her toes pointed at the thin line of foam where the wavelets break on the golden sands of the beach. She is relaxed, nearly asleep.

Martel frowns, unable to forget the incident with the logo cube.

Something about the goddess is familiar, but he cannot put his finger on it.

Should you tell Rathe?

He shakes his head and stretches, letting his weight sink farther into the clinging sand. He places his right arm across the middle of Rathe's back, just below her shoulder blades, and squeezes her gently.

She turns her head on the towel and looks at him from sleepy eyes.

"You had the late shift, and I'm sleepy. How come?"

He shrugs, then grins as he realizes how meaningless the gesture is from someone lying on his stomach and half buried in sand.

"Don't know. Guess I'm still trying to get used to this place."

He squeezes her again, and she squirms the few centimeters necessary toward him until their bare legs touch.

"It's so peaceful here."

"Thanks to you," he answers. "If you hadn't found the cottage . . ."

"But you chose it."

He does not answer, but squeezes her again, then closes his eyes, trying to let himself relax.

When he wakes, Rathe is sitting cross-legged and spreading food from the basket she has brought.

"You finally hungry, sleepyhead?"

"Sleepyhead? You fell asleep first."

He props his chin up with both hands and grins at her.

Rathe uses her left hand to tousle his short and curly black hair. Then she smooths the cloth on which she sits and gestures to the space across from her, palm upward.

"Would you care to join me?"

"I'd be honored."

First, he stands and brushes the clinging sand from his legs and arms. He sits across from her, his legs to one side, for he has never been comfortable in trying to sit cross-legged, and takes her left hand and touches his lips to it.

"You're so gallant." She pauses. "However, I am—"

"Hungry," he finishes.

Not only is there Springfire, for him, but an assortment of cheeses, genuine wheat crackers, and two corm-apples.

Martel strokes her calf, finishes by squeezing her knee gently, and then picks up the beaker of Springfire.

"You have excellent taste."

"For you, anything."

She is so warm, so unlike . . . Kryn . . . the golden goddess. . . . Why does the goddess bother you, Martel?

Martel holds back his frown and takes another sip of the Springfire as Rathe picks up one of the corm-apples and begins to cut it into slices.

Before too long he will have to leave for the CastCenter, but he pushes the thought away.

XV

"And now, straight from Karnak, the day's wrap-up with Lorel Littul."

Snap. Tap. Tap. *Ease the pressure up, and fade out.* Martel's fingers dance across the board as the in-feed from Karnak blankets Aurore, letting the touries and the norms know how little had really happened with the Regency day before.

Outside the control room someone waits. Farell.

Martel touches the stud that breaks the lock circuit, although as the fax manager and senior faxer, Marta Farell certainly could override the circuits at any time.

"Greetings," he offers.

"Same to you, Martel. Have you thought about a cube project?"

She sits on one of the low ledges beneath the storage lockers.

"Hmm. I've thought about several. I guess I'm not too thrilled about any of the ideas. Every travelogue I could think of has been done, except maybe something on all of the out-of-the-way beaches—the unique ones—like the hidden sands under the White Cliffs, that sort of thing."

"Sands under the White Cliffs? I didn't know there were any." She laughs, easily, and for an instant the tightness that usually surrounds her is gone. "That might be interesting. What else?"

"People stories are always interesting. But outside of the gods, what people do here has so much less intrigue, so much less danger or strangeness, than on Karnak, or Tinhorn. People sail the seas, but the winds are so even that it's tame. We have no safaris, no treks across sandy deserts . . . are there even any deserts?" He waits, trying to provoke a reaction.

Marta Farell stays within the tight shell of her professionalism, within the barriers that say "Do not touch!" to Martel, even without his mental probing.

The quiet hum of the tie receiver is the only sound in the control center.

Martel scans the monitors, the feed time remaining, before shifting his eyes back to Farell.

"The unknown-beaches bit is a good long-term subject. The settings have to be perfect," she comments, as if no time had passed since his last question.

Martel nods, understanding what she is driving at. Offworlders are treated to exotic fax scenes every day. So his beach story will have to be not only spectacular, but artistic as well, as artistry takes time. If it works, the royalties will be substantial, and deserved.

"You're right about the human-interest angle, too," adds Farell, "but you've sealed the problem."

"Of course," Martel slips in, "there are always the gods."

"Not if you value your continued existence. And whether you do or not, remember that the gods may just decide to wipe out anyone who approves or contributes to a slot they didn't like. So forget it. Now."

Martel ignores the edge in Farell's voice, at the same time wondering.

Jumpy about the gods. Why? What has she done? Another hidden story like Rathe's?

He debates a gentle probe, then backs off. *What right do you have to dig into people's thoughts? No better than these so-called gods if you do.*

"What about something the gods favor?" he pushes.

"Anything concerned with the gods is dangerous!"

"No. There have to be things they like."

"Name one."

"What about the postulant communities? Not on candidates or demigods or priests or priestesses," he adds hurriedly, "but just on the community life, habits, what have you."

"I don't know, Martel."

"There's nothing in any of the back indexes on them, and there's nothing remotely resembling the subject on any of the closed lists."

"Look. You don't really know what you're talking about. Hasn't your lady friend, or someone, convinced you that meddling with the gods is dangerous? Especially dangerous for someone like you."

Here we go again. Someone like you.

"Would you care to explain that?" Two black glittermotes pop into view above his left shoulder as he stands abruptly.

Farell does not change position, but seems to withdraw against the storage lockers. Shrinks further into herself, and does not speak.

"Everyone seems to think I'm different. And every time I question something, people back away. But they still don't answer. Except to tell me not to question, not to challenge. So answer that, Farell. If I'm more than the simple esper I think I am, what makes me so? Why does everyone think so? And what difference does it make? If the so-called gods are so flamed powerful and if I'm such a threat ... Flame! It doesn't make sense. If I'm a threat, then they're not really that powerful. And if they're so almighty, then I'm no real threat. So answer that, Farell!"

Martel can feel the thin edge within him, the one that separates him from the darkness beneath, blurring as the now-familiar tide of inner darkness rises.

Suddenly he can see the two women that Marta Farell is. The first is a small, frightened girl, protected by a shell of professional competence. The second, not nearly so clear in focus, might better be called ... but Martel can find no words, no concepts. For the hidden Farell has a trace of wantonness, a trace of tomboyishness, an abiding warmth ...

... and in the confusion, the dark side of his own self ebbs, and he wonders why he is standing and shouting, and why Marta Farell is merely waiting. And he laughs.

"For an instant, I really got carried away. I'm sorry." He takes one step toward her, stops as he sees her shrink away. Instead, he turns and reseats himself in the console chair.

"Guess I got a little overwrought, a little carried away. Don't really understand why."

She shifts her weight, finally faces him head on.

"Because you don't understand Them, and you won't really face what you are. And no one else can afford to help you out. The costs could be far too high. I know. I know. That's why I agreed you could work here. But even I didn't—" her voice breaks off, but Martel catches the last words as unspoken thoughts, *expect this*.

Martel shakes his head. Every answer creates more questions. He decides to return to the original discussion.

"What about a slot on the postulant communities?"

"Do you really understand how dangerous it is?" Her quiet voice has a touch of resignation, desperation.

"No. But I'd like to try."

"That's obvious. If it goes right, you gain nothing. And if it goes wrong, a lot of people will suffer besides you."

Farell flips her thin legs and hips off the low ledge and alights lightly in front of the console. "But I doubt that will stop you. And, at this point, I'm not going to try to save you from yourself any longer." Her voice drops. "Martel, please be careful."

She is out the port before he can answer.

He rechecks the feed time, sets himself for the break and the return to local control.

What was that all about? Careful about what?

He shakes his head again.

A story on the postulant communities can give him a better insight into the gods, into how much real control they have, into their powers, and into the fears that everyone seems to have buried within.

We'll see, he promises.

That's right, the answer comes, but Martel cannot say whether the second thought is his or another's.

XVI

Martel peers through the peephole, although he does not need to. Gates is busy with the equipment in the off-line studio. Marta Farell is on the board in the prime studio. While the prime studio portal is locked and that peephole closed, the mental static announces her presence.

Martel shakes his head and tramps back down the narrow corridor to the lounge. He wants to run through some of the older I.D.'s, either to get some idea for new ones or to see if any appeal to him for his own programs.

"You could use the fax console in the lounge." His words are not addressed to anyone, since Hollie is busy in the front area, and the other two faxers, Dlores and Morgan, are out working on their own documentary projects.

The lounge console is serviceable, but without projecting the images full-length into the room, he will not be able to determine the technical quality of the cubes he wants to review.

Still . . . what choice is there?

His decision made, he pulls the index cube and places it in the console. He can use the screen for the first part, at least.

About half the cubes are listed as technically deficient. Four have been deleted from the records, and only a faint hesitation marks their former existence. Since the index is merely a record, he wonders why all reference to those four was removed.

From the entire cube, only six seem interesting from the three-line descriptions. Martel notes the key numbers in the console memory and returns the index to storage.

"You work too hard. It won't do a bit of good."

Hollie Devero stands inside the portal, wearing a mint-green one-piece coverall. She is too thin to carry off an outfit that severe, and the brightness of her eyes, reflecting all too obviously her cernadine habit, accentuates her angularity and the plainness of the coverall.

"Just trying to get a handle on what I'm supposed to be doing."

"You're not due in until the late swing, and it's barely twelve hundred."

Martel flicks off the screen. This is the first time Hollie has seemed friendly, and making an approach of sorts, yet. He swivels in the chair to face her, gestures to the vacant seat across from him.

"Thank you."

Wonder what she is thinking.

He touches the edge of her thoughts, recoils at the turmoil.

Is that the cernadine?

"Why do you take so much cernadine?" he blurts out, off his guard from the mental confusion he has touched.

"If you're going . . . Flame! Try to be civil, Martel! Flame you anyway!"

She has not seated herself. Rather, she draws back and puts both hands on the top of the chair. She leans forward. Martel smells the sour spice of the drug on her breath.

He tilts back, trying not to seem too obvious.

"Sorry. I'm not diplomatic. I don't know what came over me."

"You're right. You're not diplomatic. Flame! Everyone else knows. Why should you be any different? I take too much. Didn't use to. But that's my problem. It's not why I came in to see you, anyway."

She comes around the chair and plops herself into it, right across from him, oblivious to the strand of hair dangling in front of her right eye.

"Marta's afraid of you. I'm not sure why, but you're the only one she's ever been scared of. That's in the ten years since we've been stuck here. Why?"

Scared of me? Why?

Martel shrugs, trying to think of an answer.

"Is she? I thought she was very professional."

Hollie leans forward. "Believe me. She's scared of you. So am I, sort of. Except I don't matter."

. . . don't matter to anyone . . . Gates? Martel cannot ignore the stray thought fragment.

He decides to change the subject.

"You've been here ten years. Isn't that a little unusual?"

"Not necessarily. Terms range up to forty-fifty years. Some people like it here." *But not me . . . not here . . . flamed cernadine . . .*

"I didn't realize there were that many long-termers, particularly with such generous contracts. How did you get here, if I could ask . . ."

He would ask! Busybody.

Hollie crosses her arms, sits up squarely.

"That's no secret. Gates supported the Popular Front on Nalia. Did so publicly, and the Regency felt embarrassed and suggested to MatNews that Gates shouldn't be welcome. The Matriarchy agreed. So . . . I came with him" *. . . to this exotic stinkhole.*

The picture is clearer. Gates had somehow gotten tangled with Regency/Matriarchy politics, and Hollie had followed him. Now Hollie is hooked on cernadine, expensive as it is. That means that despite the lucrative possibilities for a first-class faxer on Aurore they'd never be able to leave. Not unless Hollie could kick her habit. Few do, because the addiction feeds on a poor self-image, not only physically but psychologically as well. In a word, cernadine makes the world seem more interesting and imparts an artificial sense of self-esteem to the user.

A clink from down the hallway signals the opening of a studio portal.

"You both from Nalia?"

"No. Herdian."

"But how did you get involved with Nalia?"

"MatNews covers the entire Matriarchy and reports on outsystem news."

" 'Covers' is a good word," interjects Gates from the entryway. "Like a nice warm blanket."

"I'm confused. What did your coverage on Herdian have to do with Nalia?"

"Call it a matter of politics," says Gates dryly.

"Politics?" Martel asks lamely, knowing he should see the pattern Hollie and Gates are weaving.

"You should know," Gates returns with a smile. "From what I hear, you've had a bit of a brush with politics. One of the crew, I gather."

"Well ... the Grand Duke didn't care much for me, but it wasn't for any great public display of courage." Martel shifts his weight in the chair.

Gates has moved across the lounge to the counter, onto which he levers his blocky body, equidistant from Hollie and Martel.

"Not sure my stand on the Nalian Popular Front reflected courage. Not sure I would have said what I said if I'd realized the consequences. Always easier to be brave when you're dumb."

Hollie disagrees with the tiniest of headshakes.

"Or young," adds Martel. "But why would a comment by a faxer on Herdian upset the Regency enough for the Regent to pressure the Matriarch of Halston to have you removed? Isn't that a bit farfetched?"

"I thought so at first. Of course, Herdian is the closest Matriarchy system to Nalia. Didn't think anyone would mind my comments all that much, though. Who listens to fax comments, anyway? But it turned out that the Matriarchy was behind the Popular Front, and all of a sudden that nearness became more important."

Martel shakes his head. "Wait a stan! Your government had you canned because you publicly endorsed what they were privately supporting?"

"Right. Win some, lose some."

"I still don't understand," protests Martel, half afraid that he does.

"Let's put it another way. The Matriarchy wanted to destabilize the LandRight government, which was backed by the Regency. If they came out directly in support, then the Regency would have had a pretext to act directly against Halston. At that time, and even now, who wants to take on the Empire over a fifth-rate system?"

"I understand the military aspect, but how did that affect you?"

"If the Empire could prove the Matriarchy really was behind the Popular Front, then the Empire would have had the excuse to annex the entire Nalian system as a threat to its security. If they hadn't canned me once the Empire protested, then the Matriarch would be admitting she supported the Popular Front."

Martel shakes his head. Gates is talking about webs within webs as if they were real.

"Still don't understand, do you?" rumbles Gates. "Look. Think of it this way. People never react to what's real. They react to what they want to believe. To what they believe they see or to what they want to see. What's real doesn't matter unless it coincides with their beliefs."

"So the Matriarchy kicked you out because of what they believed, rather than for what you'd done?"

"More complicated than that, but that's basically it."

Martel frowns.

"But why—"

"Martel, do you work at being dense?" snaps Hollie. *Nobody can be that stupid ... what's he playing at? Why? ... Questions about the cernadine ... after what ... deep agent ... godpawn?*

Martel spreads his hands helplessly. He has trouble following the flitting shifts in her thoughts, perhaps a result of the cernadine.

"No, he's not," says Gates. "We keep forgetting this is his first job, and right out of the Institute. And his exile was scarcely political." *Good green faxer ... but is that all?*

"It's all new. Frankly, I've been trying to figure out the

gods more than the politics." Martel tries to reinforce Gates' point.

Why do they both suspect you, Martel?

Gates trying to warn me?

Hollie's thought adds to Martel's concerns.

"You want the off-line studio?" asks Gates.

"I did have some prep I was working on."

"Fine. We're off." Gates smiles, but the smile is perfunctory. He slides off the counter, and his boots hit the flooring with a muffled thud.

"But—"

"No problem. No problem," interrupts the older man. "One thing, though. You might consider that everyone plays politics, even gods. You can't escape it." *Wish we could.*

Hollie jerks herself from the chair and follows Gates. Martel gets up from his own seat as the other two exit.

How much you need to learn, Martel. And those who know don't tell.

Martel belatedly realizes that his shields are down, that he still has not learned to keep his mental blocks in place automatically. How long have his thoughts been open to the world?

He shrugs.

Gates is right, you know . . . don't you?

Gates is right. He deserves better than Aurore . . . if he wants it.

Martel sits down again, lets himself go limp, and extends his perceptions.

Hollie and Gates are still in the front entryway. Hollie is shifting the console to full automatic, with the direct in-line straight to the live studio.

Martel power-slips under her conscious thoughts, probes for the subtle weaknesses that must exist. They do. He inserts an idea, a prohibition, a small compulsion, and what others might call an optimistic feed loop, for want of a better term. The adjustments complete, he withdraws.

Unless he has miscalculated, Hollie Devero will discover over the days and years ahead that she needs less and less cernadine, if any. Hopefully, the gradual nature of the change will let her believe that the change is hers, not his.

He takes a deep breath and climbs back to his feet.

Each time, such extensions of his abilities take less and less effort. Each time, he has a better idea of what to do and how.

Some things, Martel, some things you are learning.

He picks up the cubes he needs and heads for the vacant studio, absently noting that Gates and Hollie have left the CastCenter.

XVII

According to the datacenter, three main religious orders maintain communities and worship centers in the hills above Pamyra—the Apollonites, the Ethenes, and the Taurists. The fourth major order, the Thoradians, has a small mission at Pamyra, but lists no main community anywhere.

Martel frowns.

Even before getting into the fieldwork, he is digging up as many questions as answers. And more questions are bound to follow.

He tabs the numbers into his console, switches the fax from the datalink into the commlink, and begins his contacts.

Father Sanders G'Iobo of the Apollonites says yes, provided Martel faxes only the postulants themselves and the lay community, not the Brothers or sacred aspects.

Sister Artemis Dian agrees, if no facial close-ups or religious scenes are faxed.

Head Taurist Theseus politely explains that no internal faxshots of the community are permitted.

The Thoradian Chief Missionary grants Martel permission to fax anything he can except the interior of the Smithhall, the place of worship.

So when do you start? He blocks his own questions but nods to himself. *Now . . . before it's too late.*

Martel stands, leans over the console, and logs out. Theoretically, today is his "break" day, which gives him the time he will need before he is due back on the board.

Tonight Gates will take his shift, and Hollie will probably use the time in the spare studio to edit her slot on crafts.

Crafts? Who knows? Who knows if anyone will care about a bunch of worshipers and their offbeat gods?

Martel represses a shiver. *Maybe they'll care too much.* He recalls the warning about the logo slot by the goddess.

He pushes the uneasiness to the back of his mind and lifts the portafax unit. It will take several trips to load the flitter.

Pamyra is two stans' flight time by the CastCenter flitter, and another half-stan beyond is his first stop, the Apollonite community.

From the air the sunburst pattern is clear—radial lanes, yellow-paved, linked at the center where the temple stands, fan outward and cross regularly spaced and circular ways. The temple rises from the absolute center of the community to a pointed beacon fifty meters above-ground which pulses with a golden glow.

The last circular lane marks the perimeter between the community buildings and the supporting lands, and on it is a row of low structures, some with pens attached.

Martel circles the entire community twice, taking his wide-angle and pan shots, and ends them with a close-focused zoom in on the temple.

He drops the flitter on the pad midway between the agricultural buildings and the temple.

Father G'Iobo, clean-shaven, tanned, silver hairs streaking his golden curls, and flowing pale yellow robes not quite covering his sandals, meets Martel as he begins to unload the portafax from the flitter.

A sunburst, radiating a gentle light, hangs from a golden chain around the good Father's neck.

"Greetings, in the name of Apollo," offers G'Iobo.

Martel holds back a smile. Without probing, he can sense the priest's disapproval of his black tunic, trousers, and boots.

"Greetings to you, Father, and my thanks, both for me and for those who will have a chance to glimpse the kind of life you offer the faithful and those who would join your Order." Martel inclines his head in a gesture of respect.

"What exactly do you have in mind, my son?"

Martel finishes loading the next cube into the unit and adjusts the harness, ready to shoulder it.

"Fairly standard approach, Father. Pan shots of the community; then a mixture of shots of the secular activities . . . what people do in the way of support activities—I understand that the postulants do some crafts for the tourie trade—and perhaps a back shot or two over the shoulders of the novices of the other . . . Apollonites? Is that what those who are accepted are called?"

G'Iobo nods.

"Like a shot of them, not their faces, but from behind, as they enter the temple, with perhaps an uptake into the beacon."

"Flame," corrects the priest.

"Would any of that be a problem?" asks Martel, still balancing the fax unit on his knee, his right foot resting on the landing strut of the flitter.

"If that's all, it shouldn't be." The older man pauses, then asks, "What do you expect to get from this? What's the real purpose of your visit?"

Martel reflects. The question seems hostile, but Father G'Iobo radiates no hostility, though he wears a mindshield. Shields do not block emotions, just thoughts. Martel calculates whether he should attempt to break through the shield, decides against it.

"Twofold, I guess. First, no one has ever done a story on the religious communities. Not in any of the records. That makes it a possibility for a good story, and I need one. Second, I'm new. And I hope to learn something in the process."

G'Iobo relaxes fractionally, though his professional smile has not varied an iota.

"That seems reasonable. Please do not point your unit at any of the Brothers, the Apollonites wearing sunbursts like mine. If you feel it necessary to have some faces, a picture of a postulant or two, the ones in the plain yellow robes, would not be out of place."

Martel catches sight of a taller, more massively built Apollonite approaching.

G'Iobo turns toward the newcomer, his smile a shade

broader. "Administrative duties call me, but Brother Hercles will be your guide and adviser."

Martel again inclines his head and looks up at the giant, who towers a full two meters plus.

"Brother Hercles," says G'Iobo, "this is Faxer Martel from the CastCenter at Sybernal. He knows the guidelines, and I am sure he will do his best to follow them."

"Greetings," Martel says quietly.

"A pleasure to meet you. I've seen you on the fax." Hercles' voice rumbles like a bass organ.

"I will return to see you off," adds Father G'Iobo as he steps away toward the temple.

"Where do you wish to start?" asks the giant.

Martel hefts the fax unit into the shoulder harness.

Be nice to have his muscles to carry this, he thinks.

"I sort of thought we'd start with the outbuildings and work in, ending up with what shots I can take of the temple."

Before he finishes, Martel is talking to empty air and hurrying to catch up.

The first place where the massive Apollonite halts is in the center of a narrow barn, filled with empty stalls.

"This is the sunram barn."

Martel does a quick once-over, then focuses on a single immaculate stall.

"The sunrams?"

"Out in the fields. Not far. Do you want to see them?"

Actually, while a shot of the animals might round out the slot, Martel really wants faxtime of people. He nods.

"Not far" turns out to be across two hills. Two yellow-robed novices and another Apollonite are watching the small flock. The animals, from their black hooves to their curling golden horns and thick yellow fleece, are spotless.

As he moves closer to the sunrams Martel realizes the animals do not smell like normal sheep, but almost like flowers.

He sniffs. Sniffs again. A clean smell.

"Heather," supplies Hercles. "A good smell."

The closer sunrams raise their heads at Martel's approach. He zooms in on the head of the nearest, narrowing in on the eyes. The eye itself contains a star-shaped pupil within the golden iris.

He shifts focus from that ram to another, eating the golden grass. Neither, Martel realizes, tears at the roots the way many sheep and goats do.

The way they chew isn't your subject, he reminds himself.

Martel looks at his guide.

"Some cube on the novices?"

"I beg your pardon?" rumbles the giant.

"According to father G'Iobo, I cannot fax Apollonites, only the postulants and lay members of the community."

The herder Apollonite frowns as Martel speaks, but moves to one side before the guide gestures.

Both novices are beardless. One is fresh from academics; the other shows gray in his brown hair; laugh lines radiating from his eyes. The golden wide-link chains around their necks are plain, without the sunburst.

"Do you comb the sunrams every day?" asks Martel of the older novice at the same time as he splits the focus between the animal and the man.

The novice's eyes run to the animal, back to the faxer, and Martel catches it all on the cube.

The man shakes his head in agreement.

"Are they easy to work with?"

A more vigorous headshake.

Martel angles in on the younger. "Do you like working with sunrams?"

An almost shy smile and a headshake answer the question.

The faxer fades from the man's face to a wide pan of the flock to the nearby hilltop, as yet uncropped, where the tall grass waves against the sky.

"Thank you," he tells the shepherd Apollonite.

A fourth nod, curt, is the only response.

Martel looks to his guide.

"Vows of silence?"

"No. Nothing to say. Chatter to mortals seems unnecessary when one has beheld the grandeur of God."

"How about the furniture operation?" *Time to change the subject,* Martel thinks.

"The basket shop is closer."

"Fine. Then the furniture shop."

Once again, Martel finds himself trailing the fast-moving Apollonite.

The double time march leads to another low building. Once inside, Martel sees why the term "basket shop" is inappropriate.

On the left side of the building, nearly one hundred meters from one end to the other, stretch built-in bins, each filled with stacked and dried reeds, wickers, palms, and grasses.

Across from the nearest set of bins are three rows of short tables. Perhaps twenty are occupied. Two Apollonites rove the aisles, offering advice, assistance.

Martel concentrates his unit on the raw materials first, then on the building, and finally on the novices. Two young girls also silently weave wicker into larger baskets, but do not wear the pale yellow robes of the novices.

"Lay members of the community?" Martel half points with his free hand.

"Wards. Each community supports and aids and educates some who have no other resources, and who are too young or too disabled through no fault of their own to make their own way."

The answer raises another series of questions, which Martel chooses not to pursue, but files mentally as he focuses close-ups on the postulants. He follows the fax-ins of the younger men with shots of the girls, first of the redhead, then of the brunette.

Neither is a beauty, but each has good features, a clear complexion, and a deftness in her hands. The redhead smiles broadly as she recognizes she is the object of the fax unit.

Martel lingers on her smile before stopping.

He unshoulders the unit to check the settings. Even the girls do not look at him.

After a long moment, Martel reshoulders the fax unit.

"Furniture shop?"

This time the tall Apollonite waits for Martel to take a step before starting off with his ground-devouring strides.

The furniture shop is housed in another low building like the basket-making facility, but instead of the smell of grass, and the smells of autumn, is filled with the scents of oil and wood. Again, along the left side of the interior are bin after bin of stacked woods stretching from one end to the other.

A finished marwood chest gleams just inside the entrance. The black surfaces are so smoothly finished that even without wax, lacquer, or glaze, the wood reflects Martel and the Apollonite guide.

Martel lets out a low whistle as he admires it and plays the faxer over it from every possible angle.

"Fit for a king," he murmurs.

"Scheduled for the Matriarch of Halston," says Hercles with a laugh.

Among the workers are more Apollonites, heavy leather aprons over shortened yellow robes, than in the basket shop, and the novices all seem older.

Martel faxes a simple inlaid game table, which, for all its simplicity, could have adorned any palace, any Duke's salon.

Along with the close-ups of the novices, he adds several shots over the shoulders of the Apollonite craftsmen, careful not to appear too obvious about his intentions.

From the carpentry and cabinet making, Martel is escorted to the weavers, where the golden wool is carded, stretched, treated, woven, and tailored; to the tannery; to the clinic, which is empty except for a young man who is having his left hand treated for a gash suffered in an orchard accident; to the recreation center; to one of the living quarters; to the empty dining hall being readied for the midday meal; and finally to the administration building.

The total time on the cube reads out at close to three stans. *That ought to be enough,* Martel thinks, keeping the thought to himself as he follows Hercles back to his flitter.

Father G'Iobo, having torn himself away from his administrative duties, is waiting.

"We're sorry you could not spend more time with us, Faxer Martel."

Martel doesn't believe a word of it, and the good Father's emotions show no sign of the regret he is expressing.

"And so am I," he responds in kind, "but it's been most interesting. I hope you enjoy the program once it's aired in final fax form."

"We'll be looking forward to that," says G'Iobo.

Martel can sense the unease behind the statement, even though the priest's face carries the same warm and friendly smile.

Martel racks the one used fax cube in the storage locker, reloads the unit, thumbs the locker shut, and sets the fax unit in place for the next series of aerial shots.

As he settles behind the controls he looks up to see Father G'Iobo and Hercles standing back by the admin building, apparently waiting for his departure.

Father G'Iobo had been waiting much closer when Martel had arrived, much closer.

How about another kind of checklist? Martel asks himself, thoughts fully shielded.

He lets his perceptions range through the start circuits, mentally tracking, searching . . . and comes up with the "wrong" feeling. A small cartridge of something above the turbine blades, liquid.

Concentrating, he extends his energies, lets his thoughts remove the liquid to a small space in the bottom of the flitter.

With a touch of a stud he starts up, waves to the waiting Apollonites, and begins the short checklist.

Shortly he lifts off, heading toward the Ethene community.

Once in flight, he tries to analyze the captive liquid mentally, some sort of acid. Obviously placed to weaken the turbine blades, the acid would have loosened several blades at once, certainly exploding the engine, and possibly the whole flitter.

Martel lets the liquid eat through the bottomplate and bleed away into the open air.

What surprises will I get from the ladies?

From the air, the Ethene community shows more of a grid system, with its lanes converging in a fan toward the temple on the hillside south of everything else. The simple white stone structure, half set into the hill, lies open in the center.

Martel sees the sacred white flame from the air, takes the liberty of faxing it along with his other pan shots.

Sister Artemis Dian, the very name a position title, waits by the landing pad. She wears a white metal circlet and a veil, seemingly thin, but totally concealing. From the golden hue of her hair and the curve of her calves, which show below the three-quarter length of her off-white robes, Martel guesses she is beyond first youth, but not too far. Either that or thoroughly rejuved.

"Faxer Martel?" Well modulated, with a hint of throatiness, her voice does nothing to discourage his first impression.

"The same. Greetings, Lady."

"Sister will do, and greetings to you."

"Greetings, Sister," Martel corrected himself. "Anything I should know before we start?"

"The Goddess watches over everything, and in her wisdom will correct all that goes amiss."

Translated loosely, Martel, if you blow it, you'll get fired on the spot with celestial fury.

"I think I understand, Sister, and will follow your instructions to the letter." *Not to the spirit, however.*

The Ethene community, while laid out in a different physical pattern, bears remarkable similarity to the Apollonite village in the activities, the cleanliness, the sense of purpose and quiet. There is no furniture shop, but instead, a ceramic facility, and in place of the basket shop there is, surprisingly, the winery that produces the Springfire of which Martel has become so fond.

Sister Artemis Dian is his guide through the entire tour, even to the front steps of the temple.

"No farther," she says in her controlled contralto.

"Mind if I pan up the steps and to the mountain behind?"

"That would be acceptable."

The stroll back to the flitter is absolutely quiet, and the stillness seems to accentuate the weight of the fax unit on Martel's shoulders. Only the pad of feet and the swish of robes intrude. The Sister, like Father G'Iobo, is mind-shielded.

Her apparent young age, her young step, bother Martel, do not fit. She seems totally at ease with him, but as if he is really not present.

As he stows the used fax cube and reloads, as he resets the unit for aerial shots, she waits, far closer than the Apollonites had. Martel uses his extended perceptions to scan the flitter even before starting to climb back in.

An aura of danger clings to the power cells. But why?

Martel scans superficially, then deeply, before realizing that both original sets have been replaced with a new set, blocked somehow.

If you touch the starter, all that power will turn on itself, fuse the cells . . . and boom. No more flitter, no more Martel, and no more Sister Artemis Dian.

Ergo . . . Sister Artemis Dian wasn't. Rather some poor flunky mind-washed into being a victim. Or . . .

Martel doesn't like the second possibility. The "Sister" might be the goddess herself, able to shield herself from the fiery blast and point the finger at someone. Or claim that Martel had tried to defile the community.

Martel was either a victim or a pawn. He didn't like the possibilities, and adjusted another strap, stalling and trying to think his way out of the situation.

If he announced the problem, it would reveal abilities he really hadn't had the chance to develop fully and might open him to more scrutiny.

Slowly, carefully, he lets his thoughts disconnect the leads to the power cells, and allows the power to bleed off into the field through a "channel" he opens, until the cells are totally inert.

He finishes adjusting his harness, shifts his weight, and closes the canopy. Then, and only then, Martel touches the starter stud, and watches the "Sister" for a reaction. There is none, none that he can detect, either physically or mentally, as the flitter rises into the sky.

He shivers, partly from the effort in supplying the current needed for the start through mental ability, and partly from the strain of the undercurrents he does not understand.

He shakes his head. If everyone is so secretive about their religious communities, why haven't they all taken the stance of the Taurists and merely refused him permission to visit? He might have complained or even woven it into a faxcast, but nothing would have changed.

The Thoradian mission would be the last stop, but before landing there, he wants to complete as much of his aerial flyby and faxshot pass as he can of the Taurist community.

Every sense would have to be alert, with his mental perceptions spread as far as possible. If those who had welcomed him are trying to destroy him, what can he expect from those who declared themselves off limits from the beginning?

Nothing.

Where the Apollonite community was circular, and the Ethene a fan-shaped grid, the Taurist is rectangular, with black buildings, black-paved roads, and a central black square, in the center of which burns a strange black flame. No temple.

And no interference.

Martel rechecks the fax unit as he swings the flitter back toward the Thoradian mission.

Where the other three communities had appeared regular from the air, and orderly, the Thoradians built wherever they pleased. Some of the buildings appear to have fallen roofs, and the outlying streets are grass-choked.

No one waits at the landing stage.

Martel dons the unit, seals the flitter, not that such a precaution has been helpful before, and starts out.

Sunrams they have, unkempt and grazing around the out-buildings, but with normal, unstarburst pupils.

The scent of fire and hot metal draw him to a plain, un-painted wooden building, in good trim, but obviously old, and weathered planking that has been replaced over the years, lending the walls a patchwork impression.

Inside, two burly men, sweat pouring from foreheads into full red beards, beat out blades on the wide black anvils, to-tally oblivious to Martel and his fax unit.

Neither wears robes, but rather a short kiltlike battle skirt, with alternating leather and metal strips. Their upper bodies, outside of a reddish tan, leather aprons, and copper armbands and wristbands, are bare.

Martel focuses in on their concentration, then onto the compact and unvarying flame over which they labor.

He departs, apparently unnoticed.

More shots of abandoned structures follow.

Across the red stone lane from the log temple, distin-guished from the other buildings by the symbol of the crossed graystone hammers, Martel finds a tall figure waiting for him.

Like the others, the man is burly, muscular, tall, and dressed in battle kilt. In addition, a wolfskin cloak is thrown back over his shoulders, and hair curls from under a metal helmet decorated with twin ramhorns. From the leather loop circling his right wrist hangs the heavy graystone hammer.

"So you're the one! Upstart they all question."

"Your pardon?" asks Martel.

"Say they question. Fear what you may become. Nonsense. All of it. Thor fears none of it. Nor you. Nor what you become. Do you challenge the hammer and might?"

Martel steps back.

Thor? The so-called god himself? This barbarian rumbling gutturals?

The hammer swings and is released skyward.

A blaze of lightning follows, slashes into the suddenly dark sky.

"Doubt not Thor! Unbeliever!" The voice bellows like thunder.

Martel steps back another step, still faxing the entire incredible scene.

"That'll do. Teach them all," rumbles the old warrior, and Martel can sense the age in the god, even though the figure and the voice are those of a man in his prime.

The hammer screams back to the upraised arm, and yet another lightning bolt flares.

Martel retreats another step, aware his hands are damp, but still recording.

He stumbles, looks down to keep from letting the unit overbalance him, and when he looks up, Thor is gone. The red rock lanes are again deserted.

Martel brings the fax unit to bear on the temple, zooms in the focus, and discovers that the doors which were open are now barred.

No one stops him on his way back to the flitter, which is as he left it. Untouched.

Martel is still shaking his head as he pilots the light craft back toward Sybernal, toward the CastCenter, hoping the scenes with the thunder-god are indeed in the cube.

A small part of his mind hopes they are not, for if they are, he will use them. Must use them.

XVIII

Martel tenses.

The quartered image stands out in front of the single flat wall of the CastCenter lounge—four separate scenes, and each with its own message.

On the upper left graze a flock of sunrams, their fleeces glittering with lights of their own. On the upper right stretch long rows of golden vines, leaves half covering the ripening grapes. On the lower left extends a grass-choked pavement. Finally, on the lower right, an aerial shot of a black-walled, black-laned community.

The music wells up, subsides. A selection from *Winds of Summer*.

"The postulant communities of Aurore, as they present themselves to visitors, and to the universe ... postulants to gods who are real, and who demonstrate their powers on an everyday basis.

"Now ... a first-time-ever look at the worshipers of the living gods of Aurore ..."

The four images fade into one—the sunspire of the temple of Apollo, which fades into the white marble of the Ethene temple, which fades into an aerial shot of the black flame in the black square of the Taurist community, and then to the closed and hammer-barred front view of the Thoradian mission under sullen clouds.

"Not a bad intro, Martel," says Marta Farell.

Gates Devero nods in agreement, while Hollie makes no statement or gesture.

Martel realizes his palms are damp, rubs them on his trousers as the cube continues running through the apparently innocuous activities of the Apollonite community, and then through a similar routine in the Ethene community.

"Good shot of his expression ... really wrapped up in what he's doing."

What's he playing for? Martel picks up the thought from Marta.

"Oohhh ... the eyes on that sunram ..."

"Lot of contentment showing ..."

". . . nice view of the reflection off the marwood chest . . ."

Martel swallows, waiting for the transition from the light of the Ethenes to the aerial shots of the Thoradian mission. *Apollo!*

". . . so deserted ... old ..."

The cut from the desolation focuses down a grass-choked lane and into the blacksmith shop, with the bearded barbarians pounding, pounding out blades, the metal glowing, the heat welling out.

". . . looks like a Darian view of Hades ..."

Don't like where this is going. That thought came from Marta Farell.

From the focus on the blades the view shifts to the blank, concentrating faces of the smiths, oblivious to the watchers, robotic in their duties, and then cuts back away to the grassy pavement and what Martel had seen as he had walked through the nearly deserted community, ending up before the temple, its rough doors gaping.

The god Thor looms in the center of the scene, as if he had appeared from nowhere.

"Doubt not Thor!"

The fifth time through, Martel still marvels a bit at the swing of the magnificent graystone hammer, and the lightnings that follow, the clouds that roil in on cue from the thunder-god.

". . . don't believe it ..."

". . . how ... how did you do it?"

Fry Martel, fry us all, if this screens.

From the lightnings the fax zeroes back in on the empty square, then on the barred and closed temple, with its crossed graystone hammers.

"The Taurist community, unlike the other three," Martel's narrative rolls onward, "is closed to outsiders."

With only the low thunder of the *March of the Directorate* by Pavenne as accompaniment, the aerial view of the Taurist community unrolls, concluding with the square of the black flame.

"The postulant communities of the living gods, from light—"

The fax shows the Apollonite sunram, golden spire in the backdrop, cuts to the golden iris of the ram's eye with the dark starburst pupil. That dark star grows and grows until the entire screen is black.

"—to light—"

The scene mists from black through gray to the open Ethene square and the steps leading up to the white marble temple of the goddess.

"No farther." The words of Sister Artemis Dian roll up over the track music, and the view pans up the temple and to the dark-shadowed point of the sacred mountain. Again ... the darkness expands to encompass the entire holo image.

"—to light—"

With a quick slash view of the thunder-god's face, his lips caught twisted, the scene follows not the hammer but the lightning, on the upward stroke and the downward return. As the last lightning flash fades, the image fills with the dark clouds, which gray out and thin.

"—to dark."

From the thinning gray of the clouds the view switches to the aerial vista of the Taurist community, laid out in black, the blackness of the lanes, the blackness of the buildings, emphasized by the filters. Martel has overlaid. Steadily the focus narrows until the only identifiable object is the black flame, within its black square and centered in the middle of the holo.

The last measures of the *March of the Directorate* die away as the image blanks to black.

"Flame!" mutters Marta Farell.

"You trying a fancy form of suicide, Martel?" That from Gates.

Hollie Devero shakes her head, slowly. *Knew he was crazy.*

"But do you like it?" Martel asks, knowing the question is expected. He gets out of the narrow chair and stretches.

Silence.

"You know," says Hollie quietly, "faxers have lost their minds for less than that."

"For what? Showing a few scenes of the communities?"

"You're missing the point on purpose, Martel!" snaps Marta Farell. "Without a single negative word, without a single disparaging musical note, without a single scene of a suffering human being, you've painted the four prime gods of Aurore as petty and almost evil. And I don't want any part of it."

"How good is it?" counters Martel.

"Good enough to have the entire CastCenter leveled if we run it," retorts Hollie.

"What if you credit me with exclusive production?"

"Not good enough."

"All right. I'll can it."

"No."

Marta stretches. In her hand is a stunner.

"Unload that cube. Now. Put it on the counter."

Martel steps toward the holojector, one step at a time, narrowing his thoughts, concentrating as he does.

Hollie and Gates back away, trying to get to the side, as far from the line of fire as possible.

Martel's thoughts touch Farell's, catch the low block there, and vault into her mind.

. . . got to stop him . . . say so . . . so glorious . . . do what HE wants . . .

Martel reaches the nexus he needs, touches the nerves. Marta Farell's knees crumple. Her eyes roll up and close, and she collapses in a heap.

Martel lets himself go do in the same way, unaffected as he is. His thoughts reach out to seize Hollie and Gates Devero.

Once all three are safely unconscious, Martel climbs to his feet, fingers the bruise on his forearm where it had collided with the leg of the lounger. He unloads the cube from the holojector and carries it into the control center, where a full-stan documentary on the wind dolphins of Faldarin is concluding.

Martel keys the back-feed for Karnak, bringing the tie transmitter up full and alerting the Regency network that a new outprogram would be coming. He'd already done the attributions, foreseeing the reaction he has gotten.

As soon as the documentary finishes and the I.D. spot

plugs through, he will run *Postulants of Aurore* straight through.

With the off-planet net, once the title line alone has run there is no way that Apollo and crew will dare to stop his cube. Not before the fact.

Martel has his perceptions fully spread, but detects nothing out of the ordinary. He is banking on the fact that even the so-called gods of Aurore can handle only so many things at once, and that they do not expect him to take matters into his own hands so quickly.

Just in case anyone thinks about mechanical niceties, he wipes the cube clean of fingerprints, as well as the feeding equipment. He makes most of the adjustments by thought alone.

Once the cube runs through, without further instructions the console will pick up the KarNews feed.

The details taken care of, once the cube begins he returns to the recording studio, drains the power from Marta's stunner and from the laser knife she also carries, and resumes the position the others had seen him fall into.

He blocks off his conscious physical control and waits.

Waits until he feels someone shake him, slap him across the face. Hard. Flamed hard.

Marta, of course.

"Damn you! Damn, damn! *Damn!*"

"Wha · . . . stop . . . you . . . why . . . stun me . . ." He lets the words stumble out.

"Because I want to live. Because I want to get off this planet. Because you and your cutesy idea have ruined everything. *Everything!*"

Martel shakes his head, realizes he is swallowing something. His blood. Marta's slap has apparently caused him to bite his cheek.

He looks around. Gates, white-faced, is leaning over the counter. Hollie, leaning forward in her chair, is holding her head in her hands.

"What happened? I went to get you the cube, just like you asked. Hollie and Gates saw me. You saw me. And you stunned me, even before I got there. Now you're slapping me, and screaming that it's all my fault. You're the one who's crazy! Flamed crazy!"

"I didn't stun you. Someone else did, and they ran the cube. Ran it right out to all Aurore and back-fed to Karnak. There'll be flame to pay. And it's all on your head."

"You're crazy! You said I could try the idea. I did. You said no. I agreed, and now it's on my head. Why me? I didn't do anything."

"You made the damned cube. You made a mockery out of the Taurists, and their unnamed god can't be pleased. If he doesn't get you, then Thor will, unless the others get to you first."

"But why? It isn't our fault somebody ran the cube."

Gates says nothing, but glares at Martel, and staggers out of the studio lounge, dragging Hollie by the arm.

Marta Farell's eyes smoke. "You just might be right. And you might not. But I won't risk anyone else's life because of your stupidity. For the sake of everyone else, Martel, when you're on duty here, no one else is going to be here. Ever! You're perm night shift. Until you pack up and quit. Or until your brains, or whatever passes for brains, rot."

Martel lets a puzzled expression cross his face, as if he can't understand her hysteria. In fact, he has difficulty, although he can sense the emotional desperation welling from her.

"That's starting right now! And while you're off duty, I'll do my best to see that no one comes close to you, especially no one from any faxcast center. But don't worry. You'll get full credit for this one. Every last credit from that docuslot is yours. Even the station's cut. It should make you wealthy. If you live to enjoy it."

Martel stands there.

Marta marches toward the portal, then half turns.

"You've got about a quarter-stan before we go local. Program's on the up sheet. If I ever talk to you again, other than by fax, and that's only when necessary, count yourself flamed lucky."

Marta is gone. From the lack of mental echoes, he can tell the entire CastCenter is deserted.

"Some reaction . . ." he mutters.

He had expected concern, but not the violent paranoia they'd all displayed.

He shrugs, heals the cut inside his mouth, and heads for the on-line control center.

He leaves his mental shields up. If half of what Marta has screamed is correct, he will need them.

XIX

Dull rumbles echo, bounce, skip like flat stones over the leaden surface. Green-golden water heaves itself at the rocky fingertip of land that seems to dive into the waves.

The wind whips spray around the man standing atop the one boulder, black, that protrudes from the flat and bare rock.

The atmosphere itself shrouds the dark clouds, sulfurs the honesty of rain with the false promise of the sunlight that never has been.

Raindrops shatter as they strike the sea, fragment on crystal rocks, dissolve into the flanking beaches, nourish the high grasses on top of the cliffs above.

The difference in the fate of each raindrop is not in the rain.

Martel watches the sea, looks out across the surf that breaks below his feet and foams around his boulder perch.

A golden streak of lightning flashes, flares, flashes down at an unbroken wave climbing above its sisters.

Steam hisses, the sound audible to Martel though the crest is fully three kilos out.

Standing on the wave, appearing from nowhere, is a figure dripping cobalt water, despite the greenness of the water above which he towers, bearing a trident. He strikes the water on which he stands, and from the strike rises blue lightning toward the clouds.

Another golden bolt spears down. Hisses and steams. Haloes the sea-god.

And another.

In return comes a fainter blue upward strike.

The trident whirls, and close upon the whirling rises a waterspout, not black-green, but brilliant blue, that hurls itself toward the low-hanging clouds.

The clouds lift. The waterspout follows, howling.

Another golden bolt strikes downward, then a shower, attacking the tower of water like the arrows of a besieging army.

The tower quivers, wavers, and tilts. Drops in an instant waterfall into the sea.

Within moments, the tattered fragments of the clouds are gone, and the waves subside, the air fresh with the memory of rain.

In the distance, beyond the vision of most but clear to Martel, a pair of nymphs skates the breaksides of the remaining waves, their laughter chiming like the bells of holidays past.

The empty quarter, the empty half, the empty outside of a full beaker . . . why are these the things he looks for?

Really, it is a most unusual occurrence when analyzed—a storm to set the scene, followed by a short battle between Apollo the sun-god and the sea-god, completed with a musical finale of two nymphs with laughter. Now, hasn't that been your typical evening on your everyday deserted beach?

Oh, yes, and add to the foregoing that evening isn't evening, but everlasting day, and that most beaches away from Sybernal, Pamyra, and Alesia are usually deserted, O expert on beaches.

All quite understandable, since Sybernal had twenty kilos of perfect beach, and Pamyra another ten. The normal tourist is rich and sedentary or poor and transportationless.

The twinge in his left leg reminds Martel that he has lost track of time. Again.

The wetness of the quick rain has begun to fade with the return of full daylight, and the scent of spring fades into the perpetual golden haze that lies across the sky.

The regular beat of waves against the stone point resumes.

Martel frowns, concentrates, and a short cloak of darkness flows from his shoulders. With quick steps he crosses the flat green-gray stone, his feet leaving no trace on the damp rock.

From the back of the small peninsula rises a cliff, the gray rock cleft in the middle. The cleft is filled with broken stone.

Each boulder is roughly as wide as the armspan of an average man. None is smaller than a small table, and no sand cushions the space between the rectangular blocks. The sides of the cleft are smooth, and the gray-striped stone is scarred with black lines.

Martel jumps from the top of the bottommost stone to the next one, zigzagging his way up the jumble toward the grassy plateau.

By the time he reaches the short golden grass, the flitter he senses in the distance, coming south from Sybernal, should arrive. Piloted by Rathe Firien.

Martel drops his shadow cloak even before his first step out onto the grass. Black enough for Rathe as he stands. Black trousers, tunic, belt, and boots.

The old words rise into his thoughts and to his lips.

"Tell me now, if you can,
    What is human, what is man . . ."

He shakes his head, half aware that Rathe sees the gesture as she brings the flitter down, knowing also that she will not misinterpret, that she understands how he argues with himself.

Crooked in her left arm as she swings from the flitter is a wicker basket, the kind made by the Apollonite postulants for the tourist trade, and which would be called old-fashioned almost anywhere else in the Empire of Man.

"Flitter?" he asks, still in full stride toward her.

"Clinic's. Slow time now, and it has been for weeks. Maybe the Fuardian-Halston thing. Who knows?"

Rathe's red-silk hair is longer these days, covers her ears. With the length has come a slight wave, and a certain softness to her features.

She sets the basket on the grass. From the top she brings forth a thin cloth, which she shakes out and spreads on the ground. The basket then goes in the middle.

Rathe seats herself cross-legged and motions.

"I know you're restless, but since I've brought you the picnic dinner I don't deserve, at least sit down and enjoy it with me."

"You don't deserve?" He sits down, not cross-legged but half lying on his left side. He props his head with his left hand and looks across the top of the basket at her freckled face.

"To have dinner with one of Aurore's top faxcasters? Of course I don't deserve. And if all the rich norm ladies knew where you hid when you're not at the CastCenter, I'd never see you."

"Marta's blacked me."

"Oh, that. As long as He hasn't, I wouldn't worry."

Martel caught the anxiety beneath the bantering tone, the darkness behind the forced smile.

"You caught the special on the postulants?"

"No. But everyone's talking about it. Talking about how none of the other faxers are supposed to talk to you. I don't think it set well. Father H'Lerry is supposed to speak on it next service."

Rathe pursed her lips, returned her attention to the basket, from which she pulled a bottle of Springfire and two tulip glasses.

"I hope he's generous," Martel answers, forcing a chuckle that sounds hollow even to himself. He extends his arm for a glass. "Farell said it was on my head. Marta Farell, my dear supervisor." *How literally had Farell meant it?* He blocks the thought automatically.

Rathe licks her lips, twice catches her lower lip with her upper teeth, worries it, stares down at her half-filled tulip glass.

Martel takes a small sip of the Springfire and waits.

Rathe stares at the picnic basket.

"You're worried."

She nods, without looking up.

He can read exactly what she is thinking.

. . . not kind to the gods . . . shows them spoiled . . . Thor . . . who am I to say . . . Martel . . .

"You're thinking that I was foolish to fax it?"

"Brave. And foolish. That's why I love you. For as long as I can."

From inside the basket she pulls a small package and thrusts it at him.

"What?"

"Open it. Please."

He sets his glass on a level spot in the short grass and avoids reading her thoughts so that the gift will be the surprise she intends.

The belt, for that is what it is, uncoils from the wrappings, with the softness and jet-black of natural wehrleather. The buckle is pure silver, a simple triangle, yet hard.

Martel frowns. The buckle alone, with its monalloyed silver, represents an enormous free credit balance. Neither is wehrleather native to Aurore or easy to come by.

He gets up and kneels on both knees to don the belt, looking down at it, admiring the way it feels and fits, and the shine of the buckle, neither muted nor too bright.

"You look so good!"

"Thanks to you." He grins, looking back down at the belt, then across to her. "Rathe . . ."

His fingertips brush hers, link, and grasp her hand, draw her across the cloth to him, against him.

Lips linger. A touch of salt, a warmth radiating from lip to cheek to . . .

Yes . . . no . . . not now . . . later . . . he liked it.

Martel cradles her face in both hands as he releases her, runs his fingertips down the side of her face.

"You didn't need to."

"I know, but I wanted to." Her eyes glisten even in the pervasive indirect light, and that alone tells him that she is pleased.

"I'm hungry," he announces, not only to change the subject but because the sudden growl of his gut has reminded him that he is.

"Ha! Your stomach spoke first."

"I admit it. So what else is in the basket?"

"Sea duck and kelip."

"Then serve, wench."

"Yes, Masterfaxer. At once, sir."

Rathe does not notice the dark cloud in the distance, toward the sacred mountain behind Pamyra. Martel sees the cloud, notes it, and concentrates on the sea duck.

"Napkin?"

"At once, sir! Here you go."

"More Springfire!"

Rathe arcs the bottle across the cloth at him, but he catches it without spilling a drop. Inhales deeply of the aroma, lets it mingle with the scent of Rathe and the pinsting of the sea below.

"The days of wine and youth
 Are days of love and truth . . ."

Martel listens to the song, to the feelings behind the words, and to the hidden harmony that Rathe does not know she brings to the short song.

"Martel."

She stares at him.

He starts, realizing his cheeks are wet.

"Must have gotten something in my eyes."

Martel, crying . . . see that?

The wonder in her thoughts leeches the emotion cleanly from him.

He picks up the tulip glass from the grass and takes a swig, a long pull to empty it.

The distant cloud is no closer, but darker. Suddenly it disappears, and a chill breeze swirls the picnic cloth and is gone, and with it goes the sense of summer.

"We'd better go."

Rathe nods.

He folds the cloth while she puts the bottle and glasses away. Only crumbs from the sea duck and kelip remain, left for the shy dorles, who will flutter down to feast once the flitter and the man and the woman have left.

The myth of the "thousand ships" persists even in nontechnic cultures. . . . As a practical matter, less than seven hundred possible instances of space colonization fall within the parameters outlined by Corenth. . . . The implications of a power which could scatter a fleet of one thousand warships of advanced design obviously render the whole question moot and leave unanswered the source of an unverifiable panhumanoid myth. . . .

—*In Search of the Thousand Ships*
Pier V. RonTaur
Alphene, II, 3123 A.A.T.

XXI

The white-tipped peak juts through the white carpet of clouds like an imperfect obelisk, evenly lit and evenly shadowed at the same time.

On the empty air, close enough to reach out and touch the impossibly knife-pointed tip of the mountain, sits a man clothed in a pale sunbeam-yellow tunic, leather sandals with the straps circling his crossed and perfect legs and ankles up to his knees, and wearing a crown of light that blurs his features.

Across the peak from him stands a dark and cloudy figure, combining both the blockiness of a Minotaur and the indistinctness of a thunderstorm.

At the third vertex of the imaginary triangle appears another figure, slender, tall, feminine, and ghostly, clad in white with long golden-blond hair flowing down her back.

Martel puts another foot forward, takes another step upward through the cotton clouds, through the indistinctness, knowing the three figures above await him.

Step, step, step.

The fog swirls around him, parts in front of him, closes behind him. But it has no scent, no smell of salt and fish like sea fog, no smell of pine and rock like mountain fog, no sting of ice needles like arctic fog.

His head breaks through, and he steps clear of the fog, standing on nothing at all, to face the trio.

"Slow, Martel," observes Apollo.

The bull-god says nothing.

The golden goddess turns her head toward Apollo. Martel cannot see her eyes.

"Still ... a slow demigod is better than no demigod."

Martel does nothing. Knows he should do something. Knows he does not know what he should do.

He clenches his hands at his sides.

"If I knew ... if I only knew ..."

"But you don't, Martel. And you never will, not unless you accept that you are a god. Then you'll understand. Then you'll be just like us."

"Never! *Never!*"

Martel throws himself at the brilliance of the sun-god.

"Martel! No!"

The scene dissolves around him. The white clouds flare red, fade into a backdrop of dark wood.

He is half lying, half sitting on his bed, sweat dripping off his forehead. His left hand is falling away from Rathe's forearm.

"You started talking in your sleep again, and you grabbed me. Hard. Screamed something about knowing, and never, never ..." Her voice is filled with pain, as are her thoughts.

Martel sees the dampness on her cheeks and looks down at the arm she cradles, strangely crooked, resting below her bare and full breasts. The quilt is wound around her waist and legs still.

Her arm is broken.

Control, Martel. When are you going to get control over yourself?

"Let me see." He runs his fingers over her skin, letting his awareness build, realizing the damage is worse than Rathe knows—both bones, blood vessels, ripped muscles.

With a sudden jab at her thoughts, he takes them over, lets himself flow into her, trying to put her to sleep for what he has to do. Unlike the case with Gates Devero, this time he cares, and will spare Rathe the pain, if he can.

In slow motion, as she loses consciousness, the pictures and words float past him.

Item: "Fierce" and "gentle," coupled with a black lamb frolicking across an unfenced clearing. The lamb

> jumps and does not land. In its place glares a
> black mountain ram, black lightning for horns.

Item: A man dressed in black, standing silhouetted
      against the sea, wearing a cloak. The cloak whips
      around him, but there is no wind.

Item: Two bodies moving as one upon a bed.

Item: A man lying in a hospital bed, asleep, face con-
      torted, one hand bending the metal railing that
      rings the bed.

Item . . . item . . . item . . . item . . .

Martel breaks out of Rathe's thoughts, stares down at the
freckles on the tear-streaked face, at the closed eyes still
tight-tensed, at the smooth skin, the light nipples, the short
red-silk hair.

His own cheeks are damp, he knows. He wipes the right
side of his face with his upper right arm, still holding his unconscious lover, his unconscious greeter, and perhaps his
unconscious conscience.

Gently he moves, stretches her out on the bed, concentrates
on the arm, straightens it, using his perceptions, and gets the
bone ends aligned. Now, kneeling beside the bed, he thinks,
his thoughts reaching out to repair the damage he has
wrought, trying to mend nerves, to touch the right cells in the
right way to heal what has brought the pain and the tears.

Time stands silent as he works.

He is done.

And done, he lets go, feels himself sink toward the hard
floor, exhausted.

"Martel . . ."

A cool hand touches his face. Rathe's.

"The arm? How are you?" The words burst forth even as
he tries to uncurl from the stiff heap he has become.

"Sore, but just a little."

He heaves himself upward and sits on the edge of the bed
next to her.

Rathe pulls the quilt over her breasts, leaving her shoulders
bare, and turns to face him.

"Kiss me."

Warm lips, salty, and her eyelashes flutter against his closed eyes like butterflies.

Butterflies, but Aurore has no butterflies, and the glitter-motes are no substitutes.

The quilt drops away as two bodies meet, hold . . . and hold.

Rathe sobs, buries her head against his shoulder, sobs once more, then again. Harder and quicker, the sad shudders mount.

Martel finds himself aroused, hard against her softness, her sadness. Finds himself angry at his arousal.

He takes her face, takes her lips, kisses her once, long, evenly, trying to add heat to the salty chill, draws her to him more tightly still.

After a time, her shudders subside, and another motion begins, which he joins. And joins. And joins again.

After the joinings comes sleep.

He wakes first, leaves his arm around her, studies her body, from her full thighs through narrow waist to light-nippled and full breasts . . . smooth skin, creamy with the ubiquitous freckles of a true redhead. His eyes trace her features, the nose sharp enough for character but straight, the green eyes hidden under sleeping lids, the light eyebrows, the narrow lips that kiss so fully.

She smiles, sleeping, and the happiness lifts a corner of the darkness from him.

He thinks, finally reaches into her thoughts as narrowly as he can, makes a change, an adjustment.

After a time, she wakes. She smiles again, then frowns. Starts to pull the dark green quilt over her, then lets it drop.

"You like seeing me? You always have. Will you remember?"

"Remember?"

"Martel. Please. Be gentle. I'm not meant to sleep with gods. Not once we both know. I kept hoping you were just crazy, not divine. But you're not. It hurts too much to love you, and They'll just use me to hurt you. It's too hard . . ."

"I know."

He could feel the tears well up in his eyes again.

*Why? Cried more in the last day than in my whole life . . .
going to pieces?*

"I know you know. But that won't stop you. It can't. But
it doesn't matter."

"What will you do?"

"Now that I don't have to be a greeter?"

He nods.

"I don't know. Maybe I won't change. Maybe I will. It's
nice to have the choice."

He lies back, watches as she stands, still naked. Drinks in
each movement as she dresses. Against the dark panels of the
bedroom her skin lends her the air of a classical statue.

Her pale green tunic all in place, she comes over to the bed
and sits down next to him.

"In your own way, Rathe, dear, you're a goddess."

"Remember me that way. And don't fix my memories.
Broken arms need to be fixed, but I am what I remember."

He turns his face toward her, arms reaching to enfold her.

She plants a quick kiss on his forehead and ducks away
under his arms.

"Wouldn't be the same now."

She is gone through the portal.

Martel lies propped on the bed for a time. Then he arises
and heads to the ultrashower.

He is scheduled for his usual night shift at the CastCenter,
and lots of time for thought.

XXII

The sky outside the cottage grumbles. The room within is
dark, dimmed by clouds, which are natural, and therefore
rare. No artificial light, also rare on Aurore, or glittermotes,
which are not, intrude. Though the corner where the vidfax is
mounted gathers shadows, the man does not need light to see.

He touches the address studs, and his fingers run through
the combination with the effortlessness of habit. For he
knows the pattern by heart.

By heart, he affirms.

His hand hovers near the contact plate, ready to break the connection when she does not answer.

"Greetings," she says automatically, her eyes widening as she recognizes the caller on the screen. "Persistent, aren't you?"

"Yes," he admits, drinking in her green eyes and warm face. " 'Persistent,' I suppose, is as good a word as any."

He realizes her hair is longer now, as it could be after a standard year.

"Foolish, and blind, too," she says and he can sense the bitterness.

He waits.

"I hope this doesn't seal my death, dear one," she continues conversationally, "but you're still acting human and refusing to face what you are. Still appearing on the nightly faxcast, as if it were common for a god to broadbeam the evening trivia. Still trying to persuade a very human woman that you are, too."

"Your death?" His words sound lame.

"My death. Possibly. Possibly yours as well, although I doubt that for reasons I couldn't possibly explain." She sighs. Loudly. "Don't you understand? They want you as a god. If you won't because of me, then They'll do away with me . . . or take all my memories. Do you want to take back everything you've given me? Do you want to become just like Them?"

By now the tears are streaming down her face.

"Let me have my memories, at least. Something. Go on and be what you are! You have all I can give. I can't be some god's plaything. And I won't! If I come back to you, then that's all I'll be. Don't you understand? Don't you?"

He waits, again.

"You could come and twist my thoughts, change me into a willing tool. But you don't. Does that make you good? Or just stubborn? Or waiting until later?

"For my sake, if not for both of us, leave me alone. If you love me, if you ever loved me, please, please, let me be. If you care at all, let me alone. Let me have a memory. Before it's too late . . . already there's so little. I was stupid to fall in

love with you, and you were stupid to give me back myself
... and that's enough stupidity ..."

"All right ..." His words sound unsteady to himself.

He cannot speak more. Nods, reaches toward the contact
plate, looks once again, only to see her looking down, and
not at the screen. He presses the plate, and the screen blanks.

His room is dark, though not so dark as previously. The
storm clouds are dispersing.

He walks out onto the covered porch, then down onto the
hillside, where he stares into the distance toward a peak others cannot see. A peak called Jsalm. The sacred mountain.

He shakes his head. Once. Violently.

He turns, slowly, until he faces the small cottage. With de-
liberate and heavy steps he mounts the three risers to the
porch, crosses it, and reenters the dwelling.

A black glittermote circles the space where he had faced
the distant peak before vanishing.

The dorles, tentatively, hop to the outer branches of the
quince. The largest half-spreads her wings, then chitters a
long note that echoes, that hangs on the hillside.

XXIII

The two figures could be meeting on a mountaintop, or on a
sea bottom, or in a cloud of glittermotes that would drive a
man mad, or in the pitch darkness of the caves deep beneath
Pamyra.

Instead, they stand on a ledge over the White Cliffs.

You've bet too much on this one.

Not yet. Oaks take longer to grow.

*So do the bristlepines, but they don't challenge. Just en-
dure.*

He's young.

So you doubt already?

Sometimes, but not about the potential.

A vision of black thunderbolts passes from the lighter to
the darker.

Strong enough to take us on? Never.
Two words to avoid—"always" and "never."
If you fear, why encourage?
I don't. Just watch. The lighter one laughs, a laugh that breaks like glass against the hard rock at his back. Before the shards can reach the breakers below, he shimmers like the sun Aurore never sees and launches himself like a sunbeam into an afternoon that is not and has never seen one.

The darker one picks up a laugh crystal, studies it, ponders.

In time, he, too, departs after his own way.

Neither has noticed the white bird perched in the nearby tree, a white bird with golden eyes and dark pupils that reach back farther than any bird's should, windows into more than soul.

In turn, the bird flutters off the bristlepine branch, lands lightly next to the laugh crystal that has begun to evaporate, cocks her head as if to catch something within the frozen sound as it vaporizes.

Beneath the White Cliffs, a thousand meters below, the golden-green breakers crash, foam against sheer quartz, crash and foam, crash and foam, in even rhythm.

The white bird, larger than a dove, for there are no doves on Aurore, and smaller than a raven, takes wing, and with effortless strokes clears the cliff edge, merges with a vagrant mist that has no business so high above the waves, and disappears.

XXIV

Martel leaves his own screen blank, but taps out the code for hers.

He sighs, knowing there will be no answer. There never is, hasn't been for months.

Instead, this time, a message flashes across the screen.

FAXEE UNKNOWN. NO FORWARDING CODE.

Martel disconnects, taps out the numbers again. He must have used the wrong code.

How likely is that, Martel?

He does not answer his own question, but looks across the room at the open window, and through it sees the light breeze fluff the hillside grass.

Rathe moved? Impossible!

Besides, changing location wouldn't change the code. Permanent residents kept their codes, unless they decided to delist. If she had delisted, the screen would have told him that and indicated that her personal code was unavailable.

FAXEE UNKNOWN. NO FORWARDING CODE. The same message scripted out.

"Two options," he mutters under his breath, not liking either. Rathe has either emigrated off-planet, which is unlikely but possible, or she is dead.

How long has it been?

Martel breaks the connection and stares at the closer stretch chair, the creme one. The farther one, the black one, is where he usually sits.

Black, that's your color, not that there's much black on Aurore.

Martel picks up the faint hum of an electrobike on the coast highway, with the underlying whine that indicates it is climbing the gentle hill toward Mrs. Alderson's on its way into Sybernal.

So what do you do now? You waited too long, Martel.

He has two choices, either to see if he can track Rathe down or to finish cutting the strings right now.

Three, you can also track her down and then cut the strings.

Martel half smiles to himself.

That makes the choice.

He walks into the bedroom and sits on the end of the bed closest to the wardrobe. Off come the sandals and on go the black formboots.

He stands up and checks his tunic and trousers. Clean enough. Four stans before he is scheduled on duty at the CastCenter, certainly enough time to get to where Rathe lives—used to live—and find out what he can.

Is it really? he asks himself. *If you walk, it will take nearly a stan to get there. More. She lives/lived north of Sybernal.*

"So what are you telling yourself? That you don't have time?"

If you walk, he answers mentally.

"So don't, is that it?"

Instead of leaving through the front portal, he walks out the back way and marches over to the quince.

The resident dorle chirps once and quiets as he approaches.

You're crazy, Martel.

"Absolutely, absolutely. But you knew that before I got here, didn't you? Doesn't everyone?"

He is not certain whether he is answering himself or an intruder, but it does not matter.

Concentrating on the blackness that is somehow related to the field and yet not a part of it, he thinks of flying, of wings, and of ravens, symbols of night, symbols of that darkness.

The darkness enfolds him, washes over him, and where he stood hops a raven.

His takeoff is awkward, but with each wingbeat his flight is steadier, and he remembers to climb into the wind as he circles upward.

The southern rim of Sybernal stretches under his wings. He glides toward it, straight for an imaginary point directly over the CastCenter.

Sybernal, roughly clam-shaped, arcs around the natural harbor, which is used mainly by pleasure craft and the few fishing vessels that challenge the gold-green seas. The ring closest to the sea is the constant-width beach, from which protrudes several points, including the North and South Piers. Behind the beach is the Petrified Boardwalk, and then the town houses of the permanent touries, interspersed with a sprinkling of restaurants and shops.

Behind the narrow district of red and gold awnings and roofs that sparkle even without the direct lighting of a sun runs the Greenbelt, and through the middle of the Greenbelt the coastal highway marches.

The trade district and the residences of most natives and norms are inland of the Greenbelt, and the most affluent of those who call Aurore home have their houses on the higher grounds west and north of the town.

The poorest live closest to the trade district, where the light breezes seldom penetrate.

Martel lifts his right wing, turns more toward the west in order to cross the CastCenter directly. From above the CastCenter, the five-unit complex where Rathe lives is northwest. He had located it after she left the last time, although he'd never been invited inside.

How can you be someone's lover and never see where she lives?

The question is just another he cannot answer.

His perceptions fan outward, to sense the thermals, to soak up the feeling of being airborne, and sense a turbulence. Darkness that is not darkness looms before him, building as he flies toward the five-sided communal dwelling.

Martel simultaneously leaves his perceptions extended and builds his shields, walls of darkness, his own darkness, behind them.

While he can sense dorles, sparrows, grimmets, and other birds flying well below him, the air at his altitude is clear.

Reserved for the gods?

Martel starts to shake his head, but stops as he realizes he has lifted his left wing and lost ten meters nearly instantly.

BEAR OFF, SMALL BIRD!

Martel blinks at the power of the command, surveys the sky, and extends his perceptions further.

Directly ahead, and several hundred meters higher, circles an enormous eagle, a golden eagle, whose feathers glitter with the light of a sun.

Martel draws upon his own depths, and the raven he is enlarges, with wingtips that would cover a small flitter. He climbs, wings beating, upon a thermal he has created, until he is level with the golden bird.

So intent is he upon his efforts that he does not see the departure of the golden eagle. But when he reaches the point where the eagle had circled, the heavens are vacant, the skies absent any trace of the giant bird.

Probing the air around him, Martel finds nothing.

He circles, slowly losing altitude, extending his mental search until his probes touch the buildings below.

. . . such an enormous black bird . . .

. . . the black vulture of the gods . . .

"Did you see that? The big black one drove off the sun eagle."

. . . has to be an omen . . . god of darkness . . .

Among the jumble of thoughts he can find no trace of the warm and friendly thoughts he seeks, no sign of the woman he has known.

His shape retreats to the classical raven as he drops to the buildings below, where he alights in a fir next to the complex where Rathe lived.

Her rooms are empty. That he can tell from a quick probe.

Martel the raven launches himself from the branch toward the windowsill. He skids on the sill's smooth stone, flaps wildly for a moment to catch himself, and falls against the plastipane.

"You see that clumsy bird, Armal?"

What do you expect? Martel questions mentally, blocking the thought from any transmission. *Perfection from an instant raven?*

He peers through the clear pane. Bare is the main room. Nothing remains, not even the floor covering. The ceramic floor tiles shimmer with the cleanliness of recent scrubbing.

He casts his thoughts into the rooms, but the sterility blocks any attempt at linking anything in the four rooms to Rathe Firien. Martel casts farther. The man called Armal is the landowner and the landlord.

Martel touches his mind, feels the strangeness, and enters his thoughts. Part of Armal's memories are gone. Martel can feel the void. There are no memories of the tenant in number four. None whatsoever.

The raven who is a man withdraws his probe and tries the woman who lives with Armal. A blowsy, wire-haired brunette originally from Tinhorn, she has no memories of Rathe either.

Neither do the tenants in the other units, nor is there even a trace of such a memory in the scattered mental impressions of the guardhound.

Martel turns his bird frame on the narrow ledge, forgetting he now possesses a tail. The long feathers brush the pane, and the thrust overbalances him into the thin air of the courtyard.

"Skwawk!" *Flame!*

He instinctively spreads his wings and beats his way out of the confined space.

"Clumsiest bird I ever saw, Armal. Biggest, too. Except for that golden eagle the other day."

Martel knows the golden eagle, but short of tackling Apollo head on or sifting the minds of all Aurore one by one, what can he do?

You waited too long, Martel . . . too long if you really cared.

He does not answer himself, but flaps toward the trees in the Greenbelt. From there he can emerge as a man and walk to the CastCenter.

XXV

To whom do the beaches belong?
They are the sea's, the sands', and the land's.
They belong to the summer, the spring, and the fall,
To winter, to joy, to heartbreak, and no one at all.

The flitter, golden, with a rainbow sprayed across the lower fuselage, hovers over the beach grass at the edge of the sand, but the air from the ducts still swirls sand around the five who tumble out.

First comes a tall man in khaki shorts and blouse, wearing a leather belt hung with all the implements of the overt and professional bodyguard. Next comes a woman, wrapped in a robe that billows around her, who keeps her balance despite the interference of the robe and the softness of the sand into which she jumps.

An older woman, sharp-featured, with golden hair, and another man, younger, golden-skinned and blond, who also wears a beach robe, follow.

Last is a heavyset man who floats to the sand rather than drops.

Once the last has stepped away from the flitter, the aircraft

rises and circles to set down on the plateau above the secluded beach and wait for the return trip to Sybernal.

Secluded the beach may be, but not deserted, not as empty
as the golden sands seem.

Near the base of the cliff, south of where the beach party
disembarked, crouches a bristlepine. On the clear limb that
offers a view of the sands where the five set up their keeper,
chairs, and umbrellas waits Martel.

Today he is a raven. Tomorrow, or yesterday, a man. But
today, he has decided to watch the private party of Cordin
D'Alamay, well-known wealthy businessman from Percoln,
and rumored esper. Only rumored, for the gods of Aurore do
not permit known espers to visit without preventive quaran-
tine.

Martel is not the only watcher. That he can tell from the
number of glittermotes that flicker in and out over the surf
and around a certain ledge even closer to the bathers than the
bristlepine.

D'Alamay gestures at one of the folded chairs, all of which
are golden. The one on which his attention is riveted is the
sole chair with the rainbow across the back. The sought-after
chair rises from the pile, unfolds, and deposits itself on the
sand facing the low surf.

The heavy man wipes his sweating forehead with the back
of his black-haired and tanned arm before dropping his bulk
into the chair.

"Very impressive." The older woman, who shares the same
eagle nose, narrow face, and approximate age, places her
chair next to her brother's. "I didn't know you could handle
objects that heavy."

"It's easier here." He beckons to the other woman, who has
stripped off the concealing beach robe to display a figure,
barely covered, that would bring top prices at the Pleasure
Mart of Solipsis. Not surprisingly, since that is where Cordin
D'Alamay purchased her three-year contract. "Honey! You
and Cort set up here."

Honey nods, and favors D'Alamay with professional smile
number two—slight promise.

Cort, the male counterpart of Honey, sets up his beach

chair next to the older woman and Honey's next to D'Alamay.

The bodyguard, impassive, surveys the surf, the cliffs, the sands, the skies, one right after the other.

Atop the cliff, the flitter pilot also surveys the flat seas and the line of beach that stretches near level in both directions.

D'Alamay takes another deep breath from deep within his chair. He looks at the sand in front of him. A small hill begins to grow. Soon the rough outlines of a classical-period castle appear, along with the return of perspiration to D'Alamay's forehead.

Cort, sitting on the edge of his beach lounger, feet dug into the sand, purses his lips.

"Whew!" he whistles. "Just like Castle D'Alamay."

The slumping of the sand into rougher outlines signals D'Alamay's shift of concentration.

The heavy man's eyes settle on Honey, who views the sea from beside her lounger. His appraisal travels the length of her tanned body. Honey wears a minimal two-piece bathing suit, unlike the more conservative suit of Arabel, D'Alamay's sister. While most women of any age would be pleased with Arabel's figure and skin tone, Arabel chooses not to flaunt hers.

Cort finds his job somewhat easier because Arabel is physically attractive. No matter that the figure and the skin tone represent the best from New Augusta's medical profession.

A tenseness drops onto the beach, like an unseen dark cloud.

The raven jerks his head from side to side, but can detect no new physical arrivals.

More glittermotes flicker around the boulder behind the D'Alamay party and above the point where the waves begin to crest before they break.

Honey. Come here!

The mental command from D'Alamay is faint but clear.

Honey's cold gray eyes glaze over momentarily, but she shakes her head, and the compulsion.

Come here!

"Whatever you're doing, Cordin stop it!" Her cold eyes again glaze over.

"Remember who owns your contract." D'Alamay smiles, showing too much tooth.

Come here. Take off your suit.

"No," Honey says to the unspoken command. Her voice shakes. "I. won't."

Perspiration beads on D'Alamay's forehead.

Come here ... take off your suit.

Honey turns, takes one step toward D'Alamay, almost within his arm's reach.

"No!"

Yes! Now!

"No ..."

Yes. Now, take it off ... that's it ... like that ...

Slowly, slowly, Honey's right hand reaches to the knot at the back of her neck. Jerkily her hand tugs at it. The cords loosen, and she lets the halter fall away into the breeze. Both arms drop to her sides.

Now the bottom ...

... no ... someone, please help me ... please ... no ...

Her hands go to the tops of her bikini briefs.

CRACK!

A single bolt of golden light strikes and the damp sand between D'Alamay and Honey, throwing D'Alamay out of his chair and tossing the bare-breasted woman several meters down the beach, almost to where the waves lap against the sand.

"My god!" gasps Honey.

"Damn!" That from Cort.

But neither Cordin D'Alamay nor his sister says anything to the figure in the pale golden tunic, dark leather sandals, and sunburst crown. The god-figure stands where the light had struck.

Ten meters away, the bodyguard clutches for his stunner. He is too late.

The golden god points.

Another flash of lightning, and the bodyguard is gone, only a glassy place on the sand and the offending stunner remaining to mark his presence.

"Who are you?" snaps D'Alamay, now on his feet, but taking a step backward.

The golden figure says nothing, just stares at D'Alamay, who pales.

If you are mortal, you may not impose your mind upon others. If you seek godhood, you impose on mortals only at your own risk, challenging any god who may dispute you. Are you mortal? Or do you seek to be a god?

"Nobody makes me choose! Stettin! Stettin! Flame him!"

A narrow laser beam flares from the guard atop the cliff, but it bends away from its target.

Again the golden man gestures. Again there is a brilliant flash of light, and this time nothing remains of the cliff guard or the flitter.

D'Alamay's eyes dart from the golden crown of Apollo to the cliff and back. By the time his eyes have completed the traverse, the god is no longer there, but, instead, a whirlwind, a swirling maelstrom of dark gold and glittermotes twice the height of Cordin D'Alamay.

"Scare tactics ... scare tactics," stammers the heavy man.

Honey's eyes widen and widen, until they close, and she slumps to the sand.

Arabel shrinks away from both her brother and the whirlwind while rooting herself deeper into her lounger.

Cort stands and edges away, quickly backing down the beach toward the bristlepine, his eyes glancing from the whirlwind to D'Alamay and back again.

"Cordin D'Alamay! You must choose what you will be!" The voice of the whirlwind sounds with the power of a grand orchestra and the focused intensity of a single note.

D'Alamay shivers, shakes off the power of the whirlwind like a wet dog shaking off water, but takes a backward step.

Is that a sea-goddess that the raven alone sees beneath the face of the breakers? Just beneath a cloud of glittermotes?

Cort catches sight of something, someone, under those glittermotes and turns to face them.

Honey stretches as if she is a child waking from a long sleep and looks at her outstretched legs for a time before getting up.

Arabel sits silently.

"Choose!" demands the whirlwind.

D'Alamay shakes his head from side to side, violently.

Never!

"No one makes Cortin D'Alamay choose." But he backs farther away from the golden swirl that had been a god and may still be.

"You could run to the ends of Aurore and never escape your choice, and never escape the wind."

The man clenches his jaw and backpedals two more steps.

"Can you outrun the wind?" rumbles the whirlwind.

D'Alamay does not answer, retreats another step up the beach, his face whiter than before.

His sister Arabel shudders in her chair, which, surprisingly, still sits where she placed it. The umbrella, unnecessary as it was, under which she sat lies a good hundred meters down the beach, even beyond the bristlepine whence watches the raven. The umbrella's fabric and struts twist and tangle among themselves.

The woman called Honey stands above the high-water line of the sand and stares vacantly at the sea, a childlike look on her face.

Cort, on the other hand, stares at a vision no one else can see and takes a step into the gently lapping water.

"Can you outrun the wind?" whistles the whirlwind, its gold-and-black shape now less than twice the height of D'Alamay. "Are you a god? Or are you mortal?"

D'Alamay backs away, almost falling in the soft golden sand.

Cort takes another step into the water.

Arabel shudders.

Honey stares.

The raven watches.

D'Alamay keeps backing away from the pursuing cyclone, backing, stumbling, until his back is to the rock, the flat side of a cottage-sized boulder.

Arabel will not look, but hunches, shivering, in her chair.

Cort is now neck-deep in the water, still pushing toward a vision, his eyes bright, his progress steady.

Honey is curled up on the sand, asleep, tears drying on her face.

Three bell-like notes sound from the depths of the dark and gold twisting wind.

Bong! Bong! Bong!

"Choose what you are, what you will be!"

"No! No, no, no . . ."

"That is a choice," roars the wind, and further words, if there are any, are lost in the shrieking whine as the whirlwind rises from the sand and into the golden-hazed sky.

Silence holds, except for the ragged breathing of D'Alamay, the lapping of the sea on sand, the dry sobs of Arabel, and the sleep sounds of a grown-up child once called Honey.

D'Alamay gulps a deep breath, and another. He concentrates on a small stone at his feet. Frowns, then scowls. His face reddens, moisture popping out on his forehead, but the stone does not move.

"Gone . . ."

The heavyset man, who suddenly wears his skin like a loose cloak, looks up and across the beach.

His steps thud as he wallows toward the sobbing heap that is his sister.

Arabel does not look up as her brother stands over her, does not hear as he concentrates on her and finally mutters, "Gone, too . . ."

The only other human figure on the beach is the sleeping figure of Honey, curled into a half-circle on the dry sand above the high-water line.

D'Alamay's study turns toward the glassy patch of sand where his bodyguard had stood. The stunner lies where the guard dropped it.

D'Alamay waddles toward the weapon, staggers once, stumbles twice, and drops down on his knees to cradle the stunner in both hands.

His hands twitch, but he manages to lever the intensity setting up to lethal, and he looks squarely at the tip of the stunner before his thumbs press the firing stud.

The raven yet observes, for he knows that more will occur.

In time, less than a standard Imperial hour, two flitters set down on the hard wet sand by the sea.

The first bears the green cross of the Universal Aid Society. A man and a woman from the UAS flitter place Arabel upon a stretcher, and the body of the man D'Alamay upon a second, and the stretchers within the aircraft. As they do so, a second man polices the beach and stacks all the chairs, the foodkeeper, and the tangled umbrella, plus the scattered clothes, in the cargo bin.

The green-cross flitter lifts off toward Sybernal.

The second flitter bears the sunburst of Apollo. The two Apollonites wake the woman/child Honey and gently escort her into their conveyance. It, too, lifts off, but heads southward toward Pamyra.

The light dims on the narrow beach. Sudden thunderheads build offshore and above the beach.

Rain, driving into the sand, pools, puddles, and runs back into the sea.

Surf foams, pounds, rises, scours the upper beach, and subsides.

The raven shakes himself, waits.

Eventually, in less than a stan, the clouds break; the rain disperses; the surf lapses into a gentle lapping at the clean beach; and the eternal day returns to the again-pristine sands, which show no signs of footprints or human presence.

The raven fluffs his wings, shakes himself again, spreads his wings, and departs.

XXVI

According to the universal time, Aurore Standard, it is 0600. Not that the clock matters on Aurore, but heredity and biology are stubborn. Martel knows that, knows they are the reasons why most businesses, except for entertainment, credit, and others catering to basic needs, are closed or part-staffed.

He strides through the portal out of the CastCenter and down the glowstone steps two at a time onto the Petrified Boardwalk. Imported slab by slab, legend has it, it was carted all the way from Old Earth to appease an early demigod, Avihiro.

Martel makes a two-hand vault up and sits on the low parapet, letting his feet dangle in midair above the sand, watching the ever-parallel waves hit the surf-break, climb, and crash down onto the straight lines of the beach. The waves are higher than normal tonight, if one can call very early morning night on the planet of eternal day.

He takes a deep breath, lets it go with a long hiss which is lost, a hiss less than a transitory footnote against the text of sand, sea, and surf.

A single figure retreats farther northward along the North Promenade of the boardwalk.

Like Kryn? No ... step's all wrong ... why ... why do you keep thinking about Kryn?

He takes his eyes from the distant woman and looks down at the sand under his boots.

Why? ... You'll never see her again ... remember, Martel, she didn't protest when the Grand Duke had you Queried ... sorry, Martel, and what will you do?

He looks up at the surf.

Your unattainable bitch goddess ... that's Kryn ... that's why you lost Rathe ... wouldn't give up your impossible image.

Martel shakes his head.

How could you ever believe you meant anything to her?

Does it matter?

Does it matter?

The tight beam from Karnak has only opened the old doubts, the old questions. And the carefully phrased statements from New Augusta had only stirred the old confusions.

"The Regent is dead. Long live the Emperor!"

"Grand Duke Kirsten sits tonight at the foot of the Amber Throne, faithful to the Emperor, and faithful to the Regency, awaiting the decision of Emperor N'Troya."

That was what he, Martel the faxcaster, had announced to the tourists who wanted the news. The natives never watched faxnews. They didn't care that much about the rest of the Galaxy, and the gods knew it all before it happened. Or so it seems.

Martel still doesn't understand the Regent's "accidental" death. Was it suicide? Was Duke Kirsten, or the Duchess, that power-hungry? What of Kryn? Who attacked Karnak? How? Why? ... And what of Kryn?

He frowns, for he has no answers.

Something has happened in Karnak. Something like a black nuke cloud has appeared next to the Tree of the Regent at the daily Moment of Silence. The Guard Force attacked, and most of the park has been wiped out. An enormous crater remains.

The dislocation destroyed the majority of the convenient power grids, and the weather system collapsed. A storm followed, the father of all storms, and the crater is now a lake.

Fine enough, Martel reflects, if such an unforeseen catastrophe can be called fine ... but who would dare? Has the Brotherhood reacted at last to the Edict of Exile? Has some Brother smuggled in a mininuke? Is the whole thing an enormous hoax?

Martel shakes his head again.

No one on Aurore seems to care. Not a single call back to the CastCenter. The whole report sinking into the pond of public unawareness like a stone cast that created no ripples.

An accident with a hunting laser? Why would the Prince Regent suicide? Especially when the old Emperor is nearing the end.

The Regency Fleets are on full alert, but no unknown ships have been detected in the entire Karnak system.

No radiation has been detected in or around the lake that was the Regent's Park. Early reports mentioned a scorched faxtape recovered from the debris, but once it was turned over to the Grand Duke, all mention of it has been omitted.

And on Aurore, no one seems to care.

"No one cares," mutters Martel, knowing the words, all too self-pitying, will become one with the sound of the all-too-regular surf. "The Regent suicides. The park is destroyed, and the reports drop into Aurore like a stone into the sea."

A faint sound of bells tinkles in the back of his mind.

Martel jerks his head up, scanning both sides of the Petrified Boardwalk. He sees no one.

The off-duty newsie lets his senses slide away from his body, extends his perceptions. Nothing, except the faint feeling of bells. Silver bells. Tiny bells. Just the feeling of bells, and no sound of bells.

He shakes his head.

Ten standard hours the news has come in, and every stan

since the first, it is the same pap. The Imperial Marine Twentieth has arrived in Karnak. All's well. The Fifth, Twelfth, and Eighth Fleets patrol the system. All's well. The Grand Duke assumes the duties as acting Regent. All's well. Power is restored. All's well. Sunrise occurs without incident east of Karnak the morning following the explosion. All's well. The Emperor confirms the Grand Duke as acting Regent. The Fleets return to standby alert. All's well.

Martel frowns. Like flame all is well.

He'd been suspicious years ago when the Regent's Palace had denied reports of a confirmed power failure. The two events should be connected, and Martel gropes for the time and the details . . . not that it matters. Or does it? A corner of his mind says that it is important.

"A brooding philosopher, is that it?" With the words is the same feeling of bells, though her voice is low.

He yanks his head away from the ocean view to the woman who stands by his shoulder.

She is taller than he is, and her shoulder-length golden hair, eyes to match, and the intensity she conceals all remind him of Kryn. Yet Kryn's hair is black, he remembers. The woman is familiar . . . where has he seen her?

"I take it that Kryn is your long- and forever-lost ladylove, Martel?"

Who is she? How does she know? How had he missed her approach?

"Who are you?"

"I could be mysterious, but I won't. Call me Emily. It's not my name, but it will do for now."

"How do you know my name?" Martel feels the bells more strongly now, almost warning him. He pushes the feeling away. He needs to know more.

"Who doesn't?"

"And who is Kryn?" he bluffs.

"Martel, I know everything about you. Including the fact that you're powerful and powerless, and friend to all and friend of none."

"Fancy words . . ."

". . . and you're appealing."

Despite the sincerity in her voice, Martel senses the mockery beneath, some of which is not directed at him. He acknowledges the unstated sarcasm, ignores it, and vaults down off the wall, even though he could appear more graceful with a mental push. He still dislikes using his powers for purely physical aids; three decades have not changed that.

"Where to?" he asks.

"Wherever. Until we sleep and wake again, I'm yours. Until then, I'm yours."

There is no mockery in that statement, no warning bells to accompany it.

"All mine? Without reservations?"

"All yours. Perhaps a reservation or two, though not likely to be the ones you'd normally get to."

Martel stops in midstride, looks the golden-haired woman straight in the eyes. She meets his glance without blinking, the black depths of her pupils seeming a thousand kilos deep and a thousand years old.

"Who are you?"

"I'm Emily. Tonight. Tomorrow ... who knows?" She laughs, and the laugh carries the sound of bells and hunting horns.

"Emily ... or Diana?"

"There's a saying about gift horses ..."

"Flame ..." Martel turns and walks northward, vaguely conscious that the woman is matching him stride for stride. Her legs are longer than his, her steps effortless.

At the North Pier he stops, wipes the sweat from his forehead. She stands there, smiling, cool, golden, as crisp as she appeared four kilos back down the Petrified Boardwalk.

Martel chuckles.

"You weren't offering a choice, were you?" He pauses. "All right, I'll take you up on it. Let's drink, and be merry. At the top of the North Pier tower there's a small restaurant ... open all the time, and quiet ... not that you don't know that already."

They are the only ones there, besides the host, who seats them at the table on the seapoint of the Star Balcony. The chairs are dark leather that matches the old wood of the circular brassbound table. Both the railing and the overhanging beams lower the light level of perpetual day to that of twi-light on another planet.

The damper chill of the air is a relief to Martel, who re-fuses to use his powers to alter his metabolism, and who wonders how Emily remains so cool, unless she is indeed tapping the field. If she is, her action is at such a low level as to be unnoticeable. Martel pushes away the thought that brings.

He tries to push away the other thoughts as well, but they do not stay pushed. No one can sneak up on him. No one! But she has. No one can keep up with him for four kilos. But she has, and without breaking a sweat. Diana, not Emily, has to be the right name.

And she is familiar, but he doesn't remember how, where, and he doesn't want to think about that now, either.

"What's happening on Karnak, lady who knows every-thing?" As he finished the question, he lifts the glass, just de-livered by the unsmiling and dark-skinned host, swallows, and lets the cold Springfire ease down the back of his throat. He would prefer it from a jasolite beaker, but jasolite beakers and old Anglish decor apparently do not go together.

"You're right. They don't," responds Emily/Diana/????, "but then the old Anglish never would have created an open and paneled balcony above the sea, either."

"Karnak?" prompts Martel, consciously shielding his thoughts and taking another sip of the Springfire.

"You can take the student out of Karnak, but not Karnak out of the student. Isn't that how the saying goes? Karnak the soul of the Empire of Man . . . Karnak the Magnificent." Her lips twist slightly as she finishes.

Martel nods, looks away from the woman, all too con-scious of the tanned body beneath the thin white chiton, of the fine-sculptured neck under the antique copper choker.

The regular beat of the surf drops a level. Martel knows it will maintain the lower waves for several standard hours, un-less a sudden storm comes up, or a flurry of so-called god waves.

"Can you get there by candlelight?" he murmurs.

"Yes, and back again."

He twitches.

"I've studied you, Martel. Turned from your great ladylove Kryn, you did, to the words, to the dusty tapes of antiquity."

He pushes back his chair, puts both hands on the wide armrests.

Emily raises a hand, and he feels a gentle force pushing him back into his seat.

"You really are the bitch goddess. You really are."

"Did I say I wasn't?" She smiles.

Martel likes the smile, drinks it in, and doesn't trust it.

The candle on the table, dark green, square, winks out. Martel relights it with a thought, lets it burn, lets the flame flare, and squeezes it into a narrow column that flickers level with Emily's golden eyes, and turns the flame black. He relaxes his hold, and the golden-green flame returns to normal.

"Very impressive for a nongod."

"Flame tricks, dear bitch goddess. What's happening on Karnak?"

"You're the newsie. Tell me."

"You're the goddess. Tell me what's behind the news."

"Either an old, old god or a new god, and the gods themselves don't know."

"So the gods are only gods. Is that it?"

Martel again turns the candle flame black, this time to stay . . . at least until snuffed and relit.

"Why do you fight everything, Martel? You could be a god, and you fight that. You could have light, and you fight that. You could have me, and you fight that. Some things are meant to be."

He looks up at Emily. Even though she returns the study, her eyes open, they are hooded. But her words ring true, like gold coins dropped on a stone table.

Martel stands, walks around the table, and eases back the heavy chair for her.

"Some things I don't fight. Not forever. Shall we go?"

He reaches for her hand.

The fires crackle, black flames licking from his arms and white from hers, twining in the space and instants before their fingers touch.

A plain gold flitter crouches at the end of the pier, empty. They enter.

The hillside villa is small, five rooms in all, with limited access. The cliffs to the back are impassable to any casual visitor, and the lawns and gardens to the front stretch into what seems an endless forest, though he can spot a trail several kilos beneath the villa.

The master chamber opens to the south and to a vista including Sybernal. Martel takes another look at the sweeping emerald lawns that drop toward the distant town, toward the pine forests that seem to guard the grounds.

Emily, or Diana, reappears at his elbow, still wearing the thin white chiton and antique necklace. She is barefoot, without the white leather sandals.

"You're determined to waste all the time you have, aren't you?"

"Me?"

"You."

"Why did you find me?"

"Why not? Opposites attract."

"Oh. I'm mortal, and you're a goddess? I wear black, and you wear white?"

"Nothing that simple. You could be a god, but refuse. You could wear any color, but chose black, which is all colors or none. You could have any woman, but spurn them all."

"You make it sound so simple," growls Martel, refusing to look at her, knowing that the minute he does he will want her. "Nothing's simple."

"You, Martel, assume that everything is linked. I'm not asking for the future. I want the now."

Her hand touches the back of his wrist. He can feel the electricity build in him, holds it to himself, holds back from looking away from the view of Sybernal.

"You find me unattractive? Or are you afraid?"

The oldest ploys in the universe.

Of course she's attractive. And of course you're afraid. You're afraid of your own shadow, Martel, he thinks, not realizing that he has projected his doubts.

Emily says nothing. Stands next to him, her fingers touching his hand, letting the breeze from the open vista wash over them.

Goddesses don't need sashes or sills, do they, the half-

thought strikes him, strikes him as he feels his body respond-
ing to the desire Emily projects. Not projects, just plain has.

She wants him.

Does he want her? Really want her? Does it matter? What
about Rathe? Or Kryn?

". . . Then love the one you're with," he murmurs, and
turns toward Emily, golden Emily, gilded Diana, whose arms
come around his neck, and whose lips meet his.

Kryn, Rathe, Kryn . . . he buries the names before they
emerge as his hands tighten on the bitch goddess he holds, as
he drops into the depths and the eternities she represents.

He should feel sleepy, but doesn't, as they lie next to each
other, hands touching, arms touching, legs touching.

"What was she like, Martel?" Emily's voice is softer than
he'd imagined it could be.

"Who?"

"Your lady Kryn."

"Bitch." His voice is flat.

"If you don't want to talk, you don't have to. Were you
making love to me or to her?"

"Suppose I say both and neither? Suppose I say her?"

"Suppose you did. You still wanted me."

"Yes."

"Then that's enough for now. Now is all you have, Martel.
Unless you stop fighting it, and become a god. Or recognize
that you are."

"Do you want me just because I'm stubborn?"

She laughs, and the silver bells ring in her voice and in his
mind. "Touché."

The pines outside the marble pillars sigh with the breeze.

Her hand leaves his, touches his bare shoulder, caresses the
back of his neck.

"Martel?"

"Umm?"

"Don't waste any more time."

He rolls on his side to face her, lets his eyes run over her
slender body, over the high breasts of the huntress goddess,
over the even golden skin . . .

The second time is gentler.

He awakes alone in the bed, scrambles to his feet.

The villa is empty, except for the master chamber closet, where three identical white chitons hang, with three sets of identical white sandals beneath. In the bathing chamber, a heated bath steams as he opens the portal. A thick black towel is laid out. His tunic and trousers, immaculately clean, are hung next to the towel, with his boots beneath.

Next to his clothes hangs also a black cloak, with an attached collar pin, a black thunderbolt that glistens.

He uses his perceptions to probe the cloak and pin, but they are what they are, merely a cloak and a pin.

He steps into the bath.

Later, clad in his own clothes and the cloak he knows is a present from Emily, he walks out to the landing stage where the golden flitter waits, empty and door ajar.

Now . . . he remembers where he has seen Emily.

On the I.D. cube at the CastCenter, on that single cube that had brought the call of blasphemy and knocked poor Marta Farell right out of bed.

Of course. The goddess in one of her playful moments.

That is not quite right, he knows, but he shivers, and glances back at the white villa for a last look before he enters the flitter.

XXVII

A raven—consider the bird.

Bulky, black-feathered, wings stubby for the size of its body, raw-voiced and scratchy-toned, if you will, a scavenger, an overgrown crow. And yet a raven is more than the sum of the description.

Consider the raven, who stands for the darkness and destruction, who embodies all the forebodings of those who cannot fly, and who brings the night to day.

Is then the eagle, who is also scavenger and predator, feathered and screeching in broad daylight, whose sole superiority over the raven is size, the better bird, the more magnificent symbol?

Which would be the mightier were their sizes reversed?

Could we accept all that the raven is ... and grant him the wingspan of an eagle?

Or is it that we who eat carrion do not like to be reminded of that and revere the predator who tears bloody meat from just-killed corpses?

On planets where the sun kills and the night revives, which would be the better power symbol—eagle or raven?

—Comparative Symbols
Edwy Dirlieth
Argo, A.D. 2356

XXVIII

Taking the last steps two at a time, Martel reaches the top of the walk that leads to his cottage.

Mrs. Alderson is asleep. That he can tell from the sense of quiet around the bigger house.

The quince by the front portal of the cottage has finally decided to bloom, one of the few times since he arrived on Aurore.

As he approaches the low stone slab that serves as porch, front stoop, and delivery area, he stops. Tucked into the portal is a white oblong.

He leans forward and picks it up. The old-fashioned white paper envelope contains an equally antique handwritten letter.

The name on the envelope is his and also handwritten, but he does not recognize the hand, though it does not belong to any of his ladies. Of that he is certain.

He casts his thoughts around the cottage, but finds no one, no sense of lingering. That means the letter within the envelope was left or delivered while he was still at the CastCenter beaming forth his cubes of reassurance on behalf of Gate Seven.

Martel frowns. He sniffs the envelope. The scent, faint indeed, and overlaid with the acridity of ship ozone, is feminine.

Willing the portal to open rather than using his thumb, he steps inside.

After debating whether to open the envelope immediately, he compromises and fills a beaker half full with Springfire before retreating to the rear porch to open and read the letter.

Eridian/Halston

Martel—

I don't know whether you heard. Gates and I bought out our contracts and settled here. We never knew what you heard after Marta's "Edict." For reasons you can understand, we were afraid to risk contacting you while we were still on Aurore.

So this is sort of an apology, and a long-delayed thank-you. Long-delayed because I realized my dreams were true. They weren't dreams at all.

Gates had an accident last year. He was hit by a malfunctioning flitter and almost didn't make it. The doctor made a real fuss. They insisted Gates was fifty standard years younger than he is. His heart and arteries especially. The phrase that sticks in my mind is "almost as if his heart and aorta were rebuilt."

That's where the dreams come in. One dream I've had ever since you showed up at the CastCenter. Gates is pointing a needler at you. Stupid, I suppose, since Gates has never owned one. But you were throwing a black thunderbolt at him. Next thing, he's lying on the ground, and you are keeping him from dying. Don't ask me how.

The neurotechs tell me that they aren't dreams. I either saw it or I believe I saw it. It doesn't make any difference which. For whatever reason, you saved Gates twice, in effect.

I also wonder why I gave up cernadine. Your influence?

As always, the questions are unanswered, and I don't expect a reply.

You are what you are, and for that I am grateful now. I hope you stay that way. Your road is long, I know, and Gates and I, despite your gifts, will be dust long before you scale your heights.

Hollie

P.S. You're also the best faxer left on Aurore, whatever else you may be.

Martel leans back in the chair, places the letter on the table, and picks up the beaker to take another sip of Springfire.

A single chirp from the dorle in the back quince breaks the morning quiet.

So your road is long, Martel. How long?

He pushes his own question away and puts down the beaker without taking another sip.

As he stands the breeze from his abruptness swirls the paper letter to the floor, half under the table. Martel leaves it there and paces to the window to look up the hill at the farthest pair of quince trees.

"Even when you erase the footprints and change the memories ... just like the song." The words slip out before he thinks.

He does not sing, but, instead, the words hang in the air next to him, glowing.

I saw your footprints on the sand,
Yesterday;
I saw your smile so close at hand,
Yesterday.

Yet twenty years have come and gone,
Since then;
My hair has silvered from our dawn,
Since then.

And all my days have passed away,
All my nights are yesterday.

Martel does not look at the golden words he has wrought. Slowly they dim, and after a time the last *yesterday* fades. Only a single black glittermote circles his left shoulder.

He remembers the letter and retrieves it from under the table, looks at it as if it represents a puzzle he cannot solve. Finally, he places it on the shelf next to the book of poems by Ferlinol. The thin white sheets of paper, with their message from Eridian and the past, fold in upon each other, glow briefly, darken, and stretch into a single black rose.

Martel wipes his forehead and looks away from the flower that will outlast the cottage, and, perhaps, Martel himself.

Always harder, isn't it, when you start to care again?

He picks up the beaker from the table and downs the rest of the Springfire with a single gulp, ignoring the line of fire that sears his palate and flames down his throat.

The dorle chirps once again from the quince.

XXIX

Some stores are open at all hours, and when Martel leaves the CastCenter, his steps bear him toward the southern edge of the merchants' district, toward Ibrahim's.

He needs Springfire, perhaps some scampig, if Ibrahim has any today, and a few other, more common, items.

Good thing you've got an autochef, Martel.

Without it, the culinary monotony would have been unrelieved.

The air is quiet on this morning of eternal day and becomes even more motionless as he enters the white-gray paved lanes that indicate the area where the natives, and Martel, shop.

Aldus the bootmaker, oblivious to anyone, is letting down his awning as Martel approaches, scowling and wrestling with the heavy black iron crank.

Martel waves.

Aldus wipes the scowl from his face and, smiling a faint smile, waves back.

Across the land and three shops down from the bootmaker's is the next open doorway. As he nears it Martel can already smell the aroma of liftea and freshly baked ceron rolls.

The bakery must be new, since he does not recall it. Outside the fresh white walls and polished door he pauses, then decides to go inside.

Entering, from the corner of his eye he sees an older

woman, her brown hair shot with gray, disappear through a side door into another room, leaving only her son, a boy of perhaps eleven standard years, behind the counter where the just-baked ceron rolls are laid out.

The liftea has been brewed in an enormous samovar that stands alone on the counter next to the baked goods. Neatly racked beside the tea machine is a tray of blue porcelain mugs, each facedown on a white linen napkin.

"Good day, young man," offers Martel.

"Good day, sir. What would you like, sir?"

The youngster smiles easily, and Martel smiles back.

"Are the rolls as good as they smell?"

"I like them, but we also have the plain ones on the other tray."

"If you like them," says Martel with a laugh, "I'll have to try one, and a mug of the liftea."

He hands the boy his credit disc.

"Oh, sir. I couldn't." The boy looks away.

"Why not?"

"I . . . I . . . just . . . well . . . ah . . ." His eyes are still fixed on the floor tiles.

Flame! Flame! Flame!

"My credit's good, young man, and I would rather be charged for it."

The boy finally recovers. "It would be our pleasure, sir."

"I'm afraid I'll have to insist. If people like me eat and don't pay, how would you and your family stay in business?"

The boy's mouth drops open, only for an instant, but he takes the proffered disc and sets it in the reader, which transfers the small credit balance to the bakery.

"Thank you, sir. I hope you like the ceron. It really is my favorite, except maybe for the spice sticks, and we don't have any of those this morning."

"Ceron it is."

He picks up one of the sticky rolls and takes a bite. The orange-and-spice taste is as good as the smell, and he finishes the roll in three quick bites. He wipes his fingers on one of the small square napkins laid out on the counter next to the mugs.

The pungent liftea clears the slightly cloying aftertaste of the ceron from his mouth.

Martel looks up from the mug to see a man half enter the bakery, then abruptly back out into the lane.

Martel downs the last of the liftea and places the mug on the empty tray where, he presumes, it should go.

"As good as you said," he tells the boy, who is still alone in the room with him.

"Thank you, sir. Have a good day."

"I suppose I will. You too."

Martel leaves the shop with a smile on his face.

Ought to do that more often, Martel. You stay too much to yourself these days.

He glances toward the bootmaker's shop, but the awning is fully down and extended, and Aldus has gone back inside.

Should get another pair of boots one of these days, I suppose.

The lane is deserted, except for two girls playing in the emerald grass next to the linen shop across from the bakery.

The proprietor of the linen shop half steps out of her door, then darts back inside, as if she has forgotten something.

Martel shrugs and resumes his walk toward Ibrahim's.

A muted clanging becomes increasingly more insistent, and by the time he reaches the middle of the next row of small businesses, each with a low-fenced and trimmed side yard, the sound resembles an off-tune gong.

Behind the grassy lawn that circles a single cormapple, a double door to a metalworking shed stands open, and through the open doors Martel can see two men wrestling with what seems to be a metal tank.

For several units he stands and watches the two as they struggle to straighten the crumpled end of the tank. After the bent metal is smoothed, however, they apply the patch plate quickly, and the two lift the tank onto a small delivery wagon.

Martel looks away from the shed to discover he is being studied by a small, wide-eyed girl who hangs over the half-story railed balcony.

He looks back at her, directly.

She continues her study.

He smiles.

Her dark brown eyes widen farther, if possible.

". . . oh . . ."

The sound comes from behind him, from the metalworking shed, and he glances toward it.

Standing frozen in the double doorway is one of the two men who had been working on the tank. The sleeveless tunic emphasizes his burliness and the bronzed nature of his skin. The man is black-haired, clean-shaven, and his mouth hangs open as he stares at Martel.

For a long instant, the three of them stand locked in that triangle, unmoving.

Martel breaks the pattern by grinning at the girl, who could not possibly stand taller than his waist.

"Have a good day, young lady."

He waves and turns to continue his steps toward the food shop.

"Bye-bye." The girl's response drifts back.

There is also the sound of air being exhaled, a deep breath, as if the metalworker had forgotten to breathe.

Martel sees no one else in the two blocks before he reaches the food store.

Ibrahim's shop is empty, except for the proprietor, who is seated, as he always is, in his dark brown tunic and trousers, on the high stool behind the counter.

"Who's there?"

"Martel. I need two bottles of Springfire, a few other things."

"Heard your beach story again the other day. I wish I could have seen it."

"Thank you."

Martel picks the Springfire out of the racks and sets both bottles on the counter, then checks the meat cooler for the scampig. He is in luck; several small fillets are available. He wraps them in the transparency and places the package next to the bottles. Taking a pear from the fruit section, he adds a scoop of rice which he bags, a box of noodles, and a scattering of vegetables, all of which he has wrapped into a single package.

At last, he stands before the counter.

"What's this?" asks the shopkeeper as his fingers flicker over the package of combined and mixed fresh vegetables.

"Mixed-up vegetables. Just charge me for whatever's the most expensive. That would be the garnet beans."

"The whole thing is thirty-five credits, sir."

"That's fine, Ibrahim. Run it through."

"Yes, sir."

The entire order will fit in the collapsible pack Martel unrolls from his belt pouch. He packs the items as Ibrahim feeds his credit disc into the reader and transfer system.

As Martel lifts the pack to his back he sees a young woman, blond, green-eyed, heavyset, and wearing a burgundy overtunic, peer in the doorway and immediately back away.

"Have a good day," Martel says as he leaves the counter, placing the credit disc back in his pouch.

"You, too. I'll be listening tonight."

Not that the poor bastard could do otherwise, Martel, not both blinded and blessed for his sins.

"You're probably one of the few natives who do listen, Ibrahim, one of the very few. Take care."

Not that he has much choice there, either.

"Thank you, sir."

Martel pauses in the entranceway and looks back up the lane. As far as he can see, no one has set foot on the stones of the pavement, no one at all.

Should you remove Ibrahim's blindness? You could, you know.

Martel looks down at the white-gray stones underfoot, then back up the deserted lane. Finally he shakes his head.

Apollo would just reblind him, and, besides, where would you shop then, without everyone running away?

He sets his steps toward the south, toward the isolated house and cottage beyond Sybernal. His paces are not light, but they are quick, and eat away the distance.

XXX

The man—who wonders whether he is—sits under the covered porch.

He glances up at the wooden planks over his head, lets his eyes trace out the old, old wood from the newer old wood. To the eye, the difference is not great, though he can sense the lack of harmony that the best carpentry cannot fully disguise.

Smoothing the sundered patterns would be easy enough. Like melding into the flowing day-to-day existence of Aurore. Like forgetting dark-haired girls with golden eyes, or fire-haired women with green eyes, or demigods cast back into the sea.

"Except—" The words break as he stands, stretches.

"Except what, Martel?" he snaps at himself.

Except you're a lousy forgetter.

Shaking his head, he picks up the cup from the low table and gulps down the last of the yasmin tea.

He wears only a pair of black shorts, and is barefoot and clean-shaven. His heavy steps thud as he crosses the porch.

The cup floats from his hands and stacks itself in the cleaner.

He continues on into his sleeping quarters.

In the wardrobe are three dusty pale yellow tunics, with matching trousers, kept to remind him, and three sets of matching black tunics and their trousers.

Martel pulls on the nearest set of black pants, then the black tunic and the black belt. He sits in midair and pulls on the heavy black boots.

At one end of the closet is the black cloak. He has not worn it since it was given to him, but it repels the dust and is as fine as the day Emily left it in her villa for him.

He looks at the belt, with the triangular silver buckle that is his only ornamentation.

You wear the belt but not the cloak. Rathe, not Emily. What does that mean?

He frowns, gathers a hint of darkness around him, and, his dressing done, strides from the sleeping room back into the main room of the cottage.

The darkness, and the power it represents, both are things apart from the golden energy field of Aurore.

Just as you're a thing apart? Come off it, Martel.

He shakes his head again. Harder.

On Aurore, how can you tell what you believe from what is real? Or from what some god would have you believe is real?

He stretches out his left arm, palm open and upward, and inhales, leaving his senses to take in the faint tang of the ocean beyond the hillcrest, to take in the subdued chitter of the dorles in the quince trees.

In his open palm shimmers a black oval, a miniature doorway to ... where? Martel is not sure, releases his mental grasp on the cold depths, and lets the blackness vanish.

Is it real? Or illusion?

Real, he decides. For the hundredth time or so.

There is a feel to power, and an absolute feel to absolute power. Call it certainty, reflects Martel.

He gestures toward the inside wall, the blank one, letting his fingers trace a figure. From his hand flows the stuff of darkness, outlining a crude figure, something not seen in the indirect and omnipresent lighting of Aurore.

"Shadow, shadow, on the wall,
  Who casts the longest shade of all?
  Is it death; or yet desire?
  Is it night, tamed by fire?

"Who's the man who lights the lamp
  And calls the storm that brings the damp?
  Which the god who blocks the sun
  And fills the rivers in their run?

"Call the hammer, call the lightning ..."

He closes his mouth. The old words have power still, lifting him into the role, letting him imagine he is a god.

Not now. Not yet. Not ever.

And yet . . .

Who can say "ever" or "never" and know? Really know?

Martel shrugs.

The shadow vanishes from the wall, the only remnant the small cloud of black glittermotes that hovers above Martel before winking out.

One touches down on Martel's left shoulder, clings.

Letting his perceptions slide around the corner from where he stands, he checks the timer above the autochef.

Time to leave for the CastCenter.

Walking will give him the time to think over the puzzles.

Don't you just like to walk? Admit it, Martel. Do you really think then?

He leans to touch the light panel on his way out, cannot quite reach it, and turns it off with a mental tap.

Another black glittermote appears and settles on his right shoulder, paired nearly invisibly on the black of his tunic opposite the other mote.

As he heads down the steps to the coast highway, a dorle chitters once. He knows not why, but Rathe comes to mind.

Rathe?

Why do you keep thinking about her? She left. You didn't search, not really.

Short strides, quick strides, untiring strides bear him toward Sybernal, toward the CastCenter.

She called you a god, and you let her go.

A quick glance toward the flat surface of the ocean tells him that the waves, long and sleek in their golden greenness, are flatter than usual.

Why are you so hung up on this esper crew that calls themselves gods? Talented, yes. Gods, no. Right?

The air seems a shade more golden, along with the calm, and the highway is deserted.

Like when Rathe found you the cottage?

Stop it!

Do you love her? Honestly?

No.

Like her? Respect her?

Yes.

POWER! LIGHT!

His dialogue with his unseen devil or conscience is brought to a halt with his perception of the sheer raw energy ahead.

His legs keep pumping as he quick-steps up the paved highway and over the gentle hilltop.

Just over the crest sits the doctor/god Apollo in an insubstantial chair. The four legs of the chair are yellow snakes. The back is composed of two fanned dragon wings.

Beneath his golden ringlets Apollo's face is expressionless.

At his right foot lies the body of a man . . . young, dark-haired, facedown. Dead.

By his left quivers a redheaded woman, sobbing silently, dryly. Rathe.

Rathe.

"Balance, Martel. You do not understand the need for balance. Power must be balanced with the understanding of its impact on mere mortals. Belief is more powerful than power."

Apollo tells the truth as he sees it, Martel knows; his words ring like a flat carillon.

Martel gathers his darkness around him, bemused as the clouds of black glittermotes appear from nowhere.

"Before you try to employ that energy, Martel, be so kind as to observe."

Martel nods, reaching out a thin thread of thought to reassure Rathe.

Apollo outlines a golden square in the air. Colors swirl and resolve into a picture.

Martel watches, a corner of his mind still occupied with the huddled figure that is Rathe Firien, as the small drama comes to an end.

Rathe is helping another of Apollo's would-be demigods become accustomed to Aurore. Except . . . except this time she does not offer her body and soul.

Does not. Does not humble herself.

The man, pursuing, strikes out with all his mental force . . . and the force misses Rathe and rebounds upon him. Partly, Martel surmises, because Rathe is wearing the same shielding as when she first met him, partly because the man is a lower-level esper, and partly because . . .

Martel wonders if along with his physical gifts he had given her some shields of her own.

In the picture conjured by Apollo, the last scene shows Rathe looking down at a body, the same body that lies at Apollo's feet.

"You see, Martel, what you have done."

I? Come off it, you pious fraud!

Martel twists raw hunks of power, not from the energy field of Aurore, from his own depths, and marshals it within.

You cannot harm me, Martel.

"No! . . . No . . ." murmurs a small voice.

Martel looks at his former lover and holds his energies.

"Why not?" he temporizes.

"Because—"

Her statement is never completed, for Apollo touches her, and she is gone. A flash of flame, and she is gone.

. . . you'll be like him. Those were her last thoughts, and they fade into the golden haze.

Martel hesitates. Looks at Apollo, standing yellow-bright, smirking, daring Martel to strike.

Martel gathers his darkness even tighter into himself . . . and walks around the chair with the flickering legs, around the smirking god, and begins to trot toward Sybernal.

Step, step, step, step . . . and wipe your cheek. Step, step, step. Wipe. Step, step, step . . .

She asked you not to.

But Rathe is gone.

For what?

Gone in flame because of a mad god. And he, Martel, had not seen it coming. Had not seen the total disregard, the snuffing out of a vital woman, snap. Had not believed power so cavalierly used.

But she asked you not to.

Rathe had not asked for help, had not begged for anything . . . just for Martel not to attack Apollo. And not because she feared Martel would be hurt.

"Because you'll be like him." That was what she'd said.

Martel shudders even as he keeps trotting.

Are all gods like that?

Isn't everyone with power?

Kryn. Lovely Kryn, having her guards fire on a lonely Martin Martel just because he'd been discovered to have esper potential.

The Grand Duke, who ruled high in Karnak, throwing the Imperial Marines after a solitary student who had displeased his daughter.

Emily, the carnal goddess, taking what she wanted and leaving. No good-bye. Just the power to arouse and take and discard. And leave a black cloak as a thank-you.

Is that what becoming a god of Aurore means?

Does it have to mean that?

Step, step, step.

He lets his pace slow to a quick walk as he crosses the "official" southern boundary of Sybernal, where the Petrified Boardwalk begins.

The refrain from the *Heroes' Song* echoes in his thoughts:

Tell me now, and if you must,
That a man's much more than dust.

If Aurore is light, if Apollo is the sun-god . . . no god will I be. Not by choice, nor by accident. Not now, not ever.

Stuffing the swirling energies, the black fires, deep inside himself, Martel touches the CastCenter entry plate.

"Martel, evening shift."

That's right. Evening, evening in youth. Evening in full light. Why not? Light is a lie, promising everything and signifying nothing.

XXXI

A small, dark-haired girl stands on a half-story balcony and looks to the south. She inclines her head slightly, as if bowing to an unseen presence, then lifts it and stares into the southern distances.

"Derissa?"

She ignores the call and continues to watch the southern heavens, and their eternal gold.

"Derissa!"

The girl makes the sign of the inverted and looped cross and walks back into her bedroom to obey her mother's call.

. . . Up the lane, behind closed doors of a workroom, the bootmaker Aldus labors over a pair of black formboots.

He checks the seams of the left upper, squinting as he draws the black leather next to his eye.

He nods and puts it down, begins to check over the right upper.

The door opens behind him.

"How are you doing, dear?"

"So far, so good."

"Your supper's ready."

"I'll be there in a moment, as soon as I check this one over."

"You've checked, and checked, and checked."

"It has to be perfect."

"Would He know the difference?"

"No, probably not, but you never know. And I would. Unlike some of Them, He pays, and pays what they're worth. Almost, anyway."

The bootmaker does not lift his eyes from the black leather.

After a time, the woman looks away, shakes her head silently, and retreats to the kitchen.

. . . On a golden sand beach, across the Middle Sea, a boy, playing on the sheltered beach under the cliff on which his parents' house rests, scoops up a handful of sand for his castle.

The dark glitter catches his eye. In among the golden and silver grains of sand are black ones, sands so black that each grain seems to absorb the light, but glistens all the same.

He begins to separate the black grains from the silver and gold ones, until at last he has a small handheld heap of mostly black and glittering sand.

"Mom! See what I found!"

His mother wades in from the low surf to meet him in the ankle-deep water.

"See! See how shiny it is!"

"Pierre, put that sand down. The black ones are dangerous."

"But why?"

"Put it down. All of it."

"I want to know why."

"When you're older, I'll tell you. Put it down."

"But why?"

"I told you it was dangerous. When you are older, I will tell you why. Now ... put ... it ... down!"

"All right." He throws the black glimmerings into the water lapping around his ankles. "All right. but you'd better tell me. You promised. You promised."

"I will. I will. Now ... let's see if you can still float on your back."

... In the secret hollowed-out space beneath the old stone house, they begin to gather.

By ones, by twos, the figures drift in and take their places in the small chapel, until the requisite score has assembled.

The man in the brown robe finally approaches the cube, black on all sides, on which stands a single black candle.

He does not light it.

"Oh, hear our prayers, undeclared God of Night. God of Darkness, deliver us from Light."

"Hear our prayers."

"Oh, hear our songs, God of the Evening, God of Blackness."

In time, up wells the familiar refrain:

"... And the Hammer of Darkness will fall from the sky;

The old gods must fly, and the summer will die ..."

The black candle remains unlit on the black stone cube.

"Deliver us from Light; deliver us from the flame of our oppression, from eternal day that lets us rest not, nor slumber. Hear us, and deliver us, thy servants, from the bondage of eternal brilliance ..."

XXXII

For the third day running, the waves break over the top of the golden sand beach, and the biting spray reaches over the hill-crest and down to the porch where Martel sits.

As all mortals do, his landlady, Mrs. Alderson, had succumbed to time, even though her life had been prolonged a great deal more than she had expected. For reasons unknown to Martel, who remains uninterested in the finer details of cellular biology, his attempts to rejuvenate the gray-haired woman failed, though she was unaware of his efforts.

Surprisingly, her testament, last declared less than a standard year after he had come to live in the small cottage, had offered him the right to buy either the cottage or the house, or both.

With the continuing royalties from his reruns—both *Forgotten Beaches of Aurore* and *Postulant Communities of Aurore* are a steady source of income—he purchased both and rented the house out, preferring to stay in the cottage.

The present occupants of the house are a middle-aged couple on sabbatical from the University of Karnak. Most of Martel's renters have been outsider norms. Those who decide to stay move elsewhere.

Martel shakes his head. The mannerism is unnecessary, he knows, but he enjoys hanging on to some of his useless habits.

Martel sniffs the air, and the salt tang reminds him of the waves whose muffled crashes he can hear from the other side of the hill.

The continuing waves are unnatural, even on Aurore. After three days, they are not likely to disappear, not until they achieve their purpose.

Another challenge? Or annoyance?

He rises, his face clear, eyes hooded, dark. A stocky man, modest in height, black-haired, lightly tanned, apparently in the health of first maturity.

His steps are heavy, but they have been heavy since youth, as he descends the three steps from the porch to the hillside. He walks up the grassy slope to the top of the hill that overlooks the small bay.

At the crest he pauses.

The spray flings itself upward in misty patches, glistening in the indirect light that gives the breakers themselves a threatening yellow look.

From his vantage point he can see the outward path of at least one riptide.

He shrugs as he starts down the hillside, the shadows gathering around his black-clad form.

A dorle chitters at him, but wings over and glides across the hilltop to perch in one of the quinces and to wait.

Any close observer would note that Martel's feet do not quite touch the grass over which he marches and that there is no direct light to cast the shadows that trail him.

From the grass that does not bend under his tread to the sand that does not receive his footprints he heads straight toward the waters, and they part around him.

He walks through gold-green breakers as if they are not there, and the waters crash over the places where he has been without touching him.

Overhead, a white bird with deep golden eyes and black pupils circles, then vanishes.

His head beneath the water's surface, he follows the line of the sloping beach at least a kilo outward. By now the waves are nearly a hundred meters over his head, yet his hair is still in place, and he moves, bone-dry, over the seabed sands.

At the edge of the rocky shelf he stops, knowing that beneath his feet is the beginning of a slope that will drop nearly a kilo in several hundred meters.

By rights, that for which he searches should be near.

Out into the nearby waters he casts his thoughts, and on the first cast snares nothing.

Nor on the second. Nor on the third.

Some little patience has evolved in his years of avoiding what others regard as inevitable, and he changes his cast, refocuses his thoughts, and tries again. And again.

At last, a glimmer, a slight tug.

That is enough, and he turns his steps southward, paralleling the dropoff, striding quickly, as if the water were not surrounding him.

Above the sea the white bird, golden-eyed, circles, following his general track.

A giant sea eagle, spotting the smaller avian, stoops to kill, and is brushed aside with a sudden gust of wind. The eagle tries again and is again brushed aside, and circles in confusion before deciding on the easier prey of a flying ray. In midskim from wavetop to wavetop the ray twists. But the intended evasion is too late, and the eagle flaps heavily toward his cliff eyrie with his meal.

Circling still, the white bird follows Martel.

As Martel proceeds toward his objective the clear water becomes less clear, and then even less so, until eyesight becomes useless. Martel is untroubled and unaffected and disappears into the cloud of sediment and suspended sand.

A few hundred strides farther on, he halts.

The suspended material whirls from an ever-expanding pit. Although Martel cannot see, he knows that at the center of the pit is a restrained and chained demigod. One suffering the punishment of a major god, and perhaps, placed in such a way as to infuriate the not-quite-major goddess who rules the shallows.

Should he free the chained demigod, the one creating the turbulence in his twin efforts to escape the eternal chains and to fight off the minions of Thetis?

If he frees the unknown demigod, both may turn on him. The former because only by subduing Martel can he return to the good graces of those who chained him. By now Martel has discovered that the demigod is male and that his principal tool is the fire of lava.

In turn, Thetis may attack because Martel will have intruded and robbed her of her due. She would have all thrown to her serve her, for at least a time.

Martel steps forward and descends through the swirls of boiling water and glass rain, down until the only light is the heat that surrounds the captive, light that is dimmed a fraction of a meter from its source.

For though the eternal chains are metal, no heat will melt

them, no superhuman strength rend the unseamed black links which, no matter how deep the chained one melts away the rock, stretch yet deeper into the depths.

Do not free me unless you will pay the price.

Martel snorts at the contradiction. Any being who can free the demigod must have power superior to his.

Martel smiles, faintly, knowing the other cannot sense his humor, gathers further his own darkness, his own chill depths, and touches one link, then the other chain.

The metal draws back from his touch, glistens more blackly, if possible, then fades and is gone.

Martel gestures, and the water is crystal-clear again. Of the eternal chains there is no sign.

The onetime captive, dressed in skintight red, reaches forth across the water he has warmed to grasp the man in black. As he does his arms lengthen impossibly. Those arms burn, and the water vaporizes away from them.

Fool!

Instead of turning away, Martel glides forward into the heat, into the grasp of Hades, lets the would-be god of fire enfold him.

No!

For now Martel holds the other's arms, more tightly than the eternal chains, for yet a moment before he releases the one in red.

He steps away and points. With the shadow he dispatches through the water goes the one in red, wrapped for delivery to the Sacred Peak.

Was that wise, Martel?

Still in the depths hollowed by the demigod of fire, Martel looks up the green-glass side of the submarine amphitheater to the one who addressed him.

Thetis?

Who else?

Your pardon, but the unnaturalness of the waves beckoned.

He walks up the glass-smooth slope that would be impassable for most, as if walking up a sheer glass incline a hundred meters undersea and remaining totally dry were not at all unusual.

Thetis, at home, in her ocean, is not dry. Rather, the water enfolds her, and her clear green hair flows over her naked shoulders, front and back, like a cloak. In her right hand is a small trident. Her left is open, empty, as Martel approaches.

The unnaturalness was meant to call you. So I waited. To see what you would do.

And?

Why did you not destroy him? He would have done that to you.

And give them a reason?

Your refusal to accept godhood on their terms is reason enough.

Martel shrugs, smiles a small smile. *But I would not give them reason were I in their place. That is what is important.*

She lifts her trident halfway.

Do not, dear Thetis. For I love the sea, and I would grieve.

You mock me. You mock the gods.

No.

The energy gathers around the green goddess.

Martel gathers his darkness, the black from the depths out and beyond the field, out and beyond Aurore. The cold and the fire and the remoteness invest him. No longer a mere human figure, no longer merely immortal, he stands apart.

The water draws farther back from him, as if in fear. The sand under his feet shrinks from the soles of the black boots.

His eyes are the depths of the places where there are no stars, the distances from whence stars cannot be seen, and his eyes ... they burn. They burn black, with a light that casts shadow across the entire seabed. A light where there should be no light, and a shadow where none should be.

Still is the sea, and awful.

The trident drops, and with it the bare knee, followed by the inclined head.

For all this, Thetis, for all this, dear lady, no more am I god than this water, or that boulder.

She shivers, though she is not cold.

God of darkness, god of night, that you endure where light reigns, that you are, that you triumph, means there are no gods. Not as you would call them.

Martel nods, releases his hold on the darks and on the depths.

That may be. I am no god. Only a man who knows more than many, and a little more than some.

No. Her thought bears sadness. *Not just man. Thinking so will bring sorrow to you, to all who surround you. More sorrow than you have experienced. Already you ignore the tears. Is it not so?*

He does not answer, except with a short furrow of his brows.

Thetis belts the small trident, blows Martel a kiss, one that crosses the water between them and caresses his forehead.

If not god, accept what you are, Martel.

He salutes the departing sea-goddess with an upraised hand, and, in turn, directs his steps toward the shoreline.

The sea is flat, motionless yet as he emerges, and as his black boots touch the sand. The air is quiet, and hawks, the dorles, and the golden sea eagles all perch where perches each, waiting.

When his last step clears the water, when he turns and again salutes the mistress of the sea, only then do the gentle waves resume, the sea breezes flow, and the sea birds fly.

Martel realizes his cheeks are wet, not from the water, for no water has touched him.

In response, he presses lips to fingertips and breathes the kiss back across to the sea, back to Thetis.

XXXIII

Help!

Martel stumbles, trying to pinpoint the direction of the thought, looking around, glancing up toward the shore and the Petrified Boardwalk.

A scattered handful of people—mostly natives—make their way through the fully lit and evening streets of Sybernal. Not a one of the three within ten meters of Martel has even flinched.

Despite the faintness of the thought, the aura of the plea is familiar. He cocks his head, trying to remember, to make a comparison. Not poor lost Rathe, for even the desperation of the thought holds a hardness that Rathe would never possess.

Why dig that up? She's gone. Gone.

Martel trots to the next corner, peering around it. No one notices him in the Street of Traders, not even the old man whose boot store is yet open with its green awning overhanging the public way.

Martel darts into the narrow lane around the corner from the bootery, gathers his shadows about him, and rises into the light. He does not notice the looped sign the bootmaker traces in the air as the black raven circles up from the lane, nor the averted glance of the young girl whose balcony he passes as he flaps awkwardly northward, from where he thinks the plea for help has come.

Martel! God of the Darkness! Save me!

Martel's wings miss a beat, and he loses altitude, then converts his drop into a dive, wings folded. For the desperate prayer has indeed come from the CastCenter.

The locked portals open at his touch.

Already the center feels empty, devoid of life. Martel's thoughts precede his body through the corridors toward the main control center. An aura of power is fading, an aura that Martel recognizes, from the control room, where Martel knows he will find what he does not want to see.

In the center, in the open space before the console, which is slaved to remote and broadcasting an opera from Karnak, on that open floor are three objects.

The first is a sheet of golden parchment, scrolled, on which a name appears. The name is *Martel*.

The second is a pile of heavy gray ashes, greasy in appearance, spilling across a golden starburst that has been etched into the permaplast flooring. A starburst, Martel knows, that had not been there the day previous.

The third item, collapsed in and around the ashes, is a pale golden one-piece coverall.

There may be other small objects, such as a sunburst pin, a thin golden chain, mixed in the ashes as well, but Martel does not touch anything. Except for the sheet of parchment, which he stoops to pocket.

Martel gestures. The darkness swirls over the control room,

and the floor is as it was, unmarked. Ashes, coverall, objects, all are gone, taken into the darkness.

From darkness she came, and unto darkness will she go, now and forever.

The cold knot inside Martel does not dissolve, but reaches to chill his fingers, numb his thoughts.

"Flame!"

Darkness has fire, also, and that will I claim, for those who are mine, and those who claim me.

Martel stands, letting time swirl around him, then clamps himself back into reality.

He leaves without touching anything, departs as he came, and even young Alsitar, who is rushing through the main portal in response to the automatic alarm and who passes the one who was called God of Darkness as He steps outside the portal, even Alsitar does not see what he sees. For Martel wills it otherwise.

Believing in a god who will not accept divinity is obviously a dangerous business, reflects Martel. He shivers as his feet carry him along the Petrified Boardwalk.

He strides down the boardwalk until it becomes a patch along the back of the beachline, until Sybernal is behind him, until the roofs are less than smudges on the southern horizon.

Then he takes out the golden parchment scroll with the sunburst in the upper right corner.

Until what is proper is done,
the followers of those who challenge shall suffer,
for an undeclared god is no god,
and blasphemy is death.

Martel shakes his head. Rathe he could understand. But Marta Farell?

Does Apollo really think this would force him to take them all on?

Won't it?

Yes, but not yet, Not now.

Ever?

He touches the parchment with shadow, and it is no more.

For a time he regards the ocean in the perpetual light that could be morning or evening, and is both and neither.

At last he turns back to the south. Where his feet touch the sand, each quick step leaves a black print, each grain of once-golden sand now the color of the space between galaxies.

The line of jet footprints on the shimmering golden sands points toward a distant cottage that has become emptier by the absence of one who never lived there, and never would have.

Soon a storm will rise and scatter the dark grains. After that storm, or the next, or the following, some child will look at a black grain and wonder. For all know that the sands of Aurore are golden, and there is no black sand.

XXXIV

Rathe?

Should he re-create her? The odds are good that he can duplicate her essence.

Are they?

He twirls the beaker that contains the last of the second bottle of Springfire he has consumed since he began the debate with himself.

Would she be Rathe? Even if I caught everything? Remembered it all?

He looks from his chair on the porch up the hillside. The topmost quince is dying, he can tell.

Why don't you rejuve the quince? Re-create it?

Plants don't rejuve.

Then re-create it.

It wouldn't be the same quince. Might as well plant another.

He sips what should be the next-to-last sip from the beaker. Through two bottles the questions have not changed. Neither have the answers.

And Rathe? Would your creation be the same? Could you

bear not to make changes? Even if you didn't, would she be the same?

He does not answer the questions. Instead, his sip becomes a gulp as he downs the last drops of the Springfire from the jasolite beaker.

"Flame! Flame! Flame!"

Even as he stands and gathers the darkness to him, even as he hurls the beaker into the flooring with enough force to shatter it and embed the crystal shards into the wood, he knows the answer.

Rathe is dead.

Dead is dead.

No miraculous re-creation will restore the woman who loved him.

All you'll have is a duplicate doomed to repeat the mistakes of the real Rathe. A pale copy without the fire of the original. A living doll without the soul of the only Rathe who lived.

"A pale copy? Sure. Just a pale copy! And what are you, Martel? A pale protoplasmic copy of distant ancestors who screwed around!"

Say what you will . . . dead is dead.

"Easy enough to say. Easy enough to think. But you're alive."

Exactly.

"You can throw your thunderbolts. You can summon the eternal darkness. You can heal the sick. You can walk on air and on water. So why can't you create a new Rathe?"

You can. You just can't bring back the old.

"So why don't you?"

The darkness freezes with the question, and even outside the cottage the breeze stills and the dorles quiet.

Because she's not strong enough. Because you'd destroy her again.

"Me? You wonderful subconscious, tell me again I destroyed her."

Didn't you force her to leave and not protect her?

Martel does not answer himself in the quiet and dark that wait for his decision.

Do you want to spend every moment guarding her from

Apollo? Can you make her a goddess? And if you could, would she be Rathe?

"Flame!"

His breath comes out in a long hiss, and the silence is broken. Outside, the two dorles in the nearest quince chitter. The low waves in the bay across the hill swish once more, and the breeze ruffles his short hair. The darkness ebbs beneath the moment.

At last, he looks down and wills away the crystal shards in and on the floor. The polished wood returns to an unblemished state as the scratches erase themselves.

Although there is another bottle of Springfire in the cooler, he will not need it. Not today, not tonight, though they are one and the same on Aurore.

Even gods, even you, have limits, Martel.

He would cry, but cannot, as he looks to the hillcrest and the twilight that will be centuries in coming. Instead, he stares at the dying quince.

XXXV

Time, like a loose-flowing river, does not, will not, flow the same for all individuals, neither mortals nor immortals.

That thought flits through his mind as he takes quick step upon quick step along the narrow pathway that leads toward a white villa.

Technically, the answer is simple. Technically, the answer is not an answer, but chance. Chance alone seems to determine who lives and who dies. Some mortals become gods, and no scientist can determine why. An increasing number of mortals, even within the Empire, do not age, or age far less quickly than others.

"Miracles?" he mutters as the path begins to rise. Any demigod on Aurore can return youth to a mortal, at least in body. But whether the youth remains so for more than a few years depends again on the individual.

"My individual?" he asks the trail, both recalling and trying to forget the lady upon whom he had bestowed the gift, recalling also how he had hoped she would remain beautiful in her own way beyond her time.

Beyond her time? That time was so short.

Had he only made the effort . . . had he made the effort he had not, for the reasons he can understand but not accept.

Will you ever accept them? Will you ever fight the gods for one individual?

You can't fight them all.

Won't you have to, sooner or later?

Perhaps. But not for one individual.

Then for what? For what, for whom, will you fight, Martel?

He turns himself away from the question, lets the day enfold him, lets himself be one with the trees, the golden grass, the scrub thistles, and the meadow flowers . . . with the dorles, with the white birds that dip their beaks into the clear brooks beyond his sight.

The key is mind over matter, but not the mind of thought. Rather the mind of the mind.

He frowns. Is he rationalizing, once again, his feeling of desertion toward Rathe?

Mind over matter, indeed.

He concentrates on his pace. Quick step, quick step, and the trail unrolls before him, stretching into the low hills, beckoning him away from Sybernal.

Most of the pines, wide-trunked and long-needled, whisper in the afternoon day, murmur in the perpetual breeze that cools these hills to the north of Sybernal, and hint at the power that naps in the scattered villas that nestle on the few cleared hillsides.

Martel wipes his forehead on his short black sleeve, halts where the path forks, and casts his thoughts down both hard-packed trails.

Why are they hard-packed? No sign anyone uses them.

The right-hand path dips down toward a brook, perhaps a hundred meters beyond what he can see directly with his eyes, and leads another kilo before ending in a small parklike clearing. Although his perceptions relay no structure to him, the impression is of a small freehold left to the elements, but tidied occasionally by a passing demigod.

He casts his thoughts out along the left path, resuming his rapid pace before evaluating what he perceives.

Others may be monitoring him. That he assumes from the feather-light tendrils of power that flicker in and out of his awareness, particularly when the breeze dies to a mere ghost.

Not that you mind, Martel.

He stops and studies the hillside to his left, the abrupt clearing that slants down the slope the length of three tall pines before the old trees close in.

Old trees . . . not many young ones, nor any dead ones . . . and what does that tell you, Martel?

How old are the pines? Or the few deciduous trees that mingle with them?

Martel shakes his head, once, quickly.

The faint scent of the pines and the swish of their boughs as the breeze picks up are saying something, trying to tell him something important. What, he cannot decide.

He kicks a rock, scarcely more than a pebble. He watches as it skids down the trail before bouncing sideways and disappearing into the golden grass that he thinks of as native. This high in the hills the emerald grass of Sybernal has not penetrated, except within some estates. Yet the trees are Arthtype.

Another tendril of power, stronger, flickers over him, dismisses him, and moves on.

Martel leaves his shields fully in place and smiles as the thin probe withdraws. The prober lies along way from the path upon which he stands and does not recognize that Martel's shields conceal his darkness. But then, sentry duty is boring for most sentries in most times and places.

Martel gives the clearing beside the trial a last look before he continues onward. The scene is not quite idyllic. From between the golden grasses peer crimson flowers, while a few scattered scrub thistles ring the far edge just inside the pines.

Order . . . very definitely ordered, Martel.

The pines are all healthy. Massive. Tall. Mature, but not old, though their size lends that impression. No gnarled branches or fallen or rotten trunks detract from the evidence of strength.

He cannot recall any such evidence of decay during his entire hike from the outskirts of Sybernal.

"The trees militant," he says with a low laugh, and picks up his pace as the trail narrows and begins to turn back on itself. He cannot explain, but in their own way the pines remind him of soldiers.

The chitter of a lone dorle rises over the swish of the pine branches. Otherwise the trail is silent, as it has been all along.

"Wild chase, after something that . . ." He does not finish the sentence, for his perceptions catch the power somehow trapped on the far side of the particular hill his trail circles.

Power . . . always power . . . nowhere on Aurore it doesn't show up, sooner or later.

No . . . you draw power like a lightning rod.

Is the thought his?

It does not matter, and he proceeds along the trail until it straightens at the other side of the hill.

A stone wall, the first thing he has seen that shows lack of attention, appears on the right-hand side of the trail, which has widened into a grass-covered path.

The path meanders along the flat between two low hills. On the left continues the hill Martel has been circling, pine-covered and silent.

On the right is what he seeks. While he cannot see directly beyond the stone wall, even though several stones have toppled out of the top row and down next to the wall, he knows that behind the remaining stones are tree gardens. Behind the gardens are emerald-green lawns that rise to formal gardens and to a white villa.

Both the grounds and the villa broadcast an air of desertion, and emptiness that stretches impossibly far back in time. Since Martel has visited that villa, he knows the impression is false, strong as it is, overpowering as it threatens to become with each step he takes toward the shambling graystone wall.

To the sense of desertion, underneath it, nearly lost in the mental patina of age that the wall and the estate behind it radiate, clings a sense of danger, and of power.

Tend to be synonymous on Aurore ... danger and power do.

Martel ignores the estate, for he has found it, found it deserted. He is not disappointed.

Rather ... relieved.

And why might that be?

"I don't have to answer that," he mumbles to himself.

The clear path beckons, and with it his apprehensions.

Brushing them aside, he marches down the grassy trail that soon becomes a wider lane next to the tumbled stone wall. With each step the unseen tension tightens, although he sees nothing in front of him. His vision is limited because both lane and wall curve gently to the right.

After another quarter-stan, three separate chitters form a dorle on the far side of the wall, and after another two kilos, he sees the fountain.

As he nears the circular basin the feeling of danger mounts. Strangely, the fountain operates, for all the desertion, for all the apparent lack of life. The water does not spray from the single stone figure on the square pedestal in the middle of the deep basin, but from jets around the young man, lending the statue a curtain of mist. Likewise, all the mist falls within the basin, whose black depths stretch toward the center of Aurore.

Though the statue is that of a young man, handsome, in a simple tunic and trousers, much like Martel's, his face is contorted in agony.

Martel stands at the edge of the fountain, understanding all too well both the agony and the danger.

He probes, lets his thoughts enfold the statue, and draws from the darkness that he knows will always be near him.

Raising his left hand, he gestures. For an instant, a shadow passes over the statue. When it has fled, the curtain of mist remains, but the figure is gone.

Martel nods.

While he hopes the other will be wise enough not to return, or not to repeat his folly in another way, the irony is all too striking.

Saved him from what might have happened to you ... right, Martel?

He takes a last look at the fountain, at the jets of mist and water concealing nothing, then at the wall, and finally behind the stones at the unkempt emerald grass, the straggling gardens, and at the empty rooms and columns.

He stares at his feet.

After a time, he turns to retrace his steps back toward Sybernal, back along a trail he has already trod once without understanding why.

This time, occasionally, he whistles.

XXXVI

Should be evening. Or twilight.

Beneath his feet the golden sands stretch down to the waters of the circular bay. The golden green of the water touches the sand with a gentle swish-swash, swish-swash.

It is always twilight beneath the waters, Martel. The answering thought is faint but clear.

He looks around the bay, but no one else is present. When he first moved into the cottage, picnickers and others from Sybernal often swam in the clear waters. Over the years, its popularity has declined, and now no one comes. No one comes, except Martel, although the waters are as clear as ever, and the sands are as warm and golden as always.

With a shrug, he walks into the waters, which part around him, flowing, encircling, but not touching him.

Thetis joins him as he reaches the underwater shelf where the depths begin. The green gown flows around her like water, like liquid flame, and she bears no trident. Not this time. Her hands are open and empty.

Have you come to walk with me?

Seemed like a good idea. Don't ask me why.

Her fingertips reach out to touch his, and the warmth sends a jolt through him.

She laughs.

I'm not cold-blooded, Martel. Even my mermaids are warm and loving, for all their tails and scales.

He shakes his head, mentally contrasting the goddess beside him to Rathe ... both full-bodied, but one he pictures, holds in his mind, as red, and Thetis is green, cool and green, goddess of the sea.

... and capable of storms and cruelty ... like the sea?

He feels her stiffen at his unguarded thought, but her fingertips remain with his.

Aren't we all?

He nods, not looking at her, but aware that she is one of the few goddesses he overtops, one of the few he can physically look down at.

Ahead, rising out of the silver sands, sands unmarked by any marine growth, stands a rock cube, each pink face smooth stone, polished and glistening.

Not exactly natural.

No. This is my park, if you will.

Hand in hand, they climb on steps of nothing until they stand on the flat top of the cube.

Martel looks up. The surface of the ocean is at least fifty meters above, and it is indeed twilight where he stands.

Twilight, and it will come in turn for Aurore.

Thetis shivers, and disengages her hand from Martel's, turns to face him.

You could be more terrible than Apollo.

Me? Me? Good old Martel the wishy-washy? Who has yet to really lift a hand?

She takes both his hands in hers.

Apollo does not know what suffering is. You suffer, and do not know how to grieve. And when you have suffered enough, all Aurore will grieve.

Martel shakes his head again, strongly enough to fluff his hair out, but he does not remove his hands from hers.

Thetis drops her eyes to the pale pink of the rock underfoot.

You will be so powerful that nothing can touch you, nor your heart, except as you wish. You will have everything, and nothing.

And you?

Thetis does not look up, but shivers again.

And you? Martel presses.

When you are done, I will have only what you leave me, and a leaden shield, gray in color. Unlike some that I know. And for all his strength . . .

Thetis is sobbing silently, refusing to look up to Martel.

He frowns.

None of what she has said makes any sense, any sense at all.

. . . a leaden shield, gray in color? . . . Whose strength? . . .

Her arms drop from his hands, and she steps back and stares squarely into his eyes, her own gray eyes clear, while the tears stream down her face.

They stand there silently, both dry, yet deep in the shallows of the sea.

They stand there, neither moving.

Let us suffer together, Martel, for I see what lies before us both. Even with a companion, no one will bear what you must. And I must lose all. So let us join before we separate, for you must give me what is demanded, and I must leave you to the far future.

She steps to him, and her arms draw him down, and the green water flames that have covered her are no more, and her mouth is warm on his in the twilight that cannot elsewhere be found on Aurore.

His arms encircle her, and he tries to forget, for a moment, the ones in red, and the ones in white and blue, and to feel the cool warmth of the green goddess and the heat of her sadness, though he understands not the reasons. He will, he knows.

. . . for the son will be carried on the shield of the past, and the father on the shield of the future . . .

His fingers dig into the warm skin of her shoulders as he tries, as he succeeds in blocking away the certainty of her visions, for he knows, whatever she has seen, it will be. And he does not want to know. Not now.

And the green flame and the black flame twine in the twilight of the shallow depths of the green-golden sea, and the fires within both hold back the past and the future.

For now.

XXXVII

From his small table overlooking the Great East Beach of Sybernal, Martel can sense a wave of energy approaching the establishment.

Should you make it harder for him?

Why not? he answers his own question.

With that, he wraps the darkness around him tightly enough that only the closest observer would see him, or sense his presence.

He waits, cradling the untouched beaker of Springfire.

Steps, on the wooden entryway leading to the bar, tap lightly, are misleading, for the man who strides in with a slight wobble to his step is tall, a full head taller than the man who sits shrouded in black.

You expected something of the sort, Martel. But from a mere demigod?

He shakes his head.

The newcomer sits on a high stool at the bar and orders.

"Cherry Flare." He does not look around the room, but Martel can feel his energies probing.

Martel lets the tendrils of power slide over him, non-reacting, and waits. He takes a small sip from his beaker.

Outside, the regular waves crest, break, foam, and subside, one wave after the other. Crest, break, foam, and subside, and each time the golden-green water slips back under the crisp foam of the incoming breaker like black ice under lace.

The man at the bar, the one wearing peach trousers and tunic offset with a crimson sash, the one with the tight-curled blond hair, taps his glass on the counter.

"Another Cherry Flare. 'Nother Cherry Flare."

Martel takes another sip from his beaker. The liqueur warms the back of his throat as he swallows.

" 'Nother Cherry Flare!"

Martel says nothing as the lady keep refills the younger man's glass.

"You! You in the corner! What do you think?"

Martel raises his eyebrows and says nothing.

"I asked you what you thought!"

"I wasn't thinking, friend. I was listening and looking at the waves."

"Asked you what you thought!"

Martel sets his beaker on the table.

"So tell me what you think!" demands the man in peach.

"I'd like to hear what you think, friend." The word "friend" is clearly a courtesy.

"Think you sit there. Sit there like one of those useless gods. Dare me to say what I think."

Martel shrugs. "I'm no god. Think what you want." He looks down at the beaker.

"No difference. Gods or no gods. Too many gods. Too many demigods. Never know where they are. Never know where they are." He gulps the remainder of the second Cherry Flare as if the liquor were water.

Thud!

He slams the heavy glass on the bar. "Cherry Flare! Let's have another, lady!"

This time the woman replaces his glass with a full one almost before he has completed his demand.

"You!" he shouts at Martel. "Think I'm crazy. So do the gods."

Martel takes another sip from his beaker.

How will he play this out?

"The gods. Too many gods. Too careless. Careless, and care less about us." He laughs at his pun. "Treat us like dirt. Dirt!"

The heavy glass, still nearly full, comes down on the bar, but the speaker is oblivious to the liquor that slops onto the wood.

The keep hesitates, leans toward a concealed button, her blue eyes narrowing.

"Let him talk, Sylvia," suggests Martel.

"Very good. Let me talk. Talk about every rich norm that comes to be a god. Throws creds like light. And what we get? Nothing. Nothing but bowing and scraping, and having our brains scrambled every time we think wrong."

Not much finesse here, Martel.

Does Apollo need finesse? he responds to his own question.

Martel gestures for the other to continue.

"Even the Regent, bitch she is, doesn't follow you in and out of bed, day on day, waiting, hounding till you think wrong."

"Neither do the gods," snaps Sylvia.

"Worse!" The peach-dressed man hops off the stool, well balanced despite the slur in his speech, and wheels toward Martel. His right hand blurs as it slashes down through the heavy wood seat of the adjoining barstool.

For an instant the two halves of the barstool balance, teetering in midair. Then both sides crash to the floor.

"Ha!" The man vaults more than a meter into the air and onto the flat surface of the bar itself. "Behold the remains of Lendl the Terrible! Bar tricks! Once I could do that to any man. But here . . . here . . . one can do nothing. Nothing!"

Sylvia retreats to the far corner of the bar, away from the splash of light that sweeps out from the peach-clothed man who bestrides her bar.

"Magnificent show," comments Martel dryly, "Lendl, or whatever your real name is. Apollo at his cruelest has a sense of restraint and drama. You're merely burlesquing the whole business."

Martel finally stands, and as he speaks the darkness rises from the wood surrounding him, draws in from the corners of the room to confer a solidity upon him that leaves Lendl a tinsel shape.

"You mock me. Therefore, you mock the gods." Stars corruscate from the ends of Lendl's peach-lacquered fingertips.

"I mock no one. I merely state what is obvious. Those who consider truth mockery only mock themselves."

"Meet your end, unbeliever!" The tinsel stars at his fingertips turn brighter before they arc toward Martel.

Another one sent for an ordeal . . . or to test you, Martel.

Martel smiles, and, seeing that smile, Sylvia makes a sign, that of the looped and inverted cross, and shudders in her corner.

Lendl, lost in his madness, straightens his right arm and
flings a blaze of fire at the shadowed figure that is Martel.

The missile, though brighter than the smaller stars that die
in the darkness around Martel, slows, dims, and flickers out
long before it crosses the short distance to Martel.

A second, even brighter, starbolt flares toward Martel, and,
in turn, extinguishes itself. Lendl drags forth another from the
field of Aurore.

In turn, Martel reaches for a certain energy, turns it to twist
and isolate Lendl from his energies. He steps toward the star-
thrower.

"Do you believe in darkness, Lendl the Terrible? Have you
seen sunset in a shadow?"

The darkness crashes like a wave, like a falling cliff, over
the demigod. As it flows back to the place from which it rose,
it carries the paralyzed demigod, lacquered fingers and
starbolts included, back with it, back into the depths of time
and space.

Releasing his hold on that corner of the universal darkness,
Martel sits back down at his table and studies the flattened
waves as they break up on the Great East Beach. He sips the
last of the Springfire.

As an afterthought, he touches Sylvia's thoughts and removes the memory of a peach-and-crimson-clad demigod.
That loss of memory will protect her and confound Apollo.
For it has to be Apollo or the Smoke Bull who sends such
emissaries.

He lifts the empty jasolite beaker, knowing Sylvia will re-
fill it, waiting for the warmth of the Springfire to drown the
memories that the demigod has raised . . . again.

*So easy to strike out . . . but you don't combat fire with fire
. . . not unless you want to burn both out.*

Still, you remember, don't you, Martel?

He nods to his own thoughts and takes a sip from the latest
beaker Sylvia has placed before him.

The images flash across the dark screen within his mind.

Kryn, who was spark, and Rathe, who was fire, and Thetis, who is sea, and Emily, who is deceit, and more, and
Apollo, who is the cruelty of desert sun, and . . . and . . .

He sips the Springfire, and lets the darkness curl around him, settle deeper within.

XXXVIII

As he walks to the exit portal Martel can sense the morning shift, engineer and faxer, at the other entrance, the land-side one, waiting for the clearance that he has left.

"For all they see, I'm a myth, a creation of the nightly fax show. Martel the mysterious, featured on Path Seven and seen occasionally in Sybernal, if the rumors can be believed."

The words sound hollow, and he blocks away the memories that accompany them . . . along with one name.

Farell . . . Marta Farell.

Someday you'll have to repay that one.

Someday—but not till the time comes.

He touches the plate and steps out into the eternal day of Aurore, though the standard clock indicates it is not quite dawn on Aurore or Karnak Imperial. He pauses.

Someone else is waiting.

"Emily . . . what a pleasant surprise." Martel almost laughs as he discovers his voice has involuntarily blunted the sarcasm he meant.

"I thought I would let you recover on your own. You do insist on doing things your way."

"And you are so different?"

She smiles, and the expression is warm. "We are alike in some ways."

He nods. "But to what do I owe this unexpected courtesy?"

Goddess or not, as a woman she had approached, and it is to that approach he intends to respond.

"That's what I'd hoped for," she replies to his unthought words. The sound and thought of silver bells tinkle in his head. He pushes them away, knowing he does not want to, and takes her arm, tanned lightly, as always.

"The North Pier restaurant again?"

"Not this time." She points to a flitter landing a hundred

meters up the Petrified Boardwalk. "Not unless you miss th high cuisine terribly."

Martel reflects. If he is condemned, he might as well en joy it. For some reason, the image of Marta Farell flicker through his mind.

"Your fault, but not totally," agrees Emily.

Martel reinforces his blocks, not only frustrated at he knowing his every thought, but also angry at his own care lessness.

"Not exactly friendly."

"Neither is snooping."

She squeezes his hand. "I wasn't snooping. You wer broadcasting, and there is a difference."

He lets the outer barriers drop. What difference will i make?

The flitter looks the same, even after, what—fifty standar years? Just like Emily.

"And just like you, Martel. The world changes around you and yet you really don't notice it. You decry the gods, and th number of demigods that Apollo and the Smoke Bull are rais ing, but you're the most visible god of all."

He thinks about protesting the charge, but lets it drop.

"That's part of what makes you fascinating. Why do yo think the royalties on your shows are so high? Not tha they're not good, you understand, but how many gods in th universe are faxers?

"And why do you think Apollo is so ambivalent abou you? At the same time you oppose him, you're supporting th whole idea of the gods by your own actions."

She smiles and gestures toward the open door of the flitter

He returns the gesture. "After you, lovely lady."

She inclines her head, hesitates, then steps inside.

Martel slides in next to her.

The door swings shut behind him, and the flitter, with nei ther at the controls, lifts.

"Why is there no one who will enter the CastCenter whil you're there? Don't tell me it's because of a generation-ol edict of a defunct center chief. That provides the excuse Working with, or loving, gods is dangerous, Martel. Yo know it, and so do they."

"So why am I with you?"

"Because ... but that's beside the point. I won't answer that question until you're willing to. Until you're honest with yourself, totally honest, no one else can afford to be. In the meantime, I will take what we can both afford."

Her left hand touches his right, squeezes it, and her right reaches for his left shoulder, draws him toward her, across the golden upholstery.

Martel holds back momentarily, then lets himself slide into her, lips meeting, his arms encircling her.

The flitter shivers, shaking them. Martel lets his lips break free.

"I can't seem to concentrate on two things at once." As she struggles from half under him her laugh chimes with the bells he has heard before only in thought. Or has he?

He dredges his memories for ... what? ... as she concentrates on her mental control of the aircraft.

Presently he recognizes the villa. While the surrounding trees may be taller, little else has changed.

"It shouldn't have. Except for caretaking, I haven't been here since you were last here."

The words ring true, and that truth disturbs him. Why?

How could a goddess be interested in a mere mortal? One who shies away from even considering a trip toward godhood?

Emily frowns, but says nothing as the flitter descends toward touchdown.

"This time, the dinner choice, and it will be dinner, is mine. I'm sure you'll enjoy it."

As she finishes the last word, as if on cue the flitter settles onto the landing stage, and the door swings open.

No footman, no liveried functionary, waits as she alights. Yet the white marble columns hold the aura of expectation, as if an Imperial ball is about to occur.

Through the atrium, where not a speck of dust clings to the polished floors or to the classical columns, and through the center courtyard where the light-fountain plays in the circular basin surrounded by white flowers, she leads Martel. Only the swish of her sandals, the pad of his boots, and the splash of the fountain break the silence.

On the open portico is a table, linened, in gold and crystal and set for two.

He bows to her.

She acknowledges the bow with a faint smile. "If you will be seated . . ."

"But how can I be seated and seat you, as is proper?"

"You can't. I intend to serve you, and serve you I will."

He sits, again disturbed, unable to put his finger on the reasons for his unease.

Were Emily out to destroy him, she would not have proceeded so. His reasoning is flawed, he knows, but true all the same. Emily does not intend him harm. Far from it. Not tonight.

First is the salad, of greens sprinkled with crushed nuts. The greens are the end shoots from the yanar tree, of which there are only a handful growing at the mist line, so it is said, on less than a dozen peaks of Aurore.

The nut he does not recognize, though it brings out every spice-mint nuance of the yanar tips.

"A local variety of an old Home nut."

Martel nods. He can expect no less. Still . . . something about the dinner nags at him.

"Why did you invite me to dinner?"

"Always direct, dear Martel." She laughs, and the sound warms him. He fights the sensation. "But if I told you, it would destroy the effect."

"And you're as evasive as ever."

"There's an old saying, 'Ask me no questions, and I'll tell you no lies.' "

Martel studies her, realizes that her gown is cut lower than he remembers, that she wears nothing beneath.

Before he can speculate further, she is up.

"The main course." She disappears, to return moments later with two gossamer-thin plates, one of which she places before Martel.

The porcelain catches Martel's attention even more than the golden fish that is reputed to taste more delicate than the Emperor's cultured game trout. The porcelain is A'Mingtera, of which no complete set is known to exist.

Beside the golden fish is a thin slice of something in a light brown sauce, which Martel samples. Slightly bitter, but with a bubbling tang.

"Try the fish first."

He does, and understands the use of the thin brown mushroom, which amplifies the delicacy and sensation of the golden fish.

Even so far, goddess or not, the meal is extreme, and carries a meaning beyond seduction, though that will come, he knows, and as he knows he wants her.

Desirable as she is, sitting across from her ... Martel blocks the thought before it surfaces.

"You're upset?"

"Confused."

She finishes a last bite and wipes her lips with the silken napkin.

"Confused about you, about me," he goes on. "Any god on Aurore would be flattered by all this, all that you could offer. Why me?"

From the glint in her eyes he realizes he has not been the only one.

"No," she confirms. "What choice do I have when you turn away from me and from what you are?" Her voice is soft, with the touch of bells in it, and totally at odds with the hint of anger he has seen buried within her.

"Let's pretend I don't know anything about you, which I don't," says Martel, in an effort to retrack the conversation. "Where did you grow up and when did you discover—"

"That I was what I was? At least, you didn't ask how old I am." She pauses. "Let's just say I grew up very young long enough ago for me to be uncertain about the details."

She takes a sip of the wine, neither white nor rosé, but some of both and better than the best of either.

Martel lifts his glass to her, sips silently.

How little we know.

How little we need to know comes her answering thought.

The portico is off the bedroom Martel has been in once before.

He slips to his feet and she to hers, and they move around the linen and gold and crystal, and the white fire from her and the black from him touch and join. And join. And join.

A black shadow, more like smoke, in the upper branches of the nearby bristlepine thins and fades.

A yellow eagle hawk in the sky above circles, circles, and is gone.

This time, Martel wakes first, or Emily has let him wake first. He looks over her body, tanned, smooth as if in the first flush of young womanhood, with the high breasts, narrow waist, fine features, and high cheeks under closed eyes.

Though her hair is all golden blond, and her genes would show the same, he knows, now, that she was born with black hair like Kryn. He imagines that, changes a feature in his mind . . . and cold like ice cascades down his spine.

He shakes his head violently.

Kryn is on Karnak, the Viceroy after long positioning to succeed the Grand Duke, while Emily has been on Aurore for too long.

He also realizes another thing. Emily has never been young. Not in eons, perhaps longer. While she plays at youth, she does not love as if she were ever young, as if she had ever been fully human. And that is why he misses Rathe, why he misses Kryn, though Kryn, he knows full well, stands at the beginnings of power, at the base of ambition that will grow. Somewhere within her, he hopes with a certain sadness, she will remember being young and in love. Perhaps.

If she ever really was.

The cold thought is his own.

Emily is awake and studying him, in turn.

"And perhaps you're right. Again," she says, but her hands draw him back to her, and he does not resist. Nor is he young, either, as the fires fight and join.

XXXIX

Martel's long strides carry him up the coastal highway. The dorles chitter from the quinces and from the zebrun trees that line the empty highway.

Though he cannot hear it yet, he knows an electrobike approaches from the south, purring behind him toward the common destination of Sybernal.

Likewise, he can sense the group of young natives, perhaps five or so, who are gathered on the lane that leads to the CastCenter.

The sky is clear, as clear as it ever is under the omnipresent golden haze of the field, and the faint scent of trilia is carried from the hills on the light breeze.

Martel frowns. His stride breaks momentarily.

The youngsters are waiting for him. From his present distance he can sense no malice, no negative feelings, except a faint fear, combined with curiosity.

But waiting for you, Martel?

He shrugs and picks up his stride, letting the frown fade away.

Martel could avoid the group that awaits him, but then he would not have a clear picture of why they are interested in him, interested enough to wait, and knowledgeable enough to know where to wait.

· From a distance he can only touch the clearest of surface thoughts, and certainly not what is behind such thoughts. Besides, their actions will tell as much as their thoughts. More, if the gods are involved.

As his steps take him into Sybernal, into the long, narrow Greenbelt that surrounds the highway, he reaches out again to the young natives, but the picture is no clearer.

Again he shrugs.

Finally he tops the little hill that leads down to the lane which, in turn, leads back up to the CastCenter.

That's HIM!

Three of the male students wear the gold-and-white-striped tunics of the Sybernal Academy. One, the youngest and shortest, steps forward to block Martel's path.

Martel stops, waits.

The stillness draws out.

Martel smiles faintly, but says nothing, remains motionless.

"Honored Sir, are . . . are You . . . the One?"

"The one what?" answers Martel.

"The One . . . One . . ." stammers the boy. The top of his red hair is level with Martel's shoulder.

The Dark One . . . God of Night . . . God of Shadows . . . GOD, why me? Why . . .

Martel looks at the others.

The five, three adolescent boys and two girls, fidget, wanting to move close enough to hear his answer, but wanting to back off at the same time.

Martel does not answer, and instead takes his time to run his eyes over the entire group, one by one, letting himself pick up thoughts from each.

. . . he's strange . . . expected the question . . . Elson not forceful enough . . . little coward . . .

Dark, and the black . . . like a shadow . . . why did we listen? What if He is?

Thought it was a joke, but . . . so dark . . . moves like a shadow . . .

Silly . . . boys . . . all that way. Just has to look mysterious, and they shiver . . .

Doesn't look old. Darfid says the records don't tell . . . centuries . . . years . . . all the same . . .

Martel lets his eyes flick back over the six again. No mental sign of who, or which god, has put them up to their question.

How do you answer them, Martel? You're no god . . . why give Apollo the satisfaction? Either way?

He frowns.

They draw back, even Elson, the questioner who has blocked his path.

"A name is only what others want you to believe." He pauses, hoping that the pause will let the meaning sink in. "I am what I am, not what others would have you believe."

Martel smiles.

"And a pleasant evening to you all."

Now let Apollo figure that out!

He steps around Elson and breaks into his quick stride toward the CastCenter at the end of the lane.

Evening? What did he mean by that?

"But there isn't any evening here," protests one of the Academy students.

"So . . . you have to have evening before night. Before it gets dark," snaps the older girl, a rail-thin brunette.

"You didn't get an answer, Elson! You failed!"

"No! He gave you an answer. He really did. Don't! Don't hit me!"

Martel lifts a corner of darkness from beneath the light and flicks it toward the youngsters.

"What's that?"

"He's gone!"

"Where? He was just walking away."

"That couldn't have been a shadow ... could it?"

"Look! Up there!"

An enormous raven/night eagle circles overhead, low, glittering black, dripping shadows, dives away, and disappears behind the low hill on which the CastCenter sits.

"See!" answers Elson. "If that isn't an answer, then what is?"

... *what is* ... The thought echoes in eight minds, and Martel senses that one is not his or the youngsters'.

He emerges from behind an ancient pine, certain that no one has seen his descent, and enters the empty CastCenter. On time. Again.

XL

The hillcrest is bare. Bare except for the grass, and for the view of the lands leading northward to Sybernal and south toward the sacred peak. Bare except for the man in black who stands looking southward down at the bay.

The time is midnight, Aurore, and midnight, Karnak Standard, but irrelevant, since the eternal light varies only with the weather. Tonight there are no clouds, only the normal sea breeze.

So now she's the Viceroy?

The Grand Duke, the acting Viceroy, is dead, and the Regent's Guard has hailed the Lady Kryn as Viceroy. Not as acting Viceroy, but Viceroy.

The Third, Fifth, and Seventh Fleets have also acclaimed

her. New Augusta has accepted the inevitable and confirmed her position.

Martel draws a dark square in the air, concentrates, and is rewarded with an image of the black-haired woman, dressed in the blue and gold he has remembered for so long.

Shaking his head, he releases the picture, and it dissolves into a swirl of black glittermotes.

Emily?

This time his headshake is more violent.

Her soul is cold.

So . . . are not the souls of all gods cold?

You could become a god.

With that thought, his eyes lift toward the peak Jsalm. Though it lies beyond the reach of unaided vision, he can see its dark bulk and ice-tipped summit, can see the figures in the air above its needled tip.

So . . . Martel . . . you cannot have Kryn, for she has obtained what she has sought and will not relinquish the power and the glory that is Karnak. And you cannot have Rathe, for she is dead. Dead because of your carelessness. Or your unwillingness to make any commitment to anything. Have it either way. And you do not want Emily, or to be a god.

He turns his eyes from Jsalm toward the grass at his feet, then back to the gentle waves in the bay below the hillside. The nip of the salt air reminds him of Thetis.

Thetis?

He laughs.

No. Though a lady she certainly is.

Then what do you want?

Kryn . . . and to be me.

He turns to face the other way, down the hillside at the cottage, and at the quinces.

What are you, Martel? What are you that makes you want what you cannot have and turn from what you are?

The thought is not his, but echoes as if from a great distance.

He frowns, wondering who had been monitoring his private soliloquy, and as his eyebrows furrow, the breeze dies, and the air stills.

I am what I am, and I will have what I want!

How, pray tell?

He laughs, and the laugh echoes across the hillside, down toward the cottage on one side and toward the bay on the other. In the bay, the sound freezes the waves, holds the pair of dorles in midflight, and ripples the beach like an earthquake.

Darkness wells, and spreads, and for kilos around, night falls. At last, Martel speaks aloud, and the words rumble like thunder as they roll outward over the lands from his mouth.

"Time! Time is mine, and so is the night. Day will end, must end. And at that time comes night. Enjoy your days in the sun you cannot see, for though centuries pass, though the sons of those centuries pass, I will wait, and remember. Remember till the day when night will fall, and so will you!"

This time, this one time, Martel does not release his darkness to let it disperse. Instead, he lets it break, in waves, away from him, and in breaking that dark washes around Aurore so that all on Aurore behold a moment of night.

That darkness flies across Sybernal, across Jsalm, across Pamyra, on across the White Cliffs, across a certain white villa, across beaches, and across vacant golden waters.

That instant of night wings over the lands and waters like a night eagle whose shadowed pinions cover but briefly the ground beneath.

In certain streets of Sybernal, men crouch. Some make an obscure sign dating from the depths of history; others gape. Still others fail to notice, and others observe the strange darkness and dismiss its significance. Such it is. So has it always been.

Some notice. Some do not.

Some are pleased. Some are not.

By the time the light returns to the empty hilltop, Martel has returned to his cottage. Returned smiling, though that smile would chill most and leave their souls frozen hulks.

Outside, it is still night, despite the light of eternal day, although the clocks state it is night.

On Karnak, the Viceroy sleeps.

Part II

The Coming
of the Hammer

XLI

The Lady dreams. For now, to call her Lady is sufficient. She is that, and more.

In her dream, she falls down a long, black tunnel, shot with streaks of white. As she drops she passes point rainbows of light, all the colors she can see, and colors besides those. Colors she once could see, but knows she can no longer distinguish.

She reaches out to touch the sides of the tunnel, but they retreat from her clutching fingers.

The Lady wants to cry, but knows she must not, knows she should remember why, but cannot.

She wakes ... alone ... in a dimly lit room. To call her chamber a small hall would be more precise.

Shuddering at the all-too-familiar dream, she sits up.

"It's been a while," she murmurs, checking the time, "a long while since the last time."

"Dreams of the tunnel?" inquires her diary from the bedside table. "Yes, it has been. Nine years, eleven standard months, roughly."

"I wonder what crisis is coming," she says softly.

The diary does not answer.

The Lady resettles herself on her pillows and pulls the silksheen cover up over her shoulders, though she is not cold.

She avoids thinking about the two questions the dream has returned to her thoughts, and after some time passes into a hot and dreamless sleep.

XLII

Tap, tap.

The sound raises Martel from his study of the small beaker, which is empty, and the bottle of Springfire, which is full.

Tap, tap.

He sighs, replaces the bottle on the keeper shelf, and closes the appliance. Martel decides not to probe, hoping the intruder will leave. While the visitor does, he leaves a package.

By the time Martel reaches the front portal and opens it, no one is there. An electrobike is purring back toward Sybernal.

An envelope lies squarely on the top step.

Martel purses his lips. When was the last time he saw an honest envelope? From Hollie? Sometime in the days of the old Empire of Man? Before the fall of the Prince Regent? Before his former ladylove who wasn't seized the reins of power ... he shunts that thought away, regards the envelope.

Finally he bends and picks it up. A large envelope, to say the least, so white that the paper, parchment really, nearly blinds. His name in flowing script assures him that he is the recipient.

Martel, it reads, and across from the name, in the same black ink, is a thunderbolt, stylized, but a thunderbolt nonetheless.

He probes the inside with his perceptions, but only inert material rests there.

Closing the portal, he returns to the main room, and to the table with the beaker.

Can it be from his latest tenants?

Unlikely, for neither could write in such a flowing hand. He knows this, though he has seen neither write.

From the chief at the CastCenter, the latest of the more than several dozen for whom he has theoretically worked the "night" shift over the centuries?

Also unlikely.

He sniffs, holds the envelope up, trying to see if some perfume clings to it. For the hand proclaims that a woman wrote his name.

Emily?

He shakes his head. He cannot imagine the writing of a goddess, or the reasons why she would take the time to write. He holds the envelope, hesitates, puts it down on the table, and stands there.

Why are you afraid? You, the dark shadow of Aurore?

Not denying his fear, he walks around the table, stares out the window at the nearest quince tree, the latest of the generations he has planted, and down at the main house, rebuilt last year for the fiftieth time since he purchased it from Mrs. Alderson's estate.

After all the years, why now?

He knows the answer. He has felt it on the wind, and in his probes of what lies beyond the energy field that is Aurore.

"There is a season . . ." And after the season of light comes the season of change. Has he not said so himself?

He replaces the beaker on its shelf and walks back to his sleeping room, toward the wardrobe and the black tunics and trousers. He dons tunic, then trousers, and for the first time in many years, instead of the plain black belt, puts on the one with the triangular silver buckle. The black boots follow.

Fully dressed, he walks back to the table, regards the envelope.

After a time, he picks it up and touches the flap, which unseals at his touch, as he knew it would.

Three holos tumble out on the table, all landing face up.

Rathe Firien, snub-nosed, red-haired, full-breasted under the clinging tunic, and friendly, the warmth obvious, as if the holo had been canned the day before.

Marta Farell, not the stern-faced CastCenter chief, but smiling as if to welcome her lover, and wearing a golden gown.

And . . . at the end, Kryn Kirsten, daughter of the Grand

Duke, golden-eyed and black-haired, in tunic and trousers of blue shot with threads of gold. Slim like a bitch goddess, and bitchlike in her own way.

A narrow slip of parchment remains in the envelope.

Martel leaves it there as he studies the pictures.

Two dead women, one who loved him, and one who hadn't. Both dead because of him. And a third, possibly the most powerful person in the Empire of Light, immortal and yet not a goddess, and not on Aurore. The enigma he has not seen in more than a millennium, her holo in with that of two dead women.

An obvious conclusion to be drawn, one meant to be drawn. But why now? And by whom?

Underlying all was the assumption that he would care, that he had to care, that he could care.

The three-dimensional images looking up from the table asked a question, too. Two of them, at least, and Martel dislikes the question.

Is he going to let someone else die, as he has the other two, because he will not listen?

Or is someone using the question to force you to act?

Does it matter?

He shrugs, not sure that it does.

Who knows him well enough to ask the question in such a knifing way?

Emily. She is the only answer.

She is the goddess Dian, but Emily will do. Has always done between them.

He takes the narrow slip from the envelope, reads it.

The No-Name. 2200. My love.

Her love?

He tosses that question into his mental file with all the other unanswered questions he has ignored over the centuries, knowing that it cannot stay ignored, not this time.

He looks down at the images of the three women, all beautiful in their own way, all intelligent, and, in their own way, all dead to him.

If you believe that, Martel, you're crazier than Thor.

He wonders who expressed the thought, then realizes it is his own, not letting him lie to himself this time.

The stars have changed, and his time has come round at last, rough beast, and it may be time to slouch forward . . . he does not finish the thought, but, instead, fingers the slip and lets it burst into flame.

The ashes are light and drift from his fingertips into the still air of the room and slowly toward the floor.

Martel locks the rear portal onto the porch, as well as the front as he leaves, for the first time since he originally entered the cottage with Rathe Firien. He will not be back soon.

The three holos gaze adoringly at the wooden beams of the ceiling above the table, and the black thunderbolt on the envelope protects them.

A man who is no longer just a man, clad in two black cloaks, one fabric, one shadow, strides along the coast path toward Sybernal, and those who see him do not. But they shiver as he passes, not knowing why.

XLIII

In the strictest sense of the word, the old Empire of Man "fell" with the death of the Regent and the succession of the Grand Duke of Kirsten. Practically speaking, however, the impact was the permanent division of the Empire. Both the "eastern" Empire, ruled from New Augusta by the Emperor, and the "western" Empire, ruled from Karnak by the Viceroy, claimed to be only parts of the new Empire of Light.

In a strange way, the claims were true. In the millennium that the Empire of Light existed, never did either ruler contest a prior claim of the other, nor was there a recorded instance of the fleets of one firing upon the fleets of the other.

To the Viceroy, of course, most credit should be given. Never before or since in human history has a ruler endured, not only relatively sane, but apparently young and healthy, for a millennium. During the same period, there were twenty-four Emperors, five palace revolts, and three lineal changes associated with the Emperors of New Augusta. . . .

> —*Basic Hist-Tape*
> Hsein-Fer
> Karnak 4413

XLIV

The golden goddess glitters.

Glitters as she walks, glitters as she never glittered before, and the words she has not spoken dance across the dull air to shimmer from the darker corners created by her very presence in Sybernal. Seldom has she donned her aspect so blatantly in the city of gold sand beaches and eternal sunlight that comes from no sun and turns the seas golden-green at all hours. Seldom has she been seen in recent centuries, not since she was rumored to have consorted with the god who is and never was.

Yet she is, and she glitters as she walks from the Petrified Boardwalk down a narrow lane toward a narrower staircase. The women turn away without looking, and the men look and turn away, wishing they dared to look longer, but knowing that she has chosen the dark god, the one no one dares mention, and been rejected.

Inside the No-Name, a man dressed in black sits alone at a table. The row of tables nearest his is vacant, and the bar is slowly emptying. No one wears black in Sybernal, no one of Aurore, not without tempting the gods or the dark one, and the man in black does both.

A rumormonger who has seen better times mutters, "The Emperor kills the truth," before collapsing on the hardwood counter, and, yes, it is real hardwood, genuine steelbark from Sylvanium, that counter of the nameless bar where the media downers congregate, where they ignore the one called Martel who sits among them, where they tempt fate and gods by remaining in his presence.

Martel knows the collapsed one could not have been a

good newsie, not after spouting such garbage. The news itself kills truth, for the news media can never encompass all that happens and, by omission, present only a scattering of accurate facts sufficient to kill the truth. Rulers, among them Emperors and Viceroys, merely use the media's reported facts to ensure that the truth remains dead and buried.

In waiting, Martel has drunk too much Springfire, more than anyone should drink, he knows, and particularly more than he should drink. Still, he hesitates to change his metabolism to burn it off ... yet.

"Martel ..." The voice has a golden sound, but its fullness cannot quite hide the trace of silver bells beneath.

He turns and looks through the glitter. Even without the coruscating auras, the veil of glittermotes, and the projected sensuality, she is still impossibly impressive. Her natural, but genetically back-altered, golden hair streams over her shoulders like a cloak. The golden ruby of her lips and the clean lines of her still- and forever-young face combine with her tan and slenderness to strike a silence deeper than that at the bottom of the well of souls.

Martel, wishing again he could have remained merely a newsie, but knowing she had indeed sent him the three holos, ignores the temptation to see her as she wishes and concentrates on her as she is. Physically, of course, there is no difference, but, without all the attributes, she stands before him as a collection of clashing traits—the face of a girl with eyes that have seen Hell, the figure of a virgin with the body posture of experience, a complexion that demands dark hair with golden.

"Emily, Queen of Harlots and Whore of Gods, nice of you to pay your respects."

"Martel, your words have been nicer. Not to mention your actions."

The two newsies closest to the arched doorway scuttle through it and up the stairway into the light. Another crouches in the corner of his solitary booth.

Martel readjusts his metabolism, holds back the churning in his stomach, and wipes the instant sweat boils off his forehead as his system burns off the poisons he has so recently drunk from the jasolite beaker.

"That was then. When I was young and did not know you weren't, and when I had not learned the price. Not that I have yet paid it, but I will. Oh, I will."

"Not that one, I hope." She turns.

Martel watches, not quite ready to follow, not quite rid of the Springfire toxins.

The golden girl turns up her glitter, spraying the room with the hope that kills. The single woman, a caster from Path Five, sees that false hope and hates. Hates instantly, and dies nearly as instantly.

Martel reaches out with a twist of thought and readjusts her thoughts before her death is final, before she knows she has died. But he leaves the hatred. That is a personal matter.

Wiping off the last of the sweat-poison boils with a towel flown from across the bar, he stands away from his table and strides through the sparkling motes left by the golden girl, letting them cloak his black tunic and trousers for the instants before they understand what he is and expire.

Like a knife of night he cuts through the residues of the worthless hope left by Emily as he tracks her from the No-Name.

On the long beach called Beginning he finds her. On Aurore any beach can be a beginning, for it is on the beach that most who would be gods find their calling.

There are no shadows on the beach.

He ignores his thought and lets his steps take him to Emily, who watches the waves break, who holds her cloak of glittermotes to call attention and repel it.

His own shield of darkness wraps around him tighter than his cloak. The breeze swirls his black hair into patterns no geometrician would dare probe, but he ignores it.

"Still the same stolid Martel," observes Emily, releasing her cloak of lightmotes back into the field.

Martel looks through her shallow/deep gold eyes. Why did all those who merely accepted godhood have eyes, eyes that miss nothing but understand nothing?

Maybe that is the answer, he thinks.

"A thousand years, and you still think about eyes and philosophy?"

"How many thousand and you still don't?" he counters.

Shielded or unshielded makes no difference. Her powers have not grown.

Martel stands fractionally above the soft sand that would climb into his boots, given half a chance. The nouveaux riches of the Empire flock to Aurore to lie on the beaches, to tan, and to let the sand drift over and about them, hoping the god field would select them. And Martel stands above the sand, well above the salt.

"Philosophy is a substitute for power, or a rationale for not using it."

"Did you intrigue me out here just to insult me?" Martel knows he should have waited until Emily made her offer, whatever it is. But the time has passed, long passed, for him to take matters on her terms.

You think so?

Martel does not answer.

Emily gathers back her light cloak and draws upon the field. She expands until she is half again Martel's height, until she has a fistful of small lightnings within her right hand, until dark clouds swirl over the beach called Beginning.

Martel ignores the temptation and watches the always regular breakers coasting in to foam up on the square-lined beach that stretches kilos north and south.

The lightnings flash, and Martel accepts them, one by one, without flinching, without injury, and without expression.

From the depths of the field building around Emily comes the roaring whistle of tormented air emerging onto the sands into a sandspout that bears down on Martel. The winds die as they strike Martel, and the sands slough away.

Emily makes no other moves and says nothing. Martel is determined not to speak again.

Locking his time sense into a trance, he waits, personal defense screens alerted, only half conscious of his immediate surroundings as he feels the planet turn, if Aurore indeed is a planet, a fact contested by approximately 49.49567 percent of the physical scientists in the Empire to have studied Aurore.

Alone in his time-slowed thoughts, Martel again senses the wrongness of the beach, that wrongness he has glimpsed so many times before in passing, whether gathering background cubes for the CastCenter, or cloud-diving, or just in walking the Petrified Boardwalk.

Waiting for Emily, he ponders.

Pondering, he waits.

Multiple drains on the field around him prick his alert screens, and Martel flashes directly into double-speed awareness, without shifting a single muscle.

Item: Five full foci surround him.

Item: Emily hovers outside the pentagonal force lines.

Item: Sixteen standard hours have elapsed.

Item: All five of the foci circling him are asexual.

Never has Martel experienced an asexual focus. Theoretically, the user is either ancient or alien, but while alien gods are possible in theory, Martel has never run across one. Therefore, either the foci are ancient human-derived gods or artificial.

As a practical matter, neither is likely to be a danger, and Martel returns to normal awareness, increasing his circulation level to lessen the possibility of physical stiffness.

He blinks.

While he can sense the five foci, he can see none, only Emily hovering at an angle, her eyes shielded by her customary veil of glitter, emotions cloaked in a jangle of discordant projections.

Lust rolls in so strongly the beach air reeks of rancid trilia blossoms, so pungent that Emily would have cast a double shadow on any other planet.

Martel does not move.

"You still believe in all that ethical restraint," Emily notes as she touches down several body lengths in front of him.

"No. Or not exactly. I don't like being pushed into making decisions."

"Apollo wagered that you would break the elementals."

"And you bet I wouldn't?"

Emily makes a curious gesture in the air, and the five foci are reabsorbed into the field.

"You know, you do believe in ethical restraint. One

woman, one god, one set of beliefs, and that's what They're fearing."

Martel looks away, back at the thin edge of foam that coasts into the beach ahead of the waves.

Finally he speaks.

"Why now?"

"You've given Them a millennium. Isn't that enough?"

Since Emily never quite tells the whole truth, Martel makes the necessary translation. Apollo has finally decided that Martel is no danger and is moving against him. Either that, or Emily has decided that Apollo is no danger to Martel and is pressing Martel.

"Not necessarily."

Emily takes a step sideways, toward the water.

Martel casts around, but, outside of a few norms farther up the beach, they are alone. No gods or demigods are standing by.

"Why don't you go to Karnak, Martel?" suggests Emily.

"Why Karnak?"

Why indeed Karnak? Is she playing to your curiosity, Martel? Or trying to get you off Aurore, and away from the field?

Before he has finished the thought, the girl who glitters has bent the field and is half Aurore away, or playing with the dolphins in midocean, or reporting to Apollo.

He can go to Karnak or he can stay on Aurore.

That is not the question, but then, it never has been.

XLV

"Shuttle from the *Grand Duke Kirsten* now arriving at port ten. Passengers from Tinhorn, Accord, and Sahara. *Grand Duke Kirsten* at port ten."

One would have thought that the Viceroy would have retired the *Grand Duke* before having the former pride of the transport liners relegated to backwater runs. One might have thought, unless one knew the Viceroy. Even so, before long the *Grand Duke* would be scrap or an outsystem tramp with a new name.

Eventually, another *Grand Duke Kirsten* of the Imperial Western Flag Fleet would be built and christened—the fifth of the same name—and the cycle would repeat.

In the meantime, the fourth *Grand Duke* carries passengers on the Karnak–Tinhorn–Sahara–Accord quadrangle, and often carries far less than a full complement, for the schedule is more important than the profit, the regularity a quietly impressive reinforcement of Viceregal power cheaper than corresponding calls by appropriate fleets. Not that the fleets do not call . . . just that they call less frequently, but just as impressively as ever.

The first shuttle's passengers file down the sloping corridor toward the clearance officers and their fully instrumented cubicles.

One customs inspector fingers his power spray syringe, reviewing the small holo of a black-haired man with a young face and deep eyes, a face that seems to cast a shadow even through the holo cube. His partner should steer the man toward his station. Then it will be his job to complete the operation.

The killer, for that is an accurate description of his profession, paid as he is by the Assassins' Guild of Karnak, relaxes as he sees the man approach, mentally measures the distance between the unsuspecting traveler and his inspection console, and flexes his arm to ensure the proper function of the syringe hidden within his sleeve.

The victim wears black except for a silver triangle mounted on the plain black metal buckle of his black belt. He carries no luggage, not even a small carrying case or the effects pouch of a postulant.

The false inspector feels a twinge of unease, but stifles it with a cheerful call.

"This way, honored sir."

The traveler in black turns his gaze on the assassin, and the look alone sends a chill down the professional killer's spine, for the look is simply an acknowledgement of what is.

Nearly convulsively the assassin triggers the syringe.

For the first time in years, if ever, an assassin's weapon

fails, but the Guild insists on backup plans, and the man's hands flick to the clearance lights: green for clear, red for danger—smuggling, weapons, or attack.

Even while his hands are triggering the switch that will bring a red light while alerting the guards in the overhead blisters, he reaches for his own stunner, a special model designed to burn out enough nerves to render the question of survival academic.

The clearance light turns green, and the traveler turns to move through the opening portal to the open shuttle terminal, to Karnak itself.

Frantically the assassin jerks the stunner from inside the hidden pouch, levels it, and squeezes the firing stud. No energy flows from the circular tubes pointed at the back of the departing man in black, but the jolt to the killer's arm is enough to slam his fingers apart and let the fused hand weapon clatter on the hard flooring.

Though his arm looks intact, he cannot feel anything below the elbow.

The sound of the dropped stunner echoes through the rest of the receiving tunnel.

Three red lights blink on in the consoles above, one in each guard blister. The energy-concentration detectors focus on the heat of the discarded stunner, but the guards zero in on the figure standing above the weapon.

The assassin bites hard on a back tooth, one designed in a special way, but before the nerve poison can take full effect he collapses under three separate stun beams, one from each overhead blister.

The remaining travelers gingerly step around the twitching body, avoid looking down, and make their declarations to the other two customs officials.

The man in black does not look back.

After a time, the assassin's body is still, and, shortly, is removed. Three disposal units roll from a recess in the tunnel wall. The body is lifted into the first. The second sterilizes the floor and surrounding area. The third does nothing.

The last of the passengers from the *Grand Duke* steps around the three metallic units and presents her declaration to the sole customs officer left. By the time the clearance light has flashed green, the tunnel is empty, and the guards in their blisters have punched the standby studs, to wait for the next arrivals.

XLVI

May the wind rise in dusty rooms, rooms for sex and sensuality, and let us not call either a sin, for sinning is a term implying an absolute morality, and the gods of the Empire, the gods of Aurore, accept no morality and know no absolutes.

While they know no absolutes, they know well the power of belief in absolutes, and revel in that power.

While the winds of sex and not-sinning spin in quiet circles, rise and die, rise and die in polished sheets and damp skin, in eternal light and in eternal darkness, and in the grubby universe in between, the gods of Aurore gather upon the holy peak Jsalm.

Some glitter, like Emily, and some, like the Smoke Bull, wrap misty darkness around themselves like a cloak. Each has an individual aspect and an energy presence, but what these gods that are, beings that were, do with their appearance with the light and power they draw from the field matters little.

That they have all met on the sacred peak in person is what matters, for it was in the time of the immortal Viceroy's grandfather before the Empire of Man became the Empire of Light that they last gathered. Two have often met, perhaps three, even five, but never have all met since that time.

Apollo flares and bends the light around him, and the Smoke Bull snorts and casts little rings of darkness at the feet of those who manifest them.

"Martel has left," announces Apollo.

"Karnak," verifies the winged siren Direne, and the gods who are close enough to their maleness bend toward the lure of her voice.

Another goddess closes her eyes, thinks of her son, and wonders how soon before she will behold a leaden shield.

"I must think," thunders the hammer-thrower.

"Think ... think while you can, old throwback to antiquity," murmurs the Goat, his red eyes laughing at the prospect of chaos.

"Remember," adds Apollo, "he is still the undeclared god, and the hope of the hopeless, and all that implies."

... *and all that implies* ... The thought hangs over Jsalm long after the congregation has departed, long after they have turned their thoughts to the future, all but two, whose thoughts are on the past, and what it means.

XLVII

Martel wanders down the long parade of Emperors, past the glittering lights of the Everlight Palaces, past the modest coollights of the Longlife Homes, past even the Mausoleums of Remembrance, as the promenade narrows to a boulevard to an avenue to a street to a lane and to less than an alley among the hulks of empty walls.

One fully intact structure still stands, but the steps to the temple are barred by a laser screen. Organized religion has been banned on Karnak since the Great Upheaval, the greatness of that catastrophe attested to by the fact that not even the Empire dares to raze the temple of the Black One, only spend gigawatts of hard-earned power to shield the black marble columns with a robe of death-light.

The teletales of the sweepers flicker, throwing amber flashes on the tumbled walls outside the laser beams.

"Do I dare to touch the strings of time ... to taste the tartness of the lime ... to think no thoughts in rhyme." Martel stops. The words are in a tongue too old for even the databanks of the sweepers, and besides, the wench is not dead, but the ruler of the sweepers.

He studies the walls of fire before the temple and sighs.

" 'Tis hardest to refrain, and therein lies the paradox ... just a chatty old man you are, Martel, obsessed with your words, and knowing words are enough, and yet not enough."

He stares at the temple another long moment, then ignores the bones that crunch beneath his feet as he approaches the light knives that have claimed so many over the past millennium.

"Just a gesture, for old times' sake," he says, knowing that the banks of recorders will relay it all to the Viceroy of Karnak.

Wrapping the darkness tighter about him, he bends and picks up a jawbone, several teeth still intact, and thrusts it through the weaving net of lasers. The bone and teeth vanish in an acrid puff of smoke. Martel withdraws his untouched arm and black sleeve.

As the flashing of the teletales begins to build, the one who calls himself Martel strides into the shadows dripping from the shattered walls of the ancient dwellings that surround the Black One's temple. He is gone, gone even from the wide-angle, time-perfected spyeyes of the teletales.

XLVIII

The Viceroy watches the scene from the third teletale disc, and although the angle differs, the picture is the same. The stocky figure in black, white bone in the left hand, thrusts through the laser screens with a puff of smoke. The bone is gone, but he withdraws his untouched hand and arm and disappears into the shadows. None of the teletales have been able to catch the man's face.

"Tell me what you saw, Forde," commands the actual and titular ruler of Karnak, planet of long life and capital of the Western Reaches of the Empire of Light.

"I saw what you saw, Lady," answers the man in red, who has begun to resign himself to a drastic reduction in his life expectations.

She purses her lips, then laughs.

"Forde, you please me. That is one answer which I might accept."

Forde bows. Tall as he is, overtopping the slender figure

worn by the Viceroy, he is all too aware of how appearances deceive, all too aware his continuation rests on a patience that can be as short-lived as a laugh.

"You may go."

Forde bows again, and strides for the portal.

The Viceroy lifts her finger, then lowers it. Forde's second in command would have tried to answer the question. Better a clever schemer who knows his limits than an ambitious power-grabber who recognizes neither limits nor gods.

The man in black seemed familiar, whether she could see his face or not, and that bothers the Viceroy. The color black has unpleasant associations, reminding her of matters better left forgotten.

She represses a shudder. Perhaps she can again forget. Perhaps.

She touches the arm of the high chair that is not quite a throne.

"Query?" The well-modulated voice of the databanks forms in the empty space in front of her. She could use her screen faster than the vocal mode, but she isn't in the mood. Or she could link directly with the system, but that is not called for at the moment, she feels. Besides, she wants to be alone with her thoughts, and with the direct link she certainly does not feel alone.

"Linkage probabilities between the man in black at the temple of the Black One and the code file 'Interest Black'?"

The Throne Room is silent.

"Linkage between the recently observed man in black and the Black One variable, depending on validity of Kyre-Brackell hypothesis and associated Auroran phenomena. Range from thirty percent to eighty percent.

"Linkage between man in black and code file 'Interest Black' approaches unity.

"Linkage between the Black One and code file cannot be calculated.

"Further query?"

The Viceroy purses her lips once more.

Why would there be any linkage between the man in black and the Black One? But why would her sources on Aurore merely have suggested her agents assassinate the man in black? How had he managed the failure? For that alone he deserved to live, at least until she could discover if he had a certain method for beating the Guild. That she could use.

She frowns.

Why was his bearing familiar?

At last, she shakes her head. Maybe the familiarity was only an illusion, a similarity to someone else.

XLIX

Rydal and Commoron drift across the Lake of Dreams in a swanboat, a common swanboat with second-degree time-stretching and pleasure-lifting intensifiers. They thus prolong each instant into hours, trying to grasp the feeling of eternal life and youth.

The swanboats on the Lake of Dreams are all the two will know of long life or of centuries as frequent as sunrises. Rydal and Commoron are poor, limited to extensive wardrobes, limited in travel to the grand city of Karnak, limited to one "now," waiting for a death that will arrive long before the Viceroy has skimmed another millennium down the timetrack.

"I saw a streak of black along the far shore."

"No one walks that shore, Commoron. That's from the ruins of death."

"That's why I noticed it."

"You shouldn't be noticing such things now."

"Why doesn't the Viceroy," persists Commoron, "just level the Black One's temple?" She finishes with the symbol of the looped cross.

"Because," answers her lover, the poor Rydal, "the Black One remains trapped within the temple, like you're trapped within my boat."

Rydal ignores the fact that the swanboat is not his, as youths have done in all times and in all cultures.

"No one wears black on Karnak," Commoron muses.

"Then you didn't see a streak of black," he responds, before kissing her hand and drawing her to him.

The swanboats, including the one containing Rydal and Commoron, circle the Lake of Dreams on their preprogrammed patterns, twining their intricate paths for poor lovers clutching a moment out of time.

And yet . . . do those poor lovers know something in their blindness?

They do not. It only seems so, particularly to gods who are searching for humanity in a race that has never really had it.

Martel knows about the swanboats and favors them with a glance as he walks the ruinshore side of the Lake of Dreams, the side he had never walked as a student. He inhales the too-strong scent of trilia and novamella that crosses the water from the pleasure groves on the opposite side, beyond the dreaming couples in the swanboats.

Too much of a scent, like too much power, often has the wrong effect.

He smiles at the thought, but the smile is not a pleasant one, for his eyes are cold.

The Viceroy's Palace is at the far end of the lake, where the dark water lightens into the brilliant blue bay and where the sun always shines, even when it has set.

The swanboats do not go nearly that far, milling around as they do near the end of the Avenue of Emperors, not nearly far enough from a small square and a jet-black temple that has resisted a millennium and more of the Empire's best weapons.

The temple is guarded only because it could not be destroyed, not without taking most of the city with it, and neither the Regent nor the Grand Duke had wished that, not when the Park of Summer had already been destroyed by the Dark One and the Tree of Darkness.

The Dark One has not been seen since, excepting reports that He has reappeared on Aurore and will return to His true believers. Or reports that he has appeared on Tinhorn, or Mardreis, or Sileom, or any one of a hundred worlds outside the mainstream of the Empire.

In the interim, neither age nor weapons have changed the

temple, and the faithful still worship, though no litany exists, nor any true priests.

Martel knows these facts and quickens his pace. The Viceroy is waiting.

L

The Viceroy has a name, not that anyone has dared to use it since the Great Upheaval. She is addressed as "Lady" and other honorifics by those who must answer to her, and in other terms by those who do not.

She bites her lower lip as she gazes from her window at the morning light playing upon the blue waters of the great Lake of Dreams.

The fallen one, the man in black who is more than he seems, will arrive shortly. Of that she is certain.

Turning from the wide unglassed and open window, through which nothing but light and clean air can pass, she takes a deep breath. This day, the palace has given the air the delicate scent of sand fir.

She returns to pondering the matter of the man in black. What remains most uncertain is the purpose for which he has left Aurore and come to Karnak. His modesty also bodes ill, for the gods of Aurore, who have seldom returned to the Empire, are not known for their modesty.

The last time a god came to the people, rather than the other way around, led to the revivals that led to the Great Upheaval and the downfall of the Prince Regent. The Viceroy's edict banning organized religion still stands, although the temples, shrines, and churches are open to all—except for the one black marble temple. Anyone can worship any god, or none, but there are no priests and no services.

The precautions have worked for a thousand years.

Still . . . she shivers.

Why would anyone want to leave being a god to come back to risk death, or destruction, at the hands of the Empire?

She has no doubts that the full firepower of an Imperial

battle cruiser will turn the strange man in black to ashes and
vapor—at least away from Aurore.

So why does he court death?

Or does he?

Is that flicker of black along the far side of the lake the
man-god she expects? So soon?

She speaks to the empty air.

"A man in black will arrive shortly. I will see him as soon
as he arrives."

"Yes, Lady."

The Viceroy taps a series of studs on the wide gold belt she
wears, and she is enveloped in a coruscation of auras, each a
defense against some form of attack. She is merely testing the
system; the triggers are automatic.

The room she enters and paces is not the largest in the
Viceroy's Palace. Only a pinnace could be safely hangared
within, and the weapons that the unseen guard operators can
bring to bear on any intruder would destroy any such pinnace
as well.

Comforting herself with that thought, the cold-eyed Viceroy looks from the lake vista on the far wall to the creme-
golden hangings of the room and the gentle arch of the high
ceiling.

Should she take her seat upon the raised dais, or should she
greet the fallen one in midroom?

She decides on informality, sacrificing some of the defenses contained within the dais.

She hopes the man in black will come soon. One way or
another she can dispose of the issue, perhaps of the man, and
clear her mind for the everyday schemes necessary to keep
Karnak supplying the bodies for the Fleet, the souls for the
arts, and the young aristocrats for amusement.

Waiting, the Viceroy ponders.

Aurore, planet of eternal dawn, home of the gods, and ref-
uge for independent newsies—pondering these, Kryn does
not know which aspect of Aurore she likes least. Rulers dis-
trust dawns, gods, and independent information media, and
Aurore hosts all three.

The Lady who holds an Empire shivers and waits, knowing

she is wasting time, afraid she will recognize the man-god? in black, and afraid she will not.

"The gentleman in black has arrived and is ascending. I asked his name, but he only said he was expected."

"Thank you. Put all internal defense systems on full alert."

"It is done, Lady."

That alone would set the firevine burning with gossip, she reflects. She had not ordered full internal defenses since the previous State visit of the Prince a century earlier. Internal defenses against a man whose only attribute is sleight of hand while wearing black clothing?

Is he really the fallen one, the undeclared one, that even the gods of Aurore are rumored to oppose? The one who escaped the Assassins' Guild and her own sweepers' scans? Can she be sure? The port records missed that one's face also.

Too many questions—for that reason alone the Viceroy must see the man in black. As a Lady she is also curious. A good millennium has passed since a man has refused her his name. The last had not fared well. She smiles at the recollection, and her eyes glitter ice-bright.

She half turns at the internal warning of his approach.

The man is stocky, but not big, nor overweight, and the top of his head reaches only to the shoulders of the guardsmen who flank him into the room.

The guards halt at the arched entrance. Martel walks straight ahead to meet the Viceroy.

"Lady, a pleasure to see you again after all these years."

She smiles, even with the icy stab of fear that penetrates her. She remembers not his face, but knows she should. She cannot recall the last time she forgot an important face.

"I confess I do not recall our last meeting," she returns with a smile that includes her eyes but not her heart.

"That is not surprising, Lady. It has been some time."

He bends to touch his lips to the back of her extended hand.

"Will you continue the mystery or enlighten me before we proceed?"

"I notice you still have the lasers around the old temple," he comments.

"Yes. I see no reason to remove them. They do serve a useful purpose in attracting those who believe in death." She realizes the man will not give his name until he is ready.

"You admit that your subjects still respect death?"

"There will always be those who reject life."

"Life and death are one and the same, Lady. After more than a millennium, you certainly should recognize that."

Something about his words bothers her, rings the faint chimes of a distant memory, a cold and faraway recollection of a time before . . .

She inclines her head to the side, noncommittally.

Martel sees her struggling with the memories she has suppressed. All souls have their price. All power is bought with the stuff of the soul and paid in pain. Martel had not wanted oblivion, only occasional forgetfulness, bought with a jasolite beaker and the routine of a practicing newsie/faxer.

Never has he been more conscious, never has he realized . . .

. . . *how much Kryn and Emily are alike . . . almost as if . . .*

He thrusts the thought aside. That price he cannot pay, not now.

Martel also knows Kryn will not accept him, readies himself, drawing his cloak of darkness from the closet of time around the corner from now, preparing to use it at the proper instant.

"The Empire would not have survived without you and without Aurore and its gods, Lady and Viceroy. But the time has come for the people to accept both death and life and to create their own idols and their own rules.

"Have we not had time enough to accept that, Kryn Kirsten?" He almost added the words "my love," for she has been once, when the Lake of Dreams was the Park of Summer, and the Prince Regent had ruled Karnak.

"Strike!"

Pale skin blanching, she triggers her own shields and the palace's full internal defense/attack systems. As she begins to glow in her cocoon of energy, before the lasers flash and the disruptors scream, the hall is filled with blackness.

"Martin Martel, my god." But her words are lost in the fury that fills the blackness.

By the shore of the Lake of Dreams, Martel studies the Viceroy's Palace.

The faint green corona shifts fractionally toward the blue as the internal defense systems continue squandering millions of energons trying to destroy a man who isn't even inside the palace.

Martel begins his stroll back toward the black temple, this time along the populated and fashionable side of the lake, his feet not touching the silver sands, his black cloak flapping in the breeze like ravens' wings.

As the golden dust inside the Receiving Hall of the Viceroy's Palace finished settling into a golden carpet, as the massive heat exchangers lower the temperature to where an unmodified mortal can exist unshielded, and as the various devices within the walls begin to re-create the golden hangings and the furniture that had been turned to dust, the Viceroy releases her shields.

"I take it Martel escaped," she notes to no one in particular or to the empty air.

"No person was in the room besides yourself at the instant the disruptors focused."

She turns to the lake vista again, neither frowning nor smiling, to see if she can discern a flicker of black.

"Martel . . ."

The word dies softly in the empty hall.

LI

"He has retraced the steps of the Fallen One," observes the Goat, shedding light as a proof sheds water.

"Is *he* the Fallen One?" questions a demigod at the edge of the circle that hovers above the sacred mountain.

"How?" snorts the Smoke Bull. "When the Fallen One toppled the Regency, Martel was an apprentice newsie who had just fled the Grand Duke."

"But the holos?"

"Holos be flamed! And you, too!" With that the god who has chosen the Bull (or perhaps it is the opposite, for on Aurore those things which are lies elsewhere may be true) makes an unnecessary gesture and trusses the outspoken demigod in ropes of dark smoke that drag the impertinent to the golden-green depths of the ocean. He will emerge a decade or so hence, reflects the Smoke Bull, chastened, strengthened, and more aware of his position.

Apollo releases his hold on the rays of dawn, channels them, and stands, basked in their glow, at the center of the circle.

Cooperatively the Smoke Bull places a wreath of darkness in the air at Apollo's feet, and the brilliance of the scene creates a contrast only a grand master could fully appreciate, or convey. But there are no mortals present, and the talents of the gods do not run to mere depictions of their realities. This scene, like so many behind history, will go unpainted, unholoed, unrecorded.

"I am not concerned with what has happened, but with what may happen," begins Apollo, his musical baritone cascading down and out from the mountain.

By the time his voice reaches the resort town of Pamyra, with its homes clustered around the cove fifteen thousand meters below, all that remains is a series of carillon notes, a gentle melody that the locals have called the organ of the gods.

Apollo knows this, has cultivated his voice, and is not displeased.

"For I have monitored the field, and Martel is not drawing on it, though he maintains his link. Yet large mounts of energy are being expended in Karnak, and they center on Martel."

"Certain?" questions Emily, as curt among the gods as seductive among mortals. Deadly in both places.

"You are welcome to check yourselves. I merely call it to your attention."

"Let me summon my chariot and my hammer and end this nonsense," growls the bearded hammer-thrower, and his voice rumbles down the mountainside.

"As you please," murmurs Apollo. He sweeps his arm to encompass the group. "Should we send Thor after Martel, the hammer-thrower after the hammer?"

"Chaos!" exclaims the Goat, and his hidden red eyes dance. His meaning is not understood, or ignored. Or ignored.

"A hunt," whispers the other Huntress, savoring the blood that has not been shed . . . yet.

The handful of demigods, recalling the example of outspokenness that preceded the discussion, either nod in agreement or make no gesture.

"I will wait," mutters the Smoke Bull, and the storm clouds spin from his words.

"Then it is decided?" asks Apollo, though his tone is rhetorical.

"Decided!" claims Emily.

"Decided," adds the Huntress.

"Decided," agrees the Goat. "Decided in chaos."

The others say nothing, either through their voices or their powers. A demigod wrestles in the bottom of the sea with chains of darkness, and a tidal wave smashes the first line of houses on the beach at Pamyra, the ones reserved for the rich tourists.

"Agreed," rumbles the god of the thunder, summoning his chariot with a bolt of lightning.

"Agreed."

Decided and agreed. The thought echoes from the darkness beyond Aurore, splinters the light corona around Apollo, and vibrates in the minds of the gods and demigods.

. . . decided and agreed . . .

Emily looks at Apollo, who turns to the Smoke Bull. Their eyes meet, but not their thoughts.

Thor ignores the thought and the three and vaults into his chariot for the trip to Karnak. The goats paw at empty air, and the battle cart is gone.

LII

CLING!

The off-key alarm note of the system jolts her awake instantly. Catlike, she stretches and keys into the full command network even before pulling her lean body into the golden singlesuit.

"Report!"

"Discontinuity. Class four. Vector Aurore to Karnak. Nondrive." The disembodied voice goes directly into her nervous system through the command implant, but she prefers to believe she has "heard" it.

"Ship class?" she snaps, though a subvocalization would have been sufficient.

"Nondrive. No characteristics of known ships."

"Defenses on full alert. Response only. Response only, I repeat.

"From Aurore?" she mutters, forgetting to downgrade the commlink.

"From Aurore, Lady."

The Viceroy downplays the link and finishes drawing on the singlesuit. The full defense belt follows, then boots.

After splashing cool water over her face, patting it dry with the old-fashioned towel, she runs the styler over her hair, adjusts her complexion, and steps from her sleeping rooms into the lift shaft to the command center beneath the palace.

While she plummets, her hands recheck her defense field, and her fingers tap the belt studs one by one, touching the smooth-gritty controls with the force of ingrained habit, hardly noticing the conflicting tactile sensations produced by the smaller field that surrounds the belt itself.

The energy barrier barring the entrance to Karnak's defense center flickers green as she passes through. With the same flicker, it could annihilate anything short of a full battle cruiser not attuned to the screen.

"Lady, the center is ready," offers Forde.

"What is it?"

"The source of the discontinuity, you mean?" Forde frowns and lowers a shoulder toward the Marshal for Strategy, who stands a half-pace behind him.

"Ah ... yes ... Lady and Viceroy ... the discontinuity. Could be caused by several phenomena—a new type of ship, a natural occurrence unobserved before, a generator malfunction in an existing ship ..." His voice drags to a halt in the face of the Viceroy's glare.

"Exactly how likely are any of those ridiculous possibilities?"

"Almost nil," admits Forde, smoothing a wrinkle in the front of his rumpled red tunic.

"Something to do with the gods of Aurore?" suggests the Viceroy, twitching her nose in a frown.

Forde backs off a pace, realizing his fear-drenched sweat may have reached her. He wipes his forehead with the back of his left hand, his right hand resting on the controls of his own shields—futilely, should the Viceroy have decided to terminate his position or him.

"A possibility, admittedly," offers the Marshal. "The measured field strength might be possible, although, as you know, we have been unable to obtain any accurate readings on the powers of the so-called gods of Aurore, and, so far as we know, none has ever left Aurore."

"If this is one, Marshal, he or she will be the third," snaps the Lady.

The Marshal darts a look at Forde. Forde wipes his forehead again.

The Viceroy ignores both, steps around the two, and takes a quick dozen steps into the master control consoles and screens.

Is Martin Martel really the newsie/demigod/god named Martel? Or is Martel the god toying with her? Has he come to repay debts, old debts?

She shivers. Forde has followed her quickly enough to catch the gesture, but draws back again, wiping his sweat-streaming face. The control center air is cool, scented with lemon-orange.

Forde wipes his forehead again as the Viceroy's fingers run over the power displays.

The Marshal steps toward the board, theoretically his to command physically under the direction of the Viceroy.

Forde's long arm comes up with a snap to stop the military officer's second step. The Marshal opens his mouth, looks at Forde, then at the stiff back of the woman controlling the center, and shuts his mouth without uttering a word.

"Very sensible, Forde. Very sensible. You gentlemen may sit on the wing consoles, or leave, as you please."

Forde eases into the left wing observer's chair, the Marshal into the right.

The screen is centered on the airspace above the temple of the Fallen One, ten kilos east of the palace.

"Nothing yet to see," comments the Viceroy. "According to the energy board, some minor but nonsystemic sources are building."

"Götterdämmerung," mutters the Marshal, dredging the reference from he knows not where.

"Not exactly. More like . . ." The Viceroy halts. She wants to say Armaggeddon, but that is not it either. She sniffs. The faintly musky odor is not Forde. Rather Lady Kryn. She is afraid, and she withholds the shiver the thought could bring.

Why?

The questions leap into her head again. One she lets stay. After all, Martel had worn black. Why does she fear men in black? Why poor Martin Martel?

Except—is he still poor Martin Martel, penniless Regent's Scholar? Or does that Martin even exist? Or was he dust a millennium ago? Who is the real Martel? Does she really want to know?

A locator arrow flicks to the bottom of the screen before her, identifying a new and building energy concentration. Her eyes dart toward the red arrow, and the black dot it identifies.

"Magnification," she says quietly, heart pounding nonetheless.

She centers the screen on the dot she recognizes as Martel even before the picture is fully focused.

"The same one," whispers Forde to the Marshal.

The Marshal frowns, then raises his line-thin black eyebrows in a question, as if to ask which one.

Another locator arrow flares, and the Viceroy splits the main screen into two views. The right-hand view holds Martel in dead center, standing inside the laser screens of the temple of the Fallen One on the steps. The left-hand vision refocuses on an object sweeping out of the dawn sun.

"Goats," mumbles Forde.

"A god of Aurore, apparently," observes the Viceroy, her voice but a fraction tighter than normal, the tension unnoticed by either subordinate.

Both Forde and the Marshal stare, wide-eyed, at the apparition that fills the left screen.

Two goats, each the size of a bison, red-eyed and yoked to a four-wheeled bronze cart, paw their way through the cloudless morning skies. A red-haired, red-bearded man, armored and complete with pointed and horned helmet, leans forward in the cart and brandishes a graystone hammer in his right hand. In his left are the red leather reins.

The Regent's hands suddenly begin to play across the power controls.

CLANG! CLANG! RED ALERT! RED ALERT! FULL DEFENSE SCREENS! FULL DEFENSE SCREENS!

Another call goes to the Fifth and Seventh Fleets, not that they could accomplish anything in the space above the Vice-regal city itself, but Kryn knows they will be of help after the clash between the two gods. And their records may be of great assistance in documenting the power of the gods of Aurore.

The lights in the control center flicker.

"All power sources outside the palace screens have been diverted," reports the power center.

"Diverted? Where?" As she speaks she realizes the stupidity of the question. Martel would be grabbing power from wherever he can find it, and that may not be enough if Thor, assuming he is a god from Aurore, can draw on the entire field from that distance.

Half the controls before her are dead. Nothing outside the palace shields is operative.

She watches, merges the two screen visions into one as the

goat cart swings down out of the rising sun toward a black marble temple and a man in black. Watches, fists clenched at her sides, not knowing what outcome she wants, not knowing if either outcome is what she wants.

LIII

The Hammer
of Darkness

Though the wind joy-sings, it's a long way from here.
Though the boughs whisper, they whisper of fear.
Though the leaves linger, they lean to the wind,
And the wind, it is colder for those who have sinned.
The wind it is colder; the wind it is cold;
The wind it is colder for those who have sinned.

The ravens are winging; their wings are so black.
The lightnings are singing; the sun is turned back.
The storm clouds are drawing; the sun grows so dim;
And the dark god is coming; I know it is Him!
The dark god is coming; the dark god is coming;
The dark god is coming; I know it is Him!

Up on the hillside, where the grasses are gold,
The blossoms will fold to the touch of the cold.
The grasses love sunshine; the trees love the shade;
But neither will stand to the cold He has made.
But neither will stand to; neither will stand;
But neither will stand to the cold He has made.

The sunshine we've prayed for, but here comes the night.
The darkness is gathering to blot out the light.
The hammer of darkness will fall from the sky;
The old gods must fly, and the summer will die.
The old gods must fly; the old gods must fly;
The old gods must fly, and the summer will die.

Though the wind joy-sings, it's a long way from here.
Though the boughs whisper, they whisper of fear.
Though the leaves linger, they lean to the wind.
And the wind, it is colder for those who have sinned.
The wind it is colder; the wind it is cold;
The wind it is colder for those who have sinned.

> —Hymn, Church of the Fallen One
> Composer unknown

LIV

Martel waits. Stands on the temple steps. On the steps of the temple where he slept through the night, slept knowing the hammer-thrower has been dispatched after him, carrying the mandate of the gods, particularly of Apollo and Emily.

He does not question how he knows what transpired above Jsalm. Knowing is enough. The time to question will be later, if there is a later. As he feels the instrument of vengeance draw near, he prepares to accept the blows of the hammer-thrower.

One does not fight the blows of a single old god, not when the field of Aurore is massed behind that tottering old god. One fights all the gods.

The goat chariot clatters out of the sun, a black point in the white-gold circle of light, wheels spinning backward, and hums battle chants from a warriors' tongue forgotten longer than the languages of the obscure poets Martel has made a practice of quoting.

Thrummm! Thrummm, da-dum, da-dumm.

Martel hears the rhythm. Smiles. Husbands the energy he had drawn from his confrontation with the Lady Kryn, readies his shunts from the Viceroy's power system, and holds his darkness for the assault.

Thrumm! Thrumm, da-dumm, da-dummm.

The sound is nearer, and it rattles the looser shutters of the battered gray villas that border the black temple.

Thrummm! Thrummm, da-dum, da-dummm.

The sun darkens, though no clouds mar the blue-green of the morning sky. The Viceroy has activated the city's defense screens.

"Hsssst! Hssst!"

The breathing of the battle goats falls like rain across the pavements of the city of the Viceroy, each fragment carrying a sparkle of light that breaks as it strikes the ground or hard surface.

The sun flickers again as the goat chariot and its master hurdle through the defense screens, haloed in the energy that bathes them momentarily.

A violet pencil of light leaps from a hidden emplacement, stabs at the bearded god, touches the cart, its bronze bosses, its time-darkened wood.

The god, for it is Thor, and his graystone hammer is mighty, lifts that hammer, points it, but does not trouble himself to release it. Along the path he has pointed, back along the searing violet, strikes a bolt of lightning.

The violet light knife is no more, and above the blackened hole a small thunderstorm gathers, raining metal among the boiling water that it drops.

"Behold! Behold!" thunders Thor, his eyes burning red, his beard flaming. "Oppose not the gods!"

His words crash across the city. Two dozen men, five women, and three children die instantly from the sonic concussion. Another 231 will be permanently deaf unless major auditory surgery is performed.

"I oppose," says Martel, standing on the steps of the small black temple, and his words, scarcely more than a whisper, reverberate through Karnak, even into the sealed chambers of the Viceroy, even through the triple screens of the core-tap power stations, even into the brains of those who cannot hear, and into the awareness of those who cannot reason.

The thunderstorms, the fire vortex, and the glitter rain of the battle goats dissolve into mist at the words of the man in black.

"OPPOSE NOT THE GODS! NOR THE HAMMER OF THOR!" thunders the hammer-thrower. The chariot of the ages and its hiss-breathing goats veer leftward as they rumble down toward the temple.

Another group of unfortunates, somewhat larger now that the thunder-god is near atop the city, perish.

"I oppose."

And again, the quiet words soothe the injured, damp the thunderstorms, and enrage the hammer-thrower of Aurore.

"THEN PERISH! FALLEN ONE! RETURN WHENCE YOU CAME! *BEGONE!*"

Thor does not gesture this time. He throws his hammer, that mighty graystone hammer, and he hurls it full at the stocky man in black, who stands upon black marble steps, at that man who would seem slight beside the burliness of the ancient god. In that moment, the sun flickers, and brightens.

The hammer falls. Falls like thunder, falls like the point of massive lightning. Falls like death.

The city shakes, as if wrenched by the grasp of a wounded earth giant. Roofs crack, split asunder. Waves on the Lake of Dreams swamp the empty swanboats, spend their force in inundating the gardens bordering the lake.

The ancient oaks, brought light-years to serve no purpose but the whim of a departed Prince, bend. Bend more, then, as one, snap in two like dry sticks across a kindler's knee.

The yellow light flowers lining the paths from the lake to the palace flare, then crumble into black dust.

The lights of the city fail. Fail, reeling from the stroke of the graystone hammer. Reeling from the power of an ancient god. And darkness pounces, from house to hovel to villa to palace.

Across the void, behind a golden field, on a planet that is not a planet, the cast of the graystone hammer is felt by those gathered in the air above a sacred mountain. Two gods, a goddess, and a scattering of demigods nod. A certain shore trembles with the turning of a chained being in the depths below.

In the last nanoseconds before the hammer reaches Martel, the villas around the black temple, their walls already flattened and scattered, are pulverized into particles, and the gray dust rises. Rises to block the receptor screens, to shield the view of the teletales, those few that are self-powered and still functioning.

Before her screens, a woman finds her view blanked by the

swirled dust. The Viceroy finds tears upon her cheeks, tears unsummoned. Tears unknown since before the fall of the Prince Regent, tears unknown in a millennium.

Somewhere, a red-haired child sobs.

The man in red smashes a balled fist into his left palm, shaking his head, unaware of the shower of sweat that flies from him.

The chariot, battle goats pawing, circles the cloud of gray dust, passes over the miles of rubble and fallen towers. Thor leans over, his eyes trying to pierce the gloom where his senses cannot penetrate. His right hand is empty, though his left grasps the red leather of the reins more tightly.

He gestures with his empty right hand, calls for his hammer.

The chariot circles, a vulture above the ruins of the Vice-regal city.

The Viceroy waits, not understanding, hoping.

The man in red leans forward as the dust settles.

The sun dims, then flares even brighter, and as the dust cloud parts, the black temple emerges. Stands. Stands untouched.

"I oppose."

On the temple steps remains the man in black—not smaller, not larger, not darker, not brighter. He does not smile, nor does he frown.

In his left hand is a graystone hammer.

Martel lifts the hammer, lifts it high above his head.

"I oppose the ways of the gods, and I will break you as I will break your hammer. Behold, agent of the gods, and god no more. Behold. This hammer is your life and your strength, and it is no more."

Martel squeezes the haft, and as he does the wood cracks and the stone shatters, and the shards crumble into dust.

Thor shakes his fist at Martel, turns his battle goats and the chariot into a dive toward the man in black.

"I am of the Fallen One," admits Martel conversationally, and yet his words carry through the ruins of the city. "And the Fallen One will not be denied. Nor will He be mocked. Your hammer is gone, Thor, and you have no power over me."

The chariot is almost upon Martel, and the hiss of the battle goats is rain in his ears.

"Guess we have to make it formal, old thunder-god."

He raises his left hand again and cracks his voice like lightning across the morning.

"Begone! Forever!"

With the words flows a tidal wave of blackness. When the darkness subsides, moments later, the sky is empty.

The steps of the black temple, the only fully intact structure in the city of the Viceroy, are vacant, and the sirens begin to wail as the power returns.

LV

Martel appears in the cart, his feet planted shoulder-width apart.

The battle goats do not seem to mind, but continue their hissing breath as they paw meaninglessly at the blackness beneath their hooves.

Martel glances around the square wooden cart. In the corner floor bracket beneath his right shoulder is a built-in quiver, originally bronze, but dulled with a green patina. The horn bow is stringless and would doubtless break if strung, since Thor had never liked archery before he became god of thunder, let alone after.

If he could smell in the undertime, Martel knows, the goat cart would reek of age, and dust. Not of goat urine, for the battle goats are not goats at all, but focal elementals, harnessed through the field of Aurore.

He sighs, more of a mental reaction than a physical one, because purely physical actions really do not take place in the subwarp/subtime/subspace corridor that the gods have drilled for Thor's transit and return. With his own methods, Martel could already have been on Aurore. But then, he could not have returned as Thor.

His hair goes from black to red and lengthens. A full red

beard appears. His stockiness becomes burliness, and were he to speak, his voice would rumble.

Martel is Thor.

Presently the chariot emerges above the sacred mountain, begins a circling descent.

Martel remembers one last detail, conjures up a graystone hammer, and brandishes it, much as Thor would have done.

On the peak, or rather hovering above it, in an unnecessary expenditure of energy, reflects Martel/Thor, are Apollo, the Smoke Bull, and Emily. Assorted demigods wait beyond them.

All for the conquering hero. He blocks the thought. Thor would have thought it only his just due.

"The traitor is no more!" rumbles the returning thundergod. "He fell under the Hammer of the Gods!"

Thor vaults across the railing of the goat cart, dispatches it to an outer circle to wait, and takes three giant steps across the cloud tops toward the triad.

"Welcome back, Thor," murmurs the Smoke Bull, the darkness falling from his mouth with the words.

"Welcome," adds Apollo. And his voice chimes down the mountainside to ring through the towns below.

Emily nods. Curtly.

"No welcome from you?" growls the returned warrior. "Ah," he chortles, "but you were once fond of him."

He turns toward Apollo.

"Martel was a danger. But he didn't gloat about destruction." The words of the goddess ring in the stillness.

Thor turns back.

"Bitch goddess. Talk not to me of gloating. Talk not to me when more blood has flowed from your hands and your names than mine. Thor am I. Thor am I! Hammer and lightning, like the thunderstorms."

"Rather eloquent, Thor," adds Apollo. "Didn't know you had it in you."

"Thor?" asks Emily. "Answer one question. Did you actually see the hammer strike Martel?"

"He was there. The hammer struck, and he was not. Same as always. No draw on the field since."

"What about Karnak?"

"Flattened," admits Thor, shrugging. "You knew that would happen."

Emily frowns, and Apollo, seeing her expression, clears his throat. Even the half-cough is somehow musical.

"Is it possible, barely possible, Thor, honored hammer-thrower, that Martel ducked your blow?"

"I say he was under the hammer, and he was gone. Never has anyone escaped the graystone hammer! *Never!* NEVER!"

The three gods wince as the thunderclouds roll in at his voice, and a small tornado touches the edge of Pamyra, destroying an unoccupied cottage.

"Then it is possible," observes the Smoke Bull. "Else Thor would not be so angry."

"You old fraud!" screeches Emily. "You had him, and you missed him. Destroyed a beautiful city for nothing! Made a fool out of the gods, and left the Viceroy ready to declare war on the entire Aurore system."

"YOU LIE!" rumbles Thor, and he lifts the hammer.

"Wait!" commands Apollo, and both Emily and Thor turn to the chimes of his speech.

"Thor *may* have destroyed Martel, and he may not have. But one thing is clear. If Martel escaped and did not again confront Thor, then he does fear the hammer. Since the hammer is but one attribute of the gods, Martel may be a difficulty, but one we can handle should he reappear."

"I destroyed him," insists Thor.

"You did not," returns Emily.

"It does not matter," observes the Smoke Bull. "Apollo is right. Whether Thor destroyed Martel, or whether Martel escaped at the last instant, the result is that Thor was the stronger. Thor, by himself."

Emily almost snickers, understanding the implication behind the Smoke Bull's words.

Thor raises his hammer again.

"Put down your toy, Thor. *I* do not fear your hammer, though Martel may."

Thor glares at the Smoke Bull, raises his left hand to recall the chariot, then faces Emily.

"Bitch, best you fear the hammer of Thor!"

"Is that a challenge, old blusterer?"

Thor vaults into the chariot without answering, brandishes his hammer, and the battle goats careen across the heaven-field of Aurore, away from the sacred peak Jsalm.

"I'm not sure that sending Thor was the best idea, after all," muses Apollo.

"How soon before we can confirm what he said?" asks the god of black smoke and guile.

"You don't believe him?"

"Only that he flattened the city. No communications from Karnak."

"Why doesn't one of you go to Karnak and see?" snaps Emily.

Apollo shakes his head.

"If Thor is telling the truth, there's no need. If he isn't, then we can't afford to leave Aurore to find out."

"I'll take care of that," says Emily, "with Thor."

"Can you?" asks Apollo.

But Emily is gone, and only the glitter at the end of the rainbow remains, fading moments after she has left.

"One way or the other, you win, Apollo."

"Not if Thor wins."

"No. We both lose then. A pity about Martel. Could have been a real help, if he'd only thought more about it. Too tied up in the worldly things."

"I wonder. I wonder."

"A little late for that, now."

The two depart, each in his own fashion, and, following them, so do the demigods.

The clouds above the sacred peak are empty, and without the gods to shield, they dissipate to allow the faithful below to worship.

From Pamyra, the conical peak glows green above the shadowed slopes, for the one thing that differentiates the sacred mountain, besides its sacredness, is that its upper slopes are cloaked in shadow, unlike any other peaks on Aurore.

Thor is not hard to find, Emily discovers.

Hammer resting on his knees, the thunder-god stares down at the waves crashing against the sheer quartz cliffs that stretch kilos east and west from his vantage point. His location, across the Midland Sea from the Sacred Mountain, is scarcely hidden, though neither Apollo nor the Smoke Bull has ever cared for the White Cliffs. The Goat can sometimes be found nearby.

"It was a challenge, Thor."

The hammer-god does not acknowledge her presence, nor even the concentration of energy that the golden goddess, mistress of the rainbow, gathers about her.

"A challenge, Thor," she snaps.

"No, bitch." He lets the hammer fall as he stands, and it vanishes. "No challenge. You followed the behest of Apollo and the Minotaur to carry out the execution of another of their enemies. You, who could rule an Empire, cannot rule yourself."

"Flame, Thor. Apollo and the Bull rule Aurore. No one stands against them. Not Martel, not me, not you."

Thor smiles, and the smile does not suit him.

"None so blind as will not see, bitch goddess. None so deaf as will not hear."

"Quoting Martel won't help either, old blusterer."

Thor shrugs, unfastens the great bronze clasps that hold his bearskin cloak, and lets the skin drop. A gust from the sea wind carries it high over the waves.

A gesture from the hammer-thrower, and the cloak bunches, becomes a dark bird that spreads its wings and glides toward the calmer water out beyond the ridge of black rock over which the solid gold-green waves are breaking.

Emily laughs. The harsh notes knife the harmony of the surf noises. As she draws the colors to her the brilliance of the rainbow glitters, iridesces, mounts to eye-sear, a small nova at the top of the White Cliffs.

Two hundred fifty kilometers across the Midland Sea, the priests at the temple in Pamyra note the strange light and genuflect.

The rock under the feet of the golden goddess puddles, and she stands in a pool of molten stone.

"Very pretty, bitch, but is one supposed to be impressed?"

You talk too much, Thor!

The thought lances at Martel with the power of an Imperial battle cruiser.

You have forgotten nothing and learned nothing, Emily,

*and for that you shall pay. Pay with your memories, pay with
service, and pay for the love that has left your soul.*

Strong thoughts . . . And her sending falters.

*Where is my hammer, Emily? Where is my lightning? And
yet bind you will I in darkness, and in time, and away from
all you hold dear.*

A small sunburst crashes against Thor's shoulders. He does
not even bend, but darkness rises from the White Cliffs beneath his feet and through his hand toward the miniature sun
that is a goddess. As the blackness flows toward her the pool
of molten rock traps her feet as it freezes, holds her like a fly
in amber.

Thor takes one step toward the sun that has dwindled to a
rainbow, then another.

Who are you? Who . . . what . . .

The clifftop is empty. No sign remains of the two, except
three black footprints in the white rock leading toward a perfectly white and perfectly circular depression melted into the
stone.

A single raven, not native to Aurore, circles, then flaps
over the waves inland toward the lowlands.

LVI

The woman wakes, shaking, from a nightmare. The details
fade even as she tries to recall them.

Her hair is long and black, her waist narrow, breasts high
but adequate, certainly not small, nor large enough to merit
the term voluptuous.

All her physical characteristics, from golden eyes to lightly
tanned skin, from black hair to oval face, are irrelevant to her
at this particular moment.

She does not know who she is, where she is, or why.

In the starlight, she looks at her hands. The nails are neatly
trimmed, short, unadorned. The hands are uncallused, but not
soft.

She looks down at her body, discovers she is wearing a

light blue one-piece coverall of a luxurious material, but without underwear, she can sense, and formfitting boots a shade or two darker than the singlesuit.

She wonders how she knows the colors in the dim light.

The gentle *terwhit* of a bird in the tree above her startles her, and she studies her location.

First, it is night. That she had realized earlier. Second, she is sitting on the ground. The grass is trimmed short, and there is no undergrowth. To her right, as she looks through the darkness, is a luminous glow, against which she can see the regular outlines of other trees and of a line of bushes, presumably bordering a walk or path that leads . . . where?

She wants to bury her face in her arms and cry, but she should not. She is too important for that, she knows. She knows not why, but she feels it nonetheless.

One moment she is alone.

The next she is not.

"It's time for me to take you to your home," says the man. A figure in black, he is no taller than she is, but well muscled, despite the swirling black cloak.

How can she tell what she cannot see? She does not know, but accepts it all the same, as she accepts the kindness in the stranger's voice. Perhaps, perhaps he is not a stranger.

She stands.

He offers his arm, and they head down the path, which turns out to have a dim light of its own and leads in a sinuous fashion toward the glow she had noticed earlier.

"Terwhit!"

She jumps, knowing she should not.

"The tercels are the only nightbirds the Regent permits in the Park of Summer."

"Why?"

"One would have to ask the Regent, I suppose."

The path winds up a gentle incline. The glow in the sky ahead increases, and the girl can see that the path is a pale yellow and that the border shrubs have small yellow flowers with white centers and are evenly spaced.

She knows that the man in black will be gone before long, and even as she trusts him she fears him. Even as she fears him she knows only he can answer the questions she has and cannot ask.

"Who . . . ?" she stutters as they approach the top of the hill.

"Am I?" he asks. He chuckles, as if he finds it amusing, but she hears the bitterness behind the sound. "Who am I? I could tell you who I really am, but that wouldn't mean anything. If I gave you a name you'd recognize, then I would have to take that, too."

She shivers, starts to pull away.

His grip is like iron, and she finds her feet marching in step with his.

"Let us say, Lady-to-be, that I am your penance and hope to be your reward, and you mine. But that lies a long time from here and now . . . if either of us survives. And you will not remember this in any case."

The path widens as they come down the hill. The two take a narrower offshoot that leads to a small gate. The main path continues toward a series of towers outlined in ghostly, pervading light. She cannot turn her head toward the towers of light, but understands they are there.

At the smaller gate stands a sentry in dark blue. His eyes are blank as the man in black leads his charge past.

"You are Lady Kryn Kirsten, the only daughter and child of the Duke of Kirsten, first loyalist behind the Prince Regent. You have suffered an accident in your return to Karnak."

The dark man smiles at her, then wipes his expression blank.

"You will find it has all happened this way, though some has yet to happen that already has. Remember, Lady-to-be, do not marry."

She stands in the courtyard, sinking to her knees, head swimming as the alarms explode around her, clutching at the memories of the man in black that fade as her thoughts lose their hold on them, finding herself left with memories of a long black tunnel and with new memories, recollections of a tall man, a forbidding woman, and towers.

The last words, words someone else has spoken, remain.

"Do not marry."

LVII

From within the tunnel he has wrapped around himself, Martel can sense a spark, a familiar flame separated from him by the thinnest of margins. He knows what the spark represents, and wills his course away from it. Too close to that spark, and the energy he controls will short-circuit across more than a millennium. Without the focus he embodies ... he pushes away the thoughts, locks his mind on the place and the time where he is heading, and the tunnel of energy trails him.

Martel pushes himself away from the spark, thoughts lashing against time, most of his energy devoted merely to keeping his links with his starting point open.

"Can't go where you haven't been, is that it?" he mutters, though he neither speaks nor is heard in the nontime nexus where he finds himself suspended, but his thoughts form as though he had spoken.

He lets himself drift forward with the tide, though that motion is an illusion, because there is no tide to time, and casts his thoughts into the real time outside his energy tunnel for an anchor.

If Kryn had been born when the Duke thought she had, when she thought she had, now she would be away at Lady Persis' School on Albion. Chronologically, in real fact, the Duke does not yet have his daughter, though she has been placed already.

Martel shakes his head.

If you can only keep track until all the pieces are in place ...

As Martel sets foot on the golden tiles, the pathway to the back gate of the Duke's holding, the one on the park, is still shrouded in mist.

"Halt!" The stun rifle is centered on Martel's midsection.

"Halted I am, my friend."

"Your business?"

"To bring a report to the Duke on his daughter Kryn."

"Daughter Kryn? The Duke has no daughters—"

Martel reaches out, holds the man's mind frozen as he supplies vague recollections of a slender, dark-haired girl ... seen from a distance practicing with a light saber, rushing by the gate on the way out to the park, smiling with a new sunkite, sulking ... and finally leaving by the main gate with four trunks and three guards.

Martel finds his vision blurring with the effort, realizes how much energy he is using merely to hold himself in this place and time.

"Oh, her ... gone away to school."

"I know. I know. The Duke asked me to report. Here are my credentials."

Martel might have been able to alter the man's memories from a distance, but no feedback would have been possible. With Kryn's life the question, he had to do as well as he could.

The guard looks at Martel's empty hands, and nods.

"Lord Kirsten won't be receiving yet."

"Realized that after I'd left the port. Anywhere I could wait?"

Lowering the blue-barreled weapon, the sentry wrinkles his forehead, chews at his lower lip with sharp upper canines.

"Don't know. Let me ask the Captain."

"You don't have to wake him. I'll wait out here." Martel eases himself onto the bench across from the guard box and ignores the stunner.

Didn't realize it would be this much of a drain ...

"He's up. Already been round once."

Martel senses the Guard Captain before the man steps from the nearer wing. Senses him and inserts the memories of Kryn, subtly different, before the security chief sees him.

"Captain Herlieu, this gent needs a place to wait 'fore he makes his report to the Duke."

Martel stands and bows.

"Averil Seine, Captain. From Albion with a report for His Grace."

Herlieu frowns.

"About?"

"His daughter."

"Would have thought Her Grace would be the one to get that."

Martel shrugs. Even with a bogus set of memories, Herlieu was rationalizing to fit the situation. Obviously, the Duchess had a great deal of power.

"Ah, yes ... perhaps it should be. My commission was signed by the Duke, and ... alas, not knowing the ways, I assumed ..."

Herlieu laughs, his voice booming in the narrow space by the gate, the echoes bouncing back from the high and totally unnecessary bluestone battlements above.

"Of course you wouldn't know. The Duke, bless his soul, signs all the documents, sits on the Regent's Council, and fine advice he gives there. But her Ladyship runs Southwich here. Still ... he's the Duke."

Martel bows again. "I understand. Thank you for setting straight the record and for keeping me from a mispresumption."

"Sure she'll see you. Early riser she is. Now, what was your name?"

"Averil Seine. From Albion."

"Just sit here on the bench, and I'll tell her myself."

Martel sits, letting his mind follow the Guard Captain, touching the Imperial Marine's thoughts.

Funny-looking fellow ... why would they want to know about Lady Kryn? Lots kept quiet on her ... him not knowing about the Duke, either ...

Martel searches for the Duchess, not that it is hard. Her thoughts are clear. Crystal-clear and strong. He recoils, but not before easing in a thought or two about the Duchess' daughter.

He waits on the bench.

"You're to follow me, Master Seine."

Martel bows again and follows Captain Herlieu up the slidechutes to the tower room that views both the park and the palace.

"You may leave us, Captain."

"Yes, Your Ladyship."

The slidedoor closes.

"You're a fraud, and soon to be a dead one, Master Seine

or whatever your real name is, unless you can tell me what your game is. Then you might have a shot at a permanent lower-level apartment."

Martel probes at her mind. Strong enough, talented enough, that she would be a goddess if she sought Aurore—and he is limited indeed by the need to hold his links to the future from which he has come. Does he dare to tap power sources of a local nature? Will they break down the insulation between him and the present?

"It's simple," he temporizes. "You have no heirs. I offer you a daughter who will become Regent and Viceroy, who will become second only to the Emperor in power."

NO!

"An interesting idea," she says aloud. "But why should I believe it? Much less from an unknown from nowhere?"

A lurid thought surfaces in her mind, an image of Martel ripping off her clothes, followed by an image of her ordering him tortured.

"I think you misunderstand, Madame. The young woman already exists. She will honestly believe that she is Kryn Kirsten. She resembles you, and, to some degree, the Duke, and she will be accepted as your daughter."

Martel surveys the room. The Duchess has set aside her breakfast, and, silver hair pulled back into a tidy knot, peers down from the meter-plus bed platform at him. The marble platform is a single slab, partly draped in blue, the fabric shot through with a gold thread glittering with a light of its own.

Martel senses she is ready to push the red button. He reroutes the energy, but does not absorb it.

"Go ahead. I'm standing in the fire zone. But it won't work. Neither will the guard call."

She jabs the button.

A weak red light pulses over Martel and dies.

"What do you really want?"

"A good home for a girl who deserves it."

"You expect me to believe that?"

"No. But you will."

He throws his mind at her, as much of it as he dares, while still holding the links foretime. Unlike the Guard Captain, the sentry, there will be no insinuating memories, not quiet manipulation.

OUT! GET OUT! SCUM! Her mental screams pound at Martel.

Martel reels, knees bending with the effort of holding the circuits diverted, the energies from future and present separate, and pressing convictions and memories upon the Duchess Marthe at the same time, without destroying her in the process.

He forces an image of Kryn at her.

Your daughter . . . your hope for the future . . .

Mental pictures of Kryn, smiling, romping in the courtyard of Southwich, pictures of Marthe holding her arms out to her daughter, pictures of a small face looking up wide-eyed.

NO! I'M THE LITTLE GIRL.

Martel feels the sweat beading on his forehead.

Should have been sneaky . . . stupid . . . never figured on this kind of strength.

The energy link back to Karnak future dwindles. He doesn't want to have to live the same millennium twice.

He staggers, still beaming images at the Duchess.

She throws them back.

NO! CHILDREN ARE PIGS. EVERYONE WOULD KNOW. NOT FOR ME TO BE DEGRADED. WON'T BE A SOW. WON'T LET THEM THINK THAT!

The temperature in the bedchamber, expansive as it is, has to have risen twenty degrees.

Martel shifts his probes toward the Duchess' nerve centers.

DIE! DIE!

His shifts and the lack of images give her the room to counterattack.

Martel feels his body crumpling, and in a desperate effort seizes the power directly from the palace sources, ignoring the emotional impact the sudden blackness creates for the staff in all the scattered and endless rooms.

With the surge of renewed energy he slams aside her defenses and feels her go unconscious.

That done, he switches his concentration to the fraying edge between his own links to the blackness of the future.

*DANGER! TWO CANNOT BE ONE, NOT NOW, NOT
EVER.*

He wrenches the two energy lines apart, somehow welds
them separate, before the blackness closes in on him.

Thud! Thud!

Martel opens his eyes. His is sprawled on the pale yellow
heatstones of the Duchess' receiving room/bedchamber.

Thud! Thud!

He wobbles as he climbs to his feet.

His forehead is wet, and he wipes it away with the back of
his left hand. His sleeve comes away with a mixture of blood
and sweat. Knees rubbery, he peers up at the bed block.

Head aching, he probes.

The Duchess Marthe is unconscious, but breathing.

His eyes water with the pain, but he keeps probing.
Stroke—the mental strain of his last probes has apparently
triggered it.

Should he leave well enough alone?

He shakes his head, regretting the motion as it drives needles into his thoughts.

Kryn will need a strong protector, and the Duchess is as
strong as they come. Besides, the Duchess, for all her bias
against motherhood, also deserves better.

Thud! Thud!

Conscious of the attempts to break through the massive
door, he returns his attention to the woman, repairing the
damage and insinuating the necessary memories at the same
time. In some ways he is lucky. The Duchess is the type of
woman who will keep precious few keepsakes of her "daughter." Those few he can supply.

He completes his work with a mental report on Kryn's
progress at Lady Persis' School, awakens the Duchess, and
lets himself collapse again.

"What's this?" demands the Lady Marthe as she keys open
the door.

Three guards and the Captain stumble through.

"You didn't answer, Milady. Even the emergency call. We
were concerned."

"You had right for your concern, I suppose, Captain, but
not for me. Master Seine had some sort of seizure, and I was

simply distracted. My controls malfunctioned, and I couldn't seem to reach you. At the same time, I certainly wasn't going to leave Master Seine."

Martel groans.

"Help the poor man up. And get someone up here to clean up the mess he made. Immediately!"

"Yes, Milady."

"Get him some attention. Put him in the Red Room. When he recovers, he should see the Duke."

That is fine with Martel. So far the Duchess is reacting as he has planned . . . after his setbacks. Martel needs the rest and a quiet place from which he can influence more of the staff and get to the Duke.

He lets himself be carried while mentally reaching out toward the Duke's sleeping quarters.

The Duke of Kirsten is still asleep. The woman with him is not, but pretends to be, bored as she is.

Martel ignores her and first plants the memory chains of Kryn in the Duke's mind, then plants a more limited set and a few vagrant thoughts in the woman's mind.

She calls herself Alicia, and officially she is the Duchess' first maid. What that means to Martel is that the Duchess chooses the Duke's mistresses, and carefully.

Alicia is cunning, but the shrewdness is realistic.

Old bloat, she thinks, *some lover. Sort of kind, but the Duchess pushes him around. Still, a good thing for me. And when he's satisfied, she lets me alone.*

Martel pushes an image of Kryn at her.

Never could figure out how they got together long enough for even one. She's sharp, sharp like the Duchess. Little nicer, maybe, but when they're young you never know.

Martel relaxes, lets himself go limp as the two guards ease him into the oversized stratobed, drifts his thoughts back from the palatial sleeping room where the Duke snores and Alicia the bored and blond young maid pretends with closed eyes.

"The medtech should be here in a couple of units."

"Gerson," orders the Captain, "you wait."

"Yes, sir."

Once the door has irised shut, Martel opens his eyes.

The title Red Room is appropriate. Fabric walls, red with gold threads, twinkling like the ones in the fabric hangings of the Duchess' bedchamber. Red coverlet on the square stratobed. Red heatstone tiles on the floor. The arched ceiling overhead is red, as are the silksheen sheets that show at the upper edge of the bed.

Martel wonders at the picture—a religious figure from the ancient times before the Empire—then realizes it has been chosen because the man is dressed in red robes . . . merely for the color.

Gerson, the guard, sits in a red slouch chair, facing the door.

"Oh," moans Martel, "my head."

Gerson says nothing.

Martel eases up into a sitting position, looking around the room.

"What happened? Where am I?"

"You had a fall. Duchess had us bring you here. Red Room," supplies Gerson.

"I remember telling her about her daughter, Kryn." As he spoke Martel supplied a set of memories for Gerson as well, tinted to match the guard's underlying prejudices and experiences.

This is getting too complicated, Martel. The more people you meet, the more memories that seem necessary . . . could spend months at this.

Martel squints, thinking about all the records involved, the possible travel to Albion to make sure that records exist at Lady Persis' School and in the minds of the necessary teachers, as well as a few "classmates." Plus the Prince Regent's court and the society media.

He groans again, not entirely acting.

Will the result be worth it?

Do you have any choice?

He shakes his head, wincing at the jab of pain, leaning back and letting his thoughts set about the tasks of self-repair.

You don't have to do it all today, you know. You've got a few years . . . maybe.

He tests his energy link foretime. So far, the use of present-time energies hasn't damaged the linkage. But he can sense the limits to his control and to the total energy he can command here in the backtime. He cannot handle as many focal points, nor with as much precision.

Does it have to do with his location, the development of Aurore later on, or with the energy shunts backtime?

He shakes his head again. This time the ache is gone, but the questions remain.

Life had been much simpler as a simple newsie, playing at a minor god in the wings, coming up for breath every few decades, and avoiding any real commitment or involvement.

Now there is the question of Emily. He has taken care of her immediate future, but he still knows nothing of her past.

Does it matter?

He dozes, pushing aside the questions that hammer at him.

"Master Seine?"

He jerks to alertness.

"Medtech Nerril. Let's take a look at that business on your forehead."

Martel sits and lets the medtech clean the scrape. He could have healed the superficial damage, but what would have been his excuse for staying? Besides, a look at the Regency society from inside, even from the semiservant's position he has created, might be helpful and interesting. Might make his next efforts easier.

Might be stalling, too. Martel pushes away his own doubts, knowing the mental reservations will return, and return.

As Nerril cleans the cut with the sonic spray, Martel injects a series of memories of Kryn. He also plants the compulsion for the medtech to update Kryn's medical records. Nerril will actually be creating the records, while thinking that he is merely adding to them.

Martel catalogues all he must do . . . at a bare minimum.

The Hall of Records must be visited for the official record of Kryn's birth to be created, plus the peerage registry and the social lists. A few references would slip by, but Kryn would have years to mend the gaps by her physical presence, and who would deny her existence, when she was so obviously present and the records showed her birth? Particularly with such a powerful mother and respected and doting father?

"I said . . . that's all, Master Seine."

"Oh ... sorry ... daydreaming."

"Are you sure you're all right?"

"Fine. Fine."

Nerril packs up his equipment, collapsing it into the ubiquitous green bag.

Gerson stands by the door, twiddling his thumbs.

"Why don't you report back to Captain Herlieu that I'm fine?"

"Orders. Wait for him."

"All right."

Gerson leans back against the wall, eyes running from Martel to the picture on the wall and back again.

"Where are you from originally?" asks Martel.

"Newhebb. Isle of Narrows. Joined the Impies. When my term was up, followed the Captain here. There he was a Force Leader. One of the best. Should have seen him at New Reimer. Something, it was. Took the entire crivet, himself. Well ... him and two others. Got the Marshal's Cross for it."

Herlieu didn't look that old. That meant part of his contract with the Duke was the cost of rejuv treatments. Probably worth it to the Duchess, since Herlieu ran a tight operation.

Gerson was saved from the need for further conversation by the arrival of a young woman. Blond, dressed in the blue-and-gold tunic and trousers, in the colors of Kirsten, she was narrow-waisted, slim-hipped, and large-breasted.

After an instant Martel realizes he is seeing Alicia, maid to the Duchess and bed partner to the Duke.

"Master Seine?"

Martel inclines his head.

"The Duke would like to see you, sir. In his study."

Martel puts his feet on the floor, gingerly. The floor stays firmly underfoot. Running a quick check on himself, he decides he is in surprisingly good shape for all the energy he has expended.

Alicia leads the way.

The hallway, windowless, is lit with a uniform glow from the high ceiling and from the pale yellow heatstone flooring.

The fabric-covered walls display a pale cream-and-blue pattern of intertwined lilies and swords.

The Duke's study is in the tower opposite the Duchess'

morning receiving room. Unlike the other rooms through which Martel has passed, the walls are of dark wood, or wooden bookshelves, though each shelf is permaglassed over and sealed.

The Duke, standing behind a massive and all-wooden desk of a design centuries old, wears a dark green dressing robe and white silksheen shirt, open at the neck.

"How's Kryn, Master Seine?" The Duke's voice booms as he extends his hand down toward Martel from his near-two-meter height.

Alicia, notes Martel, does not leave, but seats herself in a window seat in the far corner of the book-lined room. She will report to the Duchess.

Martel reaches out, taking in the man's thoughts, and freezes time for them both for an instant.

Do I really have a daughter? My own daughter? All seems so vague. . . . And Seine . . . why . . . who is he? What report? Why can't I remember more? Damned rejuv. Takes the good memories with the bad.

Duke Kirsten will be good to Kryn. Perhaps too good, but the Duchess' hardheaded approach will provide balance.

Martel supplies more memories . . . image after image . . . thought after thought . . . Kryn as a dark-haired, serious-faced infant; Kryn taking a first step, holding on to the Duke's hand; Kryn drawing a squiggly tower meant to be Southwich; Kryn stamping her foot in the courtyard; Kryn . . . Kryn . . . Kryn . . .

. . . and the Duke's mind laps them up, image after image.

Martel stretches his reach further and time-freezes Alicia as well. Then he walks to the desk, places a small album on the corner. The cover is plain blue, bordered in gold, with the Duke's seal in the center.

Inside are copies of holos he remembers from the Kryn of so long ago and some he has done just for this purpose. The Duke would have had such an album, since he lives in the past as much as the present. The Duchess would not. She believes she has had a daughter for her husband, most reluctantly, and while she will ensure that Kryn meets her standards, meaning excellence in everything, the Duchess lives in the present and future. No sentimental holos for her!

Martel retreats to where he had stood and unlooses the moment he has held in check.

"She's fine, Your Lordship. Just fine. Adapting well, and doing excellently. Frankly, I don't see why you were so concerned, or why you hired me for a personal report. I'm certain Lady Persis is giving you much the same information, or will. She's an outstanding young woman and could go far if she chooses."

"Like her mother," muses the Duke. He looks down at the album quizzically, opens it, sees the first holo, smiles fondly, and shuts the cover.

"Her studies?"

"She excels, particularly in languages and in science. Very strong-minded."

"Don't know if I should have sent her away, Master Seine. I don't know, but I probably spoil the girl too much. She needs a wider perspective, and I know the Duchess feels that way."

"Are you asking me for a recommendation, sir?"

"No ... but what would you do?"

"I cannot recommend, sir. Lady Persis runs a fine school. No school is home. But then, private tutors cannot teach the interplay of other fine minds, nor the relations between one's peers."

"Good points."

Martel waits.

The Duke looks across at Alicia, as if to mark her presence, then looks back down at the album, which he picks up, fingers, and sets down again before continuing.

"All damned confusing ..." he muses.

His face clears, and he looks straight at Martel.

"Would you join us for dinner, the main meal of midday here?"

"Your offer is most generous, and I would enjoy that."

"Fine, just fine."

Martel coughs, gently.

"Your Lordship ... I did not anticipate such an invitation, and, alas, can wear only what I have on."

"We're not that formal. Wear what you have on. Black's

appropriate most places, anyway ... except the Regent doesn't seem to like it. Doesn't bother me, though."

The Duke looks at Alicia.

"Alicia, will you escort Master Seine back to his quarters ... but first get him a bite to eat, and then give him a tour of the place. I'll be late getting back."

The Duke returns his eyes to Martel. "Sorry I can't chat longer, but due at the Regent's Council meeting. Sure you understand."

"Most assuredly, Your Lordship. Most assuredly."

Alicia rises to her feet and departs, letting Martel follow as he will.

Kryn? What about me if she comes back? I'm for his pleasure and her convenience. He lives for Kryn. Was it always this way? Don't remember it like this ... Black scares me. Master Seine ... master of what? They all accept him ... from nowhere ... why?

Martel understands her questions and her fears. He tries to disarm some of them with another question he places in her thoughts.

What woman could show Kryn love?

Alicia frowns.

Love? Who knows love? Not her, not the Duke ... for his daughter ... maybe ... for me? Just lust.

Martel decides to make a few more arrangements. He touches the Duke's mind, even as the Grand Duke Kirsten is entering the flitter to take him to the palace. Alicia will be safe ... and loved.

Next ... a quick touch to the Duchess' thoughts, giving her relief that the Duke loves the maid she has so conveniently provided.

How do you know, Martel, he asks himself, *that your thoughts haven't been rearranged the same way?*

He drives the cold chill into his own deeps and pushes the thought away.

By the time they reach the kitchen, Alicia has thawed and Martel is ready for the warmed rolls and juice that are shoved at him in the back pantry.

From the kitchen the tour begins, and Alicia is thorough. For that Martel is thankful, though his feet hurt long before they finish, because virtually everyone at Southwich has a memory of Kryn. And if some of the staff wonder at the bemused look on Master Seine's face, so be it.

Once he leaves the environs of Kirsten, he will have to cover the palace, as well as some nobles and key staff in the Houses of Gatwick, Ngaio, and Sulifer. After that will come all the peerage records, and the records of Lady Persis' School.

Along the way he will plant as many memories as he can with the general populace, the gossip columnists, and the opinion leaders. Not that total coverage is necessary, particularly when the subject is the daughter of a Duke renowned for his privacy in a Regency court society that revolves around the Prince Regent and his latest boyfriend.

Dinner is served promptly at 1300 hours in the family dining room to exactly five people—the Duke, the Duchess, Captain Herlieu, Madame Herlieu, and Master Seine.

"How was the Council meeting this morning?" That is the Duchess, uninterested, but trying to break the silence.

"Same. Interesting problem, you know." The Duke pauses to slurp his red-turtle soup. "Prince Edwin asked the Council to suggest ways to increase revenues while reducing taxes. Little difficult, would you say, Master Seine?"

"I'm not an expert in high finance, Your Lordship. It does seem rather paradoxical."

"Polite way of saying it's confusing. Those ninnies sat there and hee-hawed. Perhaps this . . . perhaps that." The Duke frowns, puts down his soup spoon.

The Duchess takes another delicate sip of her soup, almost a consommé, lays her spoon on the Blackshire china, and surveys the table. The softness of the glow lights and the dimness of the exterior light, blocked as it is by the heavy draperies, reduce the sharpness of her nose, display her face as ten years younger or more, hinting at the beauty she once had been. Her silver hair, maintained by cosmetology, adds to the regal impression.

"Did the Council make any decision?" Martel asks.

"Of course! They made a decision to study the request. That's what happens most of the time."

"How did you vote?" asks the Duchess.

"Last," rumbles the Duke, "and for it—the study, that is. Stupid study, but stupid to oppose it now. Right, Milady?"

The Duchess nods.

"Don't they see the danger?" That comes from Herlieu.

"Which danger?" questions the Duchess. Her soft voice carries, silken with the feel of iron behind it. "The danger from within or the danger from without?"

"I'm a simple fighting man," answers Herlieu, "and I worry about the dangers from outside. Once they're taken care of, you always have a chance to set your own house in order."

"But doesn't a weak or disorderly house invite attack, and a strong one discourage it?"

"Makes my point, Your Ladyship. You have to be ready to fight in either case. If your house is disorderly or if it isn't."

Martel adds nothing. The last time around, he hadn't cared to try understanding the intricacies of Regency infighting, and he still doesn't. The Duke admits voting for something that is worthless with a total stranger present, and the Duchess agrees.

Martel lets his mind soak up the loose thoughts.

Few escape from the Duchess . . . a loose mélange from Herlieu . . . and a surprisingly ordered progression from the Duke. Martel zeroes in on the big man.

Edwin . . . not half the man his father the Emperor is . . . queer . . . doesn't understand economics or military power . . . amused by politics . . . way to favor is to amuse him, and they all do . . . from Mersham to Stelstrobel . . . the Fuards pour credit after credit into R&D, ships, men . . . and Edwin asks about financing his annual carnival . . . Karnak, guard of the Empire's Marches, does nothing. You, admit it, Kirsten, you do nothing either . . . too many jackals . . . all ready to pull you down . . . amusing, they'd find it . . . and they're younger . . . maybe Kryn . . . if it's right . . . haven't thought that . . .

"Does Councilor Mersham feel more committed to internal or external problems?" ventures Martel.

"Councilor Mersham is gravely concerned about all problems, as they all are."

"And the reaction to the Fuards?"

"Ha! We all are deeply concerned . . . deeply concerned . . . but also we are deeply concerned about the unrest caused by the latest tax levy which went to expand the Regent's Palace and for a ten percent increase in the basic dole."

"Did the increase make people happier?" asks Martel, remembering full well how his mother had snorted.

He is rewarded by a sniff from Madame Herlieu, a thin-faced redhead, a snort from the good Captain, and a raised eyebrow from the Duchess.

"I can see why you sent your daughter away."

"Not sure I agree now," mumbles the Duke. "Seemed good at the time. Now I wonder."

"Experience in other milieus might give her a broader outlook," comments the red-haired woman.

The Duchess nods again, and Martel reaches for the thoughts behind the nod.

Needs a lot more experience . . . maybe trip to New Augusta itself when she gets back. Then a cadet tour. Not many women do, but she can. Kryn will handle it.

For not having had a daughter until that morning, the Duchess is certainly busy plotting the path Kryn will take, Martel thinks to himself, a bit sadly.

"Why so downcast, Master Seine?" booms the Duke.

"Thinking about your daughter, I just wondered. My children," he lies, having none, "won't have to worry about high finance and privy councils, and sometimes I think they'll be the happier for it. Lady Kryn will become our outstanding Duchess, maybe more, but I wonder if she'll be happy."

"Are any of us ever really happy?" replies the Guard Captain.

"Maybe not. Maybe we delude ourselves into thinking so. Is happiness everything? And can anyone stay happy if someone isn't out guarding, and someone else ruling?"

What's he want?

The Duchess is sharp, too sharp, and Martel keeps forgetting it. The sooner he leaves the better, and the less he says the better.

The main course is scampig, roasted and lightly basted with Taxan brandy. Martel enjoys it and says little.

". . . 'course the Prince got the next bird with that needle

rifle. Not at all sporting. Single-action, but never have to re-
load. Real sport would do it with an old-style shotgun. . . .
You hunt, Master Seine?"

"Not my province. Travel too much. Can't do something
well, usually don't care to do it."

I'll bet there are some exceptions your wife knows. The un-
expectedly salacious thought from Madame Herlieu catches
Martel off guard, and he barely keeps from flushing.

The Duke doesn't notice.

". . . and the time he decided to use a bow against the
dualhorn. Sounds fair, but he used an explosive arrowhead.
What's the difference between that damned electronic con-
traption he called a bow and a full-bored laser? Oh, so he
could say he got the beast with a bow and arrow . . ."

Martel takes it all in, notes the names, and listens.

The dinner drags into the early afternoon, and later, and
later.

It is close to 1600 before Martel walks out through the
park gate, down the slight hill toward the Regent's Palace,
and into nowhere.

He has several days, weeks, of hard work ahead. But this
time, damned if *anyone* is going to see him!

LVIII

What the hammer? What the forge?
What the bellows? From what gorge
Came the fire, came the light,
Came the beasts that sowed the night?

Martel knows that the gods on high, specifically on Aurore,
do not know he is backtime. Knows, also, that they do not
believe travel backtime is possible.

In his wrapping of time energy, he debates his next move.
Which player next? Or players? The Fallen Ones, the
Brotherhood, the Prince Regent? All the pieces need to

moved quickly, before the disappearance/destruction of the hammer-thrower can be verified.

The Brotherhood is the choice.

Brother Geidren. The image of the brown-robed "brother" slips into his mind as clearly as if it had been yesterday when he confronted her across the shield wall in the underground headquarters of that secretive and now-exiled group.

None of his experiences on Aurore have shed much more light on his knowledge of the Brotherhood, and the questions have only grown with their banishment and disappearance.

Are the Fallen Ones an adjunct to the Brethren? Allies? Antagonists with mutual goals? All three rumors have persisted for a millennium ... without answers.

Martel knows only when and where Brother Geidren had been once, and the single logical possibility is to relocate that position and follow with an appearance—once the Martel he had been has left for Aurore.

First, the underground and shielded quarters of the Brotherhood. That is simple.

More difficult is locating Geidren after Martin Martel has left for Aurore. Meeting himself would be catastrophic, in more ways than one. The energy release would render the entire point of the search moot, but not in any way in which Martel would be around to appreciate.

Are you ready for this?

Do you have any choice?

The answer to both questions is no.

From the requisite undertime distance, he tracks the departure of one young and stunned Martin Martel, and thence hastens back to the bunker of the Brethren, emerging in a silent corridor, wrapped in darkness, cloaked in his energies, and invisible to all but the most talented of espers.

Geidren is not alone, rather unsurprisingly, but with two others in a room which could only be described as a communications and command center.

Martel observes from a corner, bemused that the three, all espers, are so wrapped in their own dynamics and so trusting of their mechanical detectors and guard technicians that his presence goes unnoticed.

As an afterthought, he reaches out and puts the three guards who scan the command center into a deep sleep.

Kirsten? Main threat? Overthrow the Regent? Those thoughts come from the thin-faced blond and bearded man. Call him Aquinas.

More than meets the eye. Foreboding ... doom on the horizon. Aurore? From the older man. Call him Mystic.

The Master Game Player? Or God? One choice or the other. Or your fears? Doesn't matter. We're outlawed. Queried Scholar pretext. How do we fight? Raise the Brethren? Underground? Passive resistance over time? Religion? Gerri Geidren's thoughts ring with a soft chime.

Martel is impressed. Aquinas and Mystic are definitely second-raters next to the woman.

Religion ... the great crusade, offers Aquinas.

Put the Unknowable against the Empire? Pervert the sacrament of Faith?

Would it work? asks Geidren.

Yes.

No.

NO! Martel lets himself become visible, half shading his face in a shadow of his own, and offers an observation.

"The problem with relying on religion is that you give the temporal authorities the power to ban it. Banned religions are effective only in limited circumstances—like when the god involved is willing to use force on behalf of his or her followers or when the oppression of the regime approaches terrorism."

His last half-sentence is lost in the blaze of the lasers concentrated on the corner where Martel stands.

He absorbs what he can, diverts the rest into his personal undertime/underspace reservoir that grows with each appearance and reduces his need to tap his own foretime reserves.

The way things are going, Martel, you're going to have your own fields back- and foretime, that is, if everyone keeps throwing energy at you.

Geidren stops the waste of energy with her own mental override of the controls she had activated. Mystic and Aquinas blanch as they see Martel still stands untouched.

"Trite, but who are you?"

"It doesn't matter. I'd like to offer some observations. One: The Prince Regent will fall, but the Regency will remain, more powerful than before. Two: Despite whatever you do, and it may be a great deal, the power of the House of Kirsten will wax, not wane. Three: There is a Master Game Player. Three at least, as a matter of fact. Four: You will not even attempt any injury to Martin Martel. It might make him angry, and it will definitely make me angry."

Him? Master Game Player?

Can't be!

Three of them?

Martel decides to emphasize his points, and amplifies his next message to the split point.

THERE IS A FALLEN ONE. CALL HIM THE MASTER GAME PLAYER I REPRESENT. CALL THE TWO OTHERS APOLLO AND THE SMOKE BULL, IF YOU WILL.

Mystic and Aquinas crumple, both twitching heaps. Geidren leans heavily against the commset.

Don't overplay . . . your . . . hand.

Martel smiles, points at the commset, lets the energy flow from his fingertips, and waits until the equipment is a molten heap of slag.

At the first blast, Gerri Geidren has staggered back, staring as if to penetrate the shadow that surrounds Martel's face.

No esper . . . that power.

"As I said," Martel resumes conversationally, ignoring the twitches of the two on the floor, "the Brotherhood will have to live with reality."

What would you do?

Oppose the Empire.

"But," she breaks out verbally, "you said that wouldn't do any good!"

"That is not what I said. I said the Regency would fall, but that Kirsten's power would not. In opposing the Regency and what follows, the Brethren can do a great deal of good by placing some checks on tyranny. The times will demand raw power. An organization based on promoting the best development of each individual's abilities is restricted by its very ideals from exerting the kind of power necessary. And if you

give up your ideals, you lose the power you have. So . . .
don't."

Damned philosopher.

Few would call me that.

"Two facets work better than one," he continues aloud.
"You might call the churchly half the Church of Man, and in
turn the Regency will come to regard its priests as the servants of the Fallen One, who has not really fallen yet. That
should not frighten you, because the Fallen One is of and for
the people, which should indeed frighten them."

He is distracted by the shuddering gasp of Aquinas, who
stops breathing. Martel turns his attention to the man, makes
a few adjustments, and lets Aquinas slip into a deep sleep. He
repeats the pattern with Mystic, and makes similar changes in
the metabolism and body of Geidren.

You merely represent a Master Game Player?

"In a manner of speaking."

Merely represent?

No man is a god, no matter how powerful!

Martel lets his thoughts check the area again, scanning the
monitors that guard the control center. Still under the control
of his earlier meddling, they show nothing amiss, and the
guard technicians sleep peacefully.

"The other half," he plods on, "the Brethren, could act as
the temporal government in exile, doing what it can to remind the Empire and the Regency of the human rights of
their people. Remember, neither will last forever, and some
organized group should be there to guide the way when they
fall."

They? They fall? Why should we do what you suggest?
They? Only one Empire . . .

Martel smiles.

"You can do whatever you want. But remember that your
strength lies in your ideals."

Still the damned philosopher-god.

No god, no philosopher, and a damned prophet, corrects
Martel in the instant before he vanishes.

The next step is forty years forward in time and to the palace of the aging Prince Regent.

LIX

3. And it came to pass in those days, when the son of the King of Kings sat upon the gilded throne of Karnak and ruled, and saw naught, that upon that night that was declared the servants brought food to the great table. When it was served, the lamps flickered. Flicker did the lamps twice, and after the third flicker were they extinguished, though no man had laid hands upon them.

4. Light! Let there be light! commanded the Prince, who was mighty and beholden in all the universe only to his Father, the King of Kings, the Emperor of Man. But the darkness remained, and the servants fell to their knees, and the courtiers were struck speechless.

5. Let there be light! demanded the Prince, and he stamped his boots, and the echo filled the halls, but there was no light.

6. In the midst of the darkness then appeared a light, and in that light was a demon in the likeness of a man, and he wore the black of a prophet.

7. What mean you, miserable creature, to deny a Prince of Princes light in his own hall? So saying, the Prince cast a thunderbolt at the demon. But the demon raised his hand, and the thunderbolt returned to the Prince and struck him dumb.

8. Mark well what I say, responded the demon, and low was his voice, yet all in the great halls of Karnak that was heard it, from the kitchens to the dungeons and even unto the towers that speared the heavens and called unto the stars.

9. Mark what I say, for thy days are numbered, even as the hour after the opening of the seventh seal. You shall be extinguished even as I have extinguished the lights of your hall and your mightiness. And none shall mourn you. No, none shall mourn you.

10. Before this shall come to pass, I will raise a temple, which cannot be cast down, though you and your legions will try. The mightiest tree of the world shall be uprooted, and the heavens will open, and a woman shall save thy people. And she will lead them.

11. Your people will be saved, but not you. For none shall mourn you and your passing, not even the King of Kings. For though I am vested in dark, I will bring light, and though you claim light, you are a judgment of darkness.

12. Dumbstruck stood the Prince of Princes until the demon had vanished and the lamps had rekindled themselves.

13. What heard you? asked the son of the King of Kings. What heard you?

14. But of those who heard the black demon none would look to their ruler, nor would they speak.

LX

Martel holds the nexus point, hangs in the gray of not-time, thoughts seeking the true timeline to the Karnak he had known as a student, to the time when he and Kryn had strolled the ways of the great Park of Summer, Park of the Regent.

Is the true path the reedy gray line twisting into the dark that becomes black, or the pulsing red one?

The colors he perceives are all in his mind, for the gray chaos where he waits has no color, but color is how he sees them. The solid black path, almost a road arrow of time, leads back to Aurore. That aura leaves no doubts.

A green line is the one he wants, and Martel wills himself back against the current until the feel of the reality outside the undertime river matches his images. Physics says there is no flow to time, that the flow is only in the mind of man; but Martel is used to fighting his own mind, if indeed that is where the flow of time exists.

He emerges from the undertime next to a towering red-barked tree, just outside the silver glitter fence that surrounds the giant. So high is the mutated sequoia that its noon shadow covers acres.

Martel's black cloak droops over him in the windless quiet.

Cling! Cling! Cling!

The chimes from the carillon announce the beginning of the Moments of Thankfulness. Thankfulness for the generosity of the Prince Regent. A time when all stand silent. A time when the blue-uniformed proctors ensure that silence.

Martel throws his cloak over his shoulders, casts his senses out across the acres, knows he will do what he now knows he did, and draws an aura of blackness around himself.

He strides across the shadowed grass with a light step— jaunty, daring the blue proctors and their blue helmets and their blue blast rifles to incinerate him.

Fifty-one paces later—not that Martel has counted them, he knows—the first proctor has Martel in his sights. Martel pities the man, raises his hand, and points.

The blast rifle melts.

The proctor drops it, suffers a burn as a splash of molten metal splats on his lower forearm, eats through his gauntlet.

Proctors travel in pairs. His companion, seeing the damage, turns, sights, and fires.

He explodes in a column of flame as the blast bends, impossibly, and returns to him.

Martel leaves the shadow of the mighty Tree of the Regent and casts his own acres-long shadow as he marches toward the golden towers of the palace.

In their dark blue singleskits, a second set of proctors races toward the black interloper. They race from the blue cupola that stands at the corner of the ten-kilometer-square park closest to the palace.

Any military authority would deem the singleskits, armed as they are with disruptors, stunners, tanglers, and full riot-control equipment, more than a match for a single black-shadowed man who marches upon the palace.

Deeming is not sufficient.

Martel waits to see if the bluesuits are determined to

destroy him merely for moving at the time appointed as sacred to the Prince Regent.

They are.

First, they focus the longer-range disruptors, for they are well over a kilo from Martel. The disruptors refuse to operate. As the two proctors scream closer the shock waves bend the ornamental shrubs that line the carved stone walks, rustle the leaves of the trees the singleskits barely clear, and bowl over the few children who are in the park at noon.

Martel gestures, and the proctors and their vehicles are gone. Not destroyed, although that would have been easier. Gone. Thrust through the tunnels in the around time and place to the Star Room of the Marshal of Proctors. The Marshal is not present, but the defense systems are always alert, and there will be enough wreckage to confound the Prince Regent and the Marshal.

The flow of energy from another set of disruptors bouncing from his screens draws Martel from his thoughts back into the park.

Martel admires efficiency, and the kill instinct of the bluesuits is efficient.

Less than units in the Park of the Regent and six proctors have attempted to destroy him for being so inconsiderate as to ignore the ritual silence and stillness devoted to the Prince. The last two are squandering energy on yet another attempt.

Martel's cloak flaps in the energy currents swirling around him, drips bits of shadow toward the burnt grass beneath his feet as he channels the energy into the reservoir from which he draws, and walks toward the remaining two singleskits, walks through the curtain of fire, through the disruptor beams and accompanying harmonics.

Cling! Cling! Cling!

The carillon chimes the end to the five units of stillness devoted to the greatness and beneficence of the Prince Regent whose minions continue their efforts to annihilate the Fallen One, for who but a Fallen One would dare profane the sacred stillness?

Freed from the bondage of immobility, heads in the park turn to view the pillar of flame, to see the growing pool of blackness around the figure of a single man, to hear the crusty sound of energy weapons.

From the farthest corner of the great park, screeching in on another wave of wind, comes yet one more pair of single-skits, disruptors and blasters flaring.

Martel bends the energy, forces it skyward into a grotesque parody of the Tree of the Regent, into a tree of flame casting its own shadow of dark, a flame tree visible from the towers of the palace, and from far beyond. A tree visible to the sensors of the Fleet in orbit, a tree building brightness with each instant till heads that turned toward it turn away, eyes stinging from unaccustomed tears, hands shaking.

And still the proctors fire, pouring the reserves from their singleskits, drawing from the power beams of the city.

Around the Old City of Karnak, most distant from the palace, lights fail. Next the lift/drop shafts in the towers fail and draw on their emergency reserves just to shut down and to put their emergency catch nets in place.

The Pleasures Pyramid that floats over the Lake of Hopes on the outskirts of the Old City loses lift, drifting inexorably downward, its lower floors first resting on the perfumed and green water, then crumpling as more and more of the inverted structure brings its weight to bear on the smaller lower stories.

A man, wearing nothing and one of the few who can see what is happening, dives from an upper window when the restraining fields fail. The green water is less than a meter deep.

A woman, holding up an impossible long skirt, decked in copper fronds and blueglass jewels belonging to some vanished history that never really happened, climbs from a terrace once protected by an energy screen and struggles through thigh-deep water. She has waited too long. Her scream is drowned in hundreds of others as the entire Pleasures Pyramid collapses outward and down, on her, on the water, on the floating body of the dead diver.

Martel feels the deaths, feels part after part of the city die.

The flame tree darkens, soul-sucking, energy-seeking, cold, bending light away from it. But it grows, fueled by the energy Martel funnels into it, overtopping the Regent's Tree, overtopping the highest spires of the Prince's palace.

Finally, the growth halts. The black tree stands. Untouched. Silent. Silent while the singleskits pour flame at Martel, silent while the palace's long-range disruptors and lasers add their weight to the attack. Silent while the ground beneath Martel and his tree is consumed. Silent while the innocents in the park die and the city fractures.

Silent while Martel's soul screams and tallies each death with a black weight in his mind.

The tree of the black flame vanishes. So does Martel. So do the four singleskits. So does the Park of the Regent, the Park of Summer, and so does the once-mighty Tree of the Regent.

The tree? Martel bends space and time again and sends the tree back into antiquity, back to a planet long since forgotten. And that is as it should be.

The singleskits and bluesuits are sent journeying, too, to another place, where their spirits may mingle with those of their victims.

Martel hovers undertime, drawing the thunderstorms, the clouds, the rain, overriding the climate satellites, fusing their circuits.

He is done. The rains pound Old Karnak, filling the glass-lined hole that was once the Park of Summer, filling that hole that will become the Lake of Dreams, chilling the citizens who have never felt day rain, and leaving the Prince shivering in his powerless palace.

Martel twists his place in space, fractionally, and appears in a narrow street. His cloak is wrapped around him. No one notices, for attention is focused on the coal-black clouds above, on the lack of power, on the portals that will not open, on those trapped inside and out.

A small boy is squeezed between the iris edges of a portal door. His mother is begging passersby for help, but in this district, at this time, no one will stop.

Martel gestures, and the door collapses in powder. The child falls and skins his knee, falls silently, for he can barely breathe. The mother looks sideways at Martel, then darts toward her son, scoops him up, holding him to her shoulder and brushing the sticky gray powder off him. He should be dying, squeezed between industrial doors of such power, but Martel has taken care of that as well, and the child sleeps on his mother's shoulder.

In the rain, the cloak droops behind Martel. He looks nearly and merely human, a black rat looking for the darkest corner of Old Karnak.

"Mister . . . can't wear black. Bluesuits burn you spot."

Martel smiles at the urchin, dressed in faded red and yellow, his green eyes peering from under a red thatch, with a green sandal on one foot, a red one on the other.

"Death cannot burn, young man. And life is death," he replies, pleased with himself for remembering the Litany at this point.

"Maybe no. Dead you no feel."

"Which way to Old Center? Polony's mansion?"

"That wreck?"

Martel nods, lets a little blackness seep from his soul, well out around him.

"Trick neat. You magician, something?"

"Something like that. Polony's house?"

"Turn left next alley, three streets on right, and take another left . . . real narrow. Watch Gert. Hangs there with viber."

Martel reaches out with his thoughts, checks the boy, changes a few minor metabolic matters, and ambles on toward his destination.

Three streets on down, he turns right into a narrower way, barely broad enough for three men elbow to elbow.

Gert is there, removing his viber from the inert form of an unwarned man.

Time for a demonstration.

Martel bends time, again adjusts a few metabolic details. The figure on the plastistone pavement retches, groans, and sits up.

Gert is not impressed, kicks the man away, and advances on Martel. The stench of stale ale and of sweat on sweat precedes him, a weapon in itself.

Gorillalike, brown hair streaming down over his shoulders, Gert grabs for Martel, who does not move, embraces the man in black with his right arm, which is as thick as a small oak, and carves with his left, viber on full power.

Martel should collapse into a heap from either the force of the grasp or from the impact of the weapon. He does not. Neither does the viber make any impression on him or his garments.

Gert is still not impressed, and locks both hands together and brings them down in a mighty swing on Martel's head.

There is a sharp crack through the narrow passage.

"Aeiiii!"

Gert's hands break each in a half-dozen places. Martel stands unmoved.

The man who had been the victim has regained his feet, uncertain whether he can profit by picking on Gert or on the strange figure in black, uncertain whether he should run. He temporizes by darting behind a wastebloc.

Gert stares at his hands.

Martel feels some pity, but not much. He gestures, and behind the gesture makes a few adjustments to Gert and to his hands and arms.

"You sought to give death. That is not yours to give. I have returned life. But as my reminder . . . your hands will never heal."

Gert's former victim looks at the slash in his tunic, at the man in black, and slinks quietly down the alley.

Martel steps around Gert and proceeds.

At the end of the narrow way, in a small square by itself, surrounded on all sides by another street wide enough only for a handful of people to pass shoulder to shoulder, stands a ruined dwelling. Wide steps of ancient green marble encircle the structure, modeled as it was after another ancient building on a long-forgotten planet. The columns are intact, but the roof has tumbled in.

Martel surveys the wreck. No life, except the rodents, the insects, and two tarrants who, weasellike, prey on the rodents. Drawing on the enormous field of energy poured at him by the proctors, he channels a portion into Polony's house, rebuilding, restoring, turning it to the function of the building from which it was copied.

At the center, in the hall of worship, he creates a black altar, a solid black cube with each side measuring exactly his own height. At another touch, he infuses the marble walls and columns with a slight glow, while changing the stone entirely to jet-black, streaked with a few isolated shots of silver. Finally he sets up the self-sustaining energy fields that will enable it to withstand the Empire's weapons for the centuries to come. His defenses will last. Time has proven that.

A quick tour of his handiwork convinces him of the faithfulness of his artistry and of his memory. He walks down the front steps, though "front" is not exactly correct, since the central hall may be approached through the columns from any side.

A small crowd is gathered by this time: several urchins, including the one in red and yellow; the shambling figure of Gert; a woman in a privacy cloak with the hard and painted eyes of a harlot; and, of course, the habitual representative of the Thieves' Guild, standing near the front, ready to demand tribute, and backed by several others in the shadows, who are armed with old projectile weapons and one stolen blaster.

Martel ignores the thief as he leaves the steps and stops to heal the skin ulcers of one of the urchins, a job that could have been done by any corner autodoc, though not so quickly.

"Don't you have something for me, stranger?" asks the thief.

"Life and death are one. You have life, and life is death. Without death there is no meaning to life. Without life there is no death. Be content with what you have."

Martel makes the sign of the looped and inverted cross, the one he has remembered from his student days, bestowing it as a benediction, and continues up the narrow street.

The thief throws his first knife. It hits the swirls of the black cloak and drops to the pavement with a thud.

A child in stained maroon overalls scrabbles for the blade, but drops it as if it burned. It might, reflects Martel, since it is now solid rock.

The thief ignores the byplay and throws his second knife, which suffers the same fate, though none of the crowd attempts to retrieve the weapon.

The bystanders, increased by another cloaked harlot, an older unveiled woman with braided silver hair, and a bent old man with a cane who is neither bent nor old, but an Imperial agent, draws back.

The thief draws his projectile gun and sights it dramatically at Martel's back.

Martel freezes the man, turns, reverses the benediction he had made moments before, and addresses the man, whose eyes dart from side to side as he sees Martel approach.

"I withdraw my blessing, given though you had evil in your heart. Twice have you struck, and twice have you been warned. You have not turned from your wickedness, and your heart is like stone. So be it! Life and death are one, and life is death."

The man makes no outcry, not surprisingly, for he, too, has been transmuted into black stone.

The urchin in yellow and red touches the stone tunic of the thief.

"Stone! The priest of death turned him stone!"

The Imperial agent scuttles away down another alley, hurrying as he can within the limits of his cover to make a report to the palace.

Martel turns, following the route he has pursued for the Viceroy a millennium later, not sure that anyone will pick up the parallel, but leaving the clue if anyone should choose to understand.

Every block or so he pauses, either rewarding or punishing as he sees fit. From the original crowd gathered at the temple steps, only the red-haired child has followed.

At last, on the outskirts of Old Karnak, he stops and climbs atop a stone bench on the edge of a neglected park.

All the pieces are in place from the past, and the puzzle is almost complete, except for the last pieces, and for those he must return to whence he came.

He raises his left hand.

"From the Fallen One I come, and to Him I go!"

A curtain of darkness drops across the long grass and cracked stones of the park, and when it lifts, the stone bench is bare.

The red-haired boy kneels and makes the sign of the looped and inverted cross.

LXI

The Viceroy makes no move to wipe the dusty streaks from her cheeks, but centers her screens on the row of burned-out yellow glowbushes that lies both beneath her tower apartments and nearly a kilo above her head.

A walk in darkness, with bushes like those glowing yellow, and a mist over the lawn ... she had been afraid. Like a distant song, she remembers.

Afraid ... you, the Viceroy, afraid? When?

And there had been a voice ... "if I told you my name, I'd have to take that, too."

Where have you heard that voice?

She does not want to know.

"Forde! Marshal Reitre!"

"Yes, Lady," the two chorus from the observers' positions flanking her.

"It is time to do something about the interference from the so-called gods of Aurore. Assemble the Grand Fleet, with a great deal of fanfare."

"But ... my Lady ... is that wise?" That is the Marshal.

"My Lady?" That is Forde.

"No, it is not wise. Wisdom would do nothing." She looks at Forde. "Operation Suntunnel."

Reitre blanches. Forde's face remains blank.

"You disapprove?"

"Against the power I saw on your screens, my Lady," Forde draws his words out slowly, "I question the chances of success. There were only two, and well away from their base of power."

"That is why we must remove their base of power. Without Aurore, and its sun, their power will dissipate."

"Without the Fleet, so will the Regency's." Forde's face whitens another shade as his words spill out.

"That is a chance, but unless we react to those who have smashed Karnak, the Empire will fall." She gestures at the screen, which now shows the city as it appears from the palace tower. "Out there, at this moment, thousands are flocking to the temple of the Fallen One. The Brethren are emerging, and doubtless both the Fuards and the Matriarchy are mobilizing."

As if to echo her words, the screen focuses on the small black temple, its steps packed, and the streets and lanes leading to it thronged with supplicants.

"The power of an Empire is nothing to the power of a living god." She pauses and smiles a cold smile, one that Forde has not seen, ever, and one that bears a trace of godlike aloofness. "But if the Empire should destroy such a god . . ."

Forde bows.

She turns and leaves the control center to the two men and a score of technicians.

Instead of returning to her apartments, she takes the lift all the way to the top of the Regent's Tower, the highest point of the palace.

She studies the city, spending time at each battlement of the four-sided tower. Even from her height, it is apparent that the damage is nearly as bad as the time when the Fallen One destroyed the Park of Summer. Perhaps worse.

The shock waves of the graystone hammer amounted to the impact of a low nuclear airburst, whereas the energy and the crater created by the Fallen One had more the characteristics of a surface burst. In neither case had there been radiation, which made the situation more puzzling.

She tightens her lips. Maybe there had been no Fallen One, but who had created the black temple? If the Brotherhood had had the power to protect the temple, certainly they could have stood up to her father.

She frowns. The reports about the Fallen One had been all too clear. The temple had been restored and protected overnight, and the damage of the park had been inconsistent with any known weapon, not to mention the total destruction of the tree.

Before that, years before, there had been the power failure that had turned the Prince Regent into a blabbering idiot, swearing that a black demon had appeared in his private dining room, foretelling his fall.

According to the sealed records of the palace, the ones her father had kept, one tape of the appearance of the Fallen One in the park had been recovered and screened privately by the Prince, the Grand Duke, and the High Marshal. After the screening, the Prince had destroyed the tape and retired. His bodyguards found his body the next morning.

Shortly thereafter, the High Marshal had suffered a seizure and had been relieved of command by the Grand Duke, acting as Viceroy for the Emperor.

The Lady stares out at her city, the city that has been hers and hers alone for more than a millennium, while others have aged and passed away, while others have plotted and failed, while others have feared and died. She recalls what she knows, knowing again that she knows not everything, that answers to what she does not know or to the questions she asks are locked behind the sealed portal in her mind that does not let her remember growing up or the days before she returned to Karnak from her schooling.

The wind brings her the acrid scent of fused insulation and ozone, and she half shrugs. A millennium since has given her enough memories.

Then why are they so empty, Lady?

She triggers the screens and turns in time to see the energies wash over the man in black who had called himself Martel. Sees the energies dispel themselves without touching him.

"Why are you so concerned with my memories?"

"One hopes, Kryn. One hopes."

Except for the distant wail of sirens, the tower top is silent.

At last, he speaks again.

"Why are you attempting to destroy Aurore? Both the Fleet and the Suntunnel will fail, you know."

"I don't know." She looks at him levelly. "As Viceroy, I have little choice. Karnak has been attacked."

"Neither of us has any choice. Not now. And I'm not sure we ever did." He smiles faintly, a smile that barely turns the corner of his mouth. "You'll lose. In losing, both the people and you will win, and in winning, the gods will lose."

"What sort of double-talk is that?" she snaps.

"Just ask yourself three questions, Kryn. Why can't you remember growing up? Why don't you grow older? And why do you fear black?"

She triggers the screens again, futilely, she knows, as tears stream again from eyes she had thought never cried.

Martel is gone. She knows he is Martel, and that is more frightening than the thought that she will lose her Fleet.

She shudders, waits until her eyes clear, and walks toward the lift shaft back down to the command center.

First, the beginning of reconstruction. Then the attack on Aurore.

Martel will see. Flamehell, he'll see.

LXII

Again, around the sacred peak Jsalm gather the gods of Aurore. They assemble themselves for the second time in less than a standard year, the frequency in itself a remarkable occurrence.

The Regency gathers all its Fleet against Aurore.

Laughter suffuses the group.

Where are Thor and Dian? For surely Thor should stand in the forefront to defend us against the Empire, since he has caused this expedition of vengeance. And Dian should stand for Martel, who is no more.

Laughter again rains upon the assembled gods.

Apollo and the Smoke Bull cross glances, if Apollo's glance at the insubstantial substance and infinite depths of the Minotaur can be considered a crossing of glances.

Still, the meaning is plain, for each suspects the other.

No one answers the anonymous question. No one knows.

First, Martel has gone. Then Thor and Dian/Emily.

The unseen danger may be more threat than the Empire, offers Thetis, green and wet.

The Smoke Bull nods.

After a time, Apollo agrees.

But first Karnak must be smashed, taught a lesson to end all lessons. Then we will seek out the unseen danger.

The gods and demigods find Apollo's summation to their liking, and they repair to where they individually repair and begin their preparations for the Grand Fleet of the Empire.

A sleeping woman turns over in silksheen sheets, where she has dreamed what has transpired, and sobs, but wakes not, and will remember nothing of what she has dreamed.

A man in black watches from a distance, and smiles a grim smile, and begins his preparations.

The Fleet Commander touches a switch, and the Grand Fleet swings to point toward a relatively ordinary star which is circled by an extraordinary planet.

The twenty-third Emperor of the Empire of Light shakes his head as a shadow passes before his eyes, but continues his play with his latest mistress.

A man in red addresses silent prayers to an undeclared god, while the Marshal of Strategy makes sure his laser is fully charged.

A goddess watches a demigod exercise with shield and sword, trying to hold back a vision of a leaden shield wreathed in black. She shudders and turns away.

LXIII

For the importance of the mission, the ship is termed a cruiser, but, in reality, is nothing more than a corvette with a cruiser's drives and screens. The Captain, uniformed in Imperial blue, is a recently promoted full Captain looking toward a complete and distinguished career.

"Range?" he barks.

"Point five, closing at point two per stan, sir."

The Captain settles himself back into his padded command seat. Another two stans must pass before he can start the deployment. In the meantime, the main Fleet should be arriving near outsystem Aurore.

"Not for a while yet, I suspect," a strange voice intrudes.

The Captain bolts upright, grabs for his sidearm, and

points the laser at the man in black who has appeared beside him.

"My name's Martel, Captain Ellerton. You can use that if you want, but I can assure you it won't work."

The Captain, his belief in visible technology supreme, thumbs the firing stud. Nothing happens.

"Now that we've gotten that out of the way—"

"Marines! Imperial Marines to the bridge!"

Martel smiles.

The Captain looks at the rest of the bridge crew, who proceed with their routine as if nothing out of the ordinary were occurring.

For them, nothing is.

. . . mad, going mad . . . mad . . .

"No, you're quite sane, Captain. Quite."

Martel waits again, waits until the Captain is ready to accept his presence. Then he lays a hand upon the man's shoulder to emphasize his physical reality.

"What do you want?"

"Your understanding and your cooperation."

"Maybe the first, but never the second!" blusters the officer.

"Both, I think," Martel contradicts, "once you understand. You see, very shortly, in about one stan, I imagine, I'm going to appear out in empty space on your screens, and as you release the components of the Suntunnel, I'm going to blast them and their boosters out of existence. Now, without a record of that, Captain, you are going to be in very deep trouble. Even with such a record, you'll probably face a court-martial. So I would suggest two things. First, that you use the next stan to arrange to get a permanent record of what will in fact appear on your screens. Second, that you do your absolute and total best to destroy me."

"Sounds like that's what you want. Why should I?"

"Look at it this way. If I'm just a figment of your imagination, you'll have a perfect recording of your successful deployment. If not, you're covered. And if I do destroy all your hardware, and you don't make an all-out effort to destroy me, where does that leave you?"

The Captain wipes his suddenly damp brow.

"All right," the skipper concedes, "but tell me what's in it for you."

"That's simple, Captain. It just might save me the difficulty of having to destroy three or four successors to you."

The Imperial Captain looks away. "I don't understand. Who are you?"

"I'm Martel. I told you that. I don't like destroying ships, and I'd just as soon not. If the Viceroy keeps sending ships with devices to destabilize Aurore's sun, I'll eventually have to do something drastic, and I'd rather give advance warning. Then I won't feel quite so guilty."

The Captain realizes he is still holding down the firing stud on his laser, and he releases it. The ache in his thumb reminds him how long he has pressed the stud. He looks up at Martel to find the space next to himself empty. The man in black is gone.

As a believer in visible technology, he checks the charge meter on the butt of the sidearm. Empty. He knows it had been fully charged when he took the bridge, and he has only used it once . . . without effect. He tries to persuade himself that he has seen nothing and talked to no one, but after a few units he touches the commweb.

"Communications? Captain Ellerton here. Send Commander Sirien to the bridge."

Whoever, whatever, Martel is, his logic, flame it all, is unassailable.

LXIV

GERMIC: Ah, what's the bigger mystery?
        That man ever was,
        Or that he'll always be?
JORIS: Some say one night a thousand ships
        Fell across a thousand skies,
        Like hope, which always flies.
GERMIC: Dear lady, from whence we came,
        Either from the thousand ships and skies,

Or from a single orb of fame,
Matters not when each man dies.
—Excerpt from Act II, *Home Divided*
Yves N. Dorben

LXV

Martel paces across the porch, one quick step after another.

Both the problem of arrogant gods, himself among them, and an arrogant Viceroy, whom he has created, remain.

The real Empire is the Regency, not New Augusta, and its power lies in the Viceroy. The time of the Brotherhood has come, but unless both the Empire and the gods are vanquished, one will re-create the other.

"Götterdämmerung," he whispers, and it is a promise.

Not only to himself, but to his followers, for he can no longer escape them. Declared or not, gods of human societies are created in part by their worshipers, which is what Apollo has known and feared for a millennium.

Martel pictures the thousands who thronged a small black temple on Karnak, and all of the small shrines on Aurore where shadows are cast.

"Perhaps the forbidden fruit is best," he says to no one, for no one is with him, now or ever. He looks down at the silver triangle upon his black belt, then touches the glistening black thunderbolt pin that holds his cloak. Both are appropriate.

Can he do what he plans?

He does not know, for no one has ever tried. At least, it is nowhere recorded.

Colossal arrogance, Martel . . . colossal arrogance . . .

He agrees with his thought, gathers the darkness around himself, and removes himself to a point in space where he can watch the planet which is not a planet, but which is called Aurore, as if the name were the answer to everything.

First . . . to remove the base of power of the gods.

Second . . . to scatter the gods.

Third . . . to destroy the Fleet as the basis of power for the Viceroy.

Fourth . . . the Viceroy.

To begin, he looks upon Aurore, looks upon the planet that should not be, in a way that none of the gods before him has. He understands why the forty-nine percent of the human scientists who have studied Aurore and who insist it is not a planet are correct.

Or, rather, why Aurore is more than just a planet.

He imposes, for to impose is the only way to describe what he does, the imprint of darkness across the upper reaches of the golden-hazed energy field that is, that surrounds, Aurore.

ANGER!

A ray of golden haze gathers itself from the field and arrows out from Aurore toward the point of blackness, within the wider darkness, that is Martel.

Four demigods hovering around a certain sacred peak feel their powers abruptly waning and move themselves to solid ground, their faces nearly as white as the snow that caps the peak they had soared above.

The E.W. officer of the Viceroy's lead scout gulps as his power registers, focused on Aurore, peg off the scale. He hesitates, then jabs the commweb with one hand while defocusing his receivers with the other. He is not fast enough, and the power amplifiers for the last intake screen sag into molten plastics, ceramics, and metal.

Martel calls shadows from beneath the here and now, from beneath the past, and from a future that may never be, drawing as he never has, knowing that without all that he can focus, he will not be able to deflect the raw force that the field which is Aurore has directed at him.

The cold of black fires shimmers around him, both blinding and swallowing light, one and the same. And the black fires build, and build to an intensity that will befuddle astronomers across the galaxies for so long as the energies carry.

"Flamehell! See what I see?" asks the Scout Captain, who is but a subcommander.

"I think so." That is his navigator, who sees it all through unpowered screens, the forces are so great.

Both know that what they see has long since transpired, and that lends to the wrenching at their guts.

In a series of flashes, one after another, bolts of brilliant yellow flare from the "nightside" of Aurore, each one somehow brighter than the last, until each rivals momentarily the brilliance of the sun unseen by Aurore's inhabitants. Each energy bolt, millennia into the future, will confuse and confound astronomers, those few who are looking as the light recording the phenomena slips through their system, throughout the Galaxy.

Each bolt strikes the black dot, englobed in black fire, which stands in space. Each fails to splash or to penetrate, but disappears. Disappears, and with each disappearance the blackness grows, becomes more deeply luminescent.

With the energy he has summoned, and with that he has gathered, Martel does two things.

The first is a gentle nudge, enough to shake a few buildings, to raise foot-high waves on the stillest ponds, to the celestial body called Aurore.

The second is a cast of darkness around the planet that has not known it in millennia, perhaps in eons, since it was created by the energy field that has made Aurore what it is.

Apollo stands upon the portico of a vacant pale golden and marble villa west of Sybernal, where he seeks some sign. As he stands the sky dims, and dims further, until the gloom resembles twilight.

Martel, he thinks, though he knows not why, except that the darkness itself calls to mind the one whom Thor had thought vanquished, and who, Apollo knows with cold certainty, is not vanquished. Who may be triumphant. Who will triumph, the sun-god fears.

STOP!

Apollo reels under the force of the projection.

The transmission is not a word, but a massive concept rolling outward from Aurore and bouncing back from the wall of darkness which Martel has drawn around the golden sphere that has been called Aurore.

STOP!

Martel knows what he must do, if he can, and girds himself. Apollo watches from the villa as the golden haze above the sky thins, flows in ebbing sheets eastward until it coalesces into a golden ball, a dim second sun.

The western sky is black and starless, and the sungod who was shivers.

The new-formed golden-haze sun contracts, brightens, and elongates into a wedge, pointed against the darkness, finally launching itself toward that darkness.

The sky of Aurore is jet-black where the sun-god stands, and for the first time since man has been on Aurore, darkness falls. Falls like thunder, but with no flash of lightning to break the black depths that are the sky.

Martel smiles as he views the energy field that was Aurore, that created Aurore, flee the planet it built. He parts the darkness to let the golden and white glittermotes flee their planet and the energy-sucking darkness that he has fastened upon it.

From his dark heights, he tosses darkness at the golden wedge, black lightning thrust after lightning thrust. Then, as he chevies the ancient ones on their way, he opens a tunnel, a tunnel in time, back to when a certain FO star was younger, and without a planet.

The circle is complete. What is, is.

The field, the glittermotes, will remember, and when they do, they will build the planet they remember, the one human astronomers will claim is impossible.

Which it is, but that's beside the point.

Without the field, the place that is now just a planet called Aurore will not be habitable. For that reason, Martel has already nudged Aurore toward its ultimate destination. In the meantime, the cloak of darkness, which will thin over time, will protect it and its cargo until the planet reaches that stable orbit which Martel has planned for it and for the delicate organisms that inhabit its surface.

Martel, drawing on his powers of darkness again, twists time, so that what will be done is done. He withdraws the curtain of protection.

And Apollo beholds the first sunrise on Aurore and weeps. That is, before the shadow of the Raven catches him and before he is swirled back through another tunnel of time to a back-distant place where he will be worshiped.

The Smoke Bull, standing upon the heights on the far side

of the Middle Sea, observes the approaching sunset and antic-
ipates the darkness that will fall. Before this occurs, another
darkness descends upon him and carries him back to the time
when he will see sunrises above a wine-dark sea and bring
his own darkness to those who will cause his name to remain
a symbol of fear for well beyond the years he has left without
the energy field upon which he once relied.

In turn, the shadow of the Raven falls across the fallen
gods and demigods of Aurore, and they are dispatched to
generate the legends from which they sprang. All but two.

One is Martel, the Raven, the undeclared god.

The second he will deal with later, for now he must meet
the third challenge. The Grand Fleet, discounting the reports
of the scoutship, draws near, intent upon reducing Aurore to
a cinder.

Martel, in his cloud of darkness, sighs, and rises once
again into the night.

He ignores the genuflections that accompany his departure.

LXVI

Martel debates but a moment before drifting through time and
space to meet the Grand Fleet before it nears the new orbit of
Aurore, which is now merely a planet, albeit a technically impossible one with a slightly tilted axis and a too-circular orbit.

*Should I have given it a greater axial angle than a mere
seven and a half degrees?*

He shrugs. For all the powers he has mastered, he has
never learned orbital mechanics, nor the mathematics necessary. As for the distance from the sun that should be
planetless . . . that was merely the matching of energy flows.
The "year" will be longer, much longer, and the architecture
will have to change with the introduction of nights, cold
winds, seasons, and chill.

Aurore will lose much of its attraction as the resort of endless day and home of the gods and source of gods and demigods. Two called gods remain, and Martel knows he is not a

god, but merely an immortal with godlike powers in some limited areas.

Gods are omniscient and omnipresent, and Martel is neither. That is why he must crush the Grand Fleet before it splits, and before either the Marshal or the Viceroy realizes he is the last defender of Aurore.

Space fleets are not awe-inspiring. The longest line of battle cruisers, cruisers, corvettes, and scouts, even with all screens flaring, flooding the emptiness of the night sky beyond Aurore with squandered energy, is less than a needle in that sky.

All the energy contained in the metal and composite hulls of the Grand Fleet is less than a small percentage of that represented by the smallest sun, and the combined life spans of the captains and commanders and subcommanders and officers and crews are but a fraction of the life span of the briefest star. And all the energy marshaled by one immortal called a god is insignificant against the total energy of even a small corner of a small galaxy.

Nonetheless, large enough to render a certain large fleet less significant, thinks Martel, guarding his thoughts while recognizing that few are left with the power to monitor them, and none with the power to stop him.

Old habits die hard.

Martel waits in darkness beyond the new orbit of the still-impossible planet of Aurore, waits and watches, perceptions extended, as the Grand Fleet emerges from its subspace tunnel and wedges toward the FO star that is the ships' destination.

A thousand ships, fifty thousand men and women, and all because you play games with the Viceroy you created.

Martel acknowledges the debt, wondering how he can avoid the slaughter that looms before him.

The obvious strikes him.

What's good for gods . . .

He waits . . . waits as the Grand Fleet regroups.

Two basic formations, those are the options the Marshal for Strategy must consider: the Force Wedge or the Flying V to a Point.

Both formations have advantages. The wedge concentrates

defense screens and firepower at a relatively localized point in space, while the Flying V brings all the Fleet elements together at the last possible moment for such concentration, and thus requires any enemy to spread his defensive forces.

Since the number of gods on Aurore must be finite, reflects the Marshal, and since the power he had already seen can be terribly concentrated, he advises the Fleet Commander of his recommendation, the Flying V to a Point, and his reason.

CONCUR, prints the screen from the command bridge, and the decision has been made, and the Grand Fleet spreads from its subspace breakpoint.

Marshal Reitre feels a chill wind at his back, dismisses it as imaginary, but rechecks his laser sidearm all the same.

The lead scouts sprint toward the growing image of the star, toward the star and its single planet, where waits a god of darkness in darkness.

Here's where the myth came from!

The far lead scout sees the blackness, the darkness deeper than that through which it travels, and attempts to reverse its momentum.

"Captain! No indications ahead!"

"Full reverse!" commands the Lieutenant, but as he does the stars in the scout's screens wink out.

A black-shaded rainbow coruscates across the controls and is gone.

The stars, rather another set of stars, reappear on the screens.

Buzz!

"Navigation null!"

The Lieutenant scratches the back of his head. The star on which they are closing is not the FO type on which the *Bassett* had been centered instants before.

The navigation banks contain enough data to reconstruct virtually any locale within ten thousand lights of Karnak and have come up blank.

The Lieutenant wipes his forehead.

"Proceed," he creaks out, hoping they can discover where they are, somehow.

Back in another time, Martel refocuses the tunnel that he has willed into existence and picks off the rest of the lead scouts.

Leaves 985 to go.

On the command bridge far out from the FO star in question, the screen makes the reports, one after the other, sometimes separated by moments, sometimes by close to half a standard hour.

LOCALIZATION AT 10.0. ABNORMAL ENERGY CONCENTRATION OBSERVED AT TARGET.

PROCEEDING. RATE 1.5 AND CONSTANT.

PROCEEDING. TARGET AT 9.5 RATE 1.5 AND CONSTANT.

SPATIAL DISCONTINUITY, CLASS 8. INBOUND RADIAN 0.

Marshal Reitre raises his bushy eyebrows. Class-eight discontinuities were only theoretical. Six is the greatest ever observed outside an actual nova. Reitre wonders whether the Fleet Commander understands what he is getting into.

The second advance line consists of three spread chevrons of corvettes, 120 in all, and Martel prepares to spray them all into the past after the scouts.

TARGET AT 8.5.

SPATIAL DISCONTINUITY. CLASS 9.

SQUADRON 7. REPORT.

SQUADRON 7 DOES NOT REGISTER ON MASS DETECTORS. RADIATION NIL. DRIVE DISCONTINUITIES NIL.

REGROUP AND CLOSE LINE.

REGROUPING COMPLETE.

PROCEEDING. TARGET AT 7.0 RATE 1.5 AND CONSTANT.

SQUADRON 5 DOES NOT REGISTER ON MASS DETECTORS. RADIATION NIL. DRIVE DISCONTINUITIES NIL.

PROCEEDING. TARGET AT 6.0.

SQUADRON 4 DOES NOT REGISTER ON MASS DETECTORS . . .

Marshal Reitre's hand reaches for the commweb.

ABORT MISSION, he signals, knowing the Regent will have his position and possibly his head for the override of the Fleet Commander. But the transmission from the command bridge screen tells him what he does not want to see.

NEGATIVE. CLOSING AND CONTINUING, the signal returns.

Reitre sighs, wonders if he should use the sidearm on himself, hopes against hope that something, somehow, somewhere will save the Grand Fleet, for the squadrons are disappearing faster than the screen can script, and of the Fleet the Viceroy has dispatched to Aurore nothing will return to

Karnak. Of that the Marshal is absolutely certain. He returns his eyes to the screen to watch what he fears will happen.

The remaining flanks of the Grand Fleet are beginning to curl away from Aurore, and for that reason Martel concentrates his attention on the right flank, the heavy cruisers commanded by the Duke of Trinan, who certainly would not have minded being the next Viceroy.

You can be Viceroy wherever you are. No one will be there to tell you no.

Martel does not count, only continues his tunnels to the past until a single ship remains, waits until the light cruiser *Eltiran* turns and reenters its subspace tunnel back to Karnak.

The critics were right. A thousand ships didn't fall across the skies of the past. Only 999, and none of them before the time of the first flight from old Home. That would not have been fair.

Martel pauses.

Though who's to say what's fair?

He has one other task, perhaps the hardest, yet to do.

Martel hangs in the darkness, suspends himself, juggles his thoughts and the long-buried feelings he knows churn beneath.

He turns toward Aurore. His planet. His impossible planet and the home of his impossible dreams.

LXVII

Midnight cloaks the Petrified Boardwalk ... true midnight, moonless, for Aurore has never had a moon, with the stars only for light. For who had ever thought to provide outside lights for a planet that had never seen darkness?

The polished stone walks are deserted, and Martel can sense the fear. For darkness was accepted only when it was rare and isolated, but now that night has fallen, truly fallen, not a few of his worshipers are having second thoughts.

Let them.

He shrugs and surveys the low waves that still break across the night-silver sand.

Tonight there is no Emily to rescue you.

Nor Rathe.

Nor even a Marta Farrel to recall.

Hollie and Gates Devero shipped back to Halston, what—nine standard centuries ago? They're doubtless dust, or buried in some family vault.

On Karnak waits Kryn. Or Emily, if you wish to open that issue. You're an Immortal, perhaps the last who can claim godhood, or what passes for it. Now that the field of Aurore, flickering glittermotes and all, is gone, who is left?

Emily, the answer comes. Or Kryn, for they are one and the same, and both are older than Martel. Far older.

"Are they, really?" he asks the breakers in a low voice.

The waters mumble back the answer, which he cannot hear because he has lifted his eyes to the brightest star in the east.

Martel does not address a question to the star, instead drops his head and looks across the dark jumbles that are homes and shops and taverns where darkness and fear are being rediscovered again, and yet again.

A stone rattles, displaced by a cat.

Odd, a cat that has not known darkness. Does she see as well?

Martel tries to follow the small beast with his thoughts, but he is too late, and cannot locate that particular feline.

Do we seem that indistinguishable to whatever gods there are?

He smiles a hard smile as he asks himself the question, then lets his cloak flutter in the night breeze. The sea wind bears a saltier tang than it used to.

Martel takes three steps northward, recalling another night when it was night only by the clock, and perpetual day by the light. With another step, he recalls the second night like the first.

The images mix, and on top of them comes another, a young woman, dark-haired and dressed in blue leathers. And all three are the same.

Truly a goddess you are, Dian. Or Emily. Or Kryn.

He snorts, a rough bark that causes three cats and a dorle

to jump from their respective perches. The third cat pounces on the dorle, but before she can dispatch the hapless songbird, Martel throws a handful of darkness at the pair and separates them.

Do you dare to hope, Martel? Or are you still refusing to act? Turn the universe upside down on principle, but don't make the last move?

He shakes his head and observes the northward hills, his eyes centering on a space where he knows a building of white marble stands. Has stood a good millennium or longer.

Silence drops like a second darkness on the Petrified Boardwalk.

Shortly, a large raven flaps toward a white villa, dark, unlit, and deserted now for some time, though visited once by a recently created ancient god.

Martel roams from room to room, from chamber to chamber, from porch to portico, as he waits for the dawn.

Even you, last god, bringer of darkness, cannot bring the dawn quicker.

The rose color of the eastern horizon is only the first of a handful of dawns since the re-creation of Aurore. Martel sits on the columned wall above the ravine, dangling his black-booted feet over the edge.

The dampness of the dew lends a sharpness to the corel blooms that cascade from the overgrown garden and across the far end of the same stone wall on which Martel sits.

Corel . . . Emily's villa, and Kryn's scent. Can you separate them?

He reflects upon his twists in time, letting his feet drum against the stone.

Can you put them back together again? Should you?

A dorle chitters with the first ray from the rising sun.

So much smaller than on Karnak the sun was, and yet the heat was the same. Should be, since he'd planned it that way, but the visual sense was different, a touch of strangeness, with the high sky a greener shade, holding a hint of green, green seas.

In the early-morning light, the villa is still vacant, emptier now than when the white marble had stood gray in the predawn darkness.

Martel gathers his own blackness and casts it, extending himself throughout the villa and the grounds, letting time flow around him as he becomes one with the deserted structure.

As he touches the stone, reinforces it, repairs it, he rejects time itself. As he changes half the marble from white to black. As he wills the gardens back into their formal states, and the emerald grass back into the lawns, and the rose trees back into their guards. As he adds black roses among the white. As he hopes . . .

If not, someone will be most amazed.

His last effort is to bind a corner of time around what he has wrought, letting the villa sleep immaculate and untouched, until he returns. If he returns.

Once more, the raven spreads wing and departs, this time to cross the Middle Sea toward the White Cliffs.

Atop the White Cliffs the raven alights, still a black bird that perches above a smooth circular pool of whitestone. Three black footprints, inked into the white rock, yet lead to the circular stone depression that resembles nothing so much as a petrified pool.

A pair of dorles chitter. The lone sea gull has been gone for some time.

The raven stares unblinking at the white stone pool, at the black footprints.

The bird disappears, and a man stands atop the boulder.

For a space he stands. Then he walks down through empty air to the precipice, from where he looks over the edge, as if to reassure himself that the waves still crash in against the sheer stone face far below.

They do, and the water foams golden green, as it did before and will again.

Martel steps out into the emptiness. He gathers his cloak about him and is gone, replaced instantly by the wide-winged raven he also is.

The two youths who have climbed the gentle slope from the upland meadows drop their jaws open as they watch the transformation. The taller one, red-haired, recovers first and sprints for the edge, peers over, and sees nothing.

He looks up and sees the raven beating into the distance.

The shorter, brown-haired boy has found the stone pool and the black prints.

The two look at each other. The shorter makes the sign of the inverted and looped cross. They shake their heads and hurry back to tell their parents, who have not slept well in previous nights, and who will sleep even less well in nights to come.

Martel notes this as he flaps off, but does not hesitate.

His destination is a small cottage behind a larger home, south of the city called Sybernal, a cottage he once thought of as home, or the closest thing to it.

Someone has kept the quince pruned, even planted a younger tree close by the oldest, as if to ensure there will always be the same number of quinces.

Which means there will not be.

The cottage is as he left it days, or has it been years, ago. Except that a black velvet rope is looped to bar access from either the porch or the front entry. A small black looped and inverted cross is mounted upon a black marble pedestal beside the pathway leading to the cottage. The cross is not new, though its location is.

Martel extends his perceptions and finds that the cottage is empty, although recently it has been cleaned.

Seeing the black velvet ropes, he does not enter, though he knows that two sets of black tunics and trousers hang in the closet in his sleeping chamber, as do three preserved sets of pale yellow tunics and matching trousers.

Instead, he crosses the hillside and stretches his steps toward the crest from where he can see both sides, the cottage and the sheltered bay. The heavy grass on the hilltop is longer now, and thicker, as if it relished the nights and grew in response.

Is that true of men and women as well?

There is no answer, not that he expected any.

The bay is calm, and only the smallest of waves lap at the golden sands.

The times when the waves roiled and beckoned he remembers, and when he walked the sea, and the seabed.

Thetis? Gone. You, too, and that demigod you tried to protect. And how many others have I banished? Yes, how many, Martel?

But she has gone where he has sent her, and there is no answer.

He recalls the last image from Thetis—a leaden shield, circled in black—cast at him as he left her and her charge next to a wine-dark sea.

Should you regret what is done? Should you undo it?

Those are not the questions. They never were, Martel knows as he gazes down at the green waters.

The time for gods, for an ever-growing pantheon of powerful beings with little restraint and less morality, has gone.

Morality now, Martel? How high and mighty you sound. Morality from you? How moral was it to force the Prince to use his hunting laser? How moral was it for you to block Emily's memory to create your own dreams? To send Thor back to the barbarians? To scatter nearly a thousand ships across desolate planets? To do nothing when Apollo snuffed out Rathe?

Morality aside, what he has done is right.

You hope.

Martel turns from the sea to the cottage, its lines as firm as when Mrs. Alderson first owned it. The dorles chitter in the quinces. The grass grows, and now there is sunlight, and a natural shadow down the slope of the lawn.

Sunlight . . . and shadow.

What more is life . . . than sunlight and shadow?

He turns back to the other side of the hill to watch the waves. They have picked up, and gnaw at the beach, already beginning to change, ever so slowly, the countours of the sand, to change what was so long unchanged.

"... Tell me now, and if you must,
 Is a man much more than dust?"

His words are low, hardly louder than the dorles, or the swish of the water against the sand. But the birds cease their twittering, as if to hear the next line of the ancient song. The waves pause. The air is still. The shadow of the cottage shortens, darkens, as the distant sun rises.

The hillcrest is empty, and not even a raven crosses the heavens.

LXVIII

"Where did you get it?" the Matriarch asks as she freezes the holo that fills the end of the hall.

More than three battle lasers are focused on the figure of a man, dressed in black and hanging in the void. Although he wears only a cloak to guard him against the chill of deep space, the power sheets around him, haloing him.

"Where did you get it?" This time her tone is sharper.

"From M-7a. The molecular patterns match those of the Viceregal forces. So do the focal lengths and energy levels."

The Matriarch takes a last look at the figure, tries to identify the face shrouded in shadow, but finally touches the control on her throne. The holo vanishes.

"Do you believe what's on the cube?"

Her Admiral turns his eyes to the floor without answering.

"Do any of you believe what you see?"

Still there is no answer.

"Then why did you bring it to me?"

"Because we dared not to do otherwise. . . ."

"What are the associated probabilities?"

"According to Stats, the probability is nearly unity that he destroyed the Grand Fleet of Karnak. We ran the series twice, with a complete systems check in between."

The Matriarch smiles, a cold smile, one that would make the poles of Tinhorn seem warm by comparison.

"There's one other thing, Matriarch. . . ." The tall woman who wears the winged stars of a Commodore waits.

"Yes?"

"Aurore has been moved."

"Impossible, I'd say. At least if the conventional wisdom is correct."

"According to conventional wisdom, Matriarch, that holo is impossible as well, but every test we can devise bears out its truth. And Stats computes that the destruction of the Grand Fleet and the removal of Aurore to its present distance from its primary are linked. Probability eighty-five percent. And Aurore was moved *before* the Grand Fleet broke subspace."

"Before? Are you positive?"

"Absolutely."

"Command the Fifth Fleet to avoid the entire Karnak system. Otherwise proceed on plan. And make it a standing order that *no* armed Matriarchy ship is to approach Aurore. *Ever.*"

"Yes, Matriarch. . . ." The quiet stretched out.

"You question my orders, or the wisdom behind them?" The Matriarch barked a sound that might have been a laugh. "Remember that the Grand Fleet of the Viceroy was ten times the size of our Fifth Fleet, and even the Grand Fleet couldn't move planets. If we're fortunate, the Fuards won't understand that in time, but I doubt they are that dense."

"Matriarch . . . I don't understand," confessed the tall Commodore.

"You will, one day. Just because some gods are men doesn't lessen their powers. Check the name Martel under the Apollo files. You might also note why he fled to Aurore."

The Matriarch gestures, and both the Admiral and the Commodore step back, bow, and depart to carry out their orders.

LXIX

Except for Forde, the Viceroy knows, the palace is vacant.

The screens will hold against small arms for a century, if necessary, although the mob has not yet formed.

The four towers strike into the morning, blunted spears glittering as they have for more than nine centuries, ever since she completed the rebuilding from the ruins of the Prince's Palace.

The gold-shot blue of the synthestone walls stands unmarred, stands on the hill above the rubble that is the city that has fallen to the vagaries of two gods.

Kryn had hoped that her city of Karnak would have stood longer than the city of the Prince Regent which it replaced, much longer. Instead, she stands on the East Tower, over-looking the tumbled chaos that had been order such a short time before.

By shifts, Forde has instructed the entire retinue, even the Generals and Marshals who have protested their undying loyalty, to depart.

In few cases, few indeed, was force required.

The reconstruction, directed from the fringes of the city by the Marshal of Strategy, the man name Reitre, is under way. Reitre has enough fear to be wise, and enough caution to deal with whoever follows the Viceroy.

A gold-winged bluetail alights on the corner of the battlement. Useless as they are, her father had liked battlements. Not that he had really been her father. The gene patterns hadn't matched, but what else could she have called him? And how else could she have been named Viceroy out of the Times of Trouble?

Her thoughts are broken by the sound of footsteps.

"All gone, my Lady."

"Thank you, Forde."

Forde, in red trousers, tunic, and boots, stands like the obsolete column he is, ready yet to support a ruler who knows her time has passed.

"Forde, you are the last. Reitre will need you, and you him. Serve him, and through him, my people."

"My Lady . . ."

His protest is formal. They both know it.

". . . do you think . . . ?"

"Yes. Shortly. And that will be between Us."

The way she says the word "Us" sends shivers down Forde's spine, and he bows.

"As you wish, Lady and Viceroy."

"Lady will do, Forde."

She inclines her head to dismiss him.

The footsteps echo as he heads for the drop shaft.

The people grieve now, she knows. They grieve and dig their own from the rubble left by two gods. When their grief is buried with their dead, then they will decide why they should blame their Ruler. Who did not protect them.

Who could not, she thinks.

The gold-winged bluetail preens, spreads his wings, and leaves the battlement.

A pair of sirens howl, and another overloaded skitter makes another emergency flight to another overcrowded health center. Shortly there will be more deaths as rejuve treatments lapse for all but the most powerful and secure, and that means those with private armies and independent power sources.

The people do not know that the Grand Fleet has failed. Or that Karnak lies defenseless. Or that the Twenty-third Emperor of New Augusta has been poisoned by his second wife. Or that the Fuardian First Fleet is on its way to declare Karnak a protectorate. As is the Fifth Fleet of the Matriarchy of Halston.

Occasionally, through the pall of smoke over the city, she can see a brown-robed figure surveying the defense lines of the palace. A scent of that smoke reaches her, and the bitterness waters her eyes momentarily.

The teletale at her belt indicates that Forde is outside the screens, that he has left the defenses intact.

Not altruism, nor loyalty, but realism is represented in that action. While an intact palace, with all its shielded weapons, should not fall into the hands of the first armed adventurer, neither should the palace, the symbol of the Viceroy, fall, or fall too easily. For then the mob will require more destruction to avenge the betrayal they will feel.

After a millennium of protection under the hand of the Viceroy, they will feel betrayed, and there are more than enough who will use that sense of betrayal as the rein to power.

"So why don't you do something?" she asks herself.

Instead, she crosses the tower top slowly until she can see the Lake of Dreams.

"I can just remember when it was the Park of Summer," she tells the redbird that chirps from the empty jackstaff.

She stretches forth a hand to the songster, but the bird takes flight.

"You should have been a blackbird," says the Viceroy. "But you couldn't be. Not here."

She turns back to the bench and sits, waiting, wondering if she should descend to the vacant strategy center to await the coming of the Fleets, to do her best to protect her people. Or would the few screens she could throw up now merely make the eventual situation worse?

The teletale chimes.

Forde, for some reason, is returning. Alone.

Reitre would need Forde. Therefore, Reitre is no more. No ships have arrived except two medical relief freighters.

Who? It can only be the Brotherhood, and they must have heavy weapons, for nothing less could have taken Reitre, even away from the shields of the palace.

She can only wait now.

Presently, Forde arrives on the parapet.

"Lady, do you have some way to depart? Unknown?"

"Is it the Brotherhood?" she asks, a faint quirk to her lips. After all, the brown-clad monks had started the whole thing, in one sense, by helping Martin to escape. Or had Martin maneuvered them into helping him? Or . . . she shrugged.

For all she knows, the man she knew as Martin Martel is more than that and has been all along. If he had been, had been that experienced, why would he have been interested in a mere slip of a woman, and one without much memory of her past at that?

Unless he knew she would be Viceroy. Unless he planned she would succeed the Prince. If he had known, had planned for those eventualities, why has he destroyed her Fleet, her capital, and left her alone in the wreckage of the Grand Millennium?

"My Lady?" Forde's voice breaks through her reverie.

"Yes, Forde. Is it the Brotherhood?"

"So they say." He pauses, then asks again, "Escape routes?"

"No, Forde. No escape routes for me. Not yet. Take the courier in the west tunnel from the strategy center."

"But you? How will you leave?"

"There is another, if I need it. I need to stay to see the curtain fall. To see if it will fall."

The man in red moves not.

"*Go!*" Her voice lashes around him and causes the wind to halt momentarily.

"Yes, my Lady. The Brotherhood has captured three armories and is turning the battle lasers against the palace."

"Let them. It will take more than that. Now go."

Her hands drop to her belt, and he turns, scurrying across the glowstones back toward the drop shaft. He reminds her of a lizard scuttling under a rock, but her laugh is mirthless.

She waits until the courier winks out overhead before returning to the battlement. A faint haze has built at the palace defense lines, and her teletales show that less than ten percent of the screens' capacity has been taxed.

A strange pair, she thinks. *The blue Viceroy and the black god. Is the only thing more deadly than a woman scorned a man still in love with the woman who scorned him?*

Purple light flares to the east.

A pulsed battle laser deflected by the shields. Her teletale shows that single pulse claimed, only momentarily, thirty percent of the screens' capacity.

Another flare follows, then another.

"The Brotherhood doesn't waste much time, does it?"

His voice carries an edge she does not remember.

There is a great deal you don't remember.

She turns to face him, not wanting to, but realizing she has little choice.

Martel stands no taller, no stockier, and his face is still unlined. And so is hers, she knows.

The blackness of his eyes is darker than deep space, and she tears her glance away, blinks with the next laser flare against the palace shields.

"You don't have to accept me, Kryn. And you don't have to accept you. That's your choice."

With his left hand he takes the black thunderbolt pin from his cloak, lays it in his right hand, and stretches his hand forth. The jet-blackness of the pin glitters.

Without looking at his face, Kryn studies the pin. She has never seen it. Yet the miniature thunderbolt is familiar.

"It is nine centuries old, Emily, and it was yours before it was mine, and if you so desire, it can be yours again."

She wants to shiver, though the laser blasts warm the air circulating across the top of the tower. She will not.

"Emily?"

"Emily. You are Kryn, but before Kryn you were Emily, and long before that you were called Dian. I knew you first as Kryn, then as Emily, and never as Dian. They think I am old, with my darkness and shadows, but your first youth lies long before the thousand ships fell, long before I scattered those hulls across the stars. No one but you knows how far back stretches your ageless youth. All you have to do is look."

Look!

Kryn feels the black wall in her mind, the one behind which who knows what is locked, splintering.

"*No!*" Her cry is involuntary.

He smiles, faintly, bends his head, almost as if in homage to her, but does not step forward.

The curtain has fallen away from the darkness, and the images leap at her, one after another, falling into her lap like the ships Martel has strewn across the stars.

She staggers. With an effort she is unaware of making, she catches her balance and sinks onto the glowstones, dark hair catching the purple highlights from the laser pulses, and shakes, the dry sobs racking her frame.

He sits down, not cross-legged, for his muscles have always been too tight for that, across from her and waits, helping her catch each memory as it tumbles forth.

. . . She stands before the four square limestone blocks that are the altar, obsidian knife in hand, and looks down at the young face. She does not hesitate, and with a clean downward stroke . . .

. . . The hunter stands across the clearing from her, arrow nocked, his blond eyebrows invisible in the gloom, but raised in puzzlement. She draws the moonlight to her and watches as he gently lets the tension off the bow, as he slowly goes down on bended knee while the light around her pulses. Then, and only then, does she gesture. She remains the only human figure in the clearing, and the harshness of her laugh chases the blond stag into the woods. The dogs begin to bay . . .

. . . Though the sedge has withered, and the wind's bitterness has stripped most of the leaves from the oaks, she stands on the hillside, barefoot and in a clinging shift. On her left arm rests the handle of a wicker basket as she waits for the horseman who picks his path up the hillside. His armor, though scarred, glitters in the late-afternoon light. Although his surcoat is ripped, the green and gold are still bright. Her black hair flows back over her shoulders as she waits for the knight to place her before him on his horse . . .

. . . She stares at the two vials, finally picking the one on the right and tucking it into the hidden space in her lace cuff. The Duke will be on her left, and he will down at least three full goblets of wine . . .

. . . She crouches next to the transmitter, waiting for the red light to blink on, eyes darting toward the berm a hundred meters away, over which she can see the top of the hangar. Inside, a young man waits for the same red light, and when it blinks will dash for his cockpit. She knows the pilot, every line of his body. The light blinks, red, and she touches the switch, does not look back as the hangar explodes in flame . . .

. . . She slides onto the bridge, wearing only a clinging white singlesuit, not even her pilot's rings. The watch officer looks up from his console, touches the standby stud, and rises to greet her. Lips meet, and his freeze as the jolt from her wrist stunner hits his spine. She lowers the unconscious form to the plastic of the sleepship's deck and seats herself at the console. Next comes the course tape, the one that will take the sleepship beyond the Federation's borders . . .

. . . She waits by the stone wall, idly studying the grain of the petrified walk. The one she seeks is sitting on a low stone wall, and she can sense the immense darkness of the energies he does not yet know he carries. He looks out over the water, oblivious to anything but his concerns about the troubles on Karnak.

"A brooding philosopher, is that it?"

He jerks his head to look at her . . .

. . . She stands in midair, hovers above a certain snow-tipped sacred peak, across from a bull figure in carved smoke, across from a hammer-bearing barbarian, across from a sun-wreathed god in pale yellow.

"Decided!" she declares . . .

* * *

... The breeze darts into the courtyard, ruffles her hair. The black-haired student stares at her, his eyes widening, as her hands touch the studs on her belt.

"I wish you hadn't, Kryn. Wish you hadn't," he says as he walks through the stunner beam that should have dropped him in his tracks. He leaves her and her guard without looking back ...

The top of the tower is darker now, surrounded with a twilight brightened intermittently with muted purple light pulses.

After a time, she lifts her eyes.

The defenses? Yours now? The Brotherhood? Her thoughts are clear again, ring with the unheard sound of silver bells.

Down. Mine for now. Yes.

Martel stands, stretches, then extends his left hand.

She takes it, though she does not need the assistance, and gets to her feet.

With her free hand, her left, she extends a black thunderbolt pin.

I meant it then. And now.

He bends his head slightly, and she can see the wetness in the corners of his eyes.

She takes two steps, until she is close enough to pin the thunderbolt back on his cloak. She does.

He waits until she finishes before placing both her hands in his.

The East Tower of the Viceroy's Palace is abruptly empty, and with that emptiness the afternoon sunlight returns, and the ravening purple glare of the Brotherhood's newly acquired battle lasers.

Shortly the tower is gone, following the rest of the palace, and the powder-fine blue dust, gold-speckled, begins to settle on what remains of the city and the parks, and their fallen trees.

From the depths of the ruins emerge the citizens, hurrying toward one of the few intact structures, a small black temple in the old section, where preside a handful of brown-clad Brothers.

None wear black, for it is sacred.

LXX

The trees are old and exude a feeling older than their height and massive trunks would indicate.

Behind the last line of trees runs a wall of unmortared rectangular stone blocks. The barrier stretches into the distance on each side and looms half again as tall as stood the tallest of the long-defunct Imperial Marines. No gates break the expanse of stone, but thin white marble columns are embodied in the blackness at regular intervals.

The small but hot noon sun has fatigued the traveler, and he sits on one of the white marble benches beneath the trees and wipes his damp forehead.

His boots are dusty, but even so clash with the faded brown tunic and trousers he wears. He wipes his forehead again, replaces the cloth in his belt pouch, and pushes a strand of gray hair back over his ear.

He stares at the wall.

Is that all?

A black-and-white stone wall? Even on a miracle planet?

He could climb the wall. After all, it is only twice as tall as he is. Despite the aches in his joints and the years in his bones, the climb would not be difficult.

The grass grows right up to the stone, but not into or between it. Nor do any of the vines that curl up some of the mossy trunks actually touch the stone.

The path he has taken, the one on which he stands, parallels the wall ahead for perhaps half a kilo before winding back into the forest.

He looks at the wall, ignoring the heavy footsteps behind him on the hard-packed earth.

"I wouldn't, if I were you."

The voice belongs to a short and heavyset man, clad in an off-white monk's robe.

The traveler looks up but does not otherwise acknowledge the statement.

"It's not called the Wall of Forgetfulness for nothing, pilgrim. You touch it, and you may forget why you wanted to. You try to climb it, and you forget Martel-near everything.

"Every couple of years, some young scientist from the Matriarchy or the Fuardian Empire shows up with a bunch of high-energy weapons to prove there's nothing unusual about it."

"And?" asks the man with the red boots sardonically.

"The Governor, whoever it is, tries to discourage them. Shows the scientist the old cubes. Sometimes that works. Mostly, it doesn't. The last one I remember. She smuggled in one of the old Imperial battle lasers. The beam just bent back off the wall. You could see it twist into the looped cross. Just came back and destroyed the laser. Her, too."

The traveler turns away. Always the superstitions. On every planet where he had searched for Her.

"Have it your way." The monk smiles and continues his patrol.

The older man eases himself to his feet and edges toward the wall. At the base of the stone is a clear line where the grass stops growing, knife-sharp.

He stretches his hand to touch the stones . . .

. . . and finds himself lying facedown in the grass. His nose is scraped. He sits up, realizing that the small, hot sun is lower in the blue-green sky.

Small dark splotches stain the front of the dusty tunic, where blood has somehow found its way.

"Nonsense," he mutters.

But he does not reach out toward the wall again as he lurches to his feet. His eyes range over the crispness of the stones, then lift to the treetops he can see above the wall.

"Nonsense," he grumbles.

His eyes travel down the pathway toward a flicker of white that may represent the monk who had warned him.

With a last look at the gateless wall, he turns and sets his steps back along the way he had already come. The hard-packed pathway will lead him back to the coast and to the extension of the Petrified Boardwalk north of Sybernal. His stride lengthens.

The shuttleport south of the old planetary capital is more than a few units away, and he wants to make the midlight lift.

"Can't believe anything anymore. Not anything. But I'll find Her someday, somewhere. Find Him, too. The bastard!"

He looks back over his shoulder at the crisp lines of the black-and-white stone wall, unmortared, that has resisted lasers and time, then shakes his head.

"Can't believe anything."

Forde's fingers stray toward the hidden shoulder holster where rests the aged but fully charged Imperial Marine blaster.

"Somehow ..." He sighs, putting one foot in front of the other. "Somehow ..."

LXXI

The man and the woman sit on the portico, savoring the short twilight.

Down the hillside and into the trees stretch the gardens and the emerald-green lawn. Beyond the forest is a simple black-and-white stone wall, and beyond that the rest of the universe.

A dorle twitters from the branches of the newest quince tree, the one the man planted a decade ago.

As one, the man and woman stand and drift to the low marble railing of the portico, arms touching.

Poor Forde. Her thoughts chime gently.

He has what he wants. If he found you, then ... he'd have nothing.

But how many years?

Close to two hundred. Hatred and longing keep him going.

Longing ... you know about that.

Without turning from the distant vision of an old and red-booted man, he knows she has smiled.

Don't forget the hatred ... some of that, too ...

She touches his fingertips with hers. In turn, his eyes refocus on the quince tree before he looks at her.

He has his vision, she adds.

Don't we all?

Some men look, and others create ...

. . . and still others think they are gods. He turns to her, their eyes nearly level. *Even for me, the temptation is great.*

The time is coming when you will have to surrender to it. Our time must come round again.

He shakes his head, for he knows it is true. She is right.

While the past few centuries have been quiet, the times are again changing, and new gods and new empires are building. Gods without understanding, who will have to be cast down, and empires without humanity, which will have forgotten their origin and their purpose.

He sighs, quietly, and looks back at the quince, which is beginning to lose its leaves as the fruit ripens.

She picks the thread of the old song from his thoughts.

> *Tell me now, and if you can,*
> *What is human, what is man.*
> *Tell me now, and if you must,*
> *Where's the god that men can trust?*

He laughs, and his laugh echoes alone above the emerald grass. The pieces fracture and float like mist above the turf, finally dissolving into the sod.

He laughs, and the haunting notes still even the crickets.

He laughs, and the twilight becomes night.

She laughs, gently, in return. Silver bells in the evening wrap themselves around the haunted notes of his rejoicing.

The two laughs mingle, build, rustle the forest leaves and needles as they carry the wind across the black-and-white stone wall, where the monks hear the sacred bells and bend their heads in worship.

On the portico of a white-and-black marble villa, a man and a woman hold hands, just like any other man and woman.

A red-booted old man boards a shuttlecraft.

Three monks in white lift their heads and finish sweeping the nave before replacing the tapers.

The evening star glitters in the eastern sky, and the man and the woman hold that brightness in their hands, and the blackness from his hands and the light from hers twine around it, the one following the other, black and white, black and white.